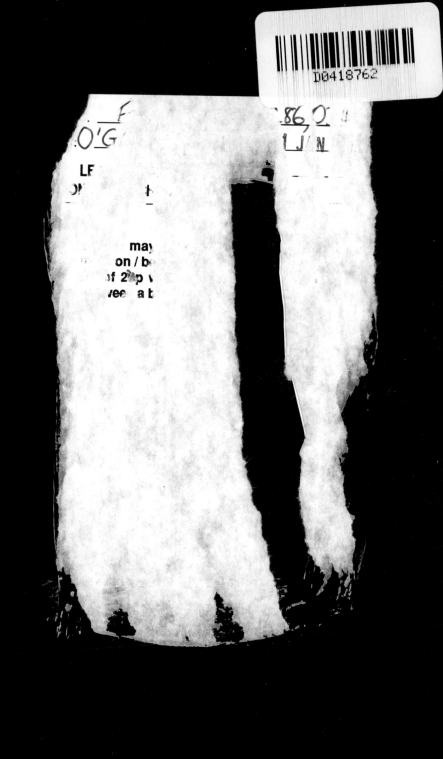

A Crooked Field

Also by Colm O'Gaora

GIVING GROUND

COLM O'GAORA

A Crooked Field

PICADOR

First published 1999 by Picador

an imprint of Macmillan Publishers Ltd
25 Eccleston Place, London SW1W 9NF
and Basingstoke

Associated companies throughout the world

ISBN 0 330 37077 4

9 8 7 6 5 4 3 2 1

A CIP catalogue record for this book is available from
the British Library.

Typeset by SetSystems Ltd, Saffron Walden, Essex
Printed and bound in Great Britain by
Mackays of Chatham plc, Chatham, Kent

For Alison and Eoin

and in memory of my grandfather

Mícheál de Búrca

Part One

WHEN THE LAST of the mourners
had been ushered out, their voices snagging on the nightwind
and the sound of their feet clattering on the hard path that
led down to the road where finally their shapes were claimed
by the darkness, the house fell silent. Helen took the brush
from where it always stood behind the kitchen door and
began to sweep the floorboards, the thick bristles upon that
wood like the sound of fingers scraping beneath. She swept
slowly, carefully, as though there were spirits present that
should not be disturbed. The clocks had been stopped, the
mirrors draped in brown felt, the curtains drawn. Candles
burned on every ledge and surface, their ghostly wax forms
like worn teeth in the darkening mouth of the room.

When she had finished she put away the brush and
cleared the table of the glasses that smelled of whiskey and
sherry. The best china cups and saucers had already been
gathered and waited now beside the sink. She filled a basin
with warm water and dipped each one in turn into the suds,
the sound of water the only tear in the blanket of silence.
Afterwards she dried them, examining the delicate swallows
hand-painted on their sides and the gold filigree turned
around the handle. She wrapped them in newspaper before
returning them to the cardboard box at the bottom of the
dresser where her mother had kept the most fragile of

things. Here were other smaller boxes, filled with old but not forgotten jewellery, odd pieces of silver, thimbles, and a christening tankard for a godchild. All were labelled in her mother's small but elegant script, refined throughout her years in a classroom. She touched them, as though her mother's care and warmth was still there amongst these mute and patient things.

One by one the candles began to drown in their own substance, the pools of molten wax petrifying as they spilled over the lips of the saucers, taking the light with them. She lit the oil lamp on the sideboard and its decorated shade cast a rosy glow across the room.

Now she could hear him making his way back to the house, his boots on the path, the tick-tick of the dog's paws on the stones as it trotted alongside him. He did not come in. When she went to the door to look for him she saw only the glow of yellow flame suspended in the darkness and, as he bent towards it, his face momentarily alive with shadows, the cigarette trapped between his lips.

'Daddy,' she said, but he did not hear her and she did not try again. He bent to pick up a stick that the dog had dropped at his feet and threw it out into the darkness, the dog turning and racing after it, the white flashes on its forelegs dissolving. When the dog returned the stick he threw it out again, pulling gently on the cigarette as he listened to the stick hooping through the air and the panting of the chasing dog. The sounds reminded her of a skipping rope in the yard at school, the thump of rope against the flags and the gasping breaths of a girl keeping time with it. A skipping rhyme entered her head and she looked forward to telling her friends about the cakes, biscuits and sweet drinks she had had during the day, and the coins pressed into her hand by relatives who could find no other way of expressing their pity for her.

She watched her father for a while longer, the puffs of

grey-blue cigarette smoke drifting in the air, the dog running back and forth as though weaving some fantastic and invisible tapestry.

A solitary candle burned in the hallway, past which the mourners had filed for four days now. It had a small red cross on its side and a metal collar that caused it to burn more slowly than the others. Father Mahon had brought it with him from the church. Helen moved her finger through the flame, each time more slowly than before until she could bear it no longer.

The door to her parents' bedroom was shut but she carefully edged it open, the cold draught upsetting the candle flame behind her. She turned on a lamp and closed the door. Someone had stripped the mattress and covered it with grey sheets instead of the yellow floral sheets her mother said had been a wedding present from a cousin in America. The pillowcases, too, had been replaced with plain white covers. In the dim light, the room looked dull and leaden, as though her mother had never set foot in it. The dressing table had been cleared, the headscarves tied to the back of the chair removed. Only the alarm clock and an empty water glass remained. The clock had been stopped and without thinking she turned the key in the back a few times. The busy ticking filled the room and she wondered how they had ever slept with that noise.

In a corner of the room she smelled a stale tobacco smell. She thought of her father, but he never smoked inside the house. Pushed up against the skirting board she found a squashed cigarette butt and she remembered then seeing Mr O'Donoghue, who owned a pub in Loughrea, coming out of the bedroom earlier in the afternoon and saying hello to her. She looked around the room in vain for traces of her mother. Only her maiden name appeared on a framed Papal marital blessing that hung above the bed; 'Elizabeth O'Shea', the black ink faded to yellow at the edges of the script.

The wardrobe, however, held more evidence of her mother's former presence: blouses, skirts, a cherry-red jacket, old shoes crumpled at the bottom along with a fox fur she had inherited from an aunt but had never worn. A solitary glass eye held her gaze through a film of dust. Pushed in at the back was one of the floral pillowcases and in it the other pillowcase and the sheets. She emptied the pillowcase and her mother's things fell in a puddle on the floor: a tattered slip, brassières, stockings, a faded-to-yellow herring-bone corset, a grey An Post savings book with eleven pounds and four shillings in it, a blank postcard from Buncrana, and finally a string of silk scarves knotted together. She bent down and lifted these things to her face. She could smell her mother from them, familiar and comforting, like the smell of earth and dry leaves. She could hear her mother's voice and see her face again. It was as though she was still there. She tied the scarves around her wrist and began bundling the other things back into the pillowcase. Amongst the clothes she found discarded cellophane and plastic wrappings from surgical instruments that smelled of newness and antiseptic. She found the broken plunger from a syringe, and there the memory of the nurse who had spent that last week with them in the house.

Helen's bed had been offered to the nurse but she had refused it and instead had slept in the front room on a bed made from a board supported on four sides by kitchen chairs and topped with an old mattress. The summer before, on their way along the coast to Screeb, her mother had pointed out the nurse's new bungalow with its view over a tidal island and the rotting iron bridge that led to it. The nurse had gone home to her new bungalow two days ago and had not come to say goodbye to Helen.

Now she found that when she pushed the floral sheets to her nose in the hope of finding more of her mother they smelled of nothing: the smell of tears. When she had finished she shut the wardrobe and turned off the light, closing the bedroom door behind her.

Kelly was moving about in the front room, throwing a couple of pieces of turf into the range so that it would hold its warmth overnight. The house grew cold at night and this night would be colder still. She listened to him from where she blindly stood in the unlit corridor. The blessed candle had been extinguished. The wind had picked up and the front door rattled in its frame.

He moved noisily between the kitchen and the other room, unsettled yet absolute in his self-containment, as though everything and everyone else had ceased to exist with her passing. Helen listened to a chair being moved from place to place across the floor and then the thin rasp of the playing cards as he shuffled the deck in preparation for a game of solitaire. Usually he played cards only to while away what little free time he had; otherwise all his hours and attention were directed towards the small-holding. The pack would be divided and split whenever a cloudburst sent him running inside, cursing as he burst through the door, stamping his boots on the doorstep to loosen the clay, the cards snapped down on the seat of the chair one after another until the sun caught the raindrops on the window and he could return to the fields. Now the cards were dealt out more slowly, deliberately, like punctuation for dark thoughts.

There was no one to put her to bed. She did not dare to disturb him by going into the kitchen and moving the kettle to the hottest point of the range so that it would boil for her hot-water jar. She undressed alone, not wanting to turn on any light that had been out all day and evening. In the darkness she could just make out the cloth that covered the mirror on her bedside table, the fluorescent hands of the stopped alarm clock, the pale light bulb hanging from the ceiling, the sound of the wind in the fields outside.

The cards had slipped from the deck. She straightened them before tip-toeing around her father to get a coin from the mantelpiece for the bus fare to school. He was slumped in the armchair, his shirt loosened at the collar, an arm fallen over the side. One cheek bore the imprint of the armchair's fabric, where his face had turned against it during the night. The forefinger of that suspended hand pointed towards the open neck of a milk bottle wrapped in newspaper. Cautiously, she bent over and the sharp smell of alcohol filled her nose. There was about an inch of the clear liquid left in the milk bottle. She took the two-penny bit and went back to the kitchen as quietly as she could.

The brown bread was difficult to cut, the knife too heavy for her to control properly. She cut enormous slices, doorsteps that her mother would have called a waste. When the knife clattered on to the counter after the second slice she froze. There was no movement from the front room. She buttered the bread and spread a thick layer of raspberry jam on top. She had less of an appetite than she thought and the second slice went untouched. She took a handful of the biscuits that the mourners had brought to the house the day before and wrapped them in a paper bag along with a small red apple that had a yellow scar where a wasp had got at it.

Kelly would be woken by the dog when it was time for it to be let out of the back of the van that served as its kennel.

The school bus rattled along the narrow road, its diesel engine revving up the steep incline past Naylor's. When Helen heard it she felt a quiver of excitement start deep down in her throat. Her hands shook and she squeezed the bundle of books tighter against her chest. The bus crested the incline and sped towards her, shaking off a Border collie that had followed it. As it slowed to a halt she took one look backwards at the gable end of the house that poked out above the dry stone walls.

'Are you all right to be going into the school today?' asked Naughton, the driver, as he leaned out of his seat and helped her up the high step.

'I am,' she nodded and looked around for a seat. Every face in the bus was turned towards hers. She felt the throb of the idling engine running beneath her feet. Behind her Naughton was asking if she was absolutely sure as he pushed the cantilever door shut. The other children looked at her like disciples waiting for a parable. Not knowing what to do or say she returned their gaze.

'Here! Here! Sit here, beside me,' squealed Sinéad Foley as the engine fired into life and within moments they were all clamouring for her attention.

After they had run from the bus and into the school yard Helen went off to the toilet, letting the others go into the classroom ahead of her. The excitement had left her out of breath and she wanted to go to the toilet all of the time. Never before had she been the centre of attention in school; her birthday always fell during the summer holidays, and although she was good at her lessons she never excelled enough to get a medal at the end of the year. The biscuits had broken up inside the bag and when she pulled out the apple its skin was coated with crumbs, many of which had pushed into the flesh that had browned at the edges.

Inside the classroom she could hear the other children's feet scuffing on the floorboards as they stood in obeyance of the teacher's command. The teacher rhymed out a prayer and the children responded, their voices boisterous and so various that no sense could be made of the words. The teacher spoke a little after each cacophonous refrain, invoking the blessings of saints and martyrs, cardinals and bishops.

Helen heard her own name mentioned and the teacher was speaking of an hour of need when Helen opened the classroom door. Sean Wallace had his hand raised high in the air seeking the teacher's attention. Again all the faces were turned towards her. She felt giddy. Sean Wallace took his hand down.

'Helen, are you all right?' Miss Mooney came towards her, stooping a little as she looked into her face. 'Do you want to come outside with me for a minute?' Helen shook her head. 'Well,' said Miss Mooney, 'won't you sit up here beside my desk for a while then?' She dragged a chair up from the back of the classroom. 'How did you get here at all?' she said when Helen sat down.

'She came on the school bus, Miss.'

'Sean Wallace, put your hand up if you want to speak in future.'

Helen spent the morning in the chair beside the teacher's desk, breathing in the smell of chalk and the freshly pared wood from the mechanical pencil sharpener she was privileged to operate when the pencils were brought to be sharpened at noon, the metal handle turning again and again as her life had begun to turn.

In the yard at lunchtime the other children crowded round, pressing in on her. The excitement began to wane once the broken biscuits had been shared out and the apple discarded in a gutter where a seagull blown inland later discovered it. The other children re-established their own allegiances after a while, grouping together in tight knots as they circled the yard. There was the sound of skipping from around the corner but the attraction of the game had dulled for her. Clouds bubbled in the sky, casting shadows that drifted slowly across the children at play. Two boys chased each other back and forth across the concrete, their mouths wide open in the silent ecstasy of a pursuit neither wished to end. Miss Mooney patrolled the yard, a book clasped in one hand and the roll-call secured to a clipboard in the other. From time to time Helen felt Miss Mooney's eyes fall upon her. After a while Miss Mooney came over.

'Did you bring some lunch with you today, Helen?'

Helen nodded, her attention more on the two chasing boys than on the teacher. Teachers asked awkward questions.

'Did your daddy make the lunch for you?'

Again Helen nodded. One of the boys made a grab for the other's jersey but missed and almost lost his balance.

'Would you not go and join in the skipping with the girls? I'll turn the rope for you if you want,' Miss Mooney said in a half-whisper, as though it was to be a secret between Helen and herself.

Helen shook her head.

'Have you lost your tongue or what?' An edge of exasperation had crept into the teacher's voice. She stared at Helen for a while longer, waiting for her to say something. 'I've got some red lemonade in the press in the classroom if you want to come in for a few minutes before I call the rest of them.'

Helen followed Miss Mooney into the classroom where two boys sat at desks in opposite corners transcribing poems from an anthology into their copybooks. Miss Mooney looked over their shoulders to make sure that they were doing what they had been told. 'That'll teach you to do your homework in future. Gearóid Seoighe and Mark Lenehan, you should be ashamed of yourselves, what should you be?' 'Ashamed of ourselves,' the boys parroted and kept their heads bowed.

'Now, Helen,' the teacher said, lifting a bottle of lemonade from the press. She poured a glass and handed it to Helen. The sweet lemonade fizzed in her mouth and she remembered the day before when she had drunk glass after glass of cola, lemonade and orange mineral. The pats on the head from relatives and the coins that were now stacked on her bedroom windowsill.

Later, when the children had come in from the yard and the lessons resumed, Helen's thoughts broke free of the classroom. She wondered what Kelly would think of her leaving for school on her own. He would be proud of her, the way she had cut the bread and taken the fare from the mantelpiece. He would be proud of her for clearing away the glasses and for sweeping the floor the night before after the relatives and friends had gone. He would pat her on the head and tell her what a great girl she was. Birds were busy in the sky beyond the classroom window. The teacher's voice seemed as distant as the birds' plaintive calls, the children's responses like those of a choir heard through heavy cathedral doors. She felt tears upon her cheeks. The birds circled the school yard, diving from time to time.

The goodbyes and good wishes of the other children followed her up the track towards the house, the hoarse engine sound dying away as Naughton coasted the school bus down the hill. The track had seen more use over the last week than it ever had. The coarse grass that grew in a strip down its centre was speckled with oil where it had brushed the underside of visiting cars. Tyre marks had not faded in the mud at the edge of the track. When she came through the gate the small farm was spread out before her, the house standing proud on a gentle rise in the middle of the four fields. The meadows at the front of the house were the most prized, their walls the tallest and most complete. The red Bedford was parked at the gable, the dog sitting on its haunches beside it. The dog lifted its nose and dipped it a few times as it caught the traces of her smell. Kelly was at home and not in the fields.

'Well now, wee madam. If Naughton hadn't dropped by to tell me you had taken the bus, sure I wouldn't have had a clue where you were.' Kelly came out to the door when he heard her feet on the stones.

'You were asleep, Daddy.'

'Blackie woke me, but he couldn't tell me where you'd gone.'

'Sorry.'

'Never mind that now. I have the kettle on to make tea, and you'll have a sandwich.'

The house was cold. A new fire had been laid in the range and also in the fireplace in the front room and the smell of damp turf hung in the air. The kettle would take a while to boil now. Helen could not remember a new fire ever being laid in the range before. Even when Kelly cleaned the flue the fire was only ever damped down so that it could be revived with newspaper.

Kelly took out the carving knife and began to hone it against a sharpening bar, the screech of the sliding metal filling the kitchen. He cut thin, pink slices of bacon from a joint that had been boiled for the mourners two days before. He peeled the waxen rind from the meat as he cut, leaving them aside for the dog.

'How was school anyway?' he said at length.

'Okay.'

'Did you do maths?'

'We did.'

'Your lessons are important you know.'

'I know.'

Questions her mother would have asked. Kelly had taken little interest in her schooling before and the words 'lessons' and 'maths' seemed strange coming from him now.

He unwrapped the butter and spread it upon the bread before placing the bacon between the slices. She came in to watch him make the tea, the pot scalded twice and the Barry's tea spooned in with all the ceremony of a religious rite. While the tea drew at the edge of the range two mugs with a red wash around their bases were taken out and milk poured in their bottoms along with a spoon of sugar. After a few moments he took the pot from the range and a small drop of tea was trickled into the first mug. Satisfied with the colour he poured until both mugs were filled. There was no need to waste a clean spoon stirring. He propped the sandwiches on top of the mugs and carried them into the front room where they sat near the growing fire and drank and ate, Kelly resting his elbows on his knees and holding the mug and sandwich while he read the sporting pages of a newspaper spread on the floor at his feet. Helen watched him.

'Would you not get out one of your textbooks to be looking at?' Kelly said later, reaching to turn a page on the the floor. The sun had begun to set and its light cast a faint red glow across his face as he turned to her.

Helen shook her head.

'All right then. Suit yourself.'

Silence like the night fell upon them almost without their knowing. Helen grew uneasy, the only sound the turning of the newsprint and the crackle of the flames in the hearth which her father now read by. Still she sat next to him, waiting for she knew not what, watching the dusk fold in on itself and become wholly night.

When the fire fell in with a whoosh of sparks he folded away the newspaper and took more turf from a box in a corner of the room that was itself in almost complete darkness. The dog began to scrape at the door and its whining carried into the room where they sat.

'Would you believe that!' Kelly said. 'I forgot about poor old Blackie.'

This raised a smile from Helen and he turned the switch on the lamp upon the mantel. The brightness hurt her eyes and she blinked it away.

'Come on 'til we feed the poor creature.'

They took the bacon rinds out to the doorstep where the dog was circling in anxiety. It set about leaping for his hand as Kelly lifted the rinds and dropped them on to the flags. Helen came back from the kitchen with a bowl of water which she set down on the doorstep. She squatted beside the dog and stroked the silken fur on its head while it fed.

'Do you think, Daddy,' she said suddenly, 'that Blackie could stay in the house tonight?'

'And why should a dog stay in the house when it has a home of its own outside?'

'No why.' She lifted her hand from the dog as though the animal itself was at fault.

Kelly went around them and out on to the apron of gravel, his shoes crunching on the rounded stones. His breath rose before his face even though it was the end of May and the nights were warming. He stood looking out into the darkness waiting for his eyes to become accustomed to it, waiting until he could discern the shapes of the world behind the screen of darkness: the stone walls, the track that trailed away towards the road, the posts of an unfinished fence like pale sentinels in the weak moonlight. An animal screamed somewhere out in the blinded landscape and he turned his face towards the sound as if able to see the stricken creature. The dog shifted uneasily at the noise, pricking up its ears and waiting a moment or two before turning its attention back to the rinds and water.

'C'mon, Blackie,' Kelly said quietly, not turning, his hand slapping against his thigh. The dog came down off the doorstep and went around the gable with him.

Helen heard the van doors being opened and her father's voice as he spoke to the animal before closing the doors again. The dog whined as Kelly walked away. 'Whist now, Blackie, whist!' he said, and the dog was still.

Within days the house had settled. The leftovers from the food that had been prepared for the visitors of the week before was used up and Helen accompanied Kelly to the shop in the village. Those men that they met touched their caps as they passed. The women came up to Kelly to tell him that they were very sorry for his trouble, and he gripped their elbows while muttering his thanks for their sympathy. He was detained by Mrs O'Neill for some time in the grocery shop until another customer arrived and Kelly was able to get away. The village was quiet; the odd tractor rumbling along the road, a man going from one telegraph pole to another fly-posting advertisements for a circus in a nearby town, a child riding an adult's bicycle in circles in front of Breffni's public house. Helen watched the boy struggling to control the bicycle, sliding from side to side across the saddle to push the pedals. Michael O'Brien came to the door of the pub and called out to the boy, who dismounted and wheeled the bicycle back to where he had found it leaning against the front window of Breffni's. Arms, shoulders, and the backs of men were pressed against the frosted glass window of the pub. Sometimes a face would almost come into focus behind the glass when someone leaned forward to set a drink on a table or to hear what another was saying.

'Hello,' said O'Brien, resting one shoulder on the door frame. 'I was very sorry about your wife.' He made a gesture with his pint as he spoke.

'I know that. Thanks, Michael.' Kelly's feet shuffled and he rattled the van keys in his pocket as he stood looking across the road at the pub and the shapes behind the window.

'Will you join us?' O'Brien asked hesitantly. 'Just for the one.'

'No, no thanks. I've to get her home and put some order on the place before it falls asunder.'

'All right then.' He touched his cap and turned back inside the pub. Kelly stood for a few moments more before taking Helen's hand and hoisting her into the front of the van. He took a glance back at the pub and lifted himself into the driver's seat, pulling the door shut. He could have done with a pint and a short, to fill some time if nothing else. He had more to do now than before and yet the days seemed empty and shapeless.

Kelly had never been one for the pub. He only took the occasional pint, always followed by a Power's to cleanse his mouth and throat. In many ways he despised the men and their idle chat that ran on and on, the conversation drawn out to no conclusion, talk for the sake of talk.

His father had moved to the area and bought the land out the road shortly before he died and Kelly had been thrust into his role as head of the household when he was just nineteen. He had been too busy working to keep the family's head above water to fall in with the other youths of the parish, the same youths who as grown men occupied the stools at the bar and the benches behind the frosted glass. To them he was still an outsider, dedicated to his land that was commonly known as the worst for miles around. He was not admired for what small successes he had on the farm. The salad vegetables he brought on under plastic did not count for much amongst men who grew barley, potatoes and sugar beet, grazing livestock in their large meadows. They exchanged hello's and the odd word about the weather, and that was it.

When she came in from school Helen changed and went into the kitchen. The counters had been cleared and the dresser was filled with plates, mugs and cups. The table had been scrubbed and the floor swept. A pall of turf smoke that stung her eyes hung in the front room and she pulled a chair over to the window so that she could reach it and let the smoke disperse. The room was warm and cosy, almost everything was in its place, where it had always been. Kelly was outside at the gable of the house, anchoring the plastic sheeting on the cloches beneath which he brought on his crops of vegetables. She could hear the sheeting snapping to and fro in the wind as Kelly struggled to fix it to the hoops of black Wavin piping that served as supports for the cloches. The dog was standing nearby, its fur blown forward. Kelly secured the sheeting with lengths of fuse wire that he pushed through the plastic and turned around the Wavin, carefully folding away the sharp ends with an attention to detail that was at odds with other elements of his nature. His donkey jacket flapped about him, the buttons long since torn off. He stepped gingerly through the rows of young vegetables as he worked, cursing and swearing to himself when his movements bruised the leaf or stem of any living thing.

Helen lifted the heavy steel plate and threw a sod of turf into the range before moving the clothes iron from the back to the front of the range where it was hottest. Kelly had dumped the damp linen dishcloths on the counter so she folded them over the bars of the range to dry. They began to steam within seconds. She spread an old scorch-marked grey blanket on the table and went to get her school jumper and skirt. By the time she came back the iron was hot enough and the dampness had gone from the dishcloths. She took the iron to the table and set it on the broken brick she had put on the corner of the table. As she smoothed the creases from her skirt she remembered watching her mother do the ironing, the clothes quickly pressed and turned so that the iron would not need re-heating, water sprinkled on to stiff linen from a hand dipped in a mug at her side, the same hand that enclosed and guided her own along the sleeves and seams of her father's shirts. The hot iron pressed against the inside of her wrist and scattered the memory. Pain seared up along her arm and it was all she could do not to drop the iron. The burn had lifted skin from the flesh. Already it was puckered into tiny blisters. She tried to squeeze back the tears but they ran down her face as she hobbled across to the sink with her wrist pressed into the palm of her other hand. She ran water from the tap and danced her wrist under it, teeth clenched against the stabs of pain. From outside came the sound of Kelly calling the dog back from where it had pursued a blackbird along a wall: 'Come on, Blackie! Get away out of that!' He seemed part of another world altogether; oblivious of her pain, oblivious of anything but his fields, the cloches, the dog.

When she was able she took the iron back to the range and set it to heat yet again. She found a small bottle of iodine and dabbed some on the burn, flinching at the sting. She took one of her father's clean shirts from where it hung on the back of his bedroom door and ironed it along with her skirt and jumper.

When Kelly came in Helen was sitting at the table, her pencil poised over the blank page of a copybook, a poetry reader spread open beside her, but all her attention was on her father. His gaze was fixed on a pair of stray lambs in a distant field as he washed his hands in the sink. She listened out for him: the sloshing water, the kettle slid from the back to the front of the range, other things idly lifted and replaced as he waited for the kettle to boil.

She so much wanted him to notice. But what was there to notice after all? He had paid little heed to his wife's efforts around the house, except when she took it upon herself to move an item or two of furniture to give a room a fresh look and release it from the stale aspect of familiarity. Then he would come in from the fields and look about him, trying to figure out what had changed. 'What did you want to be moving the dresser for?' he would say as he fell back into the armchair and waited for a mug of tea to be brought. 'A change is as good as a rest,' she would counter from the kitchen. 'I saw no need for it anyways.' 'Left to your own devices you'd change nothing,' she would jibe, setting the tea down next to him on the armrest. Now, nothing in the room had changed and there was nothing for him to notice. The ironed shirt had been returned to the wire hanger on the back of his bedroom door and the cuff of her sleeve concealed the iodine-stained burn.

'Aren't you the great girl to be paying heed to your lessons? Aren't you?' He rested his fists on the table next to her and peered at the poetry book.

'I will arise and go now, and go to Innisfree,
And a small cabin build there, of clay and wattles made:
Nine bean-rows will I have there, a hive for the honeybee
And live alone in the bee-loud glade.'

'Don't I remember doing the same poem in school myself, and that wasn't today nor yesterday.' Kelly smiled and turned the page to read the remaining stanzas. 'God! and isn't it powerful stuff altogether.' His mood was as bright now as it had been for weeks, the spare verses untethering him from the house and fields. He read on as though Helen was not there, his eyes flickering across the print, pausing only where he struggled with a word, rolling the syllables across his lips as he deciphered it. His breath caught Helen's ear, the slow draughts as he breathed in and out. 'I had little interest in it then, mind you. I had more time for the hurling and the handball than for books when I was your age.' He turned the page. 'As for your mother . . .' and the spell was broken. His voice died to a whisper and she caught nothing of what he said. The ticking of the kettle could be heard in the kitchen before it broke into a squeal. Kelly went in to make the tea.

Days followed one after another. Kelly made her sandwiches every evening so that they would be ready for her the next morning and he draped her school clothes on a cord hung from two nails over the range. Kettle steam caused the creases to fall from the fabric. He woke her with a rap on her bedroom door, but would never come in to pull back the curtains.

She could still see her mother standing at the end of the bed, an edge of the curtain in her hand, squinting against the stark glare of early morning light, or grey projected raindrops streaming across her face.

Often she was awake before his knock, listening to him feeding the dog or searching through the house for some tool or other, but still she would wait for his signal that it was time to get up.

On Sundays Kelly left out the purple velveteen dress for her, while he wore a blue shirt and charcoal tie with his best black jacket and patent shoes. His hair was slicked to one side and he smelled strongly of talcum powder. He took a newspaper with him to the van and spread a few pages of it over the seats to keep the dog hairs from their good clothes.

At the church, however, where once the three of them strode proudly towards the front rows, Kelly now hung back amongst the men who surrounded the table where the donations to the parish were made, bright coins chinking on to the dull wooden surface. Their faces turned upward whenever a pound note fluttered down amongst the coins, the name of the donor registered in a ledger so that prayers might be said for them. Helen was a stranger amongst the men at the rear of the church, where Father Mahon's sermon was never heard except when he raised his voice to admonish the sins of sloth, greed, and adultery. The front rows of the church were empty except for Miss Mooney who sat on one side, while on the other and immediately beneath the lectern, his face turned upwards like a moonflower, sat Gerard Nealy, a simple youth who roamed the roads from dawn until dusk, his reflective armband catching a blade of sunlight that made its way through the leaded window above the altar.

After Mass the men stood at the galvanized gate nodding to various members of the congregation as they passed through, making boxing feints and punches at the young boys who ran giggling past them. The men scattered whenever Father Mahon appeared at the church door, a missal in his hand, guiding an elderly lady down the two steps and on to the broken concrete path.

Kelly took to visiting Breffni's public house after Mass. He squeezed in amongst the shapes of other men pressed against the frosted glass window and after a while emerged with a bottle of Corrib lemonade and a straw for Helen. She would sit on the stool beneath the black public telephone just inside the door of the pub, the acrid smell of the toilets along the hall mingling with the smell of tobacco and stale beer from the saloon bar. While she waited she listened to the infrequent telephone calls and afterwards pressed the A and B buttons furiously in the hope that a coin or two might be released. Sometimes, when the shop next door had shut, men would go into the saloon bar and emerge a while later with a loaf of bread, a half-pound of Denny's sausages, or a quart of engine oil, patting her on the head as they paused to pull back the front door. Finally, Kelly would wobble out of the pub, belching repeatedly as he crossed the road to the van, the dog barking crazily in the back as they travelled the empty road.

The men came in the middle of June. Helen noticed the Opel parked in front of the house when she came up the track after the school bus had dropped her off. The dog was circling it, barking and baring its teeth at the doors. The car was empty.

'Daddy,' she called when she opened the front door.

'Daddy,' she called again, but there was no answer. His boots stood inside the door, caked in fresh clay. She waited beside them. She could hear the hoarse barking of the dog outside and the ticking of the range in the kitchen. Fear crept inside her; a trembling started. She ran in through the kitchen with her eyes half closed and her arms outstretched for fear of what she might find there, and ran into Kelly who was standing in the middle of the front room.

'Daddy, Daddy!' She threw herself around him. 'I was afraid!'

'It's okay now,' he said, but there was little warmth or comfort in his voice and she drew away.

Three men were walking across one of the fields that the house backed on to. She recognized Mr Sweeney, who lived in a big house out on the Tuam road, but she had never seen the other two before. Kelly's stare followed them through every field and across every dry stone wall which they had to help each other over. He stood away from the windows so that he could not be seen from outside, but their every movement and gesture was registered. If he could have read their lips he would have.

'Do you know those men, Daddy?' she asked. 'That's Mr Sweeney, isn't it?'

'Aye, it is,' he answered at length. 'And Packie Folan, and his brother-in-law, Mick Costelloe.'

'Why are they in the fields then?'

Kelly said nothing, moving around the room so as not to lose sight of them, careful enough not to be seen. He had a face like thunder, cheeks darkened with blood, broken veins standing out on either side of his nose and on his chin.

Helen looked out at the men through the kitchen window. Every so often they stopped and one of them would point towards the house or a nearby wall or a telegraph pole that stood between one field and the next. Another would pace out a line with large, goose-stepping movements through the grass. The walking was tiring Mr Sweeney out. His large frame moved slowly and ungainly alongside the two younger men. He took off his cap and folded it into his hand and carried it there.

'Come away from that window now. I wouldn't want them seeing you.' Kelly stood at the door between the kitchen and the front room.

'Will they be coming in when they're finished, Daddy?'

'They'll have to if they want to deliver their verdict,' he said sourly.

'Will I make them some tea?'

'You will not. They'll get no more out of me now than is their due. Vultures they are! Nothing but vultures!' And he withdrew into the other room.

The dog was still barking at the empty car outside. Helen listened to it while she did her homework at the table. Kelly seethed in the armchair. He couldn't leave the fire alone, breaking a sod of turf into small pieces and throwing them into the flames one by one. He picked up the newspaper but could read no more than a paragraph or two at a time so he set about tearing the paper into small strips, which he rolled up and threw into the fire while he waited for the men.

When they had finished they came to the door.

'God bless all here,' Mr Sweeney called in the hallway. Even from the kitchen Helen could hear his heavy, laboured breathing.

'Indeed,' muttered Kelly as he got up and went out to them.

Helen listened to the men talking at the front door. Sometimes Kelly's voice rose loudest of all as his anger got the better of him. Mr Sweeney panted, but still his voice boomed deep and authoritative. The other two men did most of the arguing. After half an hour or so they left. Kelly slammed the front door after them. Helen watched the Opel bouncing back up the track and down to the road, the dog chasing it. Kelly had a bundle of notes in his hand when he returned to the fireside and Helen watched him in wonder as he took each note and smoothed it out on the seat of the kitchen chair that he played his cards on. He picked the dog-ears from those that had their corners folded, and counted them time and time again. It was as if he were looking for something in the money that the men had given him.

He noticed her watching.

'Never you mind this business. Keep your head in the books a while yet,' he said, licking the edge of his thumb before setting about counting the notes for the last time.

The tang of the peppers was strong upon her tongue as she licked the water from the plastic. She could feel the raised taste-buds when she ran the tip of her tongue against her teeth, the water like dew in the back of her mouth. It was warm where she crouched under the cloches, the smell of earth like a drug, the air alive and electric with creation. Small green peppers hidden beneath leaves, their insides bulging with unripe flesh and seeds; tomatoes, turning red from green, too hard and bitter to take yet. The silence was intense, as though the plants were waiting for something. She was careful not to tread on any leaf or stem; Kelly would not miss the damage. She could see him poised on the horizon, visible through the screen of plastic, pushing an empty wheelbarrow down the track towards the road. A breeze tugged at the cloche, the Wavin pipes vibrating when she held them to steady herself. With her fingers she raked the rich soil back into place as she left, erasing any sign that she had ever been there.

Kelly pushed the wheelbarrow along the road. Nobody passed him. When he reached Naylor's gate he stood beside it for a while until he was sure that he had not been seen.

He picked up the three loose breeze-blocks from behind a growth of nettles and dumped them into the wheelbarrow. He had noticed them a couple of weeks beforehand when he had gone to turn the van around in Naylor's gateway. The wheelbarrow squeaked intermittently as he wheeled the blocks back along the road and up the track to the house. He didn't look back until the blocks were safely stacked with some others at the gable end of the house. The blocks had come from everywhere and anywhere: gateposts that had fallen asunder, a broken septic tank, the old factory a few miles up the road. Kelly would store these and other things until he found a use for them. Two pool cues broken in a fight in Breffni's now supported his tomato plants, an old windscreen leaned against the gable wall beneath which he brought on seedlings, and a wooden P&T cable spool doubled as a workbench. Every item was clandestinely gathered: the van reversed up to the P&T road workings before the spool was lassoed and hauled into the back of the vehicle, the pool cues slipped beneath his coat while the barman swept broken glass from the floor, the windscreen scavenged from one of the car carcasses scattered around the parish. He dusted the grit from his hands and went into the house.

She heard him come in, the ritual stamping of the boots in the doorway with one hand on the handle and another on the frame for support. She moved the kettle to the front of the range for tea and picked up a cloth to look busy with. Kelly dawdled in the hallway and she wiped down the dresser while she waited. She could hear his breathing and the ticking as the kettle heated up.

'Only a week left for you then,' he said, coming through the door. 'You won't know what to do with yourself when it's all over with.' He had been looking at the calendar pinned to the back of the front door; school was almost finished for summer. Already some of the older boys were being called away from the classes to help in the fields. All of the Naylor children were working in other fields since their own wasn't worth a curse and there was money to be made as hired labour. The boys repaired walls and fences, greased machinery in advance of the harvest, and dosed sheep, while the girls sewed canvas seed bags together for spreading across haystacks and creels of turf. Máire and Sorcha, the youngest girls, were sent in to henhouses to recover eggs from awkward corners and the limp corpses of smothered chicks whose eyes had been pecked out by their peers.

'I'll be busy keeping house while you're working, Daddy,' she countered.

'I'm sure, now that you're a dab hand at it after me training you up, but there's other things you could be doing too.'

'Like what?'

'Ah, sure the things you always did on the summer holidays: playing in the hay fields or fishing for perch in the stream at Mullarkey's bog. Isn't there plenty to be doing when the days are so long?'

'Yes, Daddy. There is.'

The summers had been spent with her mother while Kelly worked the fields. Together they collected cress in the margins of the stream, berries that would be made into jam for spreading on sandwiches and scones, stones of different colours that Helen arranged on the mantelpiece. Flowers decked the house, plucked from the meadows and bogs and arranged in glasses. They withered in a day or two but there were always more to be picked and all of summer for the picking. Now those same months loomed long and empty before them.

'Go on in there now like a good girl and I'll make us a grand cup of tea,' he said. 'We'll have those Bolands with it that I bought in town the other day.'

Helen lingered at the range before going in, rubbing her palm along the warm metal handle of the kettle that had over the years been burnished by her mother's hands.

They ate in silence. Helen nibbled at the sweet biscuits and idly turned a cottage snowstorm upside down time and time again until Kelly told her to stop. Kelly quickly grew tired of the newspaper and shuffled through it looking for items he had missed or would otherwise have no interest in. He had filled the crossword at lunchtime and he scanned the clues once more, knowing that some of them would crop up again before the year was out. He liked to memorize as many of the clues as possible; it made for a good impression when the Sunday paper was taken out from under the bar in Breffni's after Mass and the men would crowd around and shout out their answers as Doyle the barman filled in the boxes. Kelly would bide his time and give the correct answer quietly and firmly in the knowledge that Doyle's ear, like that of any good barman in a busy pub, was tuned to one frequency only.

'How's Miss Mooney these days?' he ventured idly. The silence had cast a gloom across the room that even the flames in the hearth seemed to have retreated from. He was glad to break it now.

'She's fine.'

'I suppose she'll be looking forward to the holidays. Those teachers have an easy life of it, getting paid for their holidays and a sound pension at the end of it all.'

'She's going out to the Gaeltacht to teach a course in July and then she'll be doing a curriculum in August,' Helen defended the teacher, who knew well what was in the parents' minds and each year coached the children for it.

'Where's she off to?'

'Camus.'

'The like of those Dublin jackeens they get every year!' Kelly sneered. 'They go back up to the big smoke with less

Gaeilge than they ever had in the first place. A tour of Pearse's Cottage in Rosmuc, a brace of céilidh's and a game of hurling and they think they could be writing poetry and prose in the language. To hell with all that!'

Helen had no answer for him. The teacher was always careful to stop short of offering any opinion on the Irish courses that many teachers taught during the summer months. Once or twice in previous years Helen had seen the Gaeilgeóirs in the Gaeltacht areas, boys and girls holding hands and cuddling frantically outside the school buildings, groups of them drenching each other from the roadside water pumps, their city accents alien amidst the empty fields and roads.

'They must think we're all fools down here.' He turned back to the paper. 'If only they knew.'

Swallows dove back and forth beyond the windows. The sun was setting and in the dying of the day the birds' wings flashed like metal shards in the closing sky. Both father and daughter watched the birds squalling across the fences and the solitary winding track.

On the evening before the last day of school Kelly sat up late to write a letter to Miss Mooney thanking her for any support she had offered Helen during the last few months. Helen helped him find the old pack of Belvedere writing paper that still bore his wife's name in her own script at the bottom left-hand corner of the cover. When he set it down on the table they both stared at the name for a moment that stretched out and back to the time before they had been left so alone with each other.

'Anyways,' he broke, turning over the cover to the first white page.

The pen nib had dried and she brought him a cup of hot water to soften the ink with. The nib scratched its way across the paper for a couple of lines before the ink flowed properly. So simple and delicate an instrument as a pen looked strange and unwieldy in his hands that were more accustomed to the brute engines and tools that the calluses and ingrained dirt were testament to. He had four goes at it before he was happy with the short letter, and each time Helen took the scrunched up sheet to throw in the fire he snapped at her to return to her lessons. His wife had always written any letters that were needed but the crosswords had kept him on his toes as far as his handwriting was concerned and in the end the letter was respectable enough. He wouldn't want the teacher believing that any standards were slipping at home.

Afterwards he returned the paper to where he had found it and where it had always been kept amongst the hardbacks on the top row of the bookshelves behind the door. She was always a great one for the books, he said absent-mindedly as he thumbed open one of the novels. There was a whole row of Chambers editions of Maurice Walsh novels: *Son of Apple*, *The Key Above the Door*, *Blackcock's Feather* and others, their spines gone colourless and fragile in what little light had ever made its way into that corner of the room.

He went out to the dog with a bowl of water and stood at the door while it drank. From time to time the dog stopped and regarded him for a few moments. It was midnight and the air was still warm. A corncrake started up somewhere out in the fields, its harsh flat song seeming to carry for miles and miles in the clear unending night.

The ladybirds were easy to collect. Kelly and Helen went out into the fields with an old biscuit tin and brushed it across the tops of the bending stalks of grass. The air around them burst into clouds of flying seed and pollen as they ransacked the grass for the tiny red-shelled insects which fell into the tin with dull ticks against the metal. The pollen stung Helen's eyes and caused her to sneeze and the grass seed made her neck and underarms itch furiously but she went on collecting the ladybirds for the rest of the morning rather than let her discomfort show in front of Kelly. Too often before she had complained only to feel the keen edge of his tongue in place of any sympathy her mother might have offered. 'If you had your mind on the job in hand you'd feel nothing,' and 'If you don't get used to the itch now you'll be scratching for the rest of your days,' the skewed logic proscribing any hope of reply.

Kelly called a halt to the collecting at noon and she carried the tin back towards the house with it beating between her hands like a metal heart. When Kelly pulled back the plastic sheeting on the cloche the greenfly and whitefly shifted about from leaf to bud and stem and settled again. Helen shut her eyes against any misguided flies and laid the biscuit tin on the ground and backed off. When she had reversed out of the cloche Kelly reached past her with a straightened clothes hanger and lifted the lid from the tin. The ladybirds swarmed out like a black and red fountain and Kelly sealed the end of the cloche. For a minute or so the ladybirds threw themselves blindly against the plastic. Their ribbed and cartilaged underbellies could be seen where some of them lay trapped in condensation drops from which they would eventually free themselves.

'That'll put the wind up those blackguards, what?' Kelly stood back from the cloche and folded his arms across his chest, rocking back and forth on his heels in triumph, idly twirling the clothes hanger in his hand.

Helen watched the insects alighting on the leaves of the plants inside the cloche. 'Will they eat them all?'

'They will, every last one of them,' Kelly hummed with pride. 'Give them a couple of days and there won't be a fly left in the place.'

Later, after they had eaten, Kelly took off in the van. All afternoon and evening he had interrupted whatever he was doing to go and inspect the cloche. Instead of pulling back the plastic and looking in he would just stand gazing at it, swollen with the satisfaction of his own ingenuity. He had been full of himself, whistling as he filled in the crossword, clapping his hands together as he waited in the kitchen for the kettle to boil. He was so distracted that he didn't tell Helen where or when he was going. The first she knew was when she heard barking and looked out to see Blackie chasing the red van as it rocked down the track. The van rounded the corner on to the road to the village and Kelly slowed down so that Blackie could catch up. He often did this and would open the door to let the dog leap into the passenger side. This time, however, he began to accelerate when the dog drew level with the van. The dog chased even harder and its barking died as every ounce of effort and energy was poured into the pursuit. A little way down the road Kelly slowed again but when the dog drew level for a second time he put his foot to the floor and the van sped off. Blackie slowed and half-heartedly chased it for a couple of hundred yards.

The noise of the van's engine died in the distance and she watched the dog come back up the track to the house, its tail hung low and tongue lolling between its jaws. She brought a bowl of water out to the doorstep for it and watched it drink. She left the front door open but it would not enter; as a puppy Kelly had chased it from the hallway too often and it would not trespass now.

Lights were coming on in houses across the parish and women could be seen going from window to window drawing curtains. Trails of turf smoke rose slowly upwards in the breathless evening. She went in to switch on the lamps in the kitchen and front room, careful not to allow any light into the hallway for fear of attracting moths.

The house was empty in the morning. His bedroom was cold, the sheets unturned, the ticking of the alarm clock filling the space he had left behind.

The van stood outside with its lights on. The dog sat alert on its haunches some distance from the front of the van staring through the windscreen at Kelly, who was slumped across the steering wheel with his head resting among some papers on the dashboard. Where he dribbled in his sleep a pool of saliva had collected. When Helen opened the door the dog came to her feet but turned away at the stench of stale alcohol and tobacco that filled the van. In the cool fresh morning Kelly smelled as though he had been delivered from another world altogether. She went around and opened every door. Presently the dog returned to the van, raised itself up on its paws at the door and sniffed at Kelly's clothes. Kelly groaned and shifted but did not wake. Helen went back inside to make breakfast. The dog let itself back down and lay in the shade beside the van to wait.

The heads of the radish poked out above the fine soil and Kelly showed Helen how to rake the earth back around them so that the slugs and snails could not attack the red-skinned vegetable. They would have to be left in the ground a while yet to swell up and lose the bitterness of the too-young flesh.

In the week after the school had closed Helen was grateful for the fine weather to get out of the house. Kelly had set her small, manageable tasks in the fields and was happy to leave her to it, offering only occasional guidance when it was needed or asked for.

The fine weather had brought men to work for the first

time in the two fields behind the house that had been sold to Sweeney a couple of months before. They worked bare-backed, their skin white and freckle-daubed that would over the summer turn red and peel to a soft olive hue. They were picking stones, using small hand-rakes to drag them into piles which were then heaped into canvas sacks and carried away.

Two men worked on a boulder in a corner of the first field which Kelly had always had to cut around. The men had found a fissure in the rock and one of them held a long chisel over it while the other brought a sledgehammer to bear upon it. The man holding the chisel warned the other constantly against missing the head of it. Hammer on chisel rang out sharply in the warm afternoon like a calling to pagan ritual.

Kelly looked on from where he stood unseen in the shadows at the gable of the house. He smiled when the breeze carried the men's curses and arguments to him and triumphantly thumped one fist into the palm of the other hand each time the rhythm was broken as the hammer missed the chisel. After an hour the men changed roles and soon the point of the chisel began to make progress into the rock. Kelly turned back to the fields he still owned.

Soon after midday Thomas Naylor emerged from his house and noticed the men working in the fields behind Kelly's. He watched them awhile, shielding his eyes from the sun, wondering if he knew any of them. He could see Kelly working one of the fields at the front of his house. Never before had he seen Kelly hire labour to prepare or harvest an inch of his own land. He hurried back inside, shouting to his wife that Kelly had labour in the fields and that he was heading up to see if there was any more going. He came running from the house, buttoning a shirt across his bare chest as he ran up the track.

'Kelly, Kelly!'

Kelly pretended not to hear, making a point of stooping to pull some imaginary weed from the ground.

Thomas Naylor called out again once he had reached the edge of the field, and Kelly slowly turned to him.

'Thomas. What brings you up here?'

'I see you've got help in the fields.'

Kelly weighed the question for a moment. 'Aye.'

'I was wondering if there was any more needed, only I could do with the few bob.'

Kelly leaned on the rake and looked down towards Naylor's house where red paint peeled in patches from its asbestos roof and a listless greyhound rose then settled again under the thin shade of a windowsill.

'Well now, they seem to be making a good job of it already.' He poked at his boot with the end of the rake. 'Wouldn't you say so yourself?'

'They could always do with another set of hands on a warm day like this. The heat wears you out double quick you know.'

'Go on so. There's a few parts of the wall need repairing. If they say anything or give you any queer looks, just ignore them. They'll be jealous now of a real worker.'

'Good man, Kelly. Good man yourself,' Naylor said as he went off around the side of the house, stuffing his shirt into his trousers.

Kelly watched him go. 'That'll put the cat amongst the pigeons,' he said, but there was no one to listen.

'Will we go in for a cup of tea and a sandwich?' he called out to Helen later as he made his way back to the house. The radishes had been covered. Not a speck of red skin was to be seen beneath the bright green-leaved heads. Kelly clapped her gently on the back when they went into the kitchen. She was proud of the work she had done. She pulled the kettle to the front of the range and opened the vent to allow more air into the fire.

The day was almost gone when Kelly rose to return to the fields. Helen listened to him huffing and puffing as he laced up his boots in the hallway. She watched him make his way back to the fields, trying to shake new life into tired limbs as he bent towards his work with hoe and rake. He would struggle now more than any year to get a return on his land. The two fields that Naylor and Sweeney's men worked were lost to him and the potatoes they had traditionally yielded would be missed. The potatoes had been small for a couple of seasons and Kelly had rested the fields the previous year to let the land recover before planting again. He would have spread seaweed or bone-meal if he had been let but the fields were no longer his.

Helen looked out at the men collecting the stones. They had slowed as the day wore on and rose to straighten their backs more often now than earlier.

She remembered the shouting on a June day the year before when her father had been working that same field, using a fork to destroy the potato ridges and remove any tubers that might seed themselves during the summer. The shouting had been like that of some primal animal and she and her mother had rushed out to find him kneeling amidst the field, one hand clamped across his ear. Birds which had settled between the ridges scattered as they ran towards where he knelt. A horse fly had found its way inside his ear and had become trapped there, and when her mother prised his hand away she put her own ear to his to listen for the miraculous buzzing of that insect's useless wings. He trembled as though the engine of the fly's body had transmuted itself into his. Her mother drove him to the doctor, Kelly kneeling on the floor of the back of the van with both hands clasped over his ears and his eyes tightly shut, the dog calmly gazing out of the rear window at the walls and fields peeling away into the distance.

Thomas Naylor worked until the dew began to form upon his shoulders, his limbs long since worn out and almost worthless as he moved rock after rock along the wall, filling holes where none had ever been.

He came to collect his wage and stood there after knocking quietly on the opened front door. Kelly let him wait for a minute before calling him in.

'God bless all here.' The greeting trotted out as easily as breath. He stood in the weak light that followed him through the door, his shirt limp and insecure upon the angles of his tired frame. He had not shaved in days for want of a decent blade. He swept his hair into place with the fingers of one hand and winked at Helen. 'Máire was asking after you, Helen.' She smiled at him, unsure of how to reply to this man who had never spoken to her before. Kelly went off into the darkened hallway of the house, leaving Thomas Naylor and Helen in their awkward silence. When he returned he had a few coins in his hand.

'Now,' he said, holding out the coins for the other man to take.

Naylor looked at the coins, their edges shining in the gloom. He glanced up at Kelly and Helen saw in the nervous beginnings of a smile that Naylor thought it was a joke and that quick as a flash Kelly would pull a five or ten pound note from his breast pocket. One look at Kelly's face told him that this was not to be and that the indeterminate value of those coins was his sole reward.

When Naylor was seen coming back up the track to the house the next morning Kelly told Helen to go to her room and close the curtains. She stood in the half-darkness listening to her father moving about the other rooms in opposition to Naylor, whose boots grated on the gravel outside. Something nudged the window and she froze until it moved away again. She imagined Naylor's eyes peering through the glass and fabric and she held her breath in the hope that it might still her heart for the moments Naylor stood outside. A while later she went in to the front room where Kelly stood just out of the window frame, watching Naylor disappearing down the track to the road.

'Is there no work for him today, Daddy? Is that it?'

'No, there's no work nor money to pay for it if there was.'

They looked down at the Naylor's house where Mrs Naylor, a thin and bird-like woman, strangely bent like a sea-horse, had come out to hang washing on the line.

'No work and no money to pay for it,' Kelly repeated to himself, but Helen heard it anyway.

The Hillman Imp struggled up the track, belching black exhaust smoke as the driver shifted down gears to get up the slope. Helen and her father came to the door when they heard the noise but Kelly quickly turned back into the house once he had recognized the car.

Helen waited for her mother's sister and her husband to draw up to the house. They had not visited since the funeral and she hoped now for some news of the cousins whom she had not seen since the previous summer. Without her mother to take her there she had grown more jealous than ever of the friendship the cousins had between them, and she missed too the fun of the games and horseplay they got up to whenever she visited.

The engine of the Imp ran on for a minute or so after it had been turned off. Martin and Margaret Corcoran waited for the engine to finish hiccoughing and spluttering, Margaret turning to say something to her husband as she waved at Helen. Mr Corcoran frowned and undid his seat-belt, which was frayed where it crossed his shoulder.

'How are you, my dear?' said Margaret Corcoran, switching a tin of Jacob's biscuits to her other hand as she bent to kiss Helen on the cheek. She smelled faintly of dead or drying flowers and her kiss left a powdery feel upon

Helen's skin. She turned Helen around and walked after her into the house where Kelly had disappeared to the bathroom, his water thundering into the bowl as they waited in the hallway for him to emerge.

'Conor, you're keeping well so,' Mrs Corcoran said as Kelly came out, shaking his hands dry, the drops falling like dark freckles upon the floor.

Helen had not heard her father addressed by his forename since her mother had died. He was known to all as Kelly since there were no others of that name in the parish.

She heard now her mother's voice calling him from where she lay in bed while they put up the tinsel and paper decorations in the front room that would brighten their last Christmas together. The paper lanterns and stars she had cut out and glued together in school were strung high above the hearth, and sprigs of red-berried holly were pushed in atop the framed photographs and prints that dotted the walls of the room and kitchen. Kelly lit a Christmas candle and carried it down to her mother and she did not call out for him again that night.

'You're looking well yourself, Margaret,' Kelly said flatly. 'Won't you come through?'

'Don't mind if we do.'

Helen went to move the kettle to the front of the range and took a knife to cut back the Sellotape that sealed the tin of biscuits. In the front room Martin Corcoran was talking about the teams contesting the county hurling championship, but no one was listening and by the time the kettle had boiled he had stopped.

'Isn't this grand?' Mrs Corcoran said when the tea had been brought in on a lacquered tray, the best china cups with the painted swallows and gold filigree set alongside the teapot. 'Isn't it just dandy now?' smiling at Kelly and Helen. 'I hope the biscuits are all right, Helen.'

'They're lovely, Mrs Corcoran.' She always brought the same brand of biscuits when she visited.

'How was the drive over?' Kelly said for the sake of something to say.

'Sure now, Kelly, the Imp will take us anywhere we—'

'If it wasn't for that car the journey would have been fine. There isn't an ounce of me now, Conor, that isn't shaken to bits.' Mrs Corcoran seemed unaware that her husband had said anything at all.

'The mountings need looking after, that's all,' Mr Corcoran breathed. 'It's a wonder for its age,' he said directly to Kelly.

They exchanged news of each other's families and discussed the engraving on Helen's mother's gravestone. The Corcorans ran a guest-house near Castlebar and one of their regular visitors was a stonemason who had promised them a gravestone in return for their hospitality. Kelly held back while his sister-in-law rattled on about the wording on the headstone and the question of whether the lettering should be etched in gold paint. In time his gaze wandered towards the fields outside.

'Come on, Martin,' Kelly broke in, ''til we have a look at those mountings.' Mr Corcoran all but leapt from his seat. As they were going out the front door words were streaming from his mouth in his attempt to explain to Kelly the structure and mechanism of the engine mountings. 'We'll leave the ladies to it,' Kelly called back into the house.

'Will you have another biscuit, Mrs Corcoran?' Helen pushed the plate towards her aunt's side of the tray.

'Don't mind if I do.'

The tea was gone half-cold and Helen took the teapot into the kitchen and topped it up from the kettle. When she returned Mrs Corcoran had settled into the armchair and had opened the zip on her skirt to free her belly, which bulged through the waistband of her support tights. 'You'll let me know as soon as you hear the men coming back in, won't you?' Helen nodded and placed the teapot on the tray.

The room was too warm and Mrs Corcoran edged between sleep and wakefulness for a while as she digested the tea and biscuits. The newly warmed tea went untouched; there had been no need for it. Each time her eyes closed Helen gazed at her, examining her for any likeness or feature that distinguished her from her mother. She was some years older than her mother had been and some of the common O'Shea features had dulled upon her; the slack chin had given way to a double chin, and the once almost lobeless ears had yielded after years of being crudely pierced and hung with heavy jewellery so that they now resembled twin wrinkled and curled foetuses crouching at her temples.

Helen could hear the men at the car outside, Mr Corcoran issuing advice and instructions and Kelly's muffled replies from where he lay beneath the engine, his face turned to one side and flattened against the coarse gravel as he examined the mountings from the corner of his eye. She could tell that Kelly was already growing impatient with Mr Corcoran's stream of advice when he himself was unprepared to get even his hands dirty.

'You must come over and see the children soon,' Mrs Corcoran yawned, forcing the zip of her skirt down a couple of notches. 'They're only dying to see you, and Elizabeth can't wait for you to see her Confirmation outfit. If you leave it too long she'll have it worn out. I can't get her out of the thing.'

'I will if Daddy'll take me. He's very busy with the fields this year.'

'Sure you could come back with us now if you wanted to, you know.' Mrs Corcoran leaned forward, smiling, putting a hand on Helen's knee. 'You'd be more than welcome to stay until the weekend, or the whole summer if that's what you want. You could have your own room and all, or share the bunks with your cousins.'

Helen remembered the excitement of the bunk beds; the narrow wooden ladder to the top bunk and the way they would fix the sheets so that they hung like a screen around the lower bunk when they were changing into their pyjamas or nighties, the pillows and teddy bears that were flung around the room in the darkness. She had always been sorry when her mother came to collect her after a weekend spent with her cousins.

'Sure you'd have a great time altogether, Helen.'

'Are Elizabeth and Thomas not going on the Gaeltacht this year, Mrs Corcoran?' The two eldest children had spent three weeks on a Gaeltacht course the previous July and Helen's summer visit had had to be postponed until their return at the end of that month.

'For all the good it did them! They picked up nothing but bad habits. I don't know what they do be teaching them down there but it's certainly not Irish, I'll tell you that much.' She made a loud ticking noise with her tongue against the roof of her mouth. 'No, they'll not be going this year, nor any year for that matter. So, will you come?'

Helen heard again her father's voice, his exasperation at Mr Corcoran's fussing barely restrained as he asked for a torque wrench. He would be completely alone without her. The house would be empty each time he came in from the fields. There would be no one to help with the picking of the tomatoes or the radish or the lettuce, and no one to take the cork-stoppered milk bottle of tea out to him when he was too busy working ahead of forecast rain to return to the house. She heard the torque wrench being flung across the gravel beneath the car and then silence for a while before Mr Corcoran began to apologize.

'I don't know,' she replied. 'I'll have to ask Daddy.'

'Don't worry about that, child. I'll have a word with him for you. I'm sure he'll be delighted. That's it settled then: you can stay with us until it's time to go back to school. Isn't that great?'

Helen felt something gnawing inside her, nerves or fear, she could not tell which. She was now torn between the prospect of two exciting months with her cousins and the thought of leaving her father alone in the house for the first time in his life. She looked around her at the familiar contents and geography of the room that were comforting to her when all seemed about to change.

Mrs Corcoran stood and breathed in, zipping up her skirt as she did so. 'Come on now 'til we see what you'll need to bring with you.' She beamed at Helen and went out to the hall and down to her bedroom, her shoes clacking on the floorboards. As Helen followed her she glanced out through the front door and noticed her father's grey-trousered legs poking out from beneath the car. She could never leave him alone.

'Mrs Corcoran,' she began as her aunt rummaged through the chest of drawers beneath the window in her bedroom.

'Do you wear this one in summer?' Mrs Corcoran pulled out a cotton pinafore dress and held it up. 'Only it looks a bit heavy if we were to get any decent weather.'

'Mrs Corcoran,' Helen tried again.

'Sure you may as well take it with you anyway. What harm will it do?'

A large bumblebee drummed against the window. Time and again the glass held it back. Helen's mother used to open the window wide for the bees attracted by the warmth of the house, and for a few minutes the sweet-wrapped insect would bounce amiably around the room before finding its way out through the window which would be closed again after it.

'Now,' said Mrs Corcoran, reaching for a small red suitcase she had found in another room. There were dry sprigs of lavender in the pockets that were sewn into the lined lid of the case. She picked up a pair of Helen's shoes and bundled them into the suitcase along with a couple of dresses and some skirts. 'If we've forgotten anything there's plenty in our house that'll fit you,' Mrs Corcoran said, clicking the case shut.

She put the case in the hall in the spot where Kelly normally left his boots. Together they washed and dried and tidied away the china cups and saucers and the lacquered tray. Mrs Corcoran was fascinated when Helen took out the cardboard box that the china was kept in. 'She was always an organizer, your mother,' she sighed. 'Nothing was ever too much trouble to the poor woman.' She was stilled by the sight of the simple cardboard box with her sister's fading script on the outside. Tears welled in her eyes but did not come, and she asked Helen to hand her the china so that she might wrap and return it to the box as her sister had planned.

Kelly paused at the front door but passed no comment about the case waiting in the hallway. Mr Corcoran sat in the car and started it up, pressing on the pedal to rev the engine and check the vibrations from the newly tightened mountings. His face broke into a smile and he gave a thumbs-up sign to Kelly, who then went in to wash the oil and grease from his hands and forearms, the white bar of soap turning grey between his palms as he scrubbed.

'Hello,' he said, coming into the front room, drying his hands on a dishcloth. 'I think Martin wants to make a move, Margaret.' The car revved outside as if on cue.

'Right, right you are, Conor,' Mrs Corcoran said nervously, looking about her as if she had lost something. 'Conor,' she began, 'I've been meaning to say something to you.'

'Go on, I'll not stop you.'

'Only I was thinking that it would be better for Helen if she was to come and stay with us for a while, maybe until the school starts up again.' She had turned to look out the window with her back to him.

'Is that what the case is for in the hallway?' he probed.

'Just a few things she might need while she's away, not that she'll want for anything while she's with us of course.'

'Are you saying that there's something wanting in her own home?' Kelly rose. He bent to shake the fire with the tongs, the sudden blaze of heat red against his face. Helen saw how firmly his hand gripped the metal tongs so that the knuckles shone against the soot-black hearth.

'She wants for a mother, Conor.' Mrs Corcoran turned around to look at him. 'Only there's been a lot of talk about the time you're spending in Breffni's these days, and that wasn't happening when Lizzie was around.'

'Well, let them talk!' he defended. 'If a man can't take a drink in peace then what's the use in it?' He dropped the tongs with a loud clatter on the fireside tiles. 'Go on out the front there, Helen, like a good girl.'

Outside, the car idled and Mr Corcoran sat in the driver's seat placing his hand flat against various parts of the inside of the car, checking for vibrations. The dog came around the side of the house to her and she cradled its muzzle between her hands while she sat on the step and waited. She could hear her father and Mrs Corcoran talking inside, Mrs Corcoran's voice rising and falling, Kelly's a dull and steady monotone. A wind picked up, bringing with it the smell of cattle. In the distance people were making use of the fine evening, working the flat fields as though refusing to believe that the earth is round or that time moves on. They would stay until the light was gone and they could no longer be seen, their voices calling each other in from the darkness.

The Corcorans said nothing as they left, the car rocking back down the track to the road, the dog following it part of the way. Kelly did not come to the door to see them off, and when she went back into the house his boots stood again where the suitcase had been. She took a biscuit from the tin in the kitchen and stood in the gloam. The radio was on in the front room and Kelly sat there in the firelight listening as every week he listened to 'Colm i Sasana', the thickly vowelled language wrapped in static filling the room.

That July made its way towards August and thence September, the length so easily and steadily falling from the days it was hardly noticed. The two fields were saved, Sweeney's fields came to nothing, and before they knew it the summer had ended.

Part Two

'DADDY,' SHE CALLED between knocks on his bedroom door. 'Daddy.' She listened to him turn under the bedclothes, the clatter of a knee or elbow against the wall that brought him suddenly to waking, the day already leaking through the curtains. 'Daddy,' she called once more to make sure.

'All right! All right!' he answered, and she returned to the kitchen to make the tea.

'Christ, but that's some cold,' he said, pulling on a sweater over his shirt as he came into the kitchen.

'There's a frost,' she explained.

'Aye.' He stood with his back to the range, hands smoothing the rail. A toe poked through his stockinged foot and Helen made a mental note that it needed darning. 'It'll help break the oul' clods if nothing else,' he said at length, thoughts turning already towards the fields that needed working.

As always he was quiet over breakfast, watching the land outside the window, the new barbed wire fence that had gone up alongside the wall around Sweeney's fields, the old potato ridges that fell away towards the stream that now bore Mullarkey's name in testament to the surrender of his land to the bailiffs. Mullarkey had died since. Birds rose from a stand of copper beeches and where the sun had not caught the frost the tracks of a fox could be seen making towards it.

She cleared the table after he had taken the kettle of hot water into the bathroom to wash himself with, the rasp of the dull blade against his chin, the pools of water scattered upon the floor that she would mop later. She heated water in a saucepan to clean the two mugs and plates. Saturdays were easiest. There was no school and Kelly did not want his breakfast cooked; weekdays she rose in complete darkness. Not a word of thanks was ever offered and now none was expected.

When she reached the foot of the track she got down off the bicycle and pushed it up towards the house. Children could be heard playing somewhere; it was a cold afternoon to be out in it, she thought, and wondered whose children they were. She stopped to listen for a second then continued, the worn rubber brake blocks squealing where they touched the imperfect rim of the wheel.

Kelly was waiting for her at the door. A wind that had blown up during the afternoon took hold of her hair and streamed it out in a vane behind her head, the luxury of that hair incongruous against the poor greyness of her duffle coat. The wind pulled also at a letter Kelly held as he waited.

'You're back at last, Helen,' he greeted. 'I thought you'd never come. Were you dawdling with the others at the crossroads?'

'No. With the wind behind me I'm home quicker than I could have been. I barely had to turn the pedals the whole way,' she said, leaning the bicycle against the wall.

'Good for you, girl, good for you,' he said, high enthusiasm faltering when he saw the anxiety in her face. 'There's a letter come for you this morning, and it's great news altogether.'

'I wasn't expecting any letter at all, Daddy,' she said. 'And you've opened it. Who is it from? What does it say?' She put out her hand for the letter but he kept it from her and she went past him into the house.

'It's from the county council,' he began. 'I put in a word for you a while back when I heard that there might be a small factory opening, and now they're offering you a job as soon as it starts up. They say here that it could be open by the end of April.'

The house was warm after the January day but still she shivered. She did not know what she should say so she said nothing and went to rearrange the couple of cushions thrown into the armchair.

'Well,' he said at length, 'what do you think? Aren't you going to say anything?' Not for a moment had he considered that she might think differently to him.

'I don't know what to say, Daddy. Really I don't.' She fluffed up a pillow and let it drop. 'What type of work is it?'

'Sure, how would I know that!' he bellowed, his disappointment turning swiftly to anger. 'Will you take it or not?'

She shrunk from him. 'I don't know, Daddy.'

'What do you mean you don't know?' he rose. 'Aren't you grateful for anything I do?'

Soon there was a white cloth on the table, with salt, pepper, butter, milk. Bacon fried on the pan, the smell rising into the rooms of the house and bringing the puppy to the door, its nose dipping as it traced the smell of the cooking meat. Already Kelly had it trained not to come into the house, but he had not taught it to be quiet and it whined now at the doorstep. 'Whist!' Kelly shouted from the front room and the dog sprang away but was soon back at the door, quiet this time.

Over dinner Kelly explained that the new factory was opening up where the old car battery plant had been in Drimelogue. A grant had been obtained from Europe and the building was going to start any day now. Already notes of caution were being sounded in the village. The battery factory had been a great success for a year or two with a couple of new shops opening in Main Street to cater for the workers and the pubs packed every pay-day. But business had turned sour and the factory had shed worker after worker until it had closed, taking the new shops down with it, leaving the pubs quieter than they had ever been.

'It'll be different this time,' Kelly reassured her. 'It'll not be in the hands of locals. It's a German company that's coming to make audio cassettes. I hear the Germans are great employers altogether. It'll be a good start,' he said, knifing a wedge of butter on to his potatoes. 'You couldn't hope for better.'

'What about my lessons?'

'What about them?'

'I've my Inter Cert to do in June.'

'There'll be no need for any of that. You don't get the offer of a job like this at the drop of a hat, you know.' He pushed some potatoes into his mouth and spoke through the side of his mouth: 'I'll look after all that, never you worry.'

He took the *Sunday World* from the mantelpiece and sat in the armchair to read what had already been read on the previous Sunday afternoon. Sometimes he would read the problem page again and again, the ink blurred where his hands had rested and sweated upon on it. Helen left the paper alone until she rose early of a weekday morning, spreading it out on the floor in preparation for the ashes from the hearth, squatting to scan the questions and answers, a shovel of ashes hanging in one hand ready to be thrown on to the paper in case he should wake and disturb her. He never did, but she lived in such fear of it that the precaution had become habit.

The offer of the job had her in turmoil although she could not let it show. There was no choice. She might go through with the Inter and then if she wasn't good enough to continue for the Leaving she would have to look for a job. A shame to turn away the chance because it had come too soon.

'Is there a drop of tea on the way?'

'There is, Daddy, there is.'

'Good girl.'

It would not do to go against Kelly, but she wished that she'd had some part in the making of it. For a moment she saw her whole life framed: a white coat, rubber boots, her hair tied back in a bun, the cassettes passed from one hand to another, a life passing by.

The water hissed as it fell from the kettle spout on to the range. She scalded the pot and made the tea, bringing it in on the old lacquered tray whose surface bore the scars of teapots that had been left to draw upon the range.

'Is there a biscuit or a piece of cake at all?' he asked, not looking up from the paper which he had turned to the racing pages.

She went to the dresser and pulled back the doors. The top shelf had begun to fill with jars, each holding a sample of the crops brought on under the plastic at the gable of the house, the crude black script on a white label slapped on to each jar in turn. The ink had faded on the oldest labels but she had no difficulty in identifying their contents: beetroot, onion, asparagus, gherkin, pepper. There were no biscuits, but foil-wrapped on the bottom shelf was a piece of Christmas cake, four weeks old but not gone too dry. She cut an angled slice and brought it to him, dismay returning momentarily when she saw again how the fruit had sunk towards the bottom of the cake.

'Your mother had a great knack for getting her cakes just right, you know,' he said looking up at her, the sentence trotted out without thought but freighted with hurt.

She rushed back to the kitchen. From the front room

came the clink of his fork on the plate as he broke the cake into pieces. The spokes of light on the ceiling shortened and were gone, the rooms descending into complete and shadow-less gloom. She stood and listened to him eating. How ignorant he could be of others; that their lives should bend towards his was as natural to him as instinct.

Kelly surveyed the frost-decked fields, boots crunching on the ice flowers that had survived all day. The brown and withered stalks of the failed potato crop of the previous year were scattered across the surface. Birds picked amongst them for snails and worms. They would find little as he too had found little. The fields were worn, minerals leached down-wards by weeks of rain into a heavy grey pan that no plough would reach. He should leave the land to rest for a year but the few pounds that the crops brought could not be done without, more so this year after the potatoes had failed. Before the two fields at the back had been sold to Sweeney to pay for his wife's burial he had always let one field in turn go fallow. The money that Helen would bring home from the factory might make a difference. Another hard year was in prospect as he lifted the fork and bent towards the work.

Helen noticed the decline. The bacon he brought back from the butcher was riddled with fat; he spent a day plundering the roadsides near Maam for the remains of ricked turf, the damp shavings making the room smell sour for hours after they had been lit; a jar of honey was not replaced when it was spent; the *Sunday World* was only bought every fortnight.

With a pang she remembered that last week of August the year before when the fields were being saved and before the potatoes in the field below had failed. She had cycled to Drimelogue and then out the hill road to collect raspberries, pushing on through yellow-fingered gorse without a care, sun in her hair, a paper bag filling with the fruit. Afterwards, the making of jam, sugar heaped on the sideboard, jars scalded and lined up beside the range to warm, windows closed against the clamour of wasps. Everything had been invested in that last wonderful week before she returned to school. Nothing had come of it. The jam turned rancid before time, the potatoes were blighted, rains came.

She watched Kelly through the condensation that had lingered on the window. He leaned on the fork, considering the fields, kicking at a clod, breath rising in the limp and frozen air. The delight of that last week of summer was now so distant and strange that it seemed never to have been.

Drimelogue was busy, the new factory so much in their conversation that it appeared that every soul in the area would be working there. 'Do you think, now, that the planners will let them widen the bend at the crossroads? It's awful narrow to be turning a lorry there,' and 'I hear that they're bringing the oil for the boilers straight from the terminal at Ringaskiddy. Isn't that awful hard on poor Michael at the station, and he only pricing up a new underground storage tank the other week.' Michael's pumps, at least, were busy already as people filled cars and tractors time and again to make the extra journeys out to the factory site to see if work had started. They knew as they drove out that it wouldn't start until Easter week but the trip killed time. Such was the speculation and argument amongst them that it did not matter.

Kelly would have little of it. After Mass on Sundays the speculation was rife about who had got the jobs; some had declared their cards early and were urged to stand drinks all round, but Kelly said nothing and was not asked.

'I'd love to work on the reception desk,' young Jane

Ginn was saying behind the counter in the hardware store. 'All those handsome German men and their strange language.'

'German, my arse,' Mick Coyne laughed. 'Sure you'd see nothing but the same oul' beer-bellied gombeens from back the way, wandering round from one day to the next.'

'Come here now! Aren't they Germans that own it?'

'They are. But they'll be over in Hamburg and Bayern Munich pulling the strings. They won't want to be mixing with the bogmen at all.'

Kelly half listened, rolling his eyes to heaven at Helen, who stood reading the notices taped to the back of the door. He picked up a few spades and tested the weight and balance of each tool, liking to give the impression that he had strict criteria for the selection of a new spade or fork. 'What do you think of the turn of that?' he would ask, holding the tines of a fork upright in his hand and examining their setting. Helen never knew how to reply. 'It looks set a bit square to me, you know,' he would say and return the fork to the rack.

'Kelly,' Mick Coyne greeted as he went out of the shop.

Kelly took the cheapest fork to the counter and paid for it, returning with it to the van before setting off to buy groceries with Helen.

All along the road as far out as the factory local men were digging a trench to lay new pipes. Some of them sported new council donkey jackets and were going to great lengths so that they would not get soiled or torn, fluorescent plastic letters sewn in across the shoulders and wiped every evening with a cloth. At the head of the trench Peadar O'Tuathail was in control of the JCB, swinging the hydraulic arm around to dramatic effect, explaining to the others how difficult it was to co-ordinate the action with the levers. It seemed that a man from every home in the parish was involved in the work, and more would be taken on once the stripping out of the old factory began. The men looked up and rested on their tools to watch the red van come past.

'Would you not think of looking for some work with the rest of them, Daddy?' Helen ventured.

Kelly darkened. 'I would not,' he rose. 'I've no need of the work, and anyway it's an unholy grind.' He looked out at the men, their faces blurring past the windscreen. 'Have you ever seen the likes of them?' he said. 'Breast-feeding shovels from one day to the next, thinking they've got it made.' The van passed the last of the men. 'They'll still be the same gurriers at the end of it all.'

The men spat on their hands and returned to work.

On her last day in school Miss Mooney came to see Helen during the morning break. A palsy had struck the side of her face a couple of years back and she held a tissue to her mouth to collect the dribbles that came every few minutes. The affliction had aged her, and although in years she was still young she had never married and now never would.

'Would you not consider staying for the Inter?' she implored. 'You'd get it no bother and the Leaving too if you set your mind to it. You've got your mother's brains as well as her looks. She was a great teacher to me, you know.'

Helen had been told many times by both teachers in the school that she resembled her mother in manner as well as in appearance, but it meant little to her and in time she had come to resent the comparison.

'I'm to start in the factory on Monday,' she recited. 'It's a great opportunity and I mightn't get it again.'

'Well, as long as it's your own choice, Helen,' Miss Mooney said. 'You'll come in and see us, though?'

'Of course I will, Miss Mooney.'

Helen watched the teacher go back across the yard stuffing the dampened tissue up her sleeve. The shadows of early starlings burst upon the concrete, the paper flutter of their wings hanging in the air for moments after they had settled upon a telegraph wire. The smaller children played at skipping as she once had, their sing-song melded to the ritual thud-thud of the rope that turned in hands that would hold not pens but crayons of different colours.

The smell of fresh paint entered everything on that first day in the factory. The men had instructions from Ginn's to put as many coats on the walls as possible, a tractor and trailer having to be sent out for a dozen new tins, and Ginn had bought more than a few rounds in the Shamrock Lounge on the day that the painting was finished.

The machines were swung out of the way to create a space on the factory floor and the supervisor gave general instructions to everyone gathered there. There would be tea-breaks at eleven and three and lunch for an hour at half past twelve. Only the fitters would be working shifts so that the machinery could be kept moving overnight. The firedoors were to be kept locked and only opened when the fire officer was known to be in the area. The supervisor sent two men around the workers with small brown cards upon which they wrote each person's name. These were the timecards and it was explained to them that they were to move the cards from the rack on one side of the door to the rack on the other side, depending on whether they were coming or going. Sean Wallace raised his hand and asked how he would know if he was coming or going but he was laughed down and the question was not answered.

The work was easy: cassettes taken from a conveyor and pressed into plastic cases one after another until a box was filled, then carried to the loading bay at the rear of the building where packers would seal and stack them. For an hour of every day Helen was taken to a separate area of the factory where she was shown how to operate the press-moulding machine which turned out the cassette housings, the large hand-held control with green and red buttons that was so heavy in her hand.

The weeks built with enthusiasm: new people to meet, friends to make, the rules of commerce to learn, and each Thursday the grey envelope that bore her name, a handwritten slip, a clip of notes. The money brought home on that first Thursday, cradled against her body as a shepherd might bring home a lost lamb and offered in the blindness of that complete innocence to Kelly.

She woke each morning at six, her hair brushed at the window while the kettle boiled on the range, lard warming in the pan for his breakfast, eggs waiting on the sideboard. The ashes were cleared from the hearth, the bacon set to cook, Kelly woken only when all was ready. When his tea was poured she would take the bicycle around from the side of the house and shout her goodbyes through the front door.

One morning after she had gone Kelly took out the ball of twine he used for setting the line of the potato ridges and went out to the fields. A farmer in Castlekerrig had told him to plant across the direction of the wind for good luck so he set about making the shallow ridges for the beetroot he would be growing this year. It was a cool and windless day, the best he could have hoped for; the seeds would not scatter and the topsoil would not dry and drift after he had thrown it over the seeds to protect them from weather and birds. Again as every year at this time, all effort, imagination, and hope poured into that soil, as if history did not work here where only one man toiled in a world of his own making.

The ridges had been set, the seed sown and covered by the time Helen came back from the factory, the rattle of the bicycle carrying before her on the breeze. Kelly rolled the twine back into a ball, waving to her when she called out to him that she was home. She looked slim and graceful as she rode, trapped there against the light from the west so that the crude and heavy bicycle was transformed into some delicate instrument that bore her along.

'How was your day, Daddy?' she asked, as he sat into the table.

'Ah, grand now. It can be a hard station all the same.'

'I see that Sweeney's fields are all prepared and ready to go.'

'Why wouldn't they be with the amount of help he has these days?' Kelly said sourly. 'Anything can be got or done if you're willing to pay for it.'

The rest of the meal was taken in silence, nothing but the tap of cutlery upon a plate, the hurried breathing in and out when a too-hot potato was taken, the sound of turf hissing in the hearth.

'I've my own fields prepared and planted today,' he said as if in passing but with certain intent as she leaned over to take his empty plate.

How could she not have noticed? She trembled, the plate wobbling then steadied as she took it into the kitchen, blood running beneath her skin, urged on by a heart that beat almost in panic at the slip. The ball of twine set down upon the dinner table for her to see, the empty seed bag folded between his boots in the hallway. She had not thought to look at the fields and he had said nothing until it was too late. Her talk of Sweeney earlier had only made it worse and she knew that no matter what was said or done now it would make no difference to him.

She remembered a day when something similar had happened. Her mother was frozen just as she too was now frozen, pinned by something he had said so that no escape was possible. She remembered her mother's blue gingham apron, the casserole dish she held in both hands, a trail of dried soup laid across the back of her hand like a thin scab, the awful silence from the front room where he sat, waiting.

But her mother had the measure of him and she had let *him* wait, his demands going unanswered and no sound made until he had risen from the table and found her leaning with her back to the range, watching swallows chasing each other across the low walls.

'Is there a drop of tea on the way?' he called, scattering the memory.

'There is, Daddy. There is.'

She went out to look afterwards, when he was playing cards upon the seat of the chair, the firelight casting his indistinct shadow upon the far wall of the room. The rows had been laid out as perfectly as ever, every stone picked from the soil that had been turned and thrown into a pile at the corner of the field. Beetroot, the vegetable chosen only because of the high price it would command at the market. He was desperate to compensate for the failure of the previous year and would throw all his passion into it again this year. What did it all matter? she thought, picking a handful of soil and watching it fall away through her fingers. After she had been born and her mother had finished at the school they had survived for the most part on the hand-outs from the State and the grinds that her mother sometimes gave to those children who had gone on to study for the Leaving Certificate, their bicycles leaning against the house or simply dropped on their sides in the gravel while they studied at the table beside her mother. But Kelly had never been satisfied. It shamed him alone to make the fortnightly journey into the post office to collect the money from Dublin.

They had wanted for little but Kelly had always aspired to more, the unceasing effort of will turned in upon himself so that for many he had become bitter and twisted as the branches of a tree whose roots seek moisture and its leaves sunlight when neither is to be found.

*

The weather turned. Three weeks of rain trapped Kelly indoors, cards played again and again, old newspapers dug out of the bottoms of cupboards and scanned for any piece he had missed, but he had missed none. He stood at the window, hands sunk deep in his trouser-pockets, watching Helen leaving for the factory in the mornings, the yellow oilskin cape that stretched from the handlebars to her head keeping most of the rain off.

'It's well for you now, having a job to go to in weather like this,' he offered as she pulled on the oilskin. 'We're not all so lucky, you know.'

'I know, Daddy. Thank you.' He expected to be thanked for the job day in day out and never failed to remind her when the chance arose.

Towards the end of the three weeks he lost all patience, going outside to clear the gravel path of the weeds that had sprouted amidst the downpours, hoeing between the rows of beetroot with the blade of the hoe cutting through the sodden soil like a knife through butter. He wore an old waxed-cotton cape which over the years had given at the seams so that the rain gradually made its way inside.

Helen saw him working in the field as she came down the track on that last evening of rain, the hoe moving frantically through the rows, the useless cape thrown in a heap and trodden into the mud beneath his boots. She dropped the bicycle on its side and ran towards him.

'Daddy! Daddy! You'll catch your death!' Her feet splashed in the puddles that had collected in the field.

'Mind the rows, girl!' he warned when he saw her. 'For God's sake, mind the rows!'

He had stripped off his sodden jumper and shirt and worked barebacked, the rain beaded like dull jewels upon his white skin, flecks of mud in traces along his arms, hair plastered to his skull from which rivulets ran down his face.

'You're mad! You'll catch your death, Daddy,' she implored, picking up the cape and shaking it out.

'Leave me be now,' he grunted. 'There's work to be done.'

The rain beat down on them both, drumming on her yellow oilskin as she stood and watched her father bent over the hoe, clearing imaginary weeds from the rows, the water running down his back through his trousers and into the soil that bore it away.

He came in only when the light began to fail and the puppy began to whine from inside the red van at the gable of the house. She took the cape, jumper and shirt with her as he would have left them otherwise. They did not speak. Helen rescued the bicycle while the kettle boiled.

Dragonflies were out, emerging after the rains from the bogs where they had waited to move now in silence over the fields. Swallows pursued them with open beaks, turning sharply at the house to return for more. A cuckoo could be heard from behind Naylor's house. Everywhere was busy.

Dinner was taken late, Kelly insisting on working every minute of daylight so that the good weather would not be wasted in the fields. 'There'll be plenty of time for sitting on arses when it's pissin' down,' he coarsened, hauling a bucket of stones on to his back and taking them to throw around the sink at the septic tank. The rows of beetroot in the fields were testament to his labours: bright green-yellow shoots breaking through the dark crumbed soil like candles staked out in the gloom of a church. Not a weed in sight, the earth turned daily with the hoe.

During the weeks of summer there was the factory to occupy her, the learning that had absorbed her at the beginning now turned to habit and repetition so that she spent a great part of the day watching the clock that hung by two chains from the ceiling.

'Never mind the time now when there's work to be done,' Martin Kane chided playfully as he passed by with a load of wooden pallets on a trolley.

She took her eyes from the clockface. 'Never mind the real workers when there's dossing to be done,' she called after him, blushing at being found out.

Kane had started at the factory only two weeks before, having spent months working the stock and cellar in Breffni's. A pale and gaunt youth he moved about the factory like a spectre, ridiculed by the other men and too shy to mix with the women. He rarely spoke except in answer to a question or request. Now he had spoken to her. She looked after him, seeing only the stack of pallets drawn out through the rear doors.

The money from the factory made its way through the town. On fine Saturdays the main street was decked with ladders propped against the walls of the houses which were being re-painted in bright colours. Nesbitt's, O'Dowd's, Mulligan's, and the Shamrock Lounge were busy every evening of the weekend, and the Celtic Hotel's Green Room was fully booked every Sunday evening. The Monahans, who had a father and son employed at the factory, bought a new Fiat car, taking the train all the way to Cork to collect it from the dealer. For a time it was the only new car in Drimelogue until Dickie Redmond bought a Volkswagen after doing overtime at the factory every week for two months. A new telephone box was erected by the P&T outside O'Dowd's until a party worker informed someone in Dublin that O'Dowd's was a Fianna Fáil pub. The telephone box was quickly relocated outside Nesbitt's, who had voted Fine Gael for years. It was noticed, however, that the cabling and wiring was left in place outside O'Dowd's in case the Coalition government fell.

Breffni's, too, was busy. The goings-on in and around the factory provided a focal point for the conversation after noon Mass on Sundays. Kelly held back, biding his time in those conversations which he could have little part in since he had not been involved in the refurbishment of the factory.

'They'll need to be extending it soon, you know,' Brennan was saying. 'There's oceans of boxes stacked up in that yard out the back because they can't get the trucks in fast enough. The elements will destroy them if they're left there for any length. It would make sense to build an extension before it's too late.' He tapped his glass against the edge of the bar to emphasize his point before O'Malley cut in.

'It'd make more sense to widen the road so the trucks could get in that bit faster. It might be the cheaper option and we'd all see the benefit of it.'

A boisterous row ensued as the men took sides with Brennan or O'Malley on the merits of extending the factory and widening the road, the day and the families that waited for them forgotten in the rush of argument and counter-argument. Kelly waited until the conversation had died down.

'Did I ever tell yez about the greyhound that my uncle, God be good to him, kept? Did I?'

The men continued to mumble about the factory, nuzzling their pints and looking up at the silent television screen on a shelf above the bar.

'It was a great runner altogether,' Kelly continued. 'It was out of the traps before you knew what was going on at all. But as soon as it rounded the first bend it would start to drift off towards the other side of the track, and sure after that it was only chasing the rest of the pack.' The men were paying him scant attention but he went on. 'Well, my uncle tried this and that but he still couldn't get the poor creature to stay tight all the way around the track. The poor man was driven to such distraction that he took the animal to a vet up in Castlebar.'

Kelly looked around at the other men. Their conversation had turned to football and he wished he had never begun the tale, but he would not now be forced into silence. He grabbed hold of Brennan's forearm and held it firmly while he finished his story.

'Well, doesn't the vet take out a torch and have a good look in each of the dog's ears and doesn't he start tut-tutting away to himself like good-o. "What's wrong with the creature at all?" says the uncle. "Nothing that a lump of lead in his left ear won't cure," comes the vet's reply. "And how should I go about that?" asks the uncle. "With a hunting rifle," says the vet!'

Kelly let go of Brennan's forearm. 'Did you ever hear the like of it, what?'

'Aye,' the men muttered, nodding afterwards in faint and false expressions of lingering interest, pint glasses raised to their mouths to avoid further comment.

Kelly recognized the drawing down of the barriers. He had seen it all too often before: the hurried telling of a flat and spurious story in a bid to interest and amuse his peers, these simple men who with blanked faces waited only for him to finish and be pitched into this awful silence.

'I hear that Byrne fellow's a terrible shyster altogether,' Brennan started once a familiar face appeared on the television screen, the conversation picking up again.

Ticking of the pedals and chain that were held steady while the wheels spun carrying her down the shallow hill towards the house, the rush of air pushing the skirt along her legs to cling to her waist, sweet touch of that coolness billowing against her stomach. If her father could see her.

The brakes squealed as she slowed at the foot of the hill and she swept the skirt back into place when she noticed Mrs Naylor stepping out through the half-door with a handful of sopping clothes to hang on the short line at the gable of the house. She was more curiously bent than ever before, as if the atmosphere itself was a burden to her. She struggled to look up at the girl propped upon the high saddle sailing along the road beyond the fuchsia bushes. Helen eyed her pitifully as she brought the bicycle to a halt before wheeling it up the track. The factory had arrived too late for the rest of the Naylor family who, with their reputation for hard and honest work, would have been welcome there. All had left for England except Sorcha, the youngest, who had moved the previous New Year to Enniskillen, where she had secured a position as a dentist's receptionist.

Helen noticed on the windowsill a toolbox. It was a simple wooden box with ends like the gables of a house joined by a wooden handle, burnished by years of use to the smoothness of a beach pebble. It held now not tools and measures but soil and flowers, purple violets with blood-red hearts, their gossamer petals gaily dancing. Thomas Naylor was dead almost five years, his few possessions turned to other purposes.

The house was still as death, Kelly continuing his work in the fields beyond the glass that seemed to momentarily separate his whole existence from hers. She peeled some potatoes and set them to heat on the range. She could not understand why the memory of the candles should choose this moment to return to her; perhaps the sight of the waxen potatoes shimmering there under the water, or the purple violets fluttering in Thomas Naylor's toolbox had pricked some hidden memory. But she remembered those same candles ranged around this same room, their weak collective glow like a screen against the unwanted spirits of the dead. All was dead or dying then: the light as the candles sank into puddles, the last words of the hushed conversations that had filled the house before the mourners left, her childhood going swiftly towards its end, her father's heart.

After the simple delights of the day the memory came like a blow. She went out to the cool evening at the doorstep, her eyes swimming with unshed tears. The dog came around the gable to her and yelped at her feet but she paid it little heed. Kelly moved between the rows, thinning the beetroot seedlings. It was a perfect evening for it, not a breath of wind, a narrowing sky, the tender roots could be transferred moist and intact. She was happy for him. He worked methodically and carefully: the end of an old broomhandle pushed into the soil, each seedling dropped into place, and the soil pressed firm around it. When each row was complete he would track backwards with a bucket, scattering water from a can over each precious seedling, the can topped up in turn from the bucket.

His industry and economy amused her. The backwards shuffle, his legs spreadeagled across two rows, moving like some abominable spider, the water measured out as carefully as liquid gold. At the end of each row he stopped and straightened, gripping his sides and turning his shoulders one way and another to loosen stiffened muscles. He showed at these moments a vulnerability that he would never have wittingly displayed; the picture of a man open to weakness and failure, mercy and compassion.

Water that had boiled over from the potatoes hissed loudly on the range and she went inside to quell it.

'That's a grand bit of bacon we have here,' Kelly remarked later, as he slipped the knife under the twine around the joint and cut it free. He always believed he could tell by the cutting of the twine whether the bacon was properly cooked. This time he smiled as the twine fell away.

'It is, Daddy. The meat is better in the butcher's these days. You have to pay through the nose for it, mind. I suppose that with all the money from the factory around Gleeson reckons that his customers can afford it.'

'Does he now?' Kelly scorned. 'Well, we'll see who kills the goose that lays the golden egg this time.' The knife cut cleanly into the pink meat, exposing the narrow seams of fat from which juices ran. 'The true customers won't forget in a hurry if a time comes when things turn sour again. They'll be looking elsewhere for their Sunday joint, let me tell you.'

Helen smiled at his foreboding. There was nowhere else to look for meat. Gleeson was the only butcher for miles around. Within reason he could afford to charge what he liked.

They ate, the room growing dark and strange around them and they not caring. They spoke about the factory, and the changes in the town, but mostly Kelly spoke about the fields, the price that beetroot commanded in the markets, and whether to bring on some of the thinned seedlings for pickling beneath the cloches. Always the fields and the crops in which the future was shaped and ambitions mapped.

'They're talking about extending the factory,' Helen said as she switched on a lamp for Kelly to play his cards by.

'Are they now?' Kelly said with some disdain. 'It's well for them, then.' He gathered and boxed the cards, rapping the deck loudly on the seat of the chair.

'There's even talk amongst the girls that they might be taking on some more workers for a night shift. Some of them have their sisters lined up for the jobs already. Would you believe the brazenness of them, Daddy?' Helen smiled at the thought.

Kelly scowled as he turned over another three cards, none of which matched. 'I'd be paying as little heed now to those girls as I possibly could. There's no telling what trouble gossiping could land you in,' he pronounced firmly.

'It's only idle talk, Daddy. To pass the time.'
'A shut mouth catches no flies,' he said.

On Monday morning the other girls in the factory had so much to say to each other that the clamour of their voices could easily be heard above the machines. Every so often one of the two supervisors would saunter down the aisle between the conveyors, replacing the odd cassette that had rattled off or counting the boxes that had been filled that morning. Then the conversation would die, the girls containing themselves until the supervisor had returned to the glass-fronted office in a corner of the building.

'There's a dance in Greenford on Friday. Are we going?' came the whisper along the conveyor belt as the office door closed behind the supervisor. The girls nodded in turn as the message was passed on.

'Won't you come, Helen?' Susan Byrne nudged Helen with her elbow, neither daring to take their eyes from the conveyor and the stream of cassettes rattling past.

Helen blushed and shook her head but for the rest of the week the question was asked again and again until the dance began to play upon her mind. Kelly would not allow her to go to an afternoon dance in Drimelogue let alone an evening dance in a town that was ten or twelve miles distant, and yet now that she had the girls' friendship she was desperate that it not be weakened or lost.

After the factory had closed on Thursday she rode into Drimelogue where Ginn's were often known to keep a bucket or two of cut flowers for sale on the pavement outside their shop. Angela Ginn was just taking them in when Helen got there. She was so nervous as she travelled home with the carnations wrapped in newspaper under her arm that twice she almost lost control of the bicycle. She rehearsed the scene with Kelly over and over in her mind until she had every vowel formed and stressed perfectly. The journey that always seemed so long and lonely was now gone in no time at all and she felt her heart beat heavier than ever when the house came into view through a gap in the fuchsia bushes that lined the road.

When Kelly came in from the fields she told him, her face rising to a crimson that was disguised only by the gloom that hung in the front room where, such was her distraction, the lamps had stayed unlit.

'Daddy ... Siobhán Muldoon has asked me round to her house for dinner tomorrow evening ... I was wondering if I could go?' she blurted out all in the one breath.

'Well now that's kind of her,' Kelly said once he had asked her to repeat the request more slowly.

Helen sighed with relief.

'But what's wrong with the dinner in your own home? There's fish bought for tomorrow. It'll go off if it's left any longer,' he darkened.

She was stricken, the breath escaping her as from a punctured balloon. A vision of the girls' laughing faces in the unseen dancehall swam before her eyes. It was more than she should ever have hoped for.

'Sure why don't you go after all? What harm would it do?' Kelly said quietly and at length, reaching to turn on a light and banish the gloom.

'Oh, Daddy! Thank you! Thanks a million!' She reached for him and wrapped her arms around his shoulders and hugged him. He shrank from the contact, moving towards a copy of the *Sunday World* that had fallen down the side of the armchair.

She stood there in the front room as he eased himself into the armchair to wait for dinner. His every movement seemed precious to her for fear that he might change his mind. He bowed his head to the paper, folding it over into the lamplight, ignoring the struggling fire which he knew she would attend to before long.

'Well, go on with you,' he said.

She giggled quietly and skipped back into the kitchen to watch over the dinner cooking in the pots, every nerve alive with excitement, her limbs almost uncontrollable.

'Where did those flowers come from?' he asked a while later.

'I bought them in Ginn's today, Daddy,' she called from the kitchen. 'I thought they'd look nice on the windowsill. They're lovely colours altogether, aren't they?'

'There's nicer ones growing wild in the water meadow beyond. They wouldn't have cost you a single penny.'

All the girls took the bus together to the dance in Greenford. Helen left her bicycle chained to a gutter down an alley between the butcher's and the post office so that it would not be seen if Kelly took it upon himself to travel into Drimelogue for a Friday evening drink. She had taken a black pleated skirt and a cream blouse with her in a plastic bag. In Greenford they changed in the toilets of O'Neill's Lounge. The other girls all wore tight blue denim jeans and shirts of various colours and Helen felt embarrassed when she realized how out of place she looked alongside them. The girls crowded in front of the mirror over the broken sink, swapping mascara, eyeshadow and lipstick, while Helen brushed her hair out in long sweeps.

'Would you not try some make-up, Helen?' Susan Byrne asked, offering her the tube.

'No, no. I'll do fine as I am, thanks, Susan.'

'Go on, give it a try,' the other girls sang, and eventually she took the lipstick from Susan's outstretched hand. Her mother had never worn make-up, only a precious dab of perfume on each wrist, but she remembered seeing her Aunt Margaret applying colour to her lips during the holidays she had spent with her cousins years before. She swept the stick lightly across her lips, amazed at the redness it left behind. She stepped back from the mirror and frowned at her reflection.

'That didn't hurt now, did it?' Susan said, taking back the lipstick and bending in towards the mirror.

At first the dancehall seemed only a mass of black nothingness but as they shuffled inside figures could be made out moving across the dancefloor in time to the music. The women waited in strung-out groups along the walls, like animals caught in the glare of the men's stare from where they stood around the bar, a stare that was unflinching even as a dancing couple passed through it. As each new group of women arrived they too would be met by that stare and Helen felt it now as it roved across her body. Some of the men would come forward to exchange hello's with those they recognized, but for the most part they held back, their eyes selecting those they might approach later when drink would make it easier.

The couples that were already dancing had come there to dance. Secure in their partnership they moved with a simple, happy grace across the boards, talking quietly during the slower numbers, paying studied attention to each other's movements and to the rhythms of the music whenever the pace quickened.

The showband occupied a small stage in the corner of the hall. They looked incongruous in their white shirts, bow-ties, and dinner jackets. They were middle-aged men with wives and children, who worked on the land, as builders, or in pubs during the day, and stepped into other lives for these few hours every Friday and Saturday evening. The drummer had his eyes closed almost all of the time, the sticks finding their place from memory alone, and the saxophonist's eyes shut softly too whenever he broke into a solo. They drifted along with the music like any craft on a lazy sea, seemingly part of the throng in the small dancehall, but apart from it all the same, specks of light from the revolving glitterball catching on the instruments they played.

Helen gazed idly at the glitterball. A few of its glass mosaics were missing and it moved uncertainly on its axis but still it entranced her. One of the girls came back from the bar with a tray of drinks. Helen took the glass of vodka and orange she was handed.

One of the girls was asked to dance. She refused but when a minute later she was asked again she stepped out on to the dancefloor, proceeding slowly, deferentially, letting it be known that it was she who was doing her dancing partner the favour. Instinctively the other girls pulled closer together in her wake, closing ranks for fear that to do otherwise would be to invite all manner of men to approach them.

She chatted to Susan for a while, Susan talking about a former boyfriend who had gone to Liverpool to work on the buildings and who still wrote to her every couple of months to ask her to come over. She never once replied to his letters. She said that it was easier for both of them if she denied him any hope at all. In time she expected the letters to stop. While they talked, Helen noticed Susan's gaze wandering around the dancefloor, her eyes seeming to hold something in their grasp for a few seconds and then let go. Siobhán Muldoon came across to join them and after a short while Helen was able to move aside and see whatever it was that so held Susan's attention. As men made their way from the bar to the front door or the toilet Susan would select one of them and look into their faces until she would catch their eye. It was as if something was hurriedly being interpreted before the gaze was broken and the message lost. It seemed that for an instant they were part of another world of separate understanding. Helen watched as one of the men stopped in his tracks and came across to Susan. He leaned in between Susan and Siobhán and asked Susan to dance, his voice barely a whisper. She took his hand.

'She's a right one for the men,' Siobhán smiled after her. 'Good luck to her!' She downed the remains of her glass.

A while later it was the ladies' dance and Helen found herself alone in the corner of the hall. She retreated into the shadows to watch the other girls slowly circling the dance-floor, men clinging to them like barnacles. Susan was still dancing with the man who had approached her earlier. He was dark and strange, olive-skinned with heavy black stubble around his mouth and cheeks that led back to almost black hair. He had large brown eyes, and thick-set hands. Susan's chin rested upon his shoulder, her eyes were closed, and there was the faintest trace of a smile upon her lips. Mary Comerford danced with a man who seemed older than any other in the hall, his trousers hitched up awkwardly at his waist and the collar of his shirt frayed. His small hands rested firmly upon her bottom and their mouths were joined together like exotic fish, their feet shuffling so slowly around that they seemed to move to another music entirely.

Afterwards they waited outside the dancehall, the closing bars of 'Amhrán na bhFiann' dissolving in the air around them. Men and women were silhouetted in the double doorway as the bright strip-lights were turned on inside in an effort to clear the hall as quickly as possible. The girls peered into the brightness, hoping to recognize men they had noticed earlier, the closing of the night lending them a courage they could not summon earlier for fear that rejection would spoil what was left of the evening. Mary Comerford came through the doorway with the man she had danced with for most of the night. When the slow dances had ended they had continued to orbit the dancefloor while all around them were waltzing or jiving. Now he backed Mary up against the gable of the dancehall, his hands slipping beneath her clothes for a few warm minutes before it was time to walk to where the buses waited to take them home.

Her bicycle was still chained to the downpipe. The girls waited for her while she ran down the alleyway to fetch it. At the Square she made her goodbyes and cycled out the road to home. The night was still as death, ticking of the cycle chain the loudest thing to be heard along the road. Sometimes the brush of fern leaves when Helen strayed too near the verge. Only the cusp of a moon showed through thin clouds, dusting the fields with the faintest light. Everything was in darkness. She felt too that her soul was steeped in darkness. The high excitement of the evening at the dance had worn off and she felt now a clawing guilt that made her sick to her stomach. Never before had she deceived Kelly so. She trembled and grew cold as she made her way home through the soot-black fields.

A rusted Texaco sign creaked on its hinges as she wheeled past Michael Raftery's petrol station. Raftery, a bachelor, lived in a home for the demented near Ballinasloe, and the Scotsman who had taken the station over returned to Grangemouth within a year. The station had been empty ever since.

Martin Kane was leaning on the handlebars of his bicycle and looking out over Rosheen Lake when she came around the bend. He stood up when he saw her, the paleness of his face and hands gleaming even in that veiled moonlight. Although she knew it was him her heart raced and she slowed the bicycle with her foot, crumb-like stones skipping along the road beneath her shoe.

'Never mind the time now,' he said, echoing perfectly the first words he had spoken to her. He said it with such grace, his voice so gentle that any suspicion in her heart disappeared.

'You're out late, aren't you?' she said, bringing the bicycle to a halt.

'I might ask the same question myself,' he said softly, not turning his gaze from the lake. Two swans were marked out on the surface there like smears of white paint on a black canvas.

'I was invited to dinner at one of the girls' houses,' she lied. 'I hadn't noticed the time.' She watched him smile. 'And you?' she asked.

She kicked at the rubber bicycle pedal and listened to it spinning while she waited for his answer.

'It's nice here at this time of night,' he deflected. 'You wouldn't believe that this same spot could be so busy during the day.' He glanced back at her. 'You just wouldn't believe it.'

No, she thought, she supposed she wouldn't, but he had not said it for her to reply to.

'The swans yonder lost a cygnet a few days back,' he said. 'Isn't it odd how the cock returned as if to comfort the mother?' As he spoke one of the swans lifted its wings from its body and stretched them out before settling again.

'Yes, I suppose it is.' It was already late and she was anxious to be home but she could not leave. It was strange to her to spend idle moments in the company of a man she hardly knew, with whom such simple conversation was slow and uncertain, but easy. She found herself hanging on his every word.

'Marty Burke found the poor creature washed up on the lakeshore there. He said that a pike might have taken it. They've been known to do that.'

Helen looked out across the surface of the lake, the still waters that held the hunting fish, its green-speckled back moving in on its prey, the long and pointed jaws snapping shut on the underbelly of the poor cygnet. It must have died of fright if nothing else. She shivered at the thought.

'Are you cold, Helen?' He started with concern for her, his pale brow furrowing.

'No, not at all,' she answered, pulling the cardigan tighter around her. 'I was just thinking of that pike.'

He told her of how he used to go to Mullarkey's stream to fish for minnows and small roach with a pin tied to a piece of string and earthworms for bait. Once a pike had taken hold of a roach as he hauled it in, the water bursting open as the pike flicked its tail and returned to the depths with the roach held firmly between its teeth, leaving only a few inches of string dangling from Martin's finger. He said that for the rest of that summer he had been too frightened to return to the stream.

Helen remembered often seeing a small, thin child sitting at the edge of the stream, the water lapping his bare feet, a dog curled asleep in the grass at his back. She had gone there with her mother to pick watercress from the shallows. He had always sat upstream of the cress beds and she had noticed the yellow flowers of field-weeds that he tossed into the water floating amidst the ripples. She remembered the sun upon his hair, his spectral presence there at the edge of the water that moved between them. He hadn't changed much.

Only as the memory faded did she understand how strange yet sweet it was; the floating flowers, a young child all alone on a riverbank; perhaps it had never been.

'I must be off,' she started. 'I'm expected home this long time.'

''Right so. I suppose you'll be in the factory on Monday morning?'

'I will,' she said, pushing forward on the pedals.

'I'll look forward to that,' he said quietly as she rolled away, the words barely audible on the nightwind.

She looked back at him but he had turned towards the lake, his face profiled against the shimmering water as he watched the swans in mourning.

She was careful to walk the bicycle up the track to the

house, treading only on the line of grass and weed that ran along the centre. The dog did not stir when she passed the van to leave the bicycle at the gable. All the lights were out, the front door left unlocked as ever. The gnawing in her stomach quickened as she opened the door and stepped inside, every muscle and tendon strained with tension. She went into the kitchen. The range was cool enough to rest her hand upon, the cloths bone-dry on the rail. He had not waited up. She sighed and went into the living room which was unnaturally cool. Usually some heat remained in the hearth no matter how early the fire had been damped down. She noticed the serried edges of the card deck set down on the table, the newspaper folded on the seat of a kitchen chair, a long wax taper used to light oil lamps abandoned on the windowsill where it would hardly be found in another darkness.

'You're home so.'

He was sitting in the armchair which had been turned away from the room so that when she wheeled around only the crown of his head could be seen in the gloom. She felt her heart begin to thump madly inside her chest, lungs panting so that she could hardly speak.

'I am, Daddy. I am,' she stuttered, involuntarily snapping the taper in two.

He was quiet. She heard him breathing, slow deep sloughs of breath that seemed to draw everything in the room towards him.

She could not tell whether he knew that she had deceived him or whether this blind and ponderous silence was his attempt to draw it out of her. To say any more about the invitation to dinner that had never been was to sink deeper into the mire of deception and guilt. She thought of the two swans gliding upon the empty lake, circling the place where the cygnet had disappeared, just as she and her father now circled that horrible and empty truth of her lie.

'You'll be tired,' he said at length, his hand seizing the edge of the armchair to raise himself up. The darkness which unnerved her seemed to rest easily with him and he stood in it awhile, almost a part of it so invisible was he in that unseen room. Finally he went to the door and closed it after him, leaving her shaking with fear and relief, clutching at her own frame as though seeking reassurance that she still existed in the wake of it all.

Once the door had closed behind the supervisor the girls' conversation rose again across the factory floor. The dance in Greenford was on all their tongues, the men they had seen and met, the speculation as to when the next dance would take place. Mary Comerford had been asked out the following week by the man she had met at the dancehall. She blushed as she revealed that he was a widower whose wife had died before their first wedding anniversary and who had been left without children. It was a blessing in many ways that he hadn't to raise children on his own, a couple of the girls said. Helen stayed quiet and retreated behind a conveyor. Mary said that the widower worked as a foreman at a grain supplies yard near Cong. 'A widower! Aren't they all seed merchants one way or another!' Siobhán Muldoon burst in. 'Get it sown now, boy, before it goes to waste!' The other girls blushed as they burst into gales of laughter that brought the supervisor rushing from his office.

'I told ye once already!'

With lightened hearts they bent back towards their work.

At lunchtime they went to sit in the patterned shade of the willow tree on the riverbank. They ate their sandwiches and shared a flask of tea. A cooler breeze ran along the river and they knew instinctively that the summer was nearly at an end. They would wear cardigans over their cotton dresses, plimsolls instead of sandals, and no longer would they sit in the welcome shade of the willow tree. The knowledge hardened the hour for them and the high tone of the conversation that morning had dulled by the time they picked up their things and returned to the factory.

Helen let the others walk on for a bit so that she could stand on a stone and look downstream along the river towards Mullarkey's meadow as if expecting to find that spectral image of the boy impressed on the bank there. She had not seen him around the factory today, had not set eyes upon him nor heard his voice for more than two days now. Only the reed beds swept back and forth, a moorhen nesting safely in their midst, the river pouring through the gathered shadows like liquid sky.

'The days are shortening on us, Daddy,' she called as she drew the bicycle to a halt at a corner of the field. Dark cloud of night had risen like a reef through the horizon, fathom upon fathom of blue sky now swept before it, shadows lengthening.

Kelly tramped across the drills towards her, lifting the points of the rake clear of the bright green beetroot heads. The vest he wore was stained yellow with sweat and brown with spilled tea, an old pair of corduroy trousers fastened at the waist with baling twine, the unfixed sole of one boot slapping as he walked.

'Aye,' he said when he reached her. 'Like they do every year. Year in year out.' He leaned on the rake and squinted out at the narrowing horizon, wheezing for breath, spittle bubbling on his lower lip. 'Well, girl,' he said after a minute or two, 'since you're here now I might as well call it a day. I'll have a lie down while you get the dinner ready – I'm beat altogether this evening.' He swung a leg over the crude stone stile and made his way back to the house, resting the rake in the porch, the dog running to him and yapping about his feet as he undid his boots at the step. 'You won't be long now, will you?' he called back once he noticed that she had not immediately followed him.

'I won't, Daddy. I won't.'

The purple beetroot bulged out of the soil, their green crowns lined up in rows like soldiers on a parade ground. Between the drills the soil was clear of any growth. Here and there were small piles of stones that Kelly had raked up, fragments of old crockery and worn glass distinct among them. Helen trod carefully, the hem of her long skirt brushing the beetroot crowns where the wind tugged at it. Only she and her father knew the true extent of the effort that had gone into producing this crop.

The breeze that tugged her skirt now hummed at the barbed wire fence that ran between Kelly's fields and another. It was a light but plaintive sound, as of a tuneless violin played with a frayed bow. She could hear too the yelping of the dog at the doorstep waiting to be fed.

As she turned at the end of the last row she noticed a small patch in the crown of one of the beetroot and she knelt down to inspect it. Tiny flies had alighted upon the brightest yellow leaves at the heart of the crown, thousands of them clambering over each other in their attempts to secrete themselves into the youngest, half-formed leaves. She brushed at the leaves with the back of her hand but the flies seemed not to be disturbed. She went to the next plant to find that it too was similarly infested, and the next also. The chain of infestation linked almost every beetroot she inspected. In some the flies seemed to have just arrived, in others they appeared well established, the leaves crawling with the living mass of winged terror.

Desperately, she looked back at the house for fear that he might have seen her and wondered what she had discovered, but he was standing at the sink with his back to her, washing his hands, eyeing Sweeney's fields that were once his own and that he still coveted.

'The swan is hatching another egg.' Martin Kane had come across to her when the other girls had drifted off a few minutes earlier once the klaxon had sounded the end of the shift. 'She'll do well to have it reared by winter.'

Helen looked around but the factory floor was deserted. In spite of herself she did not want to invite the ridicule by way of association with Martin that he suffered himself, but he had chosen his moment well. She had not seen him since that previous Friday night.

'They had me working in the warehouse for a few days since,' he explained. 'It's easy work altogether: no lifting, no hauling, nobody else around from one day to the next. Just the odd truck coming in with a load or to take a container away to the Continent. Anyone can use a forklift.'

She imagined him alone in a vast dark warehouse, surrounded by the corrugated boxes of cassettes that she and the other girls filled by day, his presence marked only by a puddle of lamplight upon a desk where he sat and read. She felt a great pity for him then, that he should be shut away from the scrutiny of other men who envied him his job at the factory when they had none.

She undid her white apron and collected her things while he locked the store-room. At the factory gate he offered to walk with her awhile along the road before doubling back to his own. After a timid protest she agreed and they wheeled their bicycles side by side, pulling them in tight against the stone walls whenever a car came past.

As they walked he told her the histories of the unre-markable places that they passed: the mound that had once been a children's burial ground, the square of stones in the corner of a field that was believed to be a fairy's well, the

copse that for years had hid a family of foxes until one
summer night when a local farmer had thrown a lighted
taper into the centre of the dry copse and shot the foxes one
by one as they fled. No fox had ever ventured into the parish
to this day. He was full of stories, endless chains of history
and anecdote.

She looked at him as he spoke, this grown man little
more than a child in appearance, thought and deed, his
shock of hair pressed by the wind against a pale forehead
beneath which eyes flickered in their sockets like night stars,
gentle lips forming word and phrase that spun story after
story.

'Helen?' He had noticed her stare and felt uncomfortable with it.

'Go on, I'm listening.' She blushed, a lump catching in
her throat.

Neither spoke in the ensuing awkward silence, the spell
broken for them. Eventually Helen remarked upon a few
local features and asked him about them but he would not
be drawn and they lapsed into silence again.

The red-dropped fuschia that lined the road lifted her
heart a little as they walked their bicycles to a small bridge
over a ditch where they simply said goodbye. She pushed
her bicycle on up the incline towards home. She looked back
after a while. He stood in the road, leaning on the handlebars
much as he had been when she had come across him on the
road that night, shielding his eyes from the sun that laddered
through a row of trees at the roadside, watching her leave.
She stopped and waited there in his gaze for a moment then
re-mounted the bicycle and pushed on home.

'You were late again today,' Kelly said evenly as they sat
down to the dinner of potatoes and salt bacon that she had
prepared.

'Again?' she queried, unwrapping the butter.

'Again,' he repeated. 'You've been home later than usual this past week. I hope you haven't fallen in with a bad crowd who gossip.'

'I haven't been home late at all, Daddy. I walked up the hills today because I was tired. Nothing more.'

'You were late,' he said firmly, putting an end to all argument. 'I don't want your own stupidity to stop you from getting on in life, that's all.' He took a corner of the slab of butter and knifed it into the potatoes where it melted.

She waited in the emptying factory. Dust spun endlessly in the ribs of sunlight that slanted through the roof on to the conveyors and machines below. The slamming of the doors as the girls left caused the dust to plume and burst in the air and she watched its listless motion while she waited.

The supervisor came out and watched her sweeping broken cassette cases from the floor before asking her why she was still there. She said that she had been in late that morning and was making up the time. 'God bless your honesty, Miss Kelly,' he praised. 'There's many others wouldn't have an ounce of it in them at all.' He picked his jacket from the the hook on the back of the door and threw it over his shoulder as he left.

She looked up each time that the door opened, only to find another member of the night-shift stepping through the door, peering back at her between the mote-spun bands of light. They greeted her as they strolled past on their way to the locker room, some clapping their hands together in mock enthusiasm for the work, others wiping sleep from their eyes. She waited until the last minute but when she could wait no longer she undid her apron and stuffed it under the conveyor housing and ran to the door, footfall echoing on the floor, dust spinning in her wake. She ran with the bicycle and almost fell as she hitched herself up on the saddle, pushing furiously on the pedals to speed her home and escape her father's anger of the night before, eyes stinging with tears.

'Is there a drop of tea on the way?'

'I'll have some for you in a minute, Daddy,' she called from the kitchen where she was cleaning up after the dinner.

'Good girl yourself.'

The kettle was heating on the range. A porter cake she had been given by one of the women at work sat wrapped in foil on the sideboard, waiting to be sliced. Often, when they learned that her mother had died when she was just a child, people would bring Helen things: cakes, tins of biscuits, loaves of soda bread, jars of honey, a tin of the Earl Grey tea that Kelly had spat into the hearth after the first mouthful. 'Don't ever try and poison me with that rubbish again!' Knowing that Kelly would never have accepted such charity, Helen was careful to claim that the gifts had been bought with her wages in the shops in Drimelogue.

'Good girl yourself,' he said again when she brought him the mug of tea and a couple of slices of the porter cake. The crossword lay half completed across his lap, the deck of cards racked perfectly upon the mantelpiece.

He took the mug from her and asked her how her day had been in the factory and what new developments, if any, there were on the building of the extension. He seemed to take a great interest in what little news there was, firing more and more questions back at her. He fixed her with his eyes as she spoke, hardly averting his gaze to sip tea from his mug or lift a piece of porter cake to his mouth. When she could think of nothing else to say she quickly drained her own mug and went back to the kitchen.

'What do you think of that, my girl?' he asked, thrusting

a crumpled yellow slip at her when she returned to collect his plate and mug.

She went to take it from him but he held it firmly between thumb and forefinger. DINNY O'TOOLE, TURF ACCOUNTANT was emblazoned in thick black letters across the top half of the slip, and she recognized Kelly's handwriting across the bottom half.

'I had an outside winner in the two-thirty at Redcar today!' he proclaimed. 'Twenty-five pence was all it cost me and do you know what I won on it? Do you know?'

'No, Daddy, I don't.'

'Go on, girl. Guess!'

'I couldn't.'

'Ah! You're hopeless altogether,' he said without any malice and she smiled.

'Twenty-seven pounds and seventy-eight pence! Isn't that just grand? Isn't it?'

'It is, Daddy. It is,' she agreed. His good humour could be infectious when it was so obviously borne. Its rarity lent it an undeniable quality.

'And I gave the silver and bronze to the Little Sisters of the Poor,' he continued. 'They have a box on the counter in Dinny's, you know.'

'That's great, Daddy,' she said as she picked up the plate and mug from the fireside. It was almost a week's wages for her and he had got it within the couple of minutes it took for a horse to run two laps of a racecourse. It seemed easy money. She had heard some of the lads at the factory discussing the horses on Mondays but she had never understood the ins and outs of the betting system and paid them little heed. It surprised her all the more that Kelly had visited the bookmakers. He was not known to risk anything unless the outcome could be guaranteed, and as he said himself, that's no risk at all.

'You know,' he started, 'but I think I'll take myself into Breffni's for a quick celebration.' He got up from the armchair and brushed the crumbs from his shirt and lap into the small flames in the hearth. 'A man could do worse for himself,' he said, pulling on his jacket.

Helen watched him go, forgetting to turn on the head-lamps until he was almost out on the road, the twin beams suddenly cutting through the bluish gloam and seeming to pull drugged moths into their stare. She stood at the window until long after the van had gone, the beams reappearing momentarily on a rise in the road a couple of miles away and then gone for good. She wondered if those twin beams might find Martin cycling along the road after visiting some lake or other, perhaps on his way to work or to the warehouse where he would spend the night alone. She wished to be with him then, to stay there in the echoing warehouse with him, to listen to his shallow breathing and imagine his generous heart working alongside those lungs to breathe life into his body and into *her* life. She could see his face, the shock of fair hair on his forehead above his bright eyes, lips moving as he spun another story, as vividly now as she saw her own face reflected in the window glass. She could hear his gentle voice in the room around her and she wanted to be with him.

She woke from a dream that had left cool tears upon her cheeks. Outside the van engine ran on and on and there was a brightness across the ceiling of the bedroom where the headlamps shone through a gap in the curtains. She waited for the light to move when Kelly found first gear and was able to rev the van up the last few yards to the house, but it did not move for the whole minute that she waited. The dog woke and began to whimper at the end of the short rope tethering it to the downpipe. She waited. Finally the engine lost momentum and rattled to a halt but the light did not dim. She lifted herself up in the bed to listen and there was the sound of feet coming slowly and uncertainly across the gravel towards the house. Suddenly everything seemed wrong and out of place and she felt the grip of fear upon her, a feverish fluttering in her heart, a struggle for breath that she tried to control so that she could listen.

The dog let out a bark.

'Whist! Blackie. Whist!'

She sighed, her heart and breathing subsiding, and she heard him slump heavily against the front door, the dull rattle of limbs falling upon wood. She thought of getting up to help him in but he always refused. There was a pause and then, instead of the door opening, she heard again the sound of his feet upon the ground. He stumbled once and then again as he made his way back to the van, dropping the keys the second time, swearing out loud as he fumbled for them in the glare of the headlamps.

'Ye lousy feckers ye! Ye lousy lousy feckers, the lot o' ye!' he was saying when she opened the front door and shielded her eyes from the light to see him better. He was slumped on the ground between the two beams like some trussed animal, the keys glinting at his back, night insects hurrying to and fro in the light. She did not move towards him, uncertain that he had even seen her, but the cursing had ceased and he was mumbling incoherently now.

'Daddy,' she called, her voice scarcely louder than a whisper. 'Are you all right?'

He gathered the keys which he had now found and lifted himself to his feet, arm by arm, leg by leg, standing swaying before the van. 'Elizabeth! Elizabeth!' he yelled. 'I promised you I'd show them what the Kellys are made of!'

She reeled backwards into the house as though he had struck her, slamming the door shut upon him, but still she could hear his yelling. She rushed to her bedroom and threw herself under the sheets, dragging them over her head and around her ears so that she could not see the light nor hear him calling her mother's name.

By morning he was in the fields. She watched him while she ate at the table, a dark figure looming in the fine grey drizzle that had settled overnight, his face obscured by the hood of an old anorak, the rain-slicked handle of the hoe gripped tightly in his hands so that it would not slip and damage the cursed yet precious beetroot. There was no wind, only the rain coming down in one long meditative silence and the day stilled by it.

The saddle of the bicycle was wet through so she pulled a plastic bag over it. She walked the bicycle up the track not looking away to the fields where he laboured so that she could not tell if his eyes followed her or the blade of the hoe that worked amongst the drills.

At lunchtime the factory workers stayed inside. They watched the rain streaking the windows of the prefab that had been added to the factory as an afterthought, and now served as a canteen or at least somewhere to sit and eat the lunches the workers brought with them. There was a dart board and a stack of board games that had never been opened. There was a rack full of German business magazines, and a pair of heavy books about injection-moulding processes which had been used to prop open the canteen door during the warmest days of summer. Helen sat with the girls and listened again to Siobhán's stories about her days in Dublin: the dances, the medical students, the Royal Hibernian Hotel. Gradually, like the rain, a silence fell upon them and their faces turned idly towards the windows, the drops waiting there to soak up their thoughts. Helen wondered where Martin Kane could be, whether he was at home after a shift at the lonely warehouse or at Rosheen Lake watching the swans hatching the new egg he had told her about. She wondered if she was in his thoughts at all, as he was so much in hers.

'Are you all right there, Helen?' one of the girls asked, tipping her elbow.

'I am, I am,' she gathered herself.

'You looked like you were miles away altogether.'

She was afraid to ask any of the other men in the factory if they knew what shifts Martin was working because she knew that they would make fun of it and take it out on them both. The duty roster in the supervisor's office was pinned up on a far wall, the names and dates too small to be read from the glass window in the door of the office. She would have to wait.

The hot needle pushed into the leather of Kelly's boots as easily as any needle into flesh, the thin bore of steel shining as he turned it in the close lamplight and drew the fishing line through the hole after it. He repaired the boot whose loosened sole had been no more than a bother in the dry but became a hindrance in the wet weather of the day, the mud oozing quickly between the seams, tiny stones and grit pressed into the soles of his feet.

Helen cleared the dresser of delft and took a damp cloth to the woodwork, wiping away the dust and crumbs that had settled. She took the good plates and the painted casserole dishes to the sink to wash them in soapy water that would lift the dust and brighten the pattern again.

They both heard the dog bark and begin to whimper before settling once more at the gable. Helen lifted her head from the sink and looked out at Sweeney's fields behind the house, hearing Kelly shift in the armchair, his concentration broken by the dog.

The knock on the front door was soft and barely heard inside the house.

'What was that at all?' demanded Kelly irritably, the needle held steady and motionless in his fingers as he listened again.

'I think there's someone at the door, Daddy.' She shook suds from her hands and reached for a towel. 'Will I go?'

But Kelly was on his feet at once, the boot set down in front of the hearth, the fishing line and needle carefully laid out so that he could pick up exactly where he left off.

'I was looking for Helen, Mr Kelly . . .'

Helen froze.

'And who might you be? I know your face from somewhere about.'

'Martin, Mr Kelly. Martin Kane is my name.' The voice washed out with uncertainty. 'Only I work down at the factory and I was wondering if Helen was here?'

'Aye, I've got you now.' Kelly darkened as he looked at the pale youth on the doorstep before him. He gazed then over Martin's shoulder, at the fields damp in the wake of the rain that had already begun to clear. The beetroot rose cleanly from the healthy soil, rows of bright green crowns glistening with wetness. He maintained his silence. Kane shifted uneasily, his hands searching the lining of his pockets as if expecting to find some answer to this silence there.

'It's okay, Daddy,' Helen said coming from the kitchen, rubbing her hands in the towel. 'I know him.' Her heart beat wildly, like a bird trapped inside her frame.

Kelly did not move for a while, drawing out the moment before he turned and went back into the front room and took up the bright needle and pushed it again through the leather sole of the boot.

The navy donkey jacket Martin wore was feathered with tiny droplets, like a hoarfrost that had settled there. The jacket had been his father's who was a much bigger man and his arms strayed within its fabric, fingers barely emerging from the cuffs when he lifted a hand to sweep damp hair from his forehead. 'Hello,' he said. 'I've been working away from the factory for a while now. I haven't seen a soul outside my own house for ages. I thought I'd come to see you.'

'That's kind of you, Martin,' she said.

Behind her came the squeak of steel and leather as Kelly repaired his boot, his silent presence stronger than anything else she felt.

'I . . . I wanted to see you anyway,' he began, his fingers knotting, 'to tell you about the swans.'

Helen leaned forward to whisper. 'That's very kind, Martin, but you'll have to go. I can't see you here, I can't.' She drew away, torn between him and her father in the front room. Martin looked at her, his face furrowed with misunderstanding, his eyes pleading for some explanation. When she imagined his journey out here to the house, along the cool, damp road, the donkey jacket heavy upon his shoulders, her heart burned with pity.

'You'll have to go,' she insisted more loudly so that Kelly could hear.

'But I care for you, Helen,' he said quietly, his voice almost at the point of breaking. It was as much as he could bring himself to say to her, as much an expression of anything that he could make.

She lowered her head, feeling at the edge of tears, drawing blindly back, searching for the frame of the door with her hands, not looking at his face, the mouth that had spoken to her, closing the door on him.

'What did he come here for?' Kelly asked, but she could not answer him for wiping tears from her face with the backs of her hands. 'What did he come here for?' he insisted, his impatient voice booming in the front room.

'He wanted to say hello,' she called, recovering herself

back in the kitchen. 'He hasn't been in the factory for a while.'

'You'd do well to steer clear of a good-for-nothing the like of him,' Kelly said. 'D'ye hear me now? D'ye hear me now, girl? Stay away from the no-hopers.'

'Yes, Daddy.'

The fuchsias were passing with the season, their belled flowers shrivelling at the first edge of cold in the morning air as she cycled to the factory. At the narrow bridge over the stream she noticed that the water was cloudy, the surface clogged with hay-cuttings where a farmer had rinsed his silage tanks into the running water. She knew that within a couple of hours the smaller fish would be turned on their sides amidst the clippings and a heron would come to gorge on them. Even now the surface was pricked with tiny rings where the fish came up to gasp in vain.

She cycled across the bridge, pushing the pedals up the hill and past the bend where Rosheen Lake came into view, the waters broken by a stiff breeze that swept the reeds and rushes back and forth. The swans were nowhere to be seen.

At the factory gate she noticed his bicycle propped against the wall with the others, the mudguard bent sideways so that the rain threw a line of wet along his spine as he rode. He had said once that he'd never had the mind to fix it, that it was as easy to take off the jacket and hang it to dry.

She left her bicycle against his and went inside, looking anxiously around as she placed her timecard in its slot. The factory was busy, the machines working through the night to fulfil the orders that were coming in. A few schoolchildren had been taken in over the summer to help with the packing, but they had returned to school by now and there was more work than ever before for the girls at the conveyor belts. As quickly as each box was filled it was taken away to the stores for stacking in preparation for the arrival of another lorry. Forklift trucks whirred around the yard outside, ferrying pallets and boxes from the stores to the loading bay and hoisting them on to the backs of flatbed trucks, the drivers scrambling across the boxes to secure the tarpaulins before driving back out on to the road.

As she tied the white apron around her waist her eyes wandered about the factory floor, past the machines, through gaps in the doors, into the loading bay, seeking him out. But he was not there. Perhaps, she thought, he had only left his bicycle at the factory to collect it later and was now at the lake searching for the swans, or watching the silver fish turning on their sides in the running stream. He had every reason to hide from her.

'Come on now, girls!' the supervisor mustered. 'Let's get cracking straight away. There's plenty more boxes where those came from!'

'Easy for him to say,' whispered Siobhán Muldoon under her breath and the others fell to laughing as the supervisor walked back to his office.

She went out alone into the flat grey day of after-rain, leaving the other girls behind in the canteen to walk across the sodden meadows to the riverbank. The willow tree had begun to lose its leaves, the narrow yellow pieces scattered on to the grass and the river, twisting and turning in the slow current that bore them away. The patch of grass where they had sat in the shade of summer afternoons was no longer flattened, the lush green stalks upright once again. The ground squeaked with wet where she walked. It was as if that summer had never been.

Martin stood some way off in another meadow, his elbow propped on a thick fence post, one hand sunk deep in his trouser-pocket. His gaze seemed fixed on some distant point and occasionally he withdrew his hand from his pocket and shielded his eyes to see better.

She lifted her apron and skirt to clamber over the low stone wall that separated the two meadows, beads of rainwater clinging to her shins as she went towards him.

'Martin,' she called gently when she was close enough.

He made a jump and turned around, his features breaking into a shadowy smile and then a frown that was slow to melt away.

She knew how much she had hurt him. 'I wanted to say how sorry I was,' she began, 'for turning you away at the door like that.'

He shrugged his shoulders and smiled weakly at her, blushing a little when they both remembered what he had said to her.

'It was cruel of me, Martin. I was cruel to you and I'm sorry.'

He leaned again on the fence post and looked away from her, tracking a few willow leaves trapped by the current against a reed bed. She apologized again but he did not respond. She asked about the swans, telling him that she had not seen them when she had passed by the lake that morning, but he simply stared out beyond the river, motionless and without expression, a grey shape in a grey landscape, alone.

She spoke to him while he stood there, sometimes saying the first thing that came to mind, sometimes telling of how she could not cross her father, how everything was his life and she a part of it and nothing could go against him as long as he lived. Her words seemed to fall from her mouth into some fathomless and untenanted depth.

Eventually she turned to leave, knowing that the klaxon would soon sound and that then they would both have to go. She could not bear to have to return with him in that barren space that had grown between them.

'I'd better get back,' she said. She tracked across the sodden meadow, lifting the hem of her skirt clear of the longer grass.

'Take my hand,' he panted as she came to the stone wall between the two meadows. He had run to catch her up.

She glanced down at his outstretched palm and slipped her hand on to it. He bore her weight as she stepped over the wall, his hand soft but unyielding, the slightest shake when she leaned heavily upon him, the simplicity of the warmth that remained when she let go. She closed her hand upon his as they walked back to the factory.

'I won't come around to your house again, Helen,' he promised. 'I wouldn't want to turn your father against me so soon.'

'I don't think that would make a difference,' Helen said, remembering Kelly's warning. 'It was kind of you, Martin, but it's best not to come to the house. We can see plenty of each other here at the factory.'

'I'll take you to see the swans' nest at the lake if you like,' he ventured.

'Yes,' she said. 'I'd like that.'

He held open the factory door for her and they went in.

Sweeney was rarely to be seen in any of the numerous fields he owned across the parish and beyond. His hired labour tended to the land, turning, sowing, and reaping as the season demanded, their wages dependent upon the yield so that Sweeney knew they would not shirk from one year to the next.

He had a policy of buying cheap, well-drained land that he would pay men to improve, clearing stones and rocks, digging in seaweed to enrich the topsoil, turning the land a foot deeper to break the grey-yellow leach-pan. The fields repaid the effort, turning out crop after crop after crop without fail.

When Kelly noticed Sweeney standing alone in one of the fields at the back of the house he went out, his mind filling with reasons for Sweeney's unexpected visit: the potatoes were blighted, the variety had not taken well, they were all stalk and no flesh, they had been attacked by slugs, they had rotted in the few days of rain.

But Sweeney was smiling, rubbing his palms together in high humour. He stretched out his hand to greet Kelly as he approached.

'Good day to you, Donal,' he said, his hands slipping around Kelly's and clasping firmly shut upon it.

'The name's not Donal at all,' Kelly said sourly, looking about him at the perfect drills of potatoes. He could tell now that there was nothing wrong with them. 'What brings you out here anyway? Doesn't oul' Mitchell report back to you at all these days?'

'He does, God be good to him, but I thought I'd cast an eye myself for a change. I like to keep up with things.' He looked out of place in his black Dunlop wellingtons and grey corduroys, an olive waxed jacket half-buttoned up over a faded shirt and a striped tie. He swept strands of hair back across a bald spot as they spoke, and Kelly took note of his perfect fingernails, not chipped or cracked from any form of labour.

After gentle prompting Sweeney told Kelly about all the crops he had planted in his larger holdings and also about the extension he had built to the bed and breakfast and which had been filled for the whole summer with German fly fishermen. It had been a powerful year for the mayfly, he said. He was hoping to buy an old railway station out in Ballynahinch with the profits and convert it into a luxury fishing lodge, but he'd wait and see how things panned out.

'"How things panned out,"' Kelly repeated to himself, smirking. 'Did you ever hear the like of the words that money can put in the mouth of a fool!'

Sweeney rattled on about how he had missed out at auction on another fishing lodge near a stretch of the Erriff up towards Westport, his voice growing ever distant to Kelly's ears until Kelly broke in:

'They tell me that the price per hundredweight is on the slide with it being a good year all round.'

'What's that?'

'The potatoes, they're on the slide at the market because of the good year.'

'I've every confidence in a good price. It always holds up well for a good variety,' Sweeney defended, buttoning the metal buttons on his waxed jacket.

Not to be put off, Kelly turned and pointed towards his own two fields where the beetroot were almost prime for harvesting.

'That's the crop to beat the band, the beetroot. There's a fair price to be had for them this year and any year.'

'There is, Donal, there is,' Sweeney said, taking a folded flat cap from his front pocket. 'But they'd have you killed with the spraying they need, and the men want paying twice over for that kind of work.' He popped the cap on his head and made his goodbyes before heading back across the stone walls to where his car waited at the road.

After he had gone Kelly went to the metal rain barrel at the side of the house. He lifted the wooden lid and peered in through the still water inside. The block he had bought in Ginn's had dissolved in time, the thick poison solution lurking greyly at the bottom of the barrel, unstirred and untouched because he had been unsure of how to apply it, and, too proud to ask another, he had not bothered with it.

*

In idle moments Helen found herself wondering about the Kane family. They lived in a well-kept two-storey house some way down the Roscommon road and they visited a store attached to a petrol garage nearby so it was rarely that they needed to come into the town where little was spoken or known about them.

What was known was that Mr Kane had spent many years working in the Durham mines until one day his back had locked in the pit-shaft and he had come home never to work again. He had tried to set himself up afterwards as a radio and gramophone repair man, but was too far out of town for people to bring their broken sets to. A faded wooden sign was still fixed to the gable of the house that faced the road. KANE DO! ELECTRICAL REPAIRS the legend humorously read, but 'No Kane Do' was what people mostly said, dropping their broken sets off at Ryan's Rentals & Repairs on the Main Street.

There had been three children, all boys. Dermot and Jim were born within a year of each other and as youngsters were rarely to be seen apart. Martin had been born ten years afterwards, conceived during the last Christmas his father had spent at home before he had locked his back in the mine. Martin's father was already an invalid when he was born, so that Bríd Kane had an infant to rear as well as a bed-ridden husband to look after for the two years that it took Mr Kane to recover sufficiently to move about the house. Some said that young Martin was remote and strange because he had been neglected as a child but others said that he was soft in the head. Helen thought she was in love with him.

A track of wet footprints ran across the floor between the bathroom and bedroom, echoes of his presence there. She watched them fade to nothingness on the fresh wooden floor that he had laid the summer before. His boots stood inside the door. From his bedroom came the sound of gentle snoring: after the day's work in the fields a warm bath had allowed sleep to overcome him. It was sometimes this way and she could remember the habit stretching back to the days when her mother was alive, cautioned by a finger pressed against the lips as she burst in the front door from school, the tiptoeing back down to her bedroom to leave her satchel and change out of her school clothes, breath held for fear of waking him when passing his door. It did not do to wake him; a door left carelessly open only to slam in the draught would bring him running in his long-johns from the bedroom, the drama of his waking exaggerated so that all might know how much he had been disturbed.

She turned to prepare the dinner, reflecting now on the slow journey home in Martin's company, the sycamore seed that had helicoptered into his fringe and hung there for minutes until he noticed and brushed it aside amidst her giggles. That nervous tension that fluttered somewhere inside her, turning like the winged seed. A chance remark might make all the difference, as it had before. Anything, it seemed, might destroy this fragile bond, and only time would seal it. The turn of easy conversation, the exchange of good humour and memories seemed now too ready and unearned. What was so easily got was easily lost, she had heard often before from her father's mouth. And yet when they had drawn their bicycles to a halt just out of sight of the house, that end had seemed to come upon them suddenly and too soon.

Potatoes were being dragged from the ground in many of the fields that rose on all sides from the lake. Men and women were bent splay-legged amongst the drills, grasping the fleshy stems and tugging sharply to free the tubers in one go. Children followed them with canvas sacks into which they tossed the potatoes. After every drill had been pulled the men would sift through the loosened soil with a fork to free those potatoes that had been missed. Their voices carried easily in the still and darkening evening, telling the children to hurry, calling neighbours across to share a cup of tea from a bottle, congratulating each other on the progress that was being made, repeatedly thanking God for the weather.

The sinking sun burned golden on the mirrored surface of the lake. All shadows were long and deep, a coolness in places where perhaps the sun had not touched since midday betraying any belief that summer had lingered into September. A boat that had seen better days strained lazily at the rotten rope tethering it to a post on the bank, mesmeric slap slap of water against the hull beating out its own time.

This silence drew the young couple towards it like moths towards a lamp. They said nothing as they walked the few hundred yards along the boreen that led down to the water's edge. Helen clasped a cardigan across her chest against a chill that was descending, prickling the skin on her cheeks, but inside she felt warm and safe. The factory had closed an hour early to allow maintenance on the conveyors and they had been sent home. Kelly would not be expecting her for another while. They had left the bicycles at the top of the boreen, where half a dozen others had also been left, dropped against the gorse or on their sides, the riders making the most of the last of the day in the fields.

'Do you come down here a lot, Martin?' she asked once they had reached the shore.

'Aye, I suppose I do,' he answered, squinting out across the lake. 'I like the water you know. It gets me thinking.'

'What do you think about then, when you're here?'

'Oh, I don't know,' he hesitated, choosing a stone and skimming it across the surface. 'Impossible things, really.' The stone came to the end of its travel and splashed beneath the water. 'Come on 'til I show you where the swans have their nest or we'll be lost in the night,' he smiled.

The nest sat amidst the thickest part of the reed bed, carefully built of straw and twigs, four eggs nestling side by side at the bottom, flecked with downy feathers. The cob trod water some yards away, seemingly unperturbed as Martin and Helen inspected the nest. Martin whispered that over time the swans had got used to his visits and only hissed whenever he came upon them too quickly. Helen leaned over his shoulder to watch, feeling the heat drawing off his back, his body shifting beneath the ill-fitting donkey jacket. While he watched the nest she watched him, marvelling at how his blond hair held the light in the dusk, pale and wondrous as any swan.

'Would you look at that!' Martin said, reaching towards the side of the nest. 'Just look!'

He held a large pine cone in his hand, a white feather caught in its petals.

'Where did that come from at all?' He grinned and held the cone up for her to see.

'Maybe the swan thinks it's an egg,' she ventured.

'No,' Martin laughed. 'They're not as stupid as the seagulls.' He dropped the cone into his pocket and stood up.

As they picked their way back across the rocks towards the bank she took his hand to balance on and did not let go when the walking became easier. She felt him try to let go and draw away from her but she would not have it and finally his hand relaxed.

'What sorts of impossible things?' she took up again.

'Oh, all sorts, all sorts,' he smiled.

She pulled him back and leaned her head against his shoulder. 'This sort, Martin?'

He cleared hair from her forehead and kissed her there, his arms folding about her so that his heat pressed against her chest and face and she drew in the smell of his skin.

This, she thought, was all she wanted now. To have him next to her, to feel the heart of another beating alongside hers, to know another and to enter into their life that was separate from the only life she had known, and that in truth was her father's life and never hers.

Their fingers entwined and she felt his breath close to her face in the closing dusk. Her mouth closed upon his for a short moment before he pulled away but still he held her close, a shudder that ran through his body now registering in hers. Again they said nothing because there was no need, and it was in darkness that they made their way back towards the boreen that would take them to their homes, their forms etched out against the silver reflecting lake.

'I'll be taking up the beetroot tomorrow, God willing,' Kelly announced, looking up from the crossword when she brought him his mug of tea. 'The weather should hold anyways. It's a bastardin' job if it rains at all.'

'There's no sign of rain, Daddy,' she humoured him. 'It was a lovely evening altogether and I'm sure everything will be fine for you.'

'Aye,' he muttered, taking a slug of tea and moving it from one side of his mouth to another as he pondered another clue.

She built up the fire, laying on the sods so that they would not spark and he could not burst out with the usual 'Sacred God! but can you do nothing right?' She filled the kettle to heat water for washing the dishes with, all the time counting the hours since she and Martin had parted, hours that seemed now to peel away into nothingness, leaving a distance that gave the illusion that nothing at all had happened and that the evening had never been, the larceny that time made on a memory that had yet to be fixed.

The ring of the church bell ran low across the fields on the Friday morning, heads turning as the workers listened to that slow tolling of the dead, fingers wiped on trouser-legs and touched to forehead, breast, and lips in turn as silent prayers were made.

Kelly did not hear the tolling, so faint had it become by the time it reached the house where he waited for the overnight dew to clear before setting out to work on the beetroot. A sack was prepared, turned inside out to shed any remains of the seed potatoes it had held before. The spade that had come from Ginn's was scraped clean with the point of an old screwdriver, shorn to bright metal in places, the plaque of rust removed from every crevice. A hammer was taken to the leading edge to even out those kinks where cursed stones had been struck in the digging of spring.

He made himself a fresh pot of tea while he waited, cupping the mug in both hands as he stood at the kitchen window and watched the men and women working in Sweeney's fields. The potatoes were coming up a bright ivory colour, the soil falling easily from them, dead stems thrown aside as the potatoes tumbled into the sacks dragged between the drills.

When he recognized one of Sweeney's labourers as a former Roscommon senior hurler he went to the back door and called out his name, waving as the red-haired man looked up quizzically. He stared at Kelly for a moment before bending down again. 'A clatter from a camán must have knocked the manners out of the man,' Kelly thought, slamming the door shut behind him. He was ready to go to work.

He took the spade, the sack, and an old bread knife with him to the two fields. The knife had been sharpened and he would use it to cut the leaved heads from the beetroot. The dog lifted itself and came to follow him diligently, squatting on its hind-quarters at the edge of the first field while Kelly set about preparing for his day's work. He rolled his shirtsleeves up to his elbows and as he stretched into the work tendons, veins, and ligaments appeared like cord laid beneath the surface of his skin.

Pushing the spade in beneath the first beetroot he lifted it free of the drill and pulled it to one side. He steadied the swollen root with one hand and brought the bread knife down heavily on the hard joint between root and leaf, the leaves coming away with a solid thock. He smiled and righted the beetroot. There where the stump whorled green into purple was a black centre, black as any ink, black as any starless night, the fecund juices oozing from the cut. As he stared aghast that dark fluid moved with the larvae of countless beings; the issue of the flies that had come to nest in the crowns of the young plants.

Kelly shook with fear and rage, the bread knife gripped solidly as though he would kill with it. There was a gnawing in his gut that he knew had been there for some time. His eye caught the old rain barrel at the gable of the house, the muslin that had been wrapped around the poison block flapping at the downpipe where it cushioned a stanchion. Beyond it the red-haired hurler toiled ceaselessly in Sweeney's fields, potatoes tumbling into the sacks one after another.

He looked out across the green heads of beetroot that fluttered gaily in the breeze. 'There's still something to be salvaged from it all!' he said against the truth, taking up the spade and plunging it beneath the next beetroot, bearing down with all his might so that it fairly sprung from its moorings. With the bread knife he halved it where it sat on the crest of drill. It was the same, as he knew in his heart it would be.

'Do you think I might see you over the weekend?' Martin ventured timidly, his eyes wandering across the lake and fields that were a mass of broken light and shadow.

'I don't know, Martin. I mightn't be able to get away at all without an excuse.' The thought of those two long days rested heavily upon her, interminable hours to be spent in the house as Kelly worked at the beetroot. The cloches had been cleared of tomatoes, which had been sold on to a Ballinasloe market trader, and most of the peppers had been pickled, the remainder left on the stalk to be used fresh when needed. There was little that had to be done until the first frosts brought the peppers to the ground and the cloches would have to be dismantled, the heavy plastic rolled up and stored away so that the winter gales would not tear it, the plot of soil dug and re-dug then spread with horse manure which would be left to rot in for the winter months.

'It'll be a long couple of days then,' he said, mirroring her thoughts.

'It will,' she agreed.

All was silent as they made their way back again along the boreen from Rosheen Lake where they had strayed hand in hand along the water's edge. The workers had left the fields early, exhausted after the week's effort of making the most of the fine weather. In the far distance they saw the red lights of the Expressway bus to Athlone moving along the main road. They watched it for a while until it was gone and invisible to them. When they reached the spot where their bicycles leaned against the gorse bushes, they stood for a long time looking back at the lake, commenting on the stillness, the curlews' song, the progress that had been made in the fields round about. A vehicle passed loudly along the road behind them, engine racing as the driver gunned the gears, thin barking of a dog that sat in the passenger seat. One of the swans swooped in overhead and came to land on the lake, pushing its feet out before it as it landed, great sweep of those wings as they barely touched the water and were gathered in.

They walked most of the distance to the house, only mounting their bicycles to freewheel down the slopes, the ticking of the chains driving their conversation. Before parting they lingered at a passing-point in the road where a willow tree swept high over the wall and provided some cover amidst the gloam.

'Close your eyes, and put out your hands,' Martin said all of a sudden.

She squeezed her eyelids shut and stretched out her cupped and trembling hands. She giggled, the sensation taking her back to a school playground when girls would hand out sweets on their birthdays.

Martin pressed something large yet light into her palm and closed her fingers over it. She opened her eyes. A pine cone rocked to and fro in her hand.

'The swans must have brought it for you the other day,' he said. 'They wanted you to have it.'

'Oh, Martin, it's lovely.' She held his shoulders and pulled him close. She felt so warm with him now that it seemed they might burn together. She held his cheek close to hers, enjoying the coolness of his skin, the silence of saying nothing because for now nothing needed to be said. Then they spoke in hushed tones for minutes then spoke no more, speech crushed and broken by the press of mouth on mouth, the closeness of skin as they sought something in each other, the quick breathing rising and falling away.

'I'll see you on Monday,' she broke, eyes now on the road for fear that her father might pass that way.

'You will,' he whispered, pulling her back to him for a final kiss.

The boots had been thrown into the hallway, smears of clay on the floor where his stockinged feet had picked it up. She called his name but the house was empty. The van was gone from the gable end and the dog with it. The old bread knife lay in the bottom of the sink, beetroot juice dried hard on the blade and splattered about the taps. The kettle was stone cold: no tea had been made for hours. A heap of grey ash lay in the hearth.

She pushed a few sods into the range and did odd chores while she waited for the heat to gather. Later she ate in the light of a solitary votive candle, her shadow moving about her upon the bleak walls. Every word she and Martin had said to each other that day replayed itself in her head. Nobody had ever spoken to her the way he did. Nobody before had called her beautiful.

The dog woke her. It was barely eleven o'clock. A thin film of condensation had formed on the window and when she wiped it away she could see the dog circling in front of the house. The van door slammed shut and she heard Kelly's feet crunching on the stones at the gable end. The dog went to one of the fence posts that shone bone-white in the moonlight and lifted its leg to it.

'C'mon, ye hooer ye! C'mon!' Kelly called the dog back coarsely.

The dog came to the doorstep, tail wagging as Kelly turned the handle and spilled into the house, his shoulder crashing into the wall.

She pulled the bedclothes back up around her and

listened, heart racing, wishing now for the simple comfort of Martin's embrace. She listened hard to Kelly gathering himself in the front hall, eyeing the boots discarded there which earlier she had not the mind to return to their usual place, painful reminders now of all that had befallen him that afternoon. He coughed heavily, a ball of phlegm rattling in his throat, and pushed the door closed, the dog setting up to whine into the darkness.

Kelly pushed into her bedroom, the door slamming back into the side of the wardrobe with a crunch as some piece of woodwork gave. In the consuming darkness he was invisible to her, the hoarse draw of his breath stealing around the room, the ticking of the door handle as he relaxed his grip upon it, the lament of the dog beyond the window. She trembled, feeling herself to be at the edge of something she would have no control over. She had never known a silence like this.

'I saw the two of you earlier.' The words slid out between his teeth and lips. Thin words freighted with anger and spite.

She swallowed. If he had seen them she could deny nothing and it would be pointless to try.

'Daddy?'

'After I telling you to keep a wide berth of that good-for-nothing bastard!' he rose. 'And I seen you coming up from the lake ... after I telling you and all!'

'Daddy!' she pleaded, but he still stood at the doorway, the smell of whiskey noticeable in the room now.

'I suppose he's had his hands all over you already, the filthy bastard.'

'I was only walking with him, Daddy,' she countered. 'Where's the harm in that?'

The door handle squeaked as Kelly in his anger drew it slowly back on its spring.

'Mind your lip, girl,' he bellowed, 'mind your lip! You weren't brought up to speak to anyone like that.' His breathing was heavy and laboured now and he leaned on the handle for support. She watched him in the darkness as he came to the end of the bed.

His hand seized her ankle and she screamed out in fright, fingers closing on the soft flesh as firmly as on a pick-handle. 'Daddy! Daddy!' but there was no one to hear that wanted to hear.

'He's been all over you, hasn't he?' he breathed, pulling her down the bed towards him.

'No! Daddy! No!'

With one hand she grabbed the corner of the mattress while the other hand desperately tried to stop her nightdress riding up her legs. The smell of stout and tobacco and whiskey was everywhere in the room. She screamed again and again as the corner of the mattress folded over and he drew her closer.

In the milky light of the window her thin bare legs and belly seemed to glow when he pulled up the nightdress. Her screams went to a silence where she could scream no more, her mouth wide open for nothing. He pushed her legs apart and looked.

'Your mother's daughter all right,' he said, raising the back of his hand to stifle a hacking cough. He let go of her ankles.

She grabbed the bedclothes and made for the far corner of the bed. She felt numb. The sharp smell of urine rose from where she had wet herself.

Through her fingers she looked up again. Kelly was gone, the door ajar. Nothing stirred. She felt cold and pulled the bedclothes tighter around her. After a few minutes had passed she heard his feet on the ground outside and a little later the smell of cigarette smoke came to her, borne on the night's breeze. He called for the dog and she listened to it dashing about his legs excitedly. 'G'wan fetch, Blackie.' The command punching through the stillness, the stick hooping unseen across the star-pricked sky, the dog stalling to listen for its fall in the longer grass. The dog panted as it returned with the stick in its mouth, belting back into the night when the stick was thrown again.

Helen pressed her cheek against the cold window to watch him where he stood in the penumbra of light thrown by the kitchen lamp, the cigarette flaring redly when he drew upon it. He seemed as much a part of the darkness now as any element of that night.

The cold reached out for her as she pulled the front door closed. The first air-frost of autumn stung her cheeks and ears and left a crisp dampness on everything. Her breath rose before her face. The chimneys of distant houses exhaled thin streams of turf smoke that hung low about the roofs as if afraid to rise into the cold.

The fields looked destroyed. When she reached them she stood in horror at the first of the stone walls. The handle of the spade had been snapped in two and both pieces forced into the ground. The once-neat drills had been ripped asunder, and scattered everywhere the remains of the precious beetroot, their livid juices splashed on soil and stone. The purple flesh wasted, useless, waiting to rot back into the ground from which it was so violently taken, like hearts torn out.

She tightened her grip on the handle of a bag she had earlier pulled out from under the bed. She had not slept for packing. At the bottom of the bag, wrapped in stockings and a corduroy skirt lay a tea service, twists of gold upon its handles, hand-painted swallows playing on its sides.

Part Three

ACROSS THE RIVER the sun fell lazily on the green domes and grey columns of the Four Courts, the trees that lined the banks turning towards copper, leaves scattering upon the broad sweep of water. In the distance O'Connell Bridge was thronged with people and vehicles, the march of footsteps from one side to another, buses throbbing as they waited for lights to turn.

It was not as her mother had ever described it. For her it had been a city of busy pubs and friendly people who would readily stop to talk in the going about of their business. For her there had been conversation on every street corner, women and children out window-shopping on Grafton Street and Henry Street, the windows of the department stores filled with wonderful things and lit up like Ferris wheels.

Some litter had caught in the space beneath a heavy metal grille set into the pavement at her feet. She stopped to watch the confetti of papers that stirred and circled in the draught thrown out by a fan. The smell of scorching fat came up to her, a smell that provoked memories of early mornings in the kitchen back home, thin lengths of streaky bacon laid out upon the smoking pan.

It was another memory that had brought her here. As the bus travelled towards Dublin she had fallen towards sleep, her eyes closing and opening with the motion of the bus, suddenly feeling cold and pulling a cardigan around her shoulders, her head resting against the window. Kelly's touch still clung to her skin like a cobweb that is walked into and never shaken off. She tried to sleep, hoping that it would be gone when she woke.

When her eyes closed she saw the foyer of the hotel just as her mother had described it. She had spent the first weekend after her wedding there, and for her then it had been the epitome of comfort and grandeur. In loving and complete detail she had described the revolving door and oak-panelled reception hall; the smell of beeswax from every inch of woodwork; the black ash piano that stood atop a short flight of stairs, where in the early evenings a young man would come to play light music; the gleam of brass and of the patent leather shoes the porters wore with a vivid red stripe that described the seam of their trousers; the polite hush-hush of voices that suggested gentility and refinement.

She pushed at the door and it moved uneasily upon its bearings. She squeezed into the compartment and pushed through into the foyer of the hotel. From a window high up in the stairwell weak sunlight leaked inside, poking through the lingering murk of dust and cigarette smoke, resting finally on the balding head of a man slumped in the corner of a banquette whose velvet upholstery had seen better days and more illustrious customers. A waitress emerged through a swing-door bearing a tray of empty glasses that tinkled and rattled as she walked. She moved a cigarette around her lips, shifting the tray on to one hand to pull back another door and disappear inside. A high reception desk stood in one corner, its wooden panels marked by the shoes of the countless customers who had waited there in the fading peal of an attention bell, the brass curves of which had dulled to the colour of rancid butter. The burgundy carpet was threadbare in places, layered with grime in others, and nearer the door a tear had been crudely repaired with what looked like baling twine. From another part of the building came the clatter of metal and the hiss of boiling water, the sound seeming to come closer as doors opened one after another until a porter appeared beside the desk.

'Madam?' he enquired politely, turning his head away to stifle a sneeze with his cuff. Beneath his double-breasted pin-stripe jacket he wore a v-neck pullover, the crushed collar of a greying shirt enclosing a black polyester tie. His hair had been slicked over to one side of his head, unbalancing his appearance and giving him a curiously slanting gait. 'Madam?' he asked again.

From out on the street she glanced back inside the hotel. The porter was still eyeing her from behind the reception desk. He picked up a telephone and began to turn the dial. She moved off, checking herself from backing into a red-faced boy who waited outside a newsagent's, wailing at the shreds of a yellow balloon that were gathered in his fist, the string hanging limply between his fingers.

She ate in a coffee house on Westmoreland Street, asking the woman at the till for directions to the ferry port. The street lights had come on, the sky lowered, buildings looming even more darkly and ominously than earlier. She felt small and helpless but determinedly set out for the ferry port on foot. At the ticket office she purchased a ticket for both the boat and the train to Euston Station. While the official took down her details she looked back at the city, lights aglow upstream, the hubbub of traffic a distant murmur that would soon be nothing to her at all.

She slept for most of the journey, the slow sway of the boat that lulled her towards a deep sleep she had feared might never come again, the purser shaking her awake as the other passengers bustled off and on to the waiting train and long-distance coaches, the sharpness of that salt air closed out by the fug of the carriage that bore her to London.

She dreamed of the swans, their necks swept perfectly back, sleek heads half-buried in the pure white feathers, adrift on the black waters of Rosheen Lake, a fair-haired boy cycling along the boreen to visit them.

'We'll be there soon enough,' a woman's voice woke her. They had stopped at a station. MILTON KEYNES the signs said through the glass that was cloudy with breath and grime. Her eyes were clotted with sleep and she wiped them with her sleeve. She could hear the woman apologizing for waking her but she was not listening really. The name of the place the train had stopped in struck her as strange, more like the names of household appliances displayed in the window at Ginn's, or a chemical drench for farm animals.

The train moved off with a jolt and pushed her back into the deep seat. A plastic cup circled on the tiny table between her and the woman. Outside the window there were roads leading everywhere; crossing each other, meeting at roundabouts, running parallel, and seeming to disappear into dead-ends where enormous sheds loomed in semi-circles waiting to swallow the trucks and vans that roamed roads that even at so early an hour were busy. The sky was full of cables suspended from enormous metal frames, and beyond them a jet could be seen carving its white vapour trail into a patch of early-morning blue. There were open spaces enclosed by roads, and then housing estates enclosed by more roads. The estates seemed vast but well planned, tidy Closes and Drives, a parking space in front of each red-bricked house, most still with their curtains drawn. The street lights were still on in the estates, orange-yellow pools fading on the concrete even as she watched. There is, she thought, too much of everything here. And almost before she knew it, it was all gone, the train crossing a fat grey motorway until there was just countryside again, field after familiar field of it.

'We're here at last,' the woman sighed as she folded away the tartan travel blanket that was cloaked over her knees during the journey. She smiled and stretched both hands out in front of her on the table. She had long slender fingers and perfect painted nails. A diamond ring nestled snugly alongside a bright gold wedding band on her left hand. Both she and Helen looked at her hands for a moment, then away and out of the window. The train was slowing, the brakes squeaking metal upon metal. There was open wasteland for a while, strewn with the wreckage of an earlier age, great fields of rusting engine and track, pools of black oil and stunted bushes, stacks of grey ballast pocked by shovel-marks. The train slid in amongst other trains and stopped.

The woman recommended that she wait until the other passengers had collected their luggage and got off the train before she should move herself, so she sat and watched the others squeezing through the doors and on to the platform, suitcases and rucksacks catching on door frames and handles. Finally the woman took down her overnight bag from the luggage rack and set it on the table. Helen followed her out on to the platform, clasping her bag to her chest to protect the china cups at the bottom.

'Over for a few days I take it?' the woman asked as they walked up the platform, Helen moving aside to let a small luggage trolley whirr past.

'Yes, I suppose so.'

'Enjoy yourself then,' the woman said as they came to the barrier where some travellers had dropped their luggage and were being greeted by friends and relatives, small children held aloft for inspection, hugs and handshakes exchanged. 'It's a wonderful place,' she added. 'Wonderful.'

Helen stopped to watch the woman move off across the

enormous concourse, heels clacking on the tiles, hair plait swinging.

It was still early morning, too early to go anywhere yet, the concourse flooded with the weak vanilla light of fluorescence, all noise echoing. Most of the benches were taken up by sleeping bearded men in soiled clothing and heavy coats, bottles of beer perched beside their heads or poking from pockets. Their ruddy and vein-webbed faces gazed blindly towards the ceiling lights, cracked lips dreaming of water, thin snores rising.

Helen found a seat beside a closed snack bar and sat down to wait. She gazed at a row of public telephones and wondered who she could telephone. She remembered the men in Breffni's hallway who had once stood over her while she waited for her father, talking loudly into the mouthpiece as though it was solely the strength of their voice that carried the signal down the line. She waited for no one now, and no one waited for her. There was nobody to telephone.

Idly, she wondered what would be said in the factory now that they had realized she wasn't coming in. How long would they leave it before the supervisor would have to get into his Opel and drive out to enquire if she was ill and why nothing had been heard from her? She could see the house, the door shut firmly, the windows empty save for his bedroom where the curtains would be drawn. And Kelly standing in that half-darkness, muzzling the dog with his fist, waiting for the supervisor to give up peering through the windows into silent rooms that bore no answer to his question. 'Quiet as the grave,' he would report back to the factory, 'quiet as the grave.'

The shutters clattered upwards at the snack bar and a small Asian man turned to smile at her. 'Good morning,' she said weakly as he dropped his keys into the plastic bag hanging from his wrist. The lights flickered on a few minutes later, accompanied by the hum of refrigerators and water-heaters. A boy in a white cap and coat arrived with a tray of fresh rolls and sliced bread and dropped them almost at Helen's feet, calling out to the Asian man as he left. The owner reappeared and took in the bread and soon he could be heard slapping the slices down on the counter and spreading them with butter.

The concourse began to fill with people as trains emptied and shops and kiosks opened up. The men on the benches stirred from their sleep, reaching for the beer bottles and coughing night-phlegm from their throats. A queue formed at the snack bar and the smell of toast mingled with steam drifted out.

A woman in a navy suit arrived and collected a cup of tea from the counter. 'Hello, Linda,' the Asian man greeted her. 'One sugar, take it away,' he laughed as the woman clicked a coin down on to the heavy glass. She wore sky-blue eyeshadow that swept up towards her eyebrows, and black eyeliner which ran into a point towards her temples. Helen stared at the woman's make-up but turned away when she was given a sharp look. She watched the woman walk over to a kiosk and unlock the door. Presently an illuminated INFORMATION sign flickered into life and the woman's face appeared behind a glass counter, a pencil held between her lips, the cup of tea steaming gently at her elbow.

'Hostels?' the woman said when Helen approached her and enquired about accommodation.

'Are there any in London?' Siobhán Muldoon had once mentioned to her that all cities had dozens of hostels for young people and others to stay while they looked for work.

'I'm quite sure that there are, dear. I'll have to look up my list and see.' The woman pulled open a drawer and drew out a suspension file bursting with papers, cards, and old envelopes. 'Is it Kilburn or Archway you're interested in?' she asked as she sorted through the contents of the file, discarding some of the papers into a bin at her feet.

'London, really,' Helen replied, peering at the cards as the woman flicked through a bundle.

The woman smiled wryly. 'Here's one in the West End for you then.' She held out a yellow card that had a drawing of the Madonna and Child on one side and an address on the other. 'St Catherine's of Victoria – if they can't put you up I'm sure they'll be of assistance in other ways.'

Helen took the card and wrote the directions to the hostel in the margins of the Madonna drawing. She thanked her and made for the escalators down to the Underground platforms, shuffling on to the metal steps alongside be-suited office workers and labourers in overalls and steel-toed boots, newspapers folded under everybody's arms, blank faces that were worn for the journey each morning.

Victoria, the directions said, and she waited on the platform. A sign hung from the roof that listed the destination of each train, the stations lighting up as the trains approached. People waited with her on all sides, newspapers unfolded and held up before their faces, the pages catching a mysterious warm breeze that coursed along the platform. She clutched the small yellow card for fear that it would blow down on to the tracks as the breeze strengthened. There was a rushing noise and then two lights could be seen hurtling down the tunnel at one end of the platform. Newspapers were refolded, people stood up, business men picked up their briefcases, secretaries brushed hair back from their faces, and the train drew in.

All the seats were taken and Helen had to stand, still clutching the bag to her chest. The train jolted as it moved off, throwing Helen into the front of the man standing facing her. 'God! I'm awfully sorry,' she apologized, struggling to regain her balance again, her hand reaching for the dangling strap. He looked back at her, straight-faced, only a slight smirk appearing on his lips after a few moments as some pleasurable thought seemed to come to him. 'I'm not used to this at all,' she offered by way of explanation but he seemed not to hear.

The train accelerated into the tunnel, taking them all with it into the darkness. Most of the faces that Helen saw had that same blank and dreamy expression, as though their souls dreamed of life on the surface, daylight, a fresh breeze, rain and real cold, while their bodies were pulled along in the ebb and flow of the trains beneath the city. She noticed how every gesture and movement they made seemed one of defence: briefcases placed in front of feet or across laps; rucksacks and handbags hugged to the chest; newspapers and books held up before their very faces; even the men who stood alongside her gripped their umbrellas like spears. Only the windows were watched, the passengers' stealthy gaze falling safely upon the faces reflected there as though to look direct would turn them to stone or salt.

The attendant in the wooden booth took her ticket and directed her up the escalator to the street. Pigeons burst into the sky as a taxi's brakes screeched. A newspaper seller called out, folding newspapers with one hand as he accepted coins in the other, print upon his palms like a black tattoo. A girl no older than herself handed Helen a piece of yellow paper. MARCH ON GREENHAM COMMON! the paper said in crude red block type, and Helen folded it into her pocket, noticing more yellow papers caught in a gutter puddle and blown under the newspaper seller's stand. The faint shadows thrown by the pigeons swarmed across the façade of a bank and into the windows of a pub, the baskets hanging over its door untended and the trailing ivy turned to rust with the season. People flooded up from the Underground and out from beneath the ornate station front that advertised trains to Brighton and the South Coast. Red buses pulled up beneath a steel and glass canopy and people queued to get on, their faces obscured by the bleary glass and grey plumes of diesel exhaust.

She found the hostel by following the directions to the letter. A squat, red-brick building beside two looming office blocks, it was marked out by the plaster dove over the door. She looked at the dove as she waited for her knock to be answered, the city's black dust and pigeon droppings collected upon it. A stout woman pulled back the door, a torn cardigan hanging from her shoulder, a red skirt unevenly hitched up beneath a velour jumper.

'Can I help you?' she asked.

Helen was struck by her Cork accent, how strange it seemed already, even though she had been in the country for less than a day.

'I was wondering ... I was wondering if there was some place for me to stay. A friend said you might have room.'

'I don't think we can help you now,' the woman said briskly, closing the door just a fraction.

'I'm just over on the boat, you know.'

'And plenty others with you, girl. We can't take them all.'

'Only Sister Frances particularly recommended this hostel,' Helen lied, producing the card from her pocket. 'She wrote the directions herself and said to be sure to call.'

'A friend, you said. A Sister.'

'Yes.'

She was shown into a small hallway with a reception booth surrounded by a glass screen. A cigarette left in an ashtray trailed grey smoke, a women's magazine lay open on the desk. The hallway was lit by a solitary bulb and on one wall hung a picture of the Sacred Heart, a blood-red electric light flickering uncertainly before it. The heat inside the building was thick and uncomfortable, a contained stuffiness that reminded her of the Underground, but here no mysterious breeze whistled to provide relief, and behind the reception booth spider-plants and cheese-plants limped towards another season that would forever be denied them.

The receptionist who had answered the door wrote Helen's details into a ledger book and slipped the yellow card into a drawer. She took five pounds as a deposit and gave Helen a key to a room on the third floor. When the receptionist had gone Helen dropped her bag on the bed and looked around the room. The bed was high and sat on castors and had come from a hospital. A St Brigid's Cross was fixed to the wall at its head. There was a small window and beneath that a large radiator on which two towels were folded. A small pine chest of drawers stood with some of its handles missing. The floor was covered in linoleum and smelled faintly of disinfectant.

In the absence of other residents who had gone out to work or to seek work the stillness was complete. She cleared a patch of condensation from the window and on tiptoe looked out at the people passing in the street below, dark shadows of winter coats against the flat grey of the paving slabs and buildings, and opposite, a cleared site filled with cars.

She sighed with relief as she swung her legs up on to the bed. Closing her eyes she tried to remember the last few months in Ireland but little of the detail emerged. Instead everything had slipped into a numbing, impenetrable blackness, and the emptiness of the memory lulled her towards sleep.

When she woke the hostel was busy. Girls were beginning to file back in, there was the noise of doors opening and closing, of running water in the bathroom along the corridor, of names being called out. It was dark in the room, the window a square of night, and she lay there listening to the sounds the girls made, the comforting presence of others. There was no effort to be made; she would not have to rise to peel potatoes or boil ham or fry black pudding, she would not have to wash up afterwards and bring a mug of tea into him at the fireside. And later she would not have to sit quietly while he did the crossword because any silence now would be her own.

Her money was running out. She had spent four days in the hostel, sleeping until mid-morning when she was woken by the women who mopped the floors and aired the rooms when most of the residents were out. Sometimes she had eaten with the other girls in the kitchen on the ground floor, but other nights she had gone to a café tucked in behind the railway station and ordered saveloys with chips and a Coke to wash the food down with. She would sit there for an hour or so, listening to the banter of the taxi drivers and railway workers who drifted in and out of the pull of the brightly lit café like moths to a flame, that space like an oasis in their working night. They knew each other by habit if not by name, clapping each other on the back and nodding across the Formica tables, trying to get a rise out of the Italian waitress who brought mugs of tea and plates of fried food to them. Sometimes tourists found their way there, maps spread out upon the table, directions asked for in competent English, their foreign tongues lending the plain café a touch of the exotic and half-known. She sat for as long as she could listening to and watching the other customers, caught up in their private and not-so-private worlds until it was time to walk the few hundred yards back to the doorway where she would always have to stand beneath the dirty plaster dove waiting to be let in.

The café kept her away from the hostel and she liked it

that way. There were so many lives there similar to her own that it was like living with mirror images, the experiences shared over the breakfast table or in the queue for the shower cubicles, the same stories of escape, the same uncertainty concealed by aggression or silence.

She chose silence, the knocks on her door that she let go unanswered, her meals quickly taken in the common room where she would sit apart from the others whenever possible, any invitations to the public house a few streets away politely refused.

A few girls dominated the space in the hostel; their evenings spent crammed into one room, a radio blaring pop music, clothes swapped and tried on for size and style, shouting and whistling through the windows at the men passing in the street below, egging each other on with shrieks and boisterous laughter. Then there were others, quieter, paler souls who hovered about the corridors in pairs or sat watching quizzes and documentaries on the television in the common room, mugs of tea cooling on the armrests beside them, letters from home poking from cardigan pockets or used as bookmarks in the fat novels they read.

Both were masks on the histories of neglect, of bitterness, of foiled ambition, lost love, or of lives bent towards the will of others.

On her first night in the hostel, having slept so much earlier in the day, she had lain awake listening to a girl coughing in a room further along the corridor, each unsuccessful clearing of the chest followed by a quiet groan of frustration. Others slept their troubled sleeps, light switches flicked on then off again a few minutes later, the patter of bare feet out in the corridor as another passed on their way to the toilet or the kitchen where a mug of warm milk could be made.

From outside had come the slow ticking of rain upon

the last of autumn's leaves, like the pulse of blood through her ears or the barely perceptible lap of water on the shore of a still lake, the smudge of swans circling in the darkness.

She tried to stop herself thinking of Martin, but there was his face before her, crouched amongst the reeds at the edge of the lake. What must he think of her now, that she had never loved him as she said she had, that she had left to escape him? She turned on her side and closed her eyes so that the image of his face drifted, a question mark in the dark around her.

People pushed against her as she idled at the newsagent's window to read the notices placed on cards there. There were advertisements for babysitters, English Language schools, landscape gardeners, plumbers, Busty Caribbeans and Disciplined Blondes. Helen looked at them all but couldn't make up her mind what she should do. She wandered from one shop to another, writing down details and telephone numbers only to scratch them out upon second thoughts a while later.

Some of the other girls in the hostel worked as waitresses or as barmaids, and others who had learned to type worked in offices or as dentists' and doctors' receptionists. One or two minded children for women who went out to work during the day, and a girl from Macroom worked in Selfridges department store selling chocolates over a glass counter.

All around her people seemed to be hurrying to or from work, briefcases gripped beneath white knuckles, smart handbags clasped under elbows, loaded trolleys pushed between van and store, taxis drawing up to the pavement and people climbing in. They seemed to be a part of another world which she could not enter. She drifted amongst them like a boat cut adrift on an ebbing tide, her shoulders butting into theirs, their breath upon her cheeks as they drew back to let her through a shop door, their shoes and boots clipping her ankles as they hurried past.

Mr Patel was sitting upon a pile of newspapers when she stopped to buy the evening paper, his chin resting on the backs of his hands, gazing fixedly at the legs and feet of the commuters who rushed past him. A dark-skinned boy handed her the paper from behind a wooden counter strewn with rubber bands and pieces of Sellotape. Mr Patel shouted something to the boy in a language Helen did not understand. The boy seemed not to hear.

'I think he wants you for something,' she said to the boy who instantly let loose a stream of words aimed at Mr Patel.

'Never mind my father, he is always an angry man,' the boy whispered to her as he slipped her coin into the plastic bowl that served as a till.

She smiled and stood for a second not knowing what to say before turning to look at the magazine rack behind her. An advertisement was fixed to the middle shelf: SHOP ASSISTANT REQUIRED REGULAR HOURS. There was no telephone number or address attached, the words stencilled on to a piece of bright green card and taped to the edge of the glass shelf.

'Where can I find out about the job?' she asked the boy, pointing at the piece of card.

The boy looked perplexed for a moment then uttered another stream of words that prompted Mr Patel to lift himself from the pile of newspapers, straightening his cardigan, a broad smile creeping across his lips.

'The position is located just here,' he said spreading his hands to indicate the shop. 'A very good position to be working in my shop. I am Mr Patel,' he said, wiping a palm on the seat of his pants before extending it to shake Helen's hand. 'Very pleased to meet you.'

Helen shook his hand and smiled nervously, wary of the sudden friendliness. In the space of a few days she had learned to be suspicious of others.

'You are interested, yes?' he asked and continued to describe the hours and conditions before she had a chance to answer. While he spoke she looked around her at the shop, which was tucked into the corner of an Underground ticket hall. At least, she thought, it would be dry and warm and there would always be people about. She remembered the shop in Drimelogue where a brass bell sat on the counter for customers to ring when they required service, the drone of the radio from a room behind the shop where Mrs Crowe often slept through the peals of the bell, emerging only to lock the door at the end of the day, sometimes finding that she had forgotten to unlock it in the first place.

'Sometimes you will be required to stay until the station is cleared at the end of the day, and if I take you into my confidence you will be allowed to close up the premises with my good self,' Mr Patel was saying.

'Yes,' Helen said tiredly. Mr Patel shuffled around her, showing her various items of stock, pointing out the shoe box where the clipped newspaper mastheads were stored before being promptly returned to the distributors, the steel box where the larger denomination notes were kept until Mr Patel pocketed them.

She took the job, reflecting as she made her way out of the station that she could easily find another if it did not suit her.

She stopped off at the café behind the railway station to celebrate. It was empty, the sauce bottles tidied into the centre of each Formica table, no haze of cigarette smoke, the hissing of a tub of fat, a fly extinguished with a snap against the violet-blue bulb above the door. She ordered chips, sausages, black pudding, and a bottle of Coke. She took her time, sitting at the window and watching shapes passing along the pavements outside, clearing the glass whenever her breath clouded it.

With the search for work over and only a few pounds in her pocket that were not already accounted for, she was forced to stay in the hostel day and night. The small room imprisoned her, the constantly fogged window with its mean view of the street below, the disturbance when the women arrived mid-morning to sweep and mop the linoleum floor, the warmth beating from the bulging radiator that dried everything out. She moved listlessly between her bedroom, the common room, and the kitchen. Other girls drifted in and out of the common room, trailing cigarette smoke, tears, and an air of boredom. They sat in front of the television, timing the day by the programmes, mugs collecting on every surface, cursing whenever the test card came up. Sometimes they broke into conversation, usually about men and sex, or the opposite altogether, nuns. 'Have you ever seen a nun in the showers?' one girl asked, provoking a silence that lingered for minutes, until another girl decamped to the kitchen and the rest followed her.

Mr Patel was waiting for his wife's aunt to return to Delhi before Helen could start work. She had stayed on in London after coming over for a family funeral, and had set about reorganizing the shop while filling in when Mr Patel's son, Hanif, was at school. Often Mr Patel would go to pick out something a customer had asked for only to find that it had been moved elsewhere and it could be some time before the item was found. It was a relief, then, when she arrived home on a Friday afternoon with a ticket to India in her handbag.

The shop was quiet when Helen turned up at noon on a Tuesday as Mr Patel had instructed. A couple of the station staff leaned against the counter chatting, their uniforms tatty

and ill-matched, smoking cigarettes as they listened to a
radio programme on Mr Patel's Roberts radio. Mr Patel
shooed them away when Helen approached and they slunk
off into the shadows near the summit of the escalators.

'Welcome, welcome! You're very welcome here!' Mr
Patel greeted, coming around the counter to her. 'You'll have
to watch out for some of those ticket collectors, you know.
They have me driven insane with their football talk. Always
football! Kevin Keegan, Francis Lee, Ray Clemence, Alex
Stepney, they go on and on all day long about it. Never
mind them. Come in behind the counter here and I will
show you what to do.'

She spent an hour peering through price lists and
magazine covers until customers began to trickle into the
shop from the street above. It was lunch hour. She watched
Mr Patel fold up newspapers for regular customers without
them having to ask for it, taking the money with one hand
while handing over the paper with the other. Some customers lingered at the glass counter, gazing dreamily at the
chocolate bars beneath until they pointed to their selection
and Mr Patel's hand flashed inside and retrieved it. He knew
the prices off by heart and, more often than not, having
guessed what coin they would offer him he would have the
correct change ready in his free hand. Mr Patel was so expert
that Helen wondered why he needed an assistant at all.

'Serving customers is the easy part,' he explained once
the lunchtime rush had died down. 'It is the other things
that need doing – ordering stock, sorting out the magazine
returns, tidying the racks, pricing the specials, telephoning
the cash-and-carry, and so on. The shop would have nothing
to sell if I served customers all day long.'

Helen remembered the packs of Kellogg's Corn Flakes
that stood on the shelves in Crowe's shop window in
Drimelogue, their faces faded to a sickly yellow in the sun,

the cardboard brittle and cracked with age. There were cans whose labels had become detached, a bottle of Robin starch, a tin of brown shoe polish, and the husks of a few dozen bluebottles and wasps. In Mr Patel's shop nothing had the chance to grow old but Mr Patel himself.

The afternoon passed in a blur. Mr Patel was eager to pass on so much information and advice that it seemed to Helen like walking into a thick fog and that the only thing to do was to go deeper into it, since turning back was not only defeat but confusion.

She was exhausted by the time the evening rush-hour was over. Her hands were blackened with newsprint and there were small stinging cuts drawn by the edges of magazines on her fingers. Her feet felt tender and swollen and the backs of her legs ached.

'It's harder work than it looks, yes?' Mr Patel asked as she swung her hips from side to side to loosen stiff muscles.

'It is, indeed it is,' she wheezed.

The city seemed a dead thing as she walked home that night, always the dry feel of newsprint upon her hands that water and soap alone could not banish. The streets dragged at her, the butter-yellow-lit buses that passed along mist-slicked streets seemed to move more slowly than ever, their brakes grating when she darted out at zebra crossings. Litter funnelled along High Holborn, trapped sometimes against bus shelters and telephone kiosks, an aluminium can rattled in a gutter somewhere, to and fro, to and fro. There were cardboard boxes stacked at the base of every lamppost and fruit trays discarded in doorways, the delicate purple wrappers joining the mêlée of blown litter.

Tiredness sank her in the end. She had walked the few miles to the shop that morning, setting out in plenty of time to save whatever the bus ride or tube fare would cost, buoyed up by the day before her. Now it told in her tired legs.

When she saw the orange light of a taxi come around Hyde Park Corner she raised her arm to hail it, the money saved that morning gone to waste.

It would, she thought, be a long, long winter. Sunlight danced between the buildings around Golden Square and pressed against the stone façades on the northern side. There were few leaves left on the branches to stand in its way. A sharp frost had left everything white when she walked out in the morning, a crisp coating on the roofs of the cars in the street below her window, the broken tarmac in the parking lot dusted with whiteness, ice in the gutters.

It was the first day of December, and the wind brought real cold with it. Mr Patel had paid her in the morning, allowing her the afternoon off to go to the shops as she had wanted. The department stores along Oxford Street were getting ready for Christmas. She went from one to another, watching the assistants dressing the windows with pictures of Santa Claus and snow scenes, goods wrapped in tinsel, clothes sprinkled with silver that sparkled under the harsh lights. There was an air of excitement on the streets refined by the cold, as though people wanted to contain and protect it, but still it escaped in bursts of laughter and conversation. Children were dragged away from toy displays, husbands stood glumly near the women's dressing rooms in the fashion departments, the restaurants in the big stores were packed, uniformed staff bawling at each other.

In the thinning of the afternoon she found escape from the clamour in a small pub near Hanover Square. The carpet was worn to nothing in places, a waxen light loomed over an empty pool table, the publican sat at the bar talking to an elderly gentleman, but it was warm and quiet, the door springing shut behind her to close out the streets.

She ordered a lemonade and a packet of crisps and sat watching the silent television on a ledge over the bar.

'Would you like it turned up, love?' the publican asked, but she said it was fine as it was. He looked at his companion and they were silent for some minutes before their conversation resumed in a hushed whisper.

The moment stretched back for her; the bar, the comforting fug of warmth welcoming, the smell of cigarettes and beer threaded back to the days when she accompanied her father to the pub after Mass on a Sunday, thud of boots in the hallway as the customers came in and out past her shelter beneath the black public phone. She knew them by their boots, shoes, and laces: the battered brogues of Thomas the postman, the cracked leather of Mr Nolan's slip-ons, the string laces of Thomas Naylor's boots that missed every second eye, the sacristan's built-up heel as he clumped inside to deliver the verdict on the morning's takings.

'Are you all right there, love?' The hand on her shoulder tapping her to wakefulness.

'Yes, yes,' she gathered herself, smoothing her hair. She had fallen asleep. 'I'm fine.'

'You were drifting off there, you were,' the publican smiled. 'I was afraid you might knock your head the way you were leaning,' he said, turning back to the bar with her empty glass. He filled it again and set it down before her. 'On the house, Sleeping Beauty,' he laughed when she offered him money. The elderly customer smiled at her and their conversation struck up more loudly this time.

Time went on, slipping past without her noticing, and in her drowsiness there was great peace. The animated conversation of the two men at the bar, the sweetness of the lemonade, the warmth, the very dullness of the lounge, all gathered together into one thing that comforted her. No longer the wait for him to return from the fields, no longer the tramp of boots upon the doorstep, no longer the dread that stole into the evenings as his mood darkened with the light and the frustration that tools and ambition had to be laid aside until dawn. No longer; the two words drawn out upon her breath.

The hostel stirred like a sleeping beast as Christmas approached. Decorations appeared from nowhere one afternoon, the girls trickling in to find the rooms and halls decked with strings of gaudy paper lanterns, bunting made from old dyed sheets, sprigs of holly over every door. The receptionist explained that the pupils in the local convent school made the decorations each year. A Christmas tree was put up inside the front door, dressed with thin silver strips and white powder from a can. With the passing of days the tree shed its needles along with the powder, dusting the coats of those who brushed past.

The various journeys home to Ireland were so much in their conversation that it seemed they were on them already. In spite of their escaping to England or leaving for a new life there they would always return, would always hunt down the home that was in their heads. Helen was silent as the other girls discussed travel arrangements and compared Christmases in each other's homes; the relatives and neighbours that would call around on Christmas morning and on St Stephen's Day, the gifts they had asked for, the friends they hoped to see again, the meals that would be prepared.

Helen tried to forget the barrenness of the many Christmases that had passed since her mother had died. The meanness of the duck that Kelly would poach from a nearby lake, its yellow bill tapping off the inside of the van where Kelly would hang the poor creature for a couple of days. Then Kelly would pluck and clean the bird before handing it to Helen to dress and roast. The meal was eaten in near-silence as the evening came on, the cooking going without praise or criticism, the importance of the feast day passing without comment, the relief when St Stephen's Day came to an end and there was other business to be getting about.

She froze when another girl's gaze fell upon her during a boisterous conversation, the silence that had protected her now marking her out, the dropped glance and turn away that let the girl know that she should not ask. There was a lull and Helen waited with pulse quickening for the girl to ask her about her Christmas but the conversation picked up again almost without missing a beat.

Mr Patel stood watching the station empty just after midnight. When the till had been reconciled, the float made up for the next morning, the mastheads clipped and stored, and the shelves tidied he would take to the small concourse to walk around and chat to the other staff that shared the station. When even they had left, he would gaze vacantly at the wooden-treaded escalators working the depths of the station, as though dredging the air, as a barge might dredge silt from a river, stirring the transient ghosts of passengers. The mechanical tread of the escalators had a yearning sound that was not lost on Mr Patel as he remembered Bombay, the swarming city of people and bicycles he was born into, more than a world and a lifetime away from the city of glass and concrete he now lived and worked in.

He clipped his nails as he dreamt, his feet sliding easily across the sole-polished floor, the sharp click of the metal clippers against the drone of the escalators and the sigh of wind along the street above.

He stood waiting to greet the night workers: the fluffers, the litter-collectors, the mop women, the poster-pasters, and finally the men who walked the tracks from one station to the next when the current had been switched off in the dead of night. He knew them all by name, and they too knew his. 'Evening, Mr Patel,' they drawled, as they hurried towards the work that showed in their pallor; skin the colour of mushrooms, features drawn by the wind that blew through the tunnels and carried the city's dust with it. They filed past and he stood to watch, like a captain in a parade ground, the orange-overalled men and women descending through the gloom into the city's marrow.

She wished Christmas to be over, and to take with it the awkwardness of the days alone in the hostel, the stillness in the streets that were too empty to walk along. She spent blank days in front of the television, sometimes with one or other of the receptionists, and they passed in a blur of TV quizzes, variety shows, and films. A shiver of bottles as an electric milk float made its way between the buildings one morning signalled the end of the holiday.

To her relief the girls returned.

She wanted to get out. She had saved some money from the wages Mr Patel gave her each Friday, and with nothing to spend it on but her lodgings at the hostel and the odd meal in the station café, it was beginning to mount up in her drawer.

Knowing that she alone had stayed behind at Christmas, some of the girls had begun to grow visibly wary of her, closing their doors as she approached, the bob of their voices lowering when she came into the common room, the hesitancy at the dinner table whenever she asked for something to be passed across. They had begun to believe, she knew, that she had been abused at home and had escaped the pawing and probing, the violation of innocent flesh, never to return. Only such a past could ever prevent her from returning to it.

There was no way back. She had to get out now, or live in the shadow of the myth they were creating for her.

She found the bedsit through an advertisement in the evening paper, tearing the page from a copy Mr Patel had left unsold on a Thursday evening, running for the Tube when she was let go after the evening rush-hour, the press of people shuffling into the Underground with her, the train that could not arrive nor travel fast enough.

Dismay slowed her pace when she turned on to the terraced street; there were others there before her, young men and women, some in nurses' uniforms, all clutching the same page from the newspaper, their breaths rising coldly into the glow of the porch light above their heads.

But the landlord seemed to take a shine to her when he saw her coming through the wooden gate. Perhaps it was the breathlessness that had brought a flush to her cheeks or the disappointment in her eyes, but he let her in before any of them, the clamour of their protest ringing in her ears as she stepped into the room. There was a bedsitting room and beyond it, through an old door frame, a kitchenette, which itself led to a toilet tacked on with sheet metal to the back of the house. There was a bed, a low table, and a narrow wardrobe of the type that might serve to hold visitors' coats in the hallway of a large house. The kitchenette had a two-ring gas cooker with a kettle and a sink, and a small cabinet fridge. There was a poster of the Small Faces stuck to the wall in a corner of the room, a tell-tale yellow tidemark creeping out along the wall behind it. A broken piece of mirror rested on two nails set into the wall above the sink. A draught caught her ankles as it moved between one room and the other. The windows ran with condensation. An electricity meter ticked urgently beside the wardrobe, waiting to be fed coins.

'Twelve pounds a week in advance,' the landlord replied when she asked how much the bedsit would cost. 'The gas is paid for, so you won't have to worry about that. The electric takes twenty pences.' He was getting impatient as she looked around the room, thumping the firm bed, opening the wardrobe whose rail was thick with bare wire hangers, a lone Mothak hanging in their midst. He rattled a few coins in his pocket while he waited, eyes darting about the room as he noticed those things that needed seeing to but could do without so long as nobody asked or complained.

'Look, will you take it or not?' he said impatiently. 'Only there's a dozen out there will if you don't want it.'

'Of course I'll take it,' she said, surprised at the turn his mood had taken.

The coins settled in his pocket and he went to straighten the curtain which was snagged on the windowsill. 'It's no palace ... but it's a grand and cosy place all the same,' he reassured. 'You know, we bought the house when we came over after the war and there was loads of work to be had. It was a sound investment, the same house.'

'It's grand, it'll do me fine,' she said, running the tap in the kitchen. The water heater burst into life with a plume of bright blue flame and the water ran hot within seconds. The warmth brought her a simple pleasure, the luxury of hot water from a tap in a home of her own. She thought of the range back home, the heating of pot upon pot of water if she or Kelly wanted a bath. She remembered, too, standing naked in a tin tub while her mother washed her down with a cloth wetted from a kettle, how the water curled outwards and made long steaming marks on the floorboards, the way she would grab the bun in her mother's hair for support as she was towelled dry before being lifted out and put to bed.

'Once I have the deposit the place is yours,' the landlord said, scattering the memory.

'The deposit,' she said. 'What deposit?'

Dismay crossed the landlord's face. 'I'll need the first fortnight's rent as a downpayment. You'll get it back when you leave — so long as there's nothing broken or what have you.' He mumbled the last few words.

Helen's heart sank. The room seemed to grow dark. She thought of the dozens of advertisements to be looked through all over again. She had not thought to save enough for a deposit.

A young man pushed into the room and asked if it was still up for grabs, and the landlord said he'd have an answer for him in a minute or two.

Helen undid the catch on the watch that had been her mother's, and offered it to the landlord.

'Ah now, I can't go accepting the likes of that,' he protested. 'It wouldn't be right at all.'

'I don't have the money saved for a deposit. I never even thought about it,' she said. 'Go on, take the watch and I'll give you the money as soon as I have it saved. I'll have it for you in no time.'

The same young man returned. 'Well?' he prompted, hopping eagerly from foot to foot.

'It's gone,' the landlord announced, showing him out to the front door where a few of the others still waited. Helen could hear them cursing as the landlord sent them on their way, telling them to call back in a week's time when one of the rooms upstairs might be free.

'All right then.' He took the watch from her and folded it into his breast-pocket. 'You'll have the money as soon as you can?'

She promised that she would and paid him the first week's rent. He locked the door behind them and they went out into the night that had grown cold and damp, the trees dripping with rain that had fallen while she had been inside. Traffic was making its way home along the High Road and she turned towards the Underground station, passing a couple of pubs, a bookmakers whose betting slips had made their way outside on the heels of customers, and a kebab shop where teenagers were gathered around a pinball machine.

Her leaving the hostel was something she kept to herself all day as she handed out newspapers, magazines, and chocolate bars, but the excitement worked away inside her so that she felt she might burst before the night-time came. She had become so skilful at taking money and handing back change that it was automatic for her. While the customers came and went she worked out her plan for leaving the hostel and moving to the bedsit; how long it would take her to save enough to get the watch back, how much money she would have left every week once the rent was paid for, what the electricity might cost. It would have been easier in many ways to stay in the hostel where most things were laid on for her, where the heat and light was free and where there were always people around. Even if you didn't want to speak to anyone, at least they were there. But it was someone else's home just as the house in Ireland was her father's. The bedsit in Hornsey would be hers alone.

'We'll be sorry to see you go,' Sister Margaret said when Helen told her that she was leaving the hostel. 'We're always sorry to see one of our girls go, but you know you're welcome back if you are ever in need of us.'

Helen thanked the Sister for her concern and watched her moving off down the corridor towards the nuns' quarters at the rear of the building, the hem of her habit gathering globs of fluff as she went, the wooden cross around her neck clacking against the pinched, proud buttons on her chest.

She packed quickly and quietly, not wanting to draw

any attention to herself. What few clothes she had were folded and dropped into the shoulder-bag where the tea service had lain undisturbed and protected since her arrival. She was not sorry to be closing for a last time the door upon the room and its tired furniture and decoration; the way it seemed to hold the dulled spirits of former occupants; the St Brigid's Cross which, like her, others had spent too much time trying to balance correctly upon a nail in the wall.

By the following evening the other girls would be wondering what had become of her. Let them, she thought, as she passed out beneath the dirty plaster dove into the cool anonymous streets where nobody would wonder who or what she was.

Byrne, the landlord, had brought a two-bar electric fire down from the attic for her, and was fitting a plug to the flex when she arrived.

'There you are now,' he smiled. 'I wasn't sure what time you said you'd come around so I found a few things to be getting on with while I was waiting. I'll be out of your way as soon as I have this yoke set up.'

Helen made a pot of tea with the groceries she had bought in the local shop and offered Byrne a cup when he had finished wiring the plug. She sat on the bed and listened to his stories about some of the people who had lived in the house over the years since his own family had moved out to Barnet. The tenants had mostly been Irish labourers and nurses who stayed for up to six or seven months at a time before they found flats to share with friends or colleagues from the sites or hospitals where they worked. He preferred to take Irish tenants because he 'knew where they were coming from' and could depend on them to pay the rent most of the time. If anything needed doing there was always one of them who was willing and able to repair a leaking cistern or nail down the odd loose floorboard themselves without calling him out at every hour of the day and night.

When the tea was beginning to grow cold the meter gave a loud click and the lights went out, the bars of the electric fire fading to dark red in seconds.

'They're a whorin' thing altogether, those meters,' Byrne cursed, looking for somewhere to put his mug. 'Will you pardon the French?' he mumbled, checking his pockets for twenty-pence pieces.

'I should have thought to get some while I was in the shop,' Helen apologized, opening her purse and shaking the coins on to the bed where they could be more easily identified in the dark, but none of the coins suited. She pulled back the curtains and the sodium glare of a street lamp cast into the room.

'That'll do the trick, girl!' Mr Byrne exclaimed.

Helen followed him outside and watched him start his car before going to a shop on the High Road to get change for the meter.

While the room warmed up she inspected the cupboards which had been emptied by the previous tenant save for a bag of long grain rice, a tin of Campbell's chicken soup, and a half-bottle of Kahlua coffee liqueur which she opened. It held a dark and rich smell, almost of molasses gone rancid, any sweetness lost. She dropped it into the bin along with the bag of rice. The soup, however, she opened and emptied into a pot to heat, putting two slices of bread under the grill to toast. While she waited she switched on the water heater again and watched the steam rise as she turned the tap on full. She liked the way the gas sparked into life without any need for a flame, the dense pop as the miasmic blue burst into the air.

When the soup and toast were ready she took them into the bedroom and sat on the bed to eat, all sorts of possibilities springing to mind as she looked around at the room. She would need a sheet and another blanket for the bed and a pillow for her head. She noted other things that she wanted: towels, a bread knife, a cloth to wipe the kitchen with, a sweeping brush.

When she had finished eating she undressed in the kitchen and soaped herself standing up, watching the rivulets of water running across the lino floor. So much had changed around her in the last few weeks, she thought, but she herself had not changed. She was the same person, inhabiting the same body, who wore the same skin that she now rinsed, the familiar marks, curves, and angles; the same breasts and inverted nipples, the same navel and shallowly domed belly, the same patch of dark hair beneath, the same dimpled knees and small feet.

She remembered how it had felt when Martin had touched her, that moment when fire seemed to race across her skin like the blue flame bursting from the water heater, a temporary sensation that gave way to a deeper warmth. He had drawn his hand back once he had traced the curve of her collar-bone and found her bra strap. It had been she who had taken his hand and pressed it to her breast so that he could feel her nipple harden into the trembling softness of his palm and understand what he had started in her.

She fingered the door key in her pocket the whole way home the next day, anxious to turn it in the lock and open the door on what was now hers. As she came up the steps from the station she noticed the small sticky buds that had begun to appear on the tall beech trees that surrounded the Green, and above them still the sky washed with indigo, the beginning of spring. The chill had begun to melt from the evenings.

As she walked along the railings past the Green she could see the shapes of children leaving the swings and see-saw in the playground, their screams and yelps striking out against the clatter of traffic. Headlights tracked through the railings, picking out mothers with push-chairs, shopping bags hung from the handles, and businessmen striding past, briefcases swinging, evening papers folded underarm. The corner shops and take-aways were busy, youngsters standing cross-armed waiting to be served, shop assistants handing groceries and cigarettes across counters. The bus stops were full, teenagers darting out into the traffic to look down the street for the next lumbering bus. When it drew up, the shadows of passengers were visible behind a curtain of condensation on the glass, names etched into it by school-children; Mark, Jason, The Clash, Samantha, and Dave loves Jenny, the letters gone fuzzy with time. The streets throbbed with abundant life. There was so much to be seen.

He smiled as he passed by, a pick-axe balanced on his shoulder, his wrist resting easily on its handle. He wore a bright yellow tunic over his blue boiler-suit that was smeared in oil and dirt. He turned to look at her as he descended the escalator into the depths of the station, his eyes a gleam of brightness against the dimness, his silence alone amongst the coarse banter of the other labourers riding the escalator with him. When their voices had gone she listened but there was only the creaking toil of the escalators and minutes later the rumble of compressors and hammer-drills working on the tracks far below.

He came to buy a bar of chocolate a couple of nights later, the coins as bright upon his soiled palms as his eyes had been in the gloom two nights before. He was undecided and asked her to pick one for him.

'A Mars,' she said, surprised at his Irish accent. 'To keep your energy up.'

'Aye, you'll need energy to keep it up,' another worker winked as he came by.

They ignored him and she took the coins. He looked at the magazines for a while, fingering the covers. He had a round face and dark curly brown hair and a few days' growth on his chin and cheeks. His shoulders were broad and he wore his watch on his right wrist, the face turned inside so that it would not scratch while he worked.

She found herself noticing these and other things about him, but could not help herself, the fascination for another holding her there as though in a trance.

'Goodbye now,' he said turning back from the magazines and leaving the shop.

She broke from her gaze and his back was turned to her, a mallet swinging in one hand. In seconds the escalator had borne him away.

There were other lives she was close to and did not know. She read their names from the post that dropped through the letter box: Mark O'Neill, Pat Donoghue, Noreen Cummins, David Compton, Dymphna Byrne, Paul Silke. They became familiar to her as the days slipped by. She heard them moving about in their rooms, music from a transistor radio seeping through the walls, the creak of beds as they shifted in their sleep, and once in the first days the sound of lovemaking from the room above, the slow gasps and groans that wound towards a minute of frantic movement as they sought their goal, the subsiding silence in which she felt her own embarrassment, flushed with it.

Otherwise they moved about the house like phantoms. She would only venture up to the shared bathroom on the first floor when she heard the door open and the pad of feet across the landing. The warm fug of the room in their wake, steam on the window, a halo of talc upon the floor, sometimes a bar of soap forgotten on the windowsill that was too intimate a thing to be used by any other.

On cold nights the walls of her room grew damp, the moisture coming through the paper and running down towards the skirting board. She had to move the bed away from the walls for fear that the mattress would rot, the bedclothes soil indelibly. To save electricity she would light the rings of the cooker, fanning the warmth out into the bedroom with a dishcloth, the heat only serving to draw more water on to the walls. She learned to ignore it, but once when she reached out in her sleep she yelped and woke as her arm brushed the cold wet paper, sweating like another's skin.

'What parts are you from?' he ventured a few weeks later, when he came into the shop as she was counting the till, Mr Patel standing guard with his nail-clippers. His voice betrayed his nerves, the way he looked away as he spoke, picking the change from her hand.

She told him, and he said that he came from Fermoy originally, but that his family had moved to Dungarvan after his father had died. He had been working in London for four years now, he said, and had never got used to it. The words flew from him as if read from a prepared statement, a résumé of an identity and state of mind in a few short sentences.

She nodded in agreement.

'Do you go to any of the pubs at all?' he changed, growing bolder now that he felt easier with her.

'I don't. I don't know my way around enough to know a good one.'

'There's grand pubs up in Kilburn, Willesden and the like. They're only black at the weekend you know. You'd swear you were back home if you closed your eyes. It's a great feeling all the same.'

'I'm sure it is,' she said, noticing Mr Patel gesturing to her that he wanted to lock up and make for home. 'I've to close up here now,' she said, rattling the plastic tray filled with coins.

'Oh, right,' he said, his mood faltering.

He lingered outside the shop, inspecting the cable on a hammer-drill. 'Would you fancy going up to the pubs one of these nights?' he blurted as she helped Mr Patel pull down the shutters. 'Just for the crack, you know.'

She couldn't refuse, snared by his good humour and the shyness that intrigued her. Why not? she thought. There was nothing to lose. They arranged to meet at the weekend outside a department store they both knew near Marble Arch.

She had set about making the bedsit her own, filling it first with things she needed: kitchen implements, a freshener for when the air grew stale during the day, a carpet-sweeper which she found in a skip, two tall glasses from a bargain shop, a plastic box to keep bread fresh in. Afterwards came the things she wanted: a glamorous cheese-plant which she stood in a corner of the room, a print of a Victorian scene with women floating on petticoats along a seafront, a colourful painted plate which she stood on the kitchen windowsill, a blue-ribbed glass bowl she found abandoned on a pillar when walking home, and finally the postcard she pinned to the wall above her head, two swans drifting on a dark lake.

She enjoyed cooking for herself, her meals no longer dictated by Kelly's likes and dislikes. She could turn some ravioli out of a tin, or boil a piece of cod in a plastic bag, knowing that he would never have approved. She cooked pasta and rice, poorly at first, but gaining confidence with experience, throwing ingredients together to make sauces. It was only as she washed up at the sink that she missed the house she had grown up in. The kitchen window gave out on to a back garden that was hardly a garden at all but a graveyard for furniture, appliances, and other things that had once served the tenants of the bedsits. A fridge lay on its side, its door open, rust-coloured water and leaves pooled inside. A gramophone poked out of a bed of nettles, a spider's web stretched across the mouth of the speaker. A baby's pram had been ditched upside down, wheels baked in rust, the fabric rotted and torn. Pipes of all sorts stood against the walls and wooden fences that enclosed the forlorn space. She promised herself that she would get a blind which she could pull down over the window so that her gaze would not fall there.

There was dereliction too in the house across the road. Corrugated steel covered the door, sprayed with graffiti, acronyms for football clubs. The lower windows had been blocked up, the frozen ooze of mortar bulging between the blocks. Pigeons passed through the upper windows and through a gaping hole in the roof, resting on window frames for hours on end, white streaks of excrement decking the walls. The front path was wildly cracked and colonized by weeds. The skeleton of a motorbike lay on its side in the garden amongst the broken bottles, drink cans and plastic bags of rubbish that had been dumped there. Sometimes dogs fought in the garden, arguing noisily over some chip wrapper or other that had found its way over the broken wall.

All week she was buoyed by the anticipation of meeting him at the weekend. As she passed papers to commuters and took their coins, keeping one eye on the magazine rack for fear that copies would go missing in the rush, she could think of little else but their arrangement for Saturday evening. Already she could see herself standing on the pavement, soft light washing around her from the huge glass windows in the department store, looking one way and another because she did not know what direction he would come from. Or she imagined that he would be there before her, leaning casually against a street sign, wearing a dark suit and a white shirt open at the collar, his heel tapping nervously against the kerb as he waited.

She had seen other girls waiting for their partners beneath the awning of the Dominion Theatre in Tottenham Court Road, elegantly smoking cigarettes, their faces upturned, the blue smoke they exhaled rising lazily towards the small lights set into the awning, standing with one leg tucked behind the other, elbow pressed into their sides. They seemed to ooze sophistication and sex, waiting as though nerves did not exist, as though they had all the time in the world.

The weekend seemed an eternity away, that stretch of time measured out by the editions of the newspapers: City Prices, one star, two star, three star, and so on throughout the afternoon until finally the van appeared upstairs with the West End Final, the twine cut free of the bale of papers that she hurriedly stacked on the counter. She could not work fast enough and Mr Patel fumed when the call of the seller on the street corner above broke out with 'West End Final' even as the delivery boy was making his way down to the station. Sometimes he would snap at her after seeing a regular customer making for the escalators with a copy of the paper tucked under their arms having by-passed the shop. Afterwards, when the throng of commuters had melted into the evening and the stack of papers had reduced to a handful, he would apologize, taking off on to the concourse with his nail-clippers, admonishing himself in his own language.

On the Saturday she was released into the city, the afternoon her own until it was time to meet him at seven o'clock. She felt renewed, the waiting of the past week almost over. The nerves that gnawed at her had all but gone now that the moment was close. To celebrate, she bought a porcelain teapot from a shop on Shaftesbury Avenue, guilt at the waste of good money only setting in as she made her way across Piccadilly Circus to the Underground, and home, where the pot was scalded and the Earl Grey made, the delicate scent of bergamot lingering until it was time to go out.

'There you are,' he exclaimed when he arrived. 'I was afraid you mightn't come, but you're early after all.'

She had been the first to arrive, pacing the footpath outside the department store, watching the staff leave through the front door, a street-sweeper stopping to chat to her, turning the conversation towards the Troubles once he had picked up on her accent. She wished for him to leave for fear that her date might think her interested in any man who stopped to talk. Eventually the sweeper pushed off, the wheels creaking on his cart, the wooden-headed brush clacking off the kerbstones. For moments afterwards she had feared that he had rounded the corner and seen her talking and had turned on his heel; but here he was.

'You're looking lovely,' he admired, his breath fogging in the cool evening air, cheeks reddened from hurrying. He wore a deep green cable-knit sweater and blue jeans beneath his coat. The black brogues had been newly polished. He was, she thought, slighter than his heavy work gear made him out to be, but his hands betrayed a powerful man.

'I still don't know your name,' she ventured, the awkwardness of the question muting her words so that she had to repeat them for him.

'Eamonn,' he said, surprised that it had never come up in conversation before. 'And yours is Helen, isn't it? I heard the shop owner call out to you once,' he explained, then laughed at the surprise upon her face.

The laughter took the edge off their meeting, the easy enjoyment of shared humour softening the defences and leading to talk about the weather and the availability of work in the city, the conversation carried to the bus stop where others waited beneath the canopy out of a thin drizzle that had begun to fall.

Conversation lapsed and some of the awkwardness returned on the bus journey, each becoming conscious of their accents amidst the silent reserve of the other passengers who stared vacantly at the pavements emptied by the drizzle, the drone of the diesel engine as the bus made its way along, throbbing when it waited at stops and traffic lights.

'We're here now,' Eamonn prompted as they approached a junction, the cooler air snapping at her cheeks when she stepped off the bus. She pulled her scarf around her neck, Eamonn walking close to shield her from the rain.

The street was lined with pubs: McDonagh's, Molly's, the Spinning Wheel, the Black Kesh, the Thatch, each vying with the other for custom, their fronts brightly lit up, the names painted in Celtic lettering, or etched into plastic signs like lettering on a gravestone, and everywhere the GUINNESS sign like a talisman. The windows were decked with posters advertising traditional music of every variety, country music performers smiled from rhinestone frames; Philomena Walsh, Big Dan The JCB Man, The Rustlers, Mary Finn & The Sunshine Band.

Three youths in Kilkenny GAA jerseys, striped like hornets, argued with a doorman at McDonagh's, the slurred buzz of their voices carrying across the street. Eventually they turned their argument upon each other until one of them was pushed back over a litter bin, all hostility forgotten as the other two rushed to rescue him, retreating down the street while swearing out loud at the doorman.

Helen stared, the whole scene seeming to her like the main streets of a few Irish towns distilled and poured out into this unwitting part of a foreign city.

'C'mon, we'll try the Spinning Wheel,' Eamonn started, his hand cradling her elbow but letting go when he felt her hesitate. 'Don't worry, you can get a quiet drink in there at the worst of times.'

They had to turn sideways to squeeze through the throng inside the door. Pints of Guinness were being passed through the crowd at head height, hands ready to take the dew-furred glass and lift it to the mouth, froth quivering on the lip as the taste was savoured before the thread of conversation would be sought for and found again. The smell of beer and tobacco hung thickly in the air, the fug entwined with the argument and talk that was everywhere. A television set perched above the optic racks played mutely to the few souls at the bar who paid it any attention. Two barmen worked the counter with ease, pints of Guinness racked up to settle, whiskey tumblers to hand beside the measures, water jugs set out at intervals along the counter, the till drawer left open so that there would be no delay.

Eamonn looked around and took her hand, guiding her through the crush, past an enormous log fire whose heat was so intense that people backed away from it, to a set of benches at the rear of the pub where a group of elderly men sat in quiet conversation, their bloodhound eyes hardly registering the young couple who came to sit in their midst.

A hatch gave on to the bar and Eamonn returned after a few minutes with a Guinness for himself and an orange juice for Helen.

'You seem to know your way around here well enough,' she remarked when he sat down.

'When I first came over I'd come up here and do the rounds of the bars,' he explained. 'I'd have a drink in one and move on to another if there wasn't any conversation or crack to be had. After a while you'd recognize the same faces and voices, the bars would take on a character all of their own, and you'd come to favour one over the other on account of the people and the crack inside. It was the only way I knew of falling in with a crowd of some sort.'

A man in his mid-thirties, his hand already reaching for his flies, saluted Eamonn as he passed on his way to the toilets. Eamonn lifted his pint from the table in reply.

'You'd learn a lot from sitting at the counter on Saturday evening listening to the goings-on around you,' Eamonn went on, clearing the pale froth from his lip. 'You'd hear where the best places to be picked up by the site contractors were, and where it was only Travellers that were picking men up to do asphalting work. Sometimes you'd fall in with a few lads who were off to a dance in the Galtymore or the Gresham. You'd get a lift there and back if you were lucky.'

Helen reflected on her own failure to fall in with any crowd, the empty souls in the hostel and those who flitted about like ghosts at the shared house, the patterns of avoidance that had begun in each place and looked set to continue. Eamonn had grasped every opportunity for contact with others, the same opportunities that she had so easily spurned.

'Will you have another?' His glass was empty, ringed with the tide-marks of stout that marked out the conversation.

'I will,' Helen replied, buoyed now by the crowd and the clamour of the pub, the easy intimacy of conversation she had not known since leaving Ireland. 'I'll have a vodka with the orange.'

Talk carried them through the evening, the exchange of

family histories and stories about their local towns, the inevitable search for common ground, as if a link between them would drag any feelings they held for each other out of the shadows and into the light where they might be allowed to flourish. Helen steered the conversation away from Kelly as much as possible, shrugging her shoulders when Eamonn asked why she had left, moving forward and back like a yacht tacking across wind and current.

'Would you think of going back at all?' he probed. 'You had a job after all, they might have you back.'

'I wouldn't go back. Not now. Anyway, I like it here.'

'I'd go back to sweep the streets of Cork tomorrow if they'd only have me, and most of these would too,' he said, nodding towards the crowd of men and women in the pub. There was an edge of anger in his voice that unsettled her, a side of him that hadn't shown itself until now when the evening was drawing to a close.

The barmen called time and there was a crush at the bar as the last orders were taken. Eamonn returned from the hatch with a glass of Guinness and another vodka and orange. They drank the last in silence, looking about them at other couples and the groups of young men and women eyeing one another up. Finally, it was time to go, the cubes of ice losing their shape in the bottom of her glass much as the conversation had melted towards nothing. It was a shame, she thought, for a few words to change the course of a pleasant evening. There was little that could recover it for them now.

The street was filled with the drunken cries of revellers as the pubs emptied. A few sat on the kerbs waiting for friends to emerge through doorways, ushered or pushed out by barmen who were anxious to clear up and make their way home. A fast-food van had drawn up outside the Thatch and an unruly queue formed for the beefburgers and hot-dogs sizzling on its pans, the waxen smell of fat and onions hanging thickly in the night. Young men, red-faced from drink, clutched women to them like trophies, the women laughing hysterically at everything that was said as they stumbled along the pavement. A navy police van cruised slowly down the street, uniform buttons and badges glinting from where officers watched the scene outside. A pint glass dropped and smashed on the flagstones, scattering those around it. The police van paused and moved off again.

'It was a grand night,' Eamonn began as they walked away. 'You were great company, you know.'

The ready flattery made her uncomfortable. The conversation had been difficult when it had turned. They both knew it yet still he persisted.

'It's not easy to spend so long with somebody you hardly know and be able to get anything out of it. Sometimes you can go for a drink with your best friend and have nothing to talk about. Have you ever found that?'

Helen nodded. It was easier to agree now than pursue the point and prolong the awkwardness.

When they came to the empty bus stop they turned to look back the way they had come for the bus, a breeze catching their faces.

'There's a place in Willesden I know that'd still be open if you're interested. It's quiet enough and I'd put you in a taxi afterwards.' He would offer anything now not to have to face into the night alone.

'No thanks, Eamonn,' she said, pitying the tone of quiet desperation in his voice. 'I'm tired enough as it is.'

The bus she was waiting for turned the corner and came into sight, slowing at the traffic lights.

'Perhaps we could go out another night?' Eamonn ventured as the bus drew up.

'We could . . . I suppose,' she faltered.

'I'll see you in the station one of these nights then,' he said as she reached for the handrail and pulled herself up on to the platform.

She smiled and thanked him for the evening, turning into the bus which was almost empty. The conductor rang the bell a couple of times and she watched through the window as Eamonn buttoned his jacket and turned for home.

It had been a pleasant evening. Looking back on it now, from where she sat in the rocking to and fro of the bus, the bitterness he had loosed in the last minutes had been rising during the whole evening. How flustered he had been when he couldn't remember his brother's birthday or his parents' wedding anniversary. Little things that had almost driven him to distraction. He had seemed such a simple character before that turn had been taken. A labourer who sought out and enjoyed the company of others, who over the years would have taken a number of women to the same pub on the same bus and had the same conversation with each of them. Had it turned so with them? Like her, he was still alone.

Blurred figures glided past on the pavements outside, moving through her thoughts, running towards the sanctuary of traffic islands, their heads down as though against the darkness, street light catching only the dull gleam of a chin or forehead. A tall, rangy woman in denim shorts and torn stockings leaned into a car window. Two youths pushed a market cart around a corner. A police car switched on its blue light and turned right around in front of the bus before speeding off. A long truck loaded with reams of newsprint had pulled up on the Finchley Road, the driver standing beside it and pouring coffee from a flask. Groups of people lingered outside fast-food outlets and beneath the revolving yellow light of a mini-cab office, static-accented voices crackling from radio-sets in the cabs that waited for business.

The stillness of nights at home in Ireland came to her, the keening of wind in the telegraph wires, the bawl of a dog or donkey, the drone of a solitary car tracking along the road, and that other silence that seemed to fall from the stars and in which you could hear your own heart beat faster and faster as the silence pushed on into the night.

Post arrived every morning for the other occupants of the house; circulars, bills, subscription magazines, letters, and air-letters with the address bordered by red and blue flashes and handwriting visible through the thin paper. But it was the postcards she enjoyed most, with their photographs of every corner of Ireland: the Giant's Causeway, a flame-haired and freckled child in a tartan skirt standing beside a donkey, a waterfall on the River Erriff, St Kevin's Kitchen, Trinity College, the Spanish Arch, O'Connell Street 'the widest boulevard in Europe'. Sometimes there were postcards from elsewhere, a palm tree from the South of France, the Statue of Liberty, a woman's breasts caked in sand from Benidorm, squid hung up to dry in Greece, 'Kiss Me Quick' from Morecambe. She read them all, the easy sentences that said little, meant nothing. They all sounded the same, the way postcards do, but it was the handwriting that preserved their otherness, the imprint of another life that she could only guess at.

She would stand inside the front door and read the cards, ready to drop them to the floor with the rest of the post as soon as there was movement on the landings upstairs. Nothing fell through the letter box bearing her name although sometimes she half-expected it to; a note from an unknown acquaintance, a letter from someone in Ireland who might have tracked her down. But she reminded herself that nobody knew she was there, that she was just another soul in a city of millions.

She grew impatient. Now that she had a job and a place of her own, her life had assumed a pattern that seemed to repeat itself week after week. The journey to work every morning, the day marked out by the arrival of the evening paper's editions, the cash counted as the station emptied, the journey home again, a meal taken in silence as the walls oozed water. Only the night out with Eamonn had offered anything else, and she had not seen him since. Some nights she waited for the track teams to arrive but he was not amongst them and she was too embarrassed to ask after him, knowing the laughs it would raise amongst the other men.

She worried that she had seemed ungrateful that night, taking the drinks he bought her yet spurning his offer of going on to the bar in Willesden. He had been keen to string out the hours with her, not seeming to notice the unease that had crept into the conversation, the enjoyment of her company submerging any ill-feeling or awkwardness. Now his absence weighed upon her.

Darkness lifted slowly from the days as winter fled the streets. A sky the colour of school-ink over the offices and shops as they emptied in the evenings, mornings lifted by sunlight slanting between buildings and across parks, dragging shadows out on to the dewed grass, the tender heads of bulbs poking through the beds, the pensioners who brought their dogs to relieve themselves.

She watched them, the flat-capped men in solid brogues and Crombie coats and woollen scarves, a leash held limply in their hands, gazing across the grass at a mongrel circling a tree or litter bin. She saw her own father take his place amongst them, Blackie following some invisible track across the park, his nose skimming drops like crystals off the bright green blades of grass. She thought of his boots standing inside the front door, their stitching caked in clay, leather gone shiny where the laces crossed.

Turning away towards the station she let it go, the world of her father that had no place in this city. It was a relief that it had so easily been set adrift, when to be part of it seemed the whole of life itself.

He appeared just when she had given up all hope of seeing him again. He was there, flicking through a magazine when she looked up from the till. She didn't know what to say, but she knew that she wanted to tell him how glad she was to see him.

'It's you,' she stumbled eventually. 'I wondered where you'd got to.'

'I've been working at London Bridge for a while. One of the gang took a knock, so I was sent down.' He put the magazine aside. 'It made a change anyhow.'

'Was he badly hurt, the other lad?'

'Broke his shoulder and his jaw. A cable-tie snapped and caught him on the way back – they said it might have taken his head clean off.'

Helen winced, feeling a weakness in her knees.

'Goes with the job. One of the perks,' Eamonn smiled.

'It's dangerous work so?' she asked, more out of something to say than any curiosity. It was easier to keep him there with idle talk than to let him go and make the effort to bring him back.

'Not if you have your wits about you.'

'He was new to the work?'

'No, not at all, but he was arrogant. He'll change his tune though, if he ever comes back.'

The boots of the other men could be heard on the tiles, the tang of their cigarettes preceding them down the stairs and into the station. One of the Underground attendants reappeared at the top of the escalators and shouted the all-clear to the men, a torch flashing in his hand. Eamonn looked round at the men making their way downstairs, raising a hand in salute.

'Back to the grind-stone, I suppose.' He was reluctant to go. 'Your own work has been okay?'

'I'm still here, as you can see. There's little that changes around here from one week to the next.'

'There's some would kill for your job back home, you know,' he smiled.

'They'd be welcome to it then,' she whispered, leaning across the counter towards him.

The touch was sudden and unexpected, her hair brushing against him as though against something electric. The way he smelled of another person, of shaving cream and the place he lived in, the way that scent marked the crossing of the boundary between them. She drew away.

He had noticed nothing. 'I'll have another one of those Mars bars to take with me,' he said, reaching for money in his breast-pocket.

'Go on,' she said, taking the chocolate from the rack, 'on the house.'

'What? There's no need . . .'

'Quick, before the boss comes back,' she laughed, glancing around the station.

'All right so.'

She knew that he would want to ask her out again, but that her not wanting to go with him to the late bar in Willesden was foremost in his mind. 'I enjoyed our night out,' she said.

He seemed taken aback, as though it was strange that she should mention it now when the night had ended with such awkwardness.

'I enjoyed it myself. It was a grand few hours.'

'We could go to the bar in Willesden which you mentioned another time.'

'There's no good reason why we couldn't.'

She felt the tension draining away, Eamonn's features seeming to soften now that he had her confidence again.

'I'm on again tomorrow,' he said. 'We could make some arrangements then.'

She watched him go down into the depths of the station alone, the other men gone before him, their laughter already echoing in the empty tunnels.

When the shop had been closed up and Mr Patel had left she went to the top of the escalator and looked down into the station at the empty concourse, the tiled floor that had been swept clean, the yellow lighting that would stay on all night.

She went down. The platforms were empty, the destination signs unlit. A kettle stood on a paraffin stove at the end of a platform, a wisp of steam sailing from its spout, three blue mugs in attendance beside it. The noise of machinery and tools coursed along the tunnels, metal upon metal upon metal. She ventured to the end of the platform where a sign on the tracks read CURRENT OFF and peered into the tunnel.

The roof of the tunnel was strung with bulbs, like the river embankments of the city above, their weak glow lighting the men who worked upon the track. Some were stripped to the waist, their backs glistening with sweat, muscle coiled like rope laid beneath their skin as they levered long sections of track back on to concrete sleepers with enormous iron bars. A couple of men worked an outsize torque wrench, moving from section to section to tighten the bolts that held the track in position. Deeper into the tunnel were those who worked with pick-axes and drills to demolish and remove the sleepers that had begun to disintegrate with the motion of the trains, the shattered concrete and twisted metal thrown into a container that ran along the tracks to another station where the debris was decanted and brought to the surface.

From where she crouched she looked for but did not see Eamonn amongst them. In the bleak light the men's bodies looked much the same, their voices blending into one with the clatter of machinery. She watched for a while, a foreman moving amongst them with a clipboard, a white hard hat askew upon his head, the men not lifting from their work as he passed.

The alarm woke her. Sun filtering through the mesh of curtains rested upon the far wall of the room. She pulled back the curtains and looked at the cherry blossoms peeking over the bedraggled hedge outside the window, pink petals fluttering in the rush of wind thrown by a passing car. Behind them the sky was blue, a cracked-ice blue that betrayed the coolness of spring mornings.

She pulled down the sash window to allow some fresh air in, the frame and pulleys squealing as the swollen wood was moved, an untenanted spider's web hanging in the angle of the window. Children's voices could be heard along the street, the sound of small feet scuffing on concrete and the thwack of a football against a wall.

Women passed by as she ate breakfast, talking of bingo, shopping, and grandchildren, complaining about bus time-tables, their voices gravelled and hoarse from cigarettes. They called out to the children playing football, warning them to watch out for cars. A taxi pulled up, the throb-throb of its diesel engine almost drowning the conversation between the driver and the man who slowly counted coins through the window into the cabbie's hand. 'All right ... lovely. Ta-da,' the taxi drawing away again, scattering the children. From somewhere the smell of spiced food drifted: chillies, turmeric, cardamon, garlic, a fat-frying smell. She remembered the Indian family who lived in the house that backed on to hers; the men's dull suits and slip-on shoes, the women's bright saris hemmed and seamed in gold and silver, daubed foreheads, sitting on each other's laps in the back of a clapped-out Austin while the men tinkered with the ignition or fan belt.

A bicycle went past, the cyclist slowing for the children, the chain stalled and set to ticking against the motion of the wheels.

She remembered pushing the bicycles with Martin up the slight hill towards her house, chatting, the dying sun at their shoulders, the road lined with fuchsia blossom. They had parted at the bridge over the ditch. She remembered him so vividly now, leaning on the handlebars with their metal brakes and using his hand to shield his eyes so that he could watch her until a bend in the road took her from sight.

A rattling of the window frame broke the memory, the same gust shredding the spider's web. She cleared and washed the few breakfast things before going out.

The High Road was crammed. Elderly women weaved between the human traffic on the pavement, trailing wheeled shopping bags after them that caught the ankles of passers-by. The warm sunshine seemed to bring the spirit of high summer to the young girls who wore short skirts and cropped tops in pastel shades, arms and legs the colour of pastry. In the shadows of buildings their limbs broke out in goosepimples. Helen shivered just to watch them. Cars, vans, and buses struggled towards the junctions, tattooed drivers' arms hanging lazily through windows, the men eyeing the pale legs of the young girls. A Turkish youth hawked costume jewellery from a bread crate upturned on the pavement. A queue had formed outside the butcher's where the customers carried blood-specked sawdust out on the soles of their shoes. At the door of almost every shop a dog was tied, gaze directed inwards, waiting on its owner. An old wooden stall was parked on a street corner, decked with bunches of flowers, a silver-haired woman calling out the prices for carnations, hands busy with the coins in her apron.

The hairdresser's was busy, housewives lined up in front of mirrors, looking as if they saw there the people they wished to be rather than these simple women who wore the years of their lives in their faces.

Kelly used to cut her hair for her, setting the chair down near the window of the lightless front room, his hand planted firmly on her head so that she could not move, the crudely sharpened scissors pulling the hair from her scalp as they cut an uneven fall upon her shoulders, a slanted fringe upon her forehead. 'Stay still now, girl,' he warned as she winced and shrunk from him. Afterwards the clippings would be swept into a paper bag and thrown on the fire, the smell of burning hair still with them as they ate a meal of bacon, turnips and potatoes hours later.

As long as she could remember her hair had been shoulder-length, like her mother's before her. Once she had found photographs of her mother sitting in a sun-trap at the back door of a house, her hair teased outwards by a breeze. It had looked so bright and supple, not the dull, brittle strands her illness had reduced it to in the months before she died. She remembered the awful feel of it then, like a paper crown upon her sweating forehead.

Again she was there before him, running her fingers through her hair, turning to look at herself in the heavy plate-glass of the shop windows. The street was almost empty of traffic. Two men appeared with a metal box on wheels and began emptying the parking meters that lined a side street. One of

the men began to whistle, the surrounding buildings ampli-
fying and twisting the tune so that it was unrecognizable. A
large concrete planter was filled with crocuses, daffodils, and
crisp packets. There was a warmth in the air that reminded
her of summer.

She watched him walk from where the bus dropped the
passengers off. 'I was wondering if it was yourself at all,'
Eamonn smiled.

They took the same bus as they had the last time, but
now, without the rain and the darkness, the evening seemed
spread out before them. She sat close to him on the double
seat, feeling his heat against her, the gentle depth of his voice
like a thrill. When they got off the bus at the High Street
she linked her arm in his. He stopped and looked at her for
a moment but when she met his gaze he walked on.

The pubs were thronged. They went from the first to
the second and then to the third, the Spinning Wheel, where
they had spent that first evening, finding again a seat at the
back amongst the old men playing cards for coppers. She
asked for a vodka and orange, tumbling the ice with a plastic
cocktail mixer as they talked.

The open fire crackled and spat, glowing embers racing
out on to the tiles. There was slate amongst the coal.

'"Polish coal!" is what my father would say if he was
here now,' Eamonn laughed. 'He was never a man to praise
the foreigners, never had a good word for them at all, God
rest him.'

The light humour carried on as the pub filled and they
drew closer across the table, other customers pressing in on
all sides. It was a busy night. Someone explained that there
had been an Irish festival in a nearby park and that people
had travelled from across the city for it.

'If we'd had our wits about us we could have gone there
ourselves,' Eamonn said. 'We could have made an afternoon
of it, you know.'

'We could. There'll be other times, I'm sure.'

His face brightened, the promise of a future engagement raising whatever hopes he had of winning her. 'There will,' he affirmed.

They talked until the fire had ceased its spitting and slumped to ashes, the slate marked out in the hearth by a fur of ash. The bar staff came to clear the tables. She remarked on the way their hands could hold so many glasses at once.

'It makes for a lot less walking, that's for sure,' Eamonn said, running the last drop of stout around the bottom of his glass before emptying it.

'We could go to a dance,' he ventured on the pavement outside. 'There's many of them that were here will be going, you know,' he offered.

'Why not?' she said, happy to link her arm with his as they set off down the street.

There was a long queue to the steps of the dancehall but it moved quickly and they were in the foyer before long. The doormen were elderly and dressed up in dinner suits and bow-ties, lapels gone green with age, white shirts that had long since lost their crispness. A crude sign tacked to the glass of the booth read: SMART DRESS ONLY/ NO PLIMSOLLS/ NO DENIMS. Helen looked around at the men invariably dressed in black or brown slacks with white or cream shirts worn open at the collar. Some wore v-neck pullovers or cardigans over their shirts, others wore Fair Isle sweaters. One of the dancegoers was picked out for the faded denims he wore, all eyes falling upon him as he remonstrated with the doormen, who eventually gave in and let him rejoin the queue.

Eamonn pushed away the money that Helen offered him at the booth and paid for them both, handing her the crudely printed ticket.

'That's too kind of you after you paid for the drinks in the pub already,' she protested, but he would not listen.

They left their coats at the cloakroom, receiving a pink docket in return. PUT YOUR TICKET IN YOUR ARSE POCKET SO THAT YOU'LL KNOW WHERE IT IS WHEN YOU'RE PISSED read the sign behind the counter, and they laughed together when Eamonn pointed it out. He led the way up the curving staircase, the burgundy carpet worn and stained on every step, the banister rail cracked and split in places. A chandelier looked down on the foyer, the shrivelled skin of a balloon trapped amongst the suspended curtains of glass that were too soiled to hold much light.

'Come on,' Eamonn beckoned to her. 'The best tables are always in the Circle.'

He led her through a set of double doors where the music rushed at them like some invisible unleashed creature and where countless lights floated magically in the darkness. Tables swept up from where they stood like terracing at a football ground, a solitary red lamp glowing on each one, the softened profiles of faces leaning into the gentle light, the ascending blue streams of cigarette smoke. They stood for a while to get their bearings and she noticed that the music held another sound in its grip, a dull buzzing that slowly resolved itself into the thick clamour of voices.

'There's a table free at the edge here.' Eamonn took her arm and pulled the chair back from the table so that she could sit down. She saw now that the red plastic lamp shades were held aloft by the statuette of a sylph-like and naked girl, head thrown back as if at the intensity of the light.

Eamonn ordered drinks from a passing waitress and they looked down at the dancefloor while they waited. The floor was thronged. So crushed were the dancers that their bodies hardly moved in time with the music, the whole tumult of flesh swelling like waves that occasionally parted to allow people to join or leave the dancefloor.

Amongst the couples on the floor were a number of girls who danced alone, dancing so freely and easily that it was as if, like butterflies, they knew that it would all end too soon.

And there were men, also, who danced alone. Like drugged moths, their eyes closed, a benign smile upon their upturned faces, they stumbled from step to step, reaching desperately for others in an attempt to stay upright.

The dancers were surrounded by onlookers vying with each other for the best vantage points, the men holding glasses to their bellies, the girls invariably laughing and chatting about the goings-on on the dancefloor.

The waitress returned with their order and again Helen attempted to pay.

'No,' Eamonn rose, grabbing the waitress's wrist as she went to take the note Helen had offered her. 'Take this now.'

After the waitress had left, Helen protested, but he would not hear of her paying for anything.

'It was I that asked you here in the first place,' he explained.

'And I was happy to come.'

'It a man's place to pay, that's that.'

He would not rise to the subject again and they were silent for a while as they watched the dancers on the floor below. She remembered the dance she had gone to with the other girls in the factory, how glamorous and exciting it had seemed that night, her bicycle chained to the downpipe in the alleyway, the risk of being found out by Kelly, the make-up she had worn. It seemed such a long time ago to her now, although scarcely a year had passed. The glamour of that night paled in comparison to *this*; the tin-roofed dance-hall was no match for the grand ballroom with its rows of tables and attendant waiters and waitresses. And there was Eamonn, who was happy just to sit and watch with her, who made easy conversation, and who wouldn't let her pay for a thing. She watched him now, sparkles thrown by a mirror-ball overhead catching in his hair, his eyes tracking the dancers across the floor, fingers tapping the railing in time to the music.

'Will we dance?' he asked later, and she was happy to take his hand and move down towards the dancefloor.

To her surprise they danced easily, keeping time with each other and the music, the smiles they exchanged at the comfort they felt in each other's company. He held her arm gently but firmly, steering her away from others on the dancefloor. A middle-aged man stumbled drunkenly across the floor, the dancers parting to allow him through, and Eamonn drew her to him out of the way. Their eyes met and they smiled. When his lips met her cheek she felt herself fill with warmth, turning her mouth to meet his, her eyes closing as his tongue sought hers out. After a few moments she drew away and rested her head against his shoulder, feeling his thick arms across her back as they circled so slowly upon the wooden boards.

At the end of the night they stood for the 'Amhrán na bhFiann', the clash of cymbals that closed the last bar jarring in her ears as Eamonn led her out by the hand, the coats which he had collected earlier draped across his forearm.

The street outside the dancehall was lined with mini-cabs, drivers smoking cigarettes in the darkened interiors. Men and women stood in groups, the women shivering as they waited for others to join them before going home or elsewhere. A fast-food van opened up on the street corner and a queue quickly formed.

'Where do you live?' Eamonn asked. 'I'll leave you home and go on from there.'

'There's no need for that,' she said weakly.

In the car he put his arm around her, his hand resting at her side and sometimes pressing against her breast when-ever they turned a corner. She accepted the stab of pleasure it caused her. She found his smell amidst that of cheap perfume and stale tobacco. She watched the driver's face and theirs framed like a curious portrait in the windscreen, street lights rushing through it. She felt carried away by the night, by the motion of the car coursing through the dark and empty streets, Eamonn's arm upon her shoulder the only thing that seemed still.

She had fallen asleep and the cold woke her as they got out of the car. Eamonn handed the driver the fare. She gave him her keys and motioned to the front door. She was aware of the revving of the car behind them as it drew away and the rattle of the brass key in the lock which had always turned badly. The hallway was empty when he switched on the light, the glare of the solitary bulb catching the stack of unclaimed envelopes on the old metal stool behind the door. Now she noticed how worn the linoleum was, faded rectangles where the sun rested upon it in the afternoons. She motioned to the door of her room and Eamonn let them inside. Street light fell across the bed and floor like a pale sheet, interrupted only by the cross of the window frame. Eamonn reached for the switch on the wall.

'No, no, I like it like this,' she said. 'It's in a mess anyway – I'd be ashamed to look upon it now.'

He checked himself. 'All right so.'

'I'll make us some tea,' she said, pressing past him. How small the room was after all, she thought, barely space between the bed and the wardrobe for them to move. The gas flame leapt into life, the dark cobalt blue ring like a spectral flower in the darkness. She set the kettle to boil.

He was still standing there inside the door when she came back into the room.

'I've no chairs so you'll have to sit on the bed.'

He sat down and she stood looking out the window at the insects busy around the street light.

'My own place isn't too much to shout about,' he began

after a while. 'It's shared with a junior doctor and a brickie. The brickie and myself have the one room and the doctor the other because the doctor snores and he does be out until all hours of the night. There isn't a pipe or a tap in the blasted place that doesn't have a rattle or a leak of some sort in it. If we could swap the doctor for a plumber we'd be laughing.'

'Only you'd probably fall sick as soon as the doctor was out the door!' Helen added, and they both laughed.

They looked at each other when they had finished laughing. There was a strange expression on Eamonn's face, as though he had been hunted down and was waiting for a blow. He stood up and she saw that he was trembling. She raised herself and kissed him on the lips. His arms enclosed her as they kissed and she felt that the room around them was trembling too. The warmth returned to her as his fingers moved through her hair and cupped the back of her head, pressing her to him. She held him close, feeling the heat of him seeping through her clothes and pressing against her skin.

They kissed for some minutes until the rattle of the kettle on the hob took her into the kitchen to turn the gas off. The tea went unmade. They kissed again and she lifted the flap of his shirt so that she could run her hands along his back. He held her closer still, almost lifting her off her feet. When he began to undo the buttons of her blouse the air came deliciously cool against her skin, which in that weak light looked dark next to the white of her bra. He slid the straps across her shoulders and her breasts fell free, his mouth reaching to find the hard nipple as though by instinct. He guided her on to the bed and she lifted her skirt. In the rush to be one he pushed her panties to one side and she felt him enter her. There was a tear which caused her to wince, and he was inside, his breath hoarse against her ear. When she felt him begin to push she gripped him and felt something coiling inside her like a soft spring. She moved with him until he came, emptying himself into her, her name repeated again and again.

He moved off her to turn on his back, chest rising and falling with the drawing of his breath, the goosepimples that flooded across his skin visible even in that grey light.

Looking into his half-closed eyes she smiled and felt the spring still coiled deep inside her. She leaned over him and kissed his chin before lowering herself on to him, taking him inside her again, pushing up and down. The spring began to coil tighter and tighter, a sensation she had not known before, a pressing sensation between her legs and a lightness in her head. Until the spring uncoiled itself in the space of a mere second or two, disengaging, dissolving, running in her blood.

When she woke he was asleep beside her on the narrow bed, turned towards the wall, thin snores lifting into the room. The sky had broken into indigo that lightened as she watched, copper-edged clouds fading as the sun rose. The room smelled ripe, the scent of sweat and sex, the sheets and their skin damp with it. She touched the wall with the back of her hand and it too was damp, condensation clinging to the surface. Their clothes were scattered on the floor, his jacket hanging from a door handle, her bra folded on the edge of the table. She couldn't think why she had stopped their lovemaking to leave it there so neatly. His shoes stood beside the door, the laces pulled from the top eyeholes. There was a film of pale clay around the edge of the sole where he must have walked beside a building site. As she looked at the muddied but otherwise shiny shoes she remembered her father and the attention he paid to his boots, which would be carefully restitched when the thread broke and water was allowed in. A jar of dubbin was kept in a kitchen drawer to be applied when they had dried out after a soaking in the fields, the boots held close to the firelight so that the dubbin softened towards oil.

Outside, a bicycle made its way along the street, the ticking of its chain stirring some memory in her. She made to sit up in the bed but stopped herself for fear of waking Eamonn. Martin's face rose before her and faded with the ticking of the chain, turning of that cycle like other larger cycles, his image gone now, only an absence felt in the room around her.

Eamonn was turned on his side, freckles spattered on his shoulders, his penis limp and wrinkled like some sea creature half-hidden in its bed of dark hair. She felt nothing for him now, and she shrank from him. She turned away but could not sleep, and eventually rose to go into the kitchen.

She brought a mug of tea back and sat on the edge of the bed to drink it, idly watching the steam rising in the cold of morning. Eamonn stirred in the bed behind her and his hand touched the small of her back, finger moving to trace the line between her buttocks. He said something she did not quite hear and moved towards her on the bed, wrapping his arm across her stomach until she felt his lips against the ridge of her shoulder-blade. She sat quite still, the mug poised before her mouth. His hand cupped her breast, teasing her nipple with his thumb. When he moved his mouth towards her ear and spoke her name she turned the other way and saw that he was hard again. She did not want him now, or ever again.

'Won't you lie down here again for a few minutes?' he implored.

'Not now. There'll be other times.' She turned to smile at him before going into the kitchen. When she returned he had pulled the covers up over himself and was lying with his hands behind his head.

'You know something, I'm so comfortable now that I could lie here like this for the rest of the day,' he said, gazing at the blank ceiling.

'I've to go out in a while, there's things to do today.' She hooked her bra across her back and stepped into her panties.

'It's Sunday, Helen,' he protested. 'Sure there's nothing to be done on a Sunday. Unless you're one for going to Mass, of course.'

'Some of us have got things to be doing anyways,' she snapped, pulling on her skirt, anxious to be clothed and less vulnerable to him.

She heard the sharp draw of breath. Her tone had taken him by surprise.

'I'm sorry,' she began. 'I've laundry to wash and the place needs a good scrub and a tidy before the week starts again. If I don't do it today, I'll never do it.'

'All right so.' He sat up in the bed to watch her move about the room, gathering the few clothes that were scattered here and there.

'Do you work on Sundays yourself?' she called from the kitchen, the heater bursting into life when she turned the tap.

'I'm on at twelve tonight all right, but none of us will arrive until half-past or even later. Sundays are the gaffer's night off so the rest of us take it easy.'

'What'll you do in the meantime?' she asked, hoping that it would prompt him to get out of the bed.

'Usually the brickie and myself go for a cooked breakfast. There's a great place up on Cricklewood Broadway that does Irish breakfasts for next to nothing. You meet all sorts up there on a Sunday; some of them are only on their way home at that hour.'

'No more than yourself,' she encouraged.

'No more than myself indeed.' He swung his legs out of the bed and stood up, reaching for his shirt.

She came out with a mug of tea and some buttered toast as he was pulling on his trousers.

'You're a great girl altogether.'

She sat on the bed and watched him eat at the table, folding the toast over on itself before taking a bite. He ate with concentration and slowness, staring at a point beyond the window.

'Do you keep in touch with your people back home?' she ventured when the silence had stretched for too long to be comfortable.

'I do, the odd time. I drop them a postcard every now and again to let them know I'm still alive. I go back often enough: Easter, Christmas, and every wedding and funeral in the parish. Sometimes you'd think I was just working here to pay the fares home. There's many in this country are in the same boat, every penny earned is saved so that they can visit the oul' sod. They'd be as fuckin' well off going back altogether.'

His bitterness rose between them so that they did not speak for some time.

'You wouldn't go back yourself then?' she broke.

'Christ, no! It'd be great for a couple of weeks, living the life of Reilly, drinks bought in the local for "the prodigal son" and all that. Soon enough though the money'd run out and the drinks would stop coming, and they'd start to wondering, and I'd start to wondering, what the feck I was going to be doing with myself.'

'Surely there's work to be had there, even on the sites in Dublin or Belfast.'

'Oh, there's work to be had all right, but half the bloody country is qualified to do it. I wouldn't stand a chance. Anyway, I might as well be in London as in Dublin. They'd be expecting me to come down on the bus at the weekends for the ploughing, the sowing, and the cutting. There'd be no end to their demands, no end.'

He set the mug back on the table with a sharp thud that made her start.

'They're happy enough, then, for you to be working the tunnels, I suppose?' she asked.

'They don't have a clue,' he admitted quietly, turning his face away from her. 'They think I'm working on the railways, not the Underground. It'd break their hearts to know I was doing the work I do. When you start they tell you it's like working in the mines, only easier. But it's not; there's no pride or tradition to it. It's soul-destroying work if you want the God's honest truth. It's easier that they don't know at all.'

When he turned back towards her there was a darkness in his face which had not been there before. She felt not pity but a remoteness from him. They had been close the previous night, had enjoyed the talk in the pub and the dancing in the dancehall afterwards, conversation had come so easily to them then. She had even allowed him inside her own body, and yet now she felt completely apart from him. The silence between them was fathomless, their words seeming to fall into its depths before reaching each other.

'The railway work is pensionable you see,' he continued eventually. 'Back home they think it's great, the security of it, the holiday and sick pay, the free travel, the money when you retire, even the feckin' uniform is a bonus as far as they're concerned. They were expecting me to be wearing it on the train home after that first time I lied to them. Could you imagine the face of the CIE ticket collector and me in a British Rail peaked cap? Well, you never saw the jaws drop so fast as when I stepped on to the platform in Waterford that day, they must have thought I'd be a few inches taller and a few inches broader, with a briefcase hanging from my left hand. Instead, I was the same gobshite coming home to them. There wasn't a word to be said on the bus back from the station.'

Rain fell suddenly, hissing on the window. They both turned to look at it running down the glass, the day darkened and destroyed before it had even begun.

'You can see now why I can't tell them that it's in the tunnels I work. Where's the pride in a uniform of sweat and dirt, or a fluorescent yellow singlet?'

She nodded, feeling momentarily sorry for him, some tenderness returning.

'It's nothing to boast about, for Christ's sake,' he breathed.

She remembered the string of bulbs along the roof of the tunnel, like inverted vertebrae, the sweat-gleamed flesh of men stripped to the waist, the spark of pick-axes against steel and rock, the bursts of hammer-drill that clotted the ears, the terrible violence in the sight and sound of that work.

As the rain fell the window steamed up until there was no rain to see and only the small sound of it falling on the glass.

'It'd take you back to the old place all the same, wouldn't it?' he said, nodding towards the clouded window.

'It would indeed,' she said quietly, recalling the countless days when the house would be stilled by rain, the snapping of cards at the fireside, Kelly's impatience rising as the hours wore on and on with no break in sight.

'I suppose I'd better be on my way,' Eamonn said eventually, reaching for his jacket. 'Will you be in the shop yourself during the week?'

'I will, as usual,' she said. 'Some things just don't change, do they?' she added.

'No, I suppose they don't. Maybe we should be grateful for it too.'

She followed him out to the front door, feeling awkward with him now and anxious for him to go so that she could gather herself and settle again. The rain had softened into a thin drizzle. Water streamed off the corrugated plastic canopy above the door and on to the broken path.

'It was a lovely evening,' he said. The bitter conversation had broken whatever was between them and he knew it now.

'It was ... it was,' she said, but his face did not change. He turned his collar up about his ears and sank his hands into his pockets before walking out into the rain, his shoulders quickly streaked with drops. She did not wait to watch him go and closed the door with relief.

The meter had run out when she got back and she sat in the grey gloom and looked around her, not really seeing anything, feeling every limb trembling with nerves, a horrible gnawing in her stomach that rose towards her throat. The tears that came stung her eyes and rolled coldly down her cheeks.

Again she heard her name repeated over and over, his hot breath on her cheek, the heat of him pouring inside as he struggled between her legs like some weakened animal trapped there.

For one moment she had wanted him, and now she wished it undone. She had wanted Martin, too. More than anything or anyone else, she had wanted *him*. She had led his hand to her breast, inviting him to explore her, inviting him to possess her in a way no man had done before. But he had held back for fear that it would destroy what they already had between them. Its fragility was as precious to him as she was.

When she had removed her jersey and released her bra Martin had gazed in wonderment at her body, his eyes seeming to soak her skin, only a trembling finger reaching to trace the line of a shoulder-blade, the curved and knuckled spine, the ridged rib-cage that surfaced each time she took a breath. 'Folded angel's wings,' he had breathed, pressing a warm cheek to her shoulder-blade, the words teased and coaxed from his thin vocabulary of love. His fingers had tenderly drawn her hair out into long strands that shone like spun silk in the light reflected from the lake. He let the strands drop one by one, drifting back towards her neck and shoulders. When he touched her breast with his hand the nipple hardened instantly, his fingers tracing the soft curves of skin, the strawberried texture of aureole, the pale and tender hollow of skin stretched across her breast-bone. He explored her like a navigator bent over the map of a land he had no desire to colonize, his sole purpose the interpretation of landscape, the position of elements, contours, shallows, depths.

A while later she filled the bath and lay back in the hot water, watching the steam twist and eddy in the draught that made its way through gaps in the ill-fitting window frame. The window fogged and the choking silence of an hour beforehand returned until she dispelled it with a swish of her hand in the water. She took the bar of soap from its plastic bag and stood up to wash herself. Guiding the soap across her skin, slowly at first but then more and more vigorously, she sought to slough his touch from her, to make herself new again. She scrubbed her breasts, where his fingers and tongue had been, her stomach where he had pressed against her, her thighs that had wrapped around him, and finally the folded flesh where he had entered her.

When she lay down in the water and the soap lifted from her skin she cried when she saw the thick red marks her own fingers had made there and she understood that nothing could be undone.

In the afternoon she took the empty satchel from the bottom of the wardrobe and filled it with clothes and the towels that were damp after the bath. When she went to strip the sheets from the bed she found the mark. Symmetrical like a butterfly's wings where the sheet had creased on to it, it looked momentarily beautiful, the dark red stain of her loss. She tore the sheet from the bed, desperate to destroy it.

> *Martin*, she wrote. *I'm sorry that I went away, but sometime in the future I'll tell you why I couldn't stay a moment longer. I've plenty of money to pay your fare to come and see me in London. Let me know when you can come over and I'll put a postal order in the post to you.*

There was so much that she wanted to say to him, but she could think of nothing more to write. She spent a while gazing at the window where raindrops were beaded. The sun began to come out, the drops to sparkle, the long grass to steam in the sudden warmth.

I miss you and I want to be with you, she finished.

The night was all but over. Mr Patel stood as he always stood on the concourse, busy with his nail-clippers, greeting the fluffers and the track workers as they arrived. Some would offer him their coats and caps in jest and for a moment the station echoed with boisterous laughter, laughter peppered with Mr Patel's tweaky accent as he attempted to extend the joke beyond its reasonable boundaries, the way people with a poor sense of humour sometimes will.

Helen counted the cash in the till and the small change in the plastic tray, leaving a float aside for the following morning. She waved to the station supervisor as he left, the torch swinging from his hand, a cigarette planted between his lips. From the depths of the tunnels came the distant rumble of the machinery starting up, the thud-thud of jack-hammers, the hiss of air-compressors. She thought of Eamonn working somewhere beneath the sulphurous light of the strung bulbs.

They hadn't spoken since he had walked out of her room and into the drizzle of a Sunday morning. She had seen him since, calling her name from the top of the escalators before he went down, but she stayed behind the counter each time, acknowledging him only with a weak smile. That Sunday was almost a fortnight ago now, but not long enough for her.

She was terrified that she would bump into him on the street or that he would call to the house some evening. She had taken to closing the curtains tightly and shading the light-bulb, stuffing newspaper into the gaps between door and frame so that the light would not show should he come looking for her.

It reminded her of how, at the approach of an unwelcome caller, Kelly would close the front door and order her to crawl under her bed while he stood unseen between the bathroom and bedroom as the caller moved from window to window, tapping at the glass and peering into every empty room, her breath held for fear they might hear it.

She saw Eamonn's clothes in every crowd about her, the black jacket and white shirt opened at the neck, the polished brogues.

'It's about time we were going home, Miss Helen,' Mr Patel smiled. He addressed her as Miss Helen when he was in his best humour. She handed him the heavy padlocks from beneath the counter and he went to start pulling down the shutters. She tidied the magazine racks and the rows of chocolate bars, glad that the day had finally drawn to a close. Gradually the days in the shop had come to weigh more and more heavily upon her. No longer could she reason or laugh away the drudgery of the handing out of papers, magazines, sweets, and chocolate, the receiving of notes and coins, the ache in her legs from standing all day, the palms of her hands hardened by paper, nickel, and copper, fingers blackened by ink.

'They're quiet down below tonight,' Mr Patel commented as she helped to turn the keys in the padlocks that secured the shutters to steel loops set in the floor.

She hadn't noticed before but now the station *was* strangely quiet. The keening noises of the escalators and nothing else. The jack-hammers stopped, the air-compressors silenced.

'Maybe they've decided to walk to the other station tonight. They don't like my chocolate any more, eh?' Mr Patel joked as he took back the keys.

'Maybe.'

Dimly she heard the intermittent sound of a siren working its way through the streets above them. There was little traffic to hold it back and the noise grew louder and louder, joined seconds later by another siren at a lower pitch. She waited for the sirens to pass by on their way to a fire or an accident but there was no change in their sound.

Mr Patel touched her elbow and she turned to see a foreman running from the top of the escalator, holding a white hard hat, a smear of blood on his forehead where he had wiped his hand. Mr Patel went to help him pull back the steel gate that secured the station entrance.

The noise of the sirens funnelled down the steps from the street and she lifted her hands to her ears. She stood and watched the firemen running past, bulky clothes restricting their limbs so that they moved like the first men on the moon. She could not bring herself to think of what might have happened in the tunnels below, remembering how Eamonn had told her of another track worker who had been struck by a steel cable. The vision of shattered bone and torn flesh that came made her feel weak.

Men rushed back and forth with large pieces of equipment, like enormous pliers with thick blades attached. Two uniformed ambulancemen took a folded stretcher down the escalator. The station supervisor appeared at the entrance and made his way uncertainly down the steps.

'What the fuck's goin' on?' he asked, his breath a fug of alcohol and tobacco.

'We don't know, we don't know,' Mr Patel eyed him with derision, appalled by his drunkenness.

'Fuckin' ... fuckin' ... ,' the supervisor mumbled but could not find the words to complete the sentence.

Helen stood in stony silence, listening to the slurred rantings of the supervisor but not hearing his words, trapped by the possibilities of what had happened in the tunnels beneath her feet.

A couple of the track workers appeared at the head of the escalators, drawing on cigarettes that glowed against their dirty sweat-streaked faces, overalls unzipped to the waist, silent, absorbed in their own thoughts and exhaustion. Gradually, more men emerged from the depths of the station to take their place amongst the others. Drained, they stood hunched and leaning against the walls, passing a cigarette between them. Mr Patel scurried across to find out what had happened.

Finally they stirred and their voices rose, cigarettes stubbed out on the tiles as a stretcher came up the narrow stairs, bracketed by ambulancemen, a fire-officer holding a drip high above their heads. A figure lay prone beneath the red blanket that was daubed with cotton-wool like shaving foam, the pale outstretched arm perfect save for an incision made to enable an intravenous tube. She recognized him beneath the translucently green oxygen mask, his eyes shut as if in sleep, no mark of pain or effort upon his face, the clear sticking plaster that fixed a tube to his nose pulling his lip out of shape, teeth bared like any terrified beast.

*

She could not sleep. Every element of the darkness held horrors for her. The creak of upstairs boards like bone on bone, water running in the pipes that brought visions of blood, the house itself seemed broken.

'He'll live,' Mr Patel pronounced when she arrived at the station the following afternoon.

It was with relief that she heard those words. The morning had been spent pacing, boiling the kettle for tea that was not drunk, cleaning where no cleaning was needed, the working away of a seed of guilt and fear. She feared that what she had felt for him in the wake of their night together could never be undone, that the whole business would be left unfinished, that he would die and that she would never find it in herself to forget the incompleteness of what had happened between them.

'His legs were crushed by a sleeper that fell on him. It took them all that time to get the sleeper off and they said he never let a sound out of him,' Mr Patel continued, tut-tutting to himself. 'It's dangerous work down there, you know.'

'I'm sure . . . I'm sure it is,' she agreed nervously, turning away as her eyes welled with tears. She had a vision of Eamonn's shattered legs, his gritted teeth, his eyes closed in pain. She remembered how quiet he had been when they had first met in the station, carefully leafing through the magazines which he replaced as he found them, the way his eyes calmly travelled about the shop, not daring to look at her in spite of himself. She looked at the magazine rack and could see him standing there in his brown cable-knit sweater and the yellow safety singlet, boots covered in concrete dust, his broad shoulders rising and falling as he breathed. The tears spilled and travelled easily down her cheeks and she pitied him now, the agony of that night and morning with him forgotten.

The customers came and went all day as every day, newspapers folded into their hands, coins taken, thanks muttered. She saw his face in every face, his tragedy in every furrowed brow. Sometimes she looked up to find someone at the magazine rack and for an instant she foolishly imagined it was him until they turned their heads, strangers. The guilt and pity had settled, erasing whatever pain she had felt at his hand.

The dandelion blossoms she had collected from amongst the junk in the back yard had yesterday served to brighten but now only emphasized the poorness of the room when she let herself in. She took the old medicine jar they stood in and dumped the livid yellow flowers in the bin. The place needed tidying but she couldn't bring herself to do anything, happy only to lie on the bed and look at the ceiling, drifting towards the light edge of sleep and back again, Eamonn's accident turned over and over in her mind so that she could not rest. Hours later, when the clock had passed midnight, the room fallen to darkness, the creak of the other occupants on the boards in the rooms above had stilled, she fell asleep, waking often during the night to find that it was still dark and the hour still early, waiting then in prone silence for sleep to reclaim her.

She woke before the alarm clock sounded, watching the thin green hand turn and turn towards nine, the seconds eaten away time and again, marking her thoughts. She stopped the tiny brass bells before the hammer could strike. For a moment it seemed like a new day, any day, until the truth returned and she fell back on the bed as if the weight of it had forced her down. Bile rose in her throat, a small acid tickle at the back of her mouth, nausea blooming in her stomach. She stumbled through the kitchen and out into the toilet, the sudden and unexpected cold numbing her skin while she retched into the bone-white bowl, the craze of green-black cracks in the glaze like witch hairs. She remembered that she hadn't eaten since the morning before as she watched her thin yellow vomit flush away, wiping her mouth with the back of her hand.

On her way out she searched amongst the unclaimed post for Martin's handwriting, her name. With regret she realized that she would never recognize his script. She had never seen it and as if it were some secret he had denied her she felt angry at him. In three weeks he had not replied to her letter, and now it seemed he never would. She remembered what she had written, *I miss you and I want to be with you*, and wished it had never been committed to paper.

The road was lined with cars parked bumper to bumper, windscreens like lozenges of reflected silver light in the narrowness of the evening sun which ripened the red-brick façade of the hospital. An elderly couple sat out on one of the iron benches that gave on to the asphalted path to the front door, her hand resting on his blanket-covered knee, shoulders gently pressing together as they leaned in to talk, a blue handbag standing half-forgotten some feet away from where they sat. A wheelchair waited at the top of the steps to the front door, a small transistor radio crudely fixed to the armrest with sticking plaster.

An orderly leaning against the reception desk directed her to the ward when she asked for Eamonn, pointing to the notice that asked all visitors to respect the needs of the patients and to vacate the wards by nine-thirty.

The corridors were hushed, the rubberized flooring absorbing all sound. Metal beds stood on their wheels along the corridors, some of them stacked high with fresh laundry, others empty but for hard mattresses and grey plastic incontinence mats marked with NHS in each corner. Pieces of disconnected equipment waited for action, cables trailing on the floor, a clipboard of data and instructions hanging somewhere. She recognized a resuscitation unit tucked under some stairs, the steel pads that would administer the current shining dully in the gloom and causing her to shudder.

The smell of disinfectant was overpowering, the floor gleaming in patches where it had been recently mopped. The smell reminded her of the poison spray Kelly had used in the vegetable cloches before discovering that the ladybirds were cheaper and just as effective. When he began to mix the poison and it was still a foul-smelling concentrated syrup, she would bring him pieces of plastic and clumps of the dog's hair that she plucked from the barbed wire fences. He dripped the poison on to the plastic and hair and they laughed in wonderment to watch it scorch and burn. Afterwards, when the spraying was finished, the left-over poison was diluted further and used to scrub down the kitchen and toilet floors, the bitumen-like smell lingering for days, its bitter taste upon skin and lips.

She struggled to slam the door of the cage-lift shut before the contraption would ascend, floors slowly appearing and disappearing beyond the crude iron grille, glimpses of corridors and windows filled with insubstantial light. It clattered to a halt on the third floor and she got out, holding the door back to allow a mute and bird-like nurse inside, her pinched face cut to diamonds as the grille slid into place.

A window was open at the end of his ward, fresh air flooding in to steal the snores of the patients who napped in the early evening. Many of the beds were empty; bare mattresses, the sheets fixed to the ends of the beds unfilled and uncharted. She looked for his face on the pillows, heart pounding in her chest, a weakness filtering through her as each shut face in turn went unrecognized. His was the last face: asleep, ash-grey, eyelids swollen and jaundiced by morphine. A metal frame sheathed in a worn red blanket covered the lower half of his body, his arms lying lamely at his sides, a green drip connection protruding grotesquely from a raised vein. Suspended from the frame of the bed by what looked like a coat hanger was a catheter bag, quarter-filled with urine, a deep golden colour beneath the strip lights. Above his head a sign read: NIL BY MOUTH. Monitoring equipment sat on a rack beside his bed but all the screens were blank, the rows of lights unlit. There were no cards, only the marks of Sellotape on the wall behind the bed where previous occupants' cards had been fixed. While she waited she wondered if those patients had recovered enough to take them to their homes where they would surely be lost in the back of a drawer or cupboard, seemingly irrelevant when rediscovered months or years later. Or had it been left to the nurses to remove the cards and bundle them along with the belongings from the bedside locker into plastic bags for a discreet hand-over to the relatives after the dust had settled?

She went to the open window to look out. Somehow her journey through the building had convinced her that the ward overlooked the back of the hospital, but now she saw the same car-lined street, the bus stop she had alighted at, the dark asphalt path. The elderly couple were gone but the handbag was still standing on the path, forgotten, no doubt, in the effort of walking the man to the door where the wheelchair was at hand. It shook now in a breeze that had risen as the evening cooled towards dusk, trapping a horse-chestnut leaf against its side. She would point it out to the orderly if it was still there when she came down. She watched a car cruise along the street, the driver craning his neck through the window to examine the numbers of the tall Victorian houses, their fronts dusted with soot and grime, but their elegance and stature undiminished. How exhausted this view was, she thought after a few minutes, like any view from a hospital window, the wonderful leafing and unleafing of the seasons meaningless in the face of pain and illness. What could it mean to them anyway, when it could not be enjoyed now, and to look upon it so was to remind oneself that it might never be again.

There was a tapping noise behind her and she turned to find his eyes upon her, their blueness taking her by surprise. She hadn't noticed them before. Perhaps it was the drugs, she thought.

'It's good of you to come,' he breathed.

'I couldn't *not* come,' she whispered, putting the bunch of violet and yellow bearded lilies on top of the equipment rack.

'Thank you,' he mouthed, motioning to the beaker of water on the bedside table. She handed him the beaker and he sipped from it, spitting the water into the cardboard container she held out to him, remarking on how it resembled an upturned bowler hat. He spluttered his laughter and it was obvious that it caused him pain.

'Sorry.'

'It's all right,' he croaked, his voice recovering from the dryness of sleep and medicine. 'You're too good to come.'

She went to find a chair to sit on the opposite side of the bed to the catheter bag, which she found embarrassing and strangely, intimately, disturbing.

'They're great in here, the staff,' he praised after a nurse had visited to take his temperature, all three of them staring at the thin glass cylinder poking from the edge of his mouth. 'They go easy on you, you know.'

He recounted the tale of the accident, how he had stepped back into the man operating the crane lever and the sleeper had crashed down, crushing his legs against the rail. He had passed out for a few seconds and when he came to he felt no pain, noticing only that none of the other track workers were there. For a moment he had thought it part of a dream, until one of the fitters came running back with a first aid box, telling him that the others had gone to the muster point to ring for help. The fitter had joked with him that they couldn't all use the two-way radio at once but they'd surely try. The pain began to seep upwards through his body, as though he was being lowered into boiling water, a searing pain that made him feel light-headed. He remembered the fitter on his knees at the side of the track, frantically emptying the contents of the first aid box on to the ballast, resorting to wiping up the blood that had run along the rail with cotton-wool soaked in surgical spirit.

The doctors had told him he was lucky, that the sleeper could easily have severed his legs clean off against the steel rail. The loss of blood had been stemmed by the shock and the quick response from the ambulance. He would walk again after a few operations to pin and mend his bones. He was very lucky, they reminded him.

Helen felt queasy as he recounted the incident, anxiously looking around her, feeling the keen guilt the healthy have when amongst the ill or incapacitated. 'Christ, that's terrible, Eamonn, really terrible,' she breathed when he had finished. He lay back on the double pillows, exhausted by the telling.

'Who else has been in so far?' she asked him when he had settled again.

'You're the first.'

She felt unbearably sorry for him to be so alone in the city. 'I'm sure I won't be the last,' she blurted, and he smiled.

'The men on the tracks wouldn't want to come anyways, and I don't blame them. Who wants a living reminder of what happens when a mistake is made?'

'Better a living reminder than a dead one,' she humoured.

'A mistake all the same,' he breathed. 'I shouldn't have been near that yoke in the first place, it was against the rules.'

'What harm? It's done now, and you're on the mend.'

'There'll be no compensation,' he countered. 'They only pay out if the rules are adhered to. The insurance won't cover them otherwise. You can see the reasoning behind it.'

'I don't see any rhyme or reason to it at all,' she rose. 'If there's an accident the company are obliged to pay compensation, that's all there should be to it.'

'Helen,' he softened. 'I know all this already, it's explained to us before we sign our contracts.'

'But . . .'

He smiled wincingly at her and she stopped, realizing how carried away with the argument she was getting.

'I'm sorry,' she said.

'Don't be. It's nice to know you're concerned. There's many would turn a blind eye to that side of it and let me battle on by myself.'

In pursuing the argument she had put off any mention of themselves, of the brief history they shared. She shifted uncomfortably on the chair, flushing at the memory of it all, hoping that he wouldn't recognize it in her, fearing that any concern she might show for him would be misinterpreted as affection, or even love.

'It's a lovely evening,' she diverted, looking at the wash of sunlight shortening on the ceiling of the ward.

'Aye, I suppose it is.' Tiredness had crept into his voice and she wondered if she should go now.

'I've to tell the family back home yet,' he started. 'The doctors were going to do it as soon as I was admitted, but I asked them not to. There's a lot more explaining to be done now that this has happened.'

For a moment she saw a life emerge from the shadow of lies, then sink back again. She could think of nothing to say to him now that would make his task any easier. She could see his mother at the end of the hospital bed, hard-faced, disappointment hanging like a veil about them as he struggled to explain himself with words that fell on unhearing ears. He might as well not bother.

The simple effort of waking showed upon his face, morphine pushing against the senses he willed to work. He smiled weakly at her.

'One way or another they would have found out,' he said. 'It would be better that it happened differently – I've dug my own hole now and I'll have to drag myself out of it in front of them all.' His words bore the imprint of a statement prepared during the long hours of recovery, the elements juggled and matched until their configuration satisfied him. The apparent ease with which an explanation would finally be offered undermined by the draining effort of preparing them, the knowledge that no explanation would offer consolation.

'You'll have their sympathy at least,' Helen nodded towards his legs.

'It'll soon go, don't worry. They've told all and sundry at home that I'm well up in the railways over here. I know what they're like; anything I've told them will have been fattened up to make an impression.'

She imagined him at home, the wheelchair pushed up at the head of the dinner table, unable to look any of them in the eye, the guilt eating away at him until he was hollow inside, the silences between them that said everything. He would have to ask them to lift him in and out of bed, to wash him and take him to the toilet, all dignity and respect gone and unrecoverable even when he could walk again.

'Gardening,' he started. 'I suppose I could take up the trowel and mower rather than the pick-axe and shovel when all this is over. None would want me back on the sites anyway after a knock the like of this.'

'You've put in your time, Eamonn,' she urged. 'There's many would be delighted to have you back working with them.'

'Not at all,' he scorned. 'I've seen it before myself, I've even been party to it and it serves me right now. As soon as a man comes back to work after an accident he's given the toughest jobs of all; heavy levering, lifting sacks of rubble on to the trucks or what have you, anything that'll put him under pressure. It might make him feel like shit, but it sure makes the rest of us feel great. It's as if we throw our own hatred of the grind on to the poor lad, knowing that if he breaks our own effort is broken too and we can take it easy for a while.'

A pair of nurses came into the ward, one of them carrying a tea-tray full of medicine tubs, another a clipboard. The clock was moving towards the end of visiting hours. The sunlight on the ceiling had faded to nothing.

'It's the teamwork that gets you through the hours down there' he continued, 'the laughs and the jokes. Any opportunity for a break in the slog is jumped upon. Why should it be any different for the worker who's trying to make his way back into it? Any dumb animal eventually makes for the weakest around it, even if it's his best friend, otherwise the others might single *him* out.'

'You've spent too long in here already, Eamonn,' she said. 'Too much time on your hands to be thinking the wrong thing altogether. You'll be fit as a fiddle before long, and all this will be far behind you.'

'I've thought it all along,' he rose. 'All of us thought it but none would admit to it. I could see it in their faces as I lay there, my neck resting on the cold metal track and my legs broken – the pity first, and then the relief that it wasn't them.'

From behind a pull-around screen one of the patients made a quiet protest as the nurses struggled to move him.

The shapes of bottoms, elbows, and heads pressed into the thin steel-coloured curtain as they lifted him. A bare and pig-hued foot poked out beneath the curtain for a moment and then the creak of springs as he settled again, the soothing vowels of the nurses as though he was an infant.

'It's only human,' she said cautiously for fear of offending him, 'to be relieved for yourself. Then the concern for the other person takes over, doesn't it?'

'I suppose so,' he said, but there was little conviction in his words.

The corridors were busy with departing visitors; children clutching handfuls of grapes, their faces smeared with chocolate, adults discreetly discussing the progress of the patient they had just left behind. Nurses hovered in white, out of earshot, talking amongst themselves, idly tucking hairs under their hats.

'It's about time I was going. It's after half past nine as it is.' She noticed the relief in her voice as she spoke and hoped that Eamonn would not hear it.

'You've been good to come, Helen. You'll be back soon?' He lifted his hand towards her as she got up and she took it. The strength of his grip surprised her, like the grip of a man slipping away towards nothingness. She looked into his face. His eyes were wet and at that moment she hated him for it, the exercise of vulnerability in the pursuit of pity that the doomed follow to the end.

'Of course I'll be back,' she said. 'Of course I will,' and she turned to go. She waved as she left the ward, but a nurse was in the way and she didn't know whether he saw her or not.

There was no warmth in the evening. The elderly woman's handbag was gone, the bench empty. A blackbird hopped along the path before her, barely visible but for the yellow smear of its beak. The lit windows of the houses opposite glowed warmly, a fat woman reaching to pull the curtains on an upper floor, the slam of a car door further along the street. She stood to wait for the bus, looking back at the hospital and trying to make out his window amongst the many windows which looked much the same. She would not be back here again. His family would come over to reclaim him and she would be forgotten amidst the bitter argument that ensued, the marking out of territory, the battle of reason and wits that he could not win. She was glad to have no part in it.

She was still looking for his window as she took her seat on the bus, folding and refolding the ticket between anxious fingers, searching in vain for one window amongst others.

The toil of the journey to work, the hour upon hour of standing behind the counter, the journey home again, stretched before her without end as she set out into the day. Would it be like this for ever, she wondered, and now that Eamonn was gone would there be anything else to break the long weeks of the summer that was beginning?

When she had returned from the hospital the night before one of the other tenants was moving out, the simple belongings stacked on the path: a bedside table, a ceramic lamp base, an electric kettle, and a small cardboard box with a radio-cassette and a few other things that were undiscernible under the street lights. She measured her own belongings against these and came up with less, the fruits of more than six months in the city. The small notes and change in her pocket were all her own, and all she had.

At first she felt restless on the Tube, fidgeting, finding herself staring at other passengers and wondering at their private lives. Some returned her stare and she would look away. The first wave of nausea seemed to come from nowhere, as though something had burst in her stomach. She clamped her hand over her mouth, desperate for the train to reach the next station, the stagger to the litter box where her vomit spilled amongst the empty drink cans and chocolate wrappers while others looked on from a distance, another curiosity amongst the dozens they saw every day. She looked back through bleary eyes as if to refute their silent condemnation.

She gagged on bile the whole way up the stairs to the street above, retching again in a doorway as people hurried past, none of them paying her any attention. Pages torn from a women's magazine circled in the doorway, the problem page staring back at her. She remembered the same page from the *Sunday World* so jealously guarded by Kelly. She retched again, the thin vomit spattering the paper at her feet.

She found a café and sat for a long time over a glass of water, afraid to drink from it at first but asking for a second glass minutes later. The water soothed her scorched throat and mouth. She stopped when she caught her reflection in the window, her cheeks and forehead pale, her hair lank, clothes dishevelled from leaning over to be sick. A bluebottle settled to feed on the film of grease inside the window and she turned away.

At home again she cooked beans on toast but could not eat, the sight and smell of the food bringing bile to her throat. She was tired after the day in the shop. Mr Patel had been annoyed when she turned up almost two hours late, screeching at her as he struggled to keep up with the lunchtime trade, folding the first editions of the evening papers, change spinning to the floor. Afterwards, as usual, he had apologized, asking what was wrong with her and agreeing that she didn't look herself. She had stayed until the very end, until the fluffers and the track workers arrived, as if to punish herself for being sick, as if the weariness would drive it away.

After she had cleared her plate into the bin she lay on

the bed, too tired to remove her shoes, waiting for sleep to overtake her, moonlight and street light draining through the trees. The house was quiet, even the hissing pipes stilled to silence. Her eyes flicked open when she smelled the tobacco smoke and she sat up. For a moment she thought she had drifted off only to wake up thinking she was back at home, but she had been awake all the time, her eyes on the ceiling and the window. She stood up and listened. A draught crossed the floor and circled her ankles. When she opened her door she saw the figure in the frame of the open front door. He barely turned to look at her, his eyes tracing the stars or the telephone wires above the street, the red glow of the cigarette cupped in his hand, grey wisps of smoke drifting back into the house. As she closed the door upon him she wondered if Kelly was at his door too, a cigarette cupped in his hand, the dog scurrying back and forth in the grass which would be long now in advance of the first cut.

Days later the doctor told her what she had not allowed herself to think: that she was pregnant. As she handed him the small flask of urine she had stopped herself asking the question why. 'Only a few weeks, mind,' he said, 'but pregnant all the same. Make an appointment to see the nurse on your way out and she'll take it from there.'

She rushed out into the street, past the startled woman on the front desk and the pensioner leaning on a shopping basket. She stopped at the pavement, gazing in wonder at the street and the life upon it that went on in spite of her pregnancy, buses groaning towards the High Street, people at the zebra crossings who did not pause to look at her, taxis and cars speeding past.

She stood on the grey flagstones and saw nothing around her, heard only the doctor's voice: 'pregnant all the same';

the casual phrase repeated over and over again in the hope that it might lose all meaning for her. But she *was* pregnant, and a child would be born in eight months time. She did not want to think about it now, but nor could she shake off the truth that was growing inside her.

When she returned the next day the receptionist gave her some leaflets and an appointment card for the nurse. She read through the leaflets on the bus to the station; leaflets from religious charities that cared for the unborn child, rubella warnings, terminations, household budgeting for mothers, genito-urinary clinics. There were no answers, the leaflets written in a blank and colourless prose that said and meant nothing to her. Nothing mattered but the child whose entire life depended upon her.

She took to walking in a foolish attempt to work off the weight she was putting on, as if she might walk the baby away, leave its ghost on the pavements behind her. She walked from the house to the station and back again, taking a map for the first couple of days and then finding her own way. The walks took her past places she had been before under different circumstances, those moments spinning together in her memory like lantern slides of her life in the city.

The streets were breaking into summer, trees in full leaf, pavements seamed with grass and the dandelions whose shuttlecocked seeds drifted in the narrow evening sun. The squares filled at lunchtime, clerks shouldering tramps from the benches to sit and eat their sandwiches and apples in the shade of plane trees and military statues, wasps arriving to feed on cores and crusts after they had gone. A boy in a striped green suit collected coins from deckchaired pensioners in a park. Two men on a platform painted the vast walls of a gasholder near a railway sidings overrun with buddleia and rust, overalls rolled to their waists, tattoos like shadows across their shoulders. She envied them all, their easy lives without care or worry, only their work to carry them from this hour to the next and the next, untouched by the despair that enclosed her days.

Bath times were the worst. Lying back in the tub, the water rolling across her skin, her breasts tender to touch and already swelling, belly rising above the tangle of dark hair. Time and again she tried to submerge the pale mound but each time the waters covered less and less, the measure of the growing child. She planted her hands on her tummy and pressed as if expecting a response to be beaten out on the distended skin, its presence silent and secure, echo of the man she had wanted to fade.

Day in day out she thought of Eamonn. It was some weeks since she had visited him in the hospital and she was certain that he would be back in Ireland by now, his mother thinking of stories to tell the relatives and neighbours to keep her dream alive. He, like they, would be completely ignorant of his child that grew inside her now. She could see him at the dinner table, involved in the banter between his younger brothers and sisters as they updated him on the goings-on in the town. He would scarcely have a thought for her, only a lingering curiosity about why she never returned to the hospital, and that too would soon be gone. He would meet another girl, possibly a local girl he knew but had never before considered, and they would walk out along the tracks and roads with never a thought for Helen and the child he would not know.

Should she have mentioned it, the child, to him before he had left the hospital? He had a right to know. It was his body, his seed, his child, and as long as it was in the world it was his as much as hers.

*

'No, miss,' the orderly at the front desk looked up from the ledger. 'He was transferred to the Royal Free for a week and then to somewhere in Ireland, I think. We could trace his address there for you if you like.'

'No, but thanks anyway.' She pushed back out of the door and on to the street. A thin, warm rain was falling. It was a half-chance, she knew, but still she was surprised to realize that she wasn't sorry not to find him there. Telling him might have extinguished all that he had felt for her, like a candle flame against a storm.

The river was still, flat grey like poured lead. Boats were moored all along the banks, and on the near bank some lay on their sides where the tide had abandoned them, mooring chains draped with green weed. The tide had turned and was filling again, those boats moored furthest from the banks welcoming the swirling and brackish waters, rising unsteadily against their chains like animals after slumber.

Helen stood on the bridge and watched the waters far below, finishing the ice cream she had bought from a van on Tower Hill. Even at this distance she could hear the chimes as it moved to a new pitch, the bells trailing through the streets like a lament.

Helen noticed a woman picking her way amongst the boats, stepping gingerly over the mooring chains, careful not to slip on the weed-slimed shale. Her hair was dishevelled, her face ruddy and pinched-looking, and she wore a soiled red sweater over a pair of baggy denim jeans. She could have been one of the vagrants Helen had often seen around London Bridge Station, blind drunk by midday, their Irish accents shaming her as they shouted and sang. The woman dragged a Border collie puppy along behind her, tethered to her wrist by a piece of string which had undergone innumerable repairs, its gangly legs splayed in a mixture of fright and curiosity.

Helen remembered how Kelly had brought the second dog home after a visit he had made to Headford, the cardboard box carried into the house under his arm and set on the table before he helped Helen make the tea. Blackie, the dog her mother had been given on her last day as a teacher in the local school, had been put to sleep months before and Helen had long-since tired of pestering Kelly to get another. As soon as she heard the scratching noise coming from the box she knew it was a puppy, since Kelly could never see the point in having a cat; 'Worthless creatures!' he would bark at cats gathered like flower petals around a saucer of milk in a farmyard. She had burst into tears as she lifted the skinny Border collie from the box, cradling him in her arms and bringing him to sit beside the fire, his eager tongue rasping against the back of her hand. 'What'll we call him, Daddy?' she begged, too excited by the surprise to utter a word of thanks. 'Blackie, like the last one,' Kelly had insisted through her protests.

Again, as she walked home, it began to drizzle lightly, rain raising the smell of dust from the streets, umbrellas sprouting everywhere like black mushrooms. The rain thickened and steadied as she went towards the station.

At the station a Salvation Army van had drawn up alongside the entrance and was dispensing cups of tea to a group of men whose stained and torn coats were soaking with rain.

She thought of the men at home who wore the seasons in their faces; the chapped lips and reddened nose and ears of winter, the furrowed brow of summer as clouds were watched and the fields silently encouraged, that unfathomable expression of autumn as the crop was saved and another year ended. But these soot-darkened men wore the whole of their lives on their faces, tragedy folded into lined features, the grey pallor of emptiness, the unmistakable sense of the last doors closing on already shut lives, their eyes like peepholes into an impossible darkness.

When the bus arrived she looked out of the window, not at the men but down at the pavements where their images were trapped in the rain with the blurred reflections of buildings and night sky like another city she did not know.

There had been a fire in the house across the road the afternoon before, a faint smell of smoke still hanging in the front hallway, pools of water standing on the pavement and in the gutter. The roof was completely gone, a solitary blackened rafter protruding grotesquely from the chimney stack, which in the heat had begun to crumble but did not fall. No pigeons roosted on the windowsill, the charred debris added to the litter in the garden. The heat had dried out the mortar and even as she watched it trickled from between the bricks. Soon the house would fall or be pulled down.

The morning sickness had gone and she felt less bloated now. The weather helped, a cool spring bursting towards summer on the last bank holiday in May, the parks filled with families picnicking, playing football, and throwing tennis balls for dogs to retrieve. Groups of young men stripped to the waist wandered the parks, beer cans in their fists, pushing and shoving into each other, roaring and whistling at the young women who steadfastly ignored them. Children on bicycles wheeled lazy circles in the heat.

With the start of the holiday season there were fewer customers in the shop, less papers to fold and hand over, less chocolate but more canned drinks. The dark skirts and suits of winter gave way to pastel cotton dresses and the men wore short-sleeved shirts, jackets slung over their shoulders, ties loosened. The evenings were warm, fragrant in places where trees gave shade. She enjoyed the walk home that took her past the parks and squares, pubs where people pulled chairs out on to the pavement, the velour upholstery and wooden legs incongruous against the grey flagstones.

She opened the bedsit window as far as it would go on its squeaky treads, propping it up with a piece of wood plundered from the back garden. The outside poured in: the scent from a stunted clematis clinging perilously to a rusting downpipe which sprouted water jets every time the bath was drained, the rich smell of cooking from the Indian family whose garden backed on to hers, bumblebees who cruised her two rooms before departing having found nothing to interest them, the scent of freshly cut grass. Sounds from the streets beyond seemed amplified in the stillness of evening; the hiss of traffic along the High Street, the slamming of front doors, a ringing telephone that went unanswered.

Mr Patel gave her the news as she was about to leave one evening: the shop was to be closed. He explained with some difficulty how the profits he made hardly covered the rent, rates, electricity, and her wages. It had always been this way, he continued, but now that he was older he felt that it was no longer worth the effort to keep the shop up. His son, Hanif, was going to study medicine in Manchester when he finished school so there was nobody to hand the running of the shop over to. His eyes tracked balefully across the tidy shelves in the shop, the glass chocolate display, the black and white tiles that he mopped every morning without fail.

'I am sorry,' he offered, shrugging his shoulders before wandering off across the concourse, unable to confront her disappointment.

Helen watched him go, the small balding head above the sleeveless beige jumper, the white shirt with the thickly knotted black tie. As she pulled on her jacket she heard again the click-click of the nail-clippers from where he stood at the head of the escalators. She felt for him, the emptiness he would face into after a half-lifetime spent building up a trade only to have to surrender it. The business would never have been more than just this shop, Mr Patel had never intended it to be otherwise, but it was taken for granted that it would always be there. She thought of telling him that she was pregnant, hoping that he might be happy for her even though she was not, but she left without saying anything.

The imminent closure of the shop cast more of a shadow upon her than she had expected. Over months when so much had changed for her the shop had remained constant, like a fulcrum to the pattern of her days. She could lose herself in the hours spent there, in the papers that were handed out, in the known and unknown faces, in the commuters' imagined lives. Mr Patel didn't mention the closing of the shop again after that night and continued as if nothing had happened, as if the shop would always be there and he with it. But Helen felt as if something had snapped inside him; his sense of humour slipped, he tired easily, and often the shop would close long before the station did.

Slowly, things began to fade. The streets emptied of children as families made for the coastal resorts; Southend-on-Sea, Broadstairs, Walton-on-the-Naze, Skegness; cars crawling their way out of the city, navigational dogs facing into the breeze, a woman holding a bird cage on her lap as the budgerigar nervously circled on its perch, children's faces flattened against windows. Signs appeared in shop windows giving notice of impending closure for the holidays, dust and litter trailed around empty school yards, policemen patrolled lazily in crisp short-sleeve shirts.

Helen fidgeted in the heat. Her clothes were tightening upon her, the bra straps cutting into her shoulders, her breasts squeezed together, waistbands that left angry red patterns on her skin. The sweat made it worse, showing in dark crescents under her arms and at the base of her neck, and her feet were swollen. She had given up walking, and it was all she could do to drag herself into the shop knowing that she would have to stand there for hours on end, waiting for the few customers who now bothered to buy a newspaper. She couldn't wait for Mr Patel to announce that he was going to call it a day and she could begin clipping the mastheads from the unsold papers and count the day's meagre takings, before the longed-for release into the cooler evening.

Helen lay on her bed listening to the sounds elsewhere in the house, feeling herself drifting off with them, her T-shirt pulled up so that her hands could frame her swelling tummy. She felt at peace. Whenever she looked down at the stretched expanse of skin and thought of the baby behind it she felt nothing but that it would be born in five and a half months time and that she would grow to love it then. There was nothing to be done now and she would simply wait like the parched leaves on the trees outside which rustled closely together in the hissing wait for rain.

She made herself a mug of tea and a couple of slices of toast and sat in bed to take them, falling asleep as soon as the mug had been drained. The mug was the first thing she saw when she woke suddenly in the early morning, the room washed with indigo and alive with her own fear. The mug, white as bone, came slowly into focus just as the pain centred upon her abdomen. The sheets clung to her skin and she could smell her own sweat, a draught rushing in to chill her. Cramps came in waves, slow drumbeats of agony, her limbs trembling with pain and fear. She pulled her legs up to her chest and wrapped her arms about her knees in an effort to still herself but even so the pain shook her.

'Daddy,' she almost called out, the word formed upon her lips but going unsaid.

Birds were going crazy in the trees outside, dense rush and flap of wings, song as sharp as needles in her ears. She clasped her hands across her ears to shut it out and rocked back and forth on the mattress.

It was then, as the room brightened, that she noticed the mark upon her nightdress, the dark-petalled flower of loss blossoming upon the cotton, an echo of the stain found on the sheets the morning after the child was conceived and returning now to reclaim what had been left behind.

Part Four

A HANDFUL OF black dog's fur had caught in the barbed wire fence at the bottom of the track, fluttering like a piece of rag left to mark where someone had died.

Her gaze moved up the track towards the house where grey turf smoke chugged out from the chimney. The cloches stood at the gable, their plastic skins rippling and snapping in the wind. The walls of the house were a sullen colour, bleached-looking, and as she walked towards the house she saw that it had been whitewashed with too weak a solution so that the wash had been rinsed from the walls by rain, the soil at her feet seamed with white. She put down her bags and looked around. The fields were silent, a few birds singing in the distance, grass and thistles bending with the breeze. The back of the van poked out from the far end of the house, its doors more eaten with rust than she remembered, an old blanket the dog slept on trapped in the hinges.

So much of that terrible last evening in this house had stayed with her that she felt now that she might be better off turning around and making for the bus again. But where would she go, she wondered, where she would not take some part of him with her?

His boots were gone from inside the front door. When she turned around the dog was racing towards her, tongue pulled back against its cheek, its coat pressed like silk. It barked and yelped excitedly as it circled her and she went down on one knee to hug it close, whispering in its ear until it stilled.

She could see him now from the step, putting his cap back on his head and taking up the fork again, animatedly loosening the soil between the potato ridges, a pair of swallows turning and diving in the sky behind him. She stood watching him for some minutes, sometimes cupping a clay-flaked hand across his mouth to cough up phlegm the pollen brought on, quickly bending back into the work in an effort to presume that she wasn't there at all. Very soon there would be too little light to see by and he would be in danger of spiking the potatoes with the tines of the fork, but she did not doubt that he was capable of standing blindly there through the night to forsake her.

The house was the same as before and the sight of it chilled her. The simple furniture that had not been moved an inch, the dull heat of the range, the towels drying on the rail, the cuckoo clock ticking on and on and on. A newspaper lay in the seat of the armchair, the crossword only half completed, the margin of the page crazed with fragments of his vocabulary. What dishes there were had been washed up, the surfaces wiped clean, a window propped to air the place. The dresser held a few more jars of preserved vegetables; this chronicle would continue in spite of everything.

The house seemed untenanted, a space into which no light could shine. The poverty of the rooms, their bare and simple furniture without adornment, no signature of clutter, the walls ringing empty and hollow. In the bathroom a grey bar of soap and a shaving brush, his razor left open like a wishbone, a facecloth dried to stiffness on the edge of the bathtub. She did not dare enter his room, but imagined the bed with its thin blankets and lifeless pillow, his shirts hanging on the angle of the wardrobe door one on another and another, the loud ticking of the alarm clock.

Her bedroom was cold, the windowsill furred with dust, the wardrobe door ajar to a rank of clothes hangers suspended like wire bats. The bedclothes were folded back, the pillow pushed up against the headboard, and for a moment she thought that he must have taken to sleeping there. But when she drummed on the mattress and a fine dust rose she knew that he had touched nothing in the room for almost a year.

His boots beat like thunder on the front step when eventually he came in from the gloaming. So long had Blackie been forced to wait in the fields with him that the dog set to whining for its food, the whole racket causing her to start from where she had dozed off in the armchair.

'Whist, Blackie! Whist!' the dog forced towards silence only to continue its whining moments later.

'You're back so,' he said, coming into the room.

'I'm back indeed,' she brightened, reaching to switch on the lamp.

'It's well for you then.' He stamped out into the kitchen, water drumming into the sink as he scrubbed his hands with the nailbrush. He cursed each time the brush slipped from his grasp on account of the soap, finally throwing it to one side and drying his hands on a cloth.

'Will I make us some tea?' she offered after a little while, going into the kitchen and finding the cloth torn asunder in his hands. They both stared at it. In his silent rage he had not known his own strength.

He flung the cloth in the old bucket that served as a bin and pulled up a paper bag spotted with dark patches of grease. He tipped the contents, a long bone and a chicken's gizzard, on to a plate and brought it out to the dog. He stood to watch the dog feeding at his feet, the unnatural crunch of the bone breaking in its jaws, gristle spilling out on to the step to be retrieved by an eager tongue. He returned to fill a bowl of water for the now panting dog, whose tail wagged metronomically back and forth as it fed, the shadow of that motion moving across the bare ground in front of the house as if to taunt the darkness that stood beyond.

Moths tumbled against the windows when she lit a second lamp, bright-winged bodies beating against the night as if to welcome her return, finding their places upon the glass from where they could watch her. She waited for him to come in, but long after the sound of the dog's eating had gone and his mug of tea had grown cold he was still outside.

She waited a while longer, her head lolling with sleep but her mind racing, and when she could bear it no longer she rose to switch off the lamps. The moonlit shadows of the window moths lay on the walls, the fire slumped to embers that would not last until dawn. The doorway was empty, a few shards of bone scattered about, but Kelly could not be seen.

She went to the van and heard the sounds of the dog settling on the old blankets. The curtains of Kelly's bedroom window were open, the bed made, shirts hanging greyly in the gloom as she had imagined. For a while she stood at the door just as he had so often stood. In the far distance a car's headlights tracked through the fields, weaving along narrow roads, rising and falling with the undulations like the lights of a ship on heavy seas. The yellowed windows of other houses winked off one by one while she stood, as though beating some soundless code out into the night. Wire fencing hummed and rattled in a breeze that had started up.

The smell of cigarettes came to her a short while later and she froze, expecting to hear him coming towards her. Still there was nothing but the smell, faint one moment, stronger the next. Her fear rose like blood rising to the surface of bruised skin and she felt his gaze upon her, imagined his eyes burning with rage out there in the blankness of that night. He would wait until *she* could wait no longer, until the fear of not knowing had consumed her. With his silent patience he would show her what he too had felt.

The trench cut through the long grass and weeds at the back of the house like a scar, stones and clay scattered wildly on either side, its bottom already colonized by daisies and chickweed.

'What's the trench for, Daddy?' she asked when he came in for the soup she had made at midday.

'What trench?' he deflected.

'The one that runs away from the back door towards the wall to Sweeney's fields.'

He looked at the slice of bread in his hand as if it were about to answer for him. His hand trembled uncomfortably and his brow furrowed. His face began to redden.

'Only there's nothing in it and I was wondering what it was for,' she added.

'You're a fine one,' he blustered, 'you're a fine one to go gallivanting without word nor warning and expect people to make an account of themselves while you're gone!' He stabbed the air with the slice of bread, cheeks swelling with the rage.

She cowered before him, eating the rest of the meal in complete silence, too afraid to reach for the salt pot that stood at his elbow.

'It was only an oul' pipe that was there for years that I was getting rid of,' he offered eventually.

Later, when she went out to hang clothes on the line,

she inspected the trench again. There was no sign that any pipe had ever lain there, the trench starting nowhere and leading nowhere.

He was washing himself at the kitchen sink when she returned, a few wooden pegs left rattling around the rust-spotted biscuit tin they had once collected ladybirds in. He smeared his forearms with soap and ran the cold tap hard to rinse his skin, water splashing everywhere and soaking his shirt. He rinsed his face loudly, blowing into the water cupped in his hands as though to warm it before it hit his face.

'Towel,' he ordered through the splashing and she rushed to get it from over the range.

As she watched him drying his face and arms she could see the trench through the window beyond and she realized then that it had been dug out of frustration. He might have cut it in a few hours one afternoon soon after she had gone, the morning spent waiting for her, wasted, hours gone to dust and nothing, the spade taken to the coarse stony ground that was slashed open until finally his energy was sapped and his anger spent.

The months of her absence were like lost time to them both, threads of the old life picked up again, running on and on as if there had been no break in the sequence of the days of their lives. Only the dog seemed to notice. It shied away from her during the first days, lifting its head from its bowl when she approached to stroke its velveteen ears. It was with much persuasion that it took once again to resting its muzzle in her lap when she sat on the doorstep to watch Kelly bent over some tool or other out in his godforsaken fields.

She found the bicycle where she had left it the year before at the gable of the house. It hadn't been touched since. An afternoon was spent tightening the brakes, pumping the tyres, oiling the stiffened chain, lubricating the axle with grease plundered from beneath the van. She took off in the evening when the dinner had been cleared away and Kelly had set out to walk the boundary of his domain, intent on replacing any stones that had been accidentally or deliberately knocked from the walls, the handle of an old hoe serving as a stick to guide him through the long fallow grass. He didn't raise an eye when she rattled off down the track in the narrow light of evening, raising clouds of midges that beat about her ears.

She was unsteady on the bicycle, the pedals heavy and her steering exaggerated as she negotiated the bends and almost unbalanced herself. The skill soon returned, as natural as walking; once learned never lost. The fields were empty, the drifting scent of cut hay evidence of the work that had been done earlier in the day. The first fields were down, the hay still spread upon the stubble in anticipation of another fine morning that would dry it. Tomorrow it would be ricked. Tractors sat abandoned in some of the biggest fields, forlorn, tines raised in surrender to impending night.

A heron sat on the bridge over the stream, taking flight when she turned the bend, long angled wings lifting it high along the course of the stream, its eyes still searching for fish. Rosheen Lake was almost hidden by the rushes, the surface disturbed by a rogue breeze thrown across it. She did not stop to look for the swans.

Her heart raced as she came down the hill towards the factory, braking to slow herself so that she could get a good look, but leaving enough pace to carry her past should she encounter any of her former colleagues. The bicycles that had always stood against the wall in the front yard were gone, the doors closed. She came to a stop and looked for a light in any of the windows, listening out for the sound of the machines. There was nothing but the lowing of cattle in the fields behind the factory, the wind in the trees and bushes. The night-shift had been stopped, she thought, the factory wound down in the summer so that holidays could be taken. She went on towards Drimelogue but stopped at the petrol station and turned back, afraid that she would meet people she knew and who would be wondering where she had been.

'I see the factory is on short hours for the summer,' she remarked to Kelly over dinner the next evening.

'Huh!' He split a potato and knifed some butter into the crevice. There was a wry smile on his lips as he watched the melted butter ooze out on to the plate.

'Are they on holidays, is that it?'

'Aye, holidays all right. A right feckin' holiday they're havin' now.' He looked out the window in the direction of the factory and the town and laughed, his eyes almost disappearing between his brow and cheeks, a smear of potato trapped on his tongue. 'Aye,' he recovered, 'holidays – I suppose you could say that.'

She realized then that the factory had closed for good, the workers laid off, moving to other towns in search of work, or retreating to the shop-counters and front rooms of Drimelogue, slumped in front of the televisions that had been bought with the first pay-packets of the previous year's spring. The girls wouldn't have the money to be going to the dances in Greenford any more. She tried to recall their names: Siobhán Muldoon, Mary Comerford, Susan Byrne . . . the only faces she could put names to. She remembered that there was a Greenford in London too. She had passed through it once on the bus, row upon row of semi-detached homes, parades of shops with red-brick council flats overhead, a wide trunk road torn through its middle.

Kelly got up from the table, collecting the bacon gristle to throw to the dog. 'You could be clearing over while I'm feeding Blackie,' he said, interrupting her daydream.

'Yes, Daddy.'

She scraped the plates clean and poured the contents of the kettle into the sink before filling it again and returning it to the range to heat for tea.

So the factory had closed as others had before it, just as Kelly and some others had predicted it would. He was triumphant when all about him were defeated; to be proved right was what mattered most, whatever misery or poverty it caused.

She pictured the roll-down shutters closing on the factory for the last time, the slow metal creak and clank as they slammed shut on the machinery which would be draped in greased cloths like funeral shrouds, the workers standing on the forecourt to watch as if in the hope that the shutters would fail to close and they could then rush inside to reclaim their positions on the production line. She saw them now as clearly as if they were standing before her in the front room, their faces closing as the door closed, the truth etched into their expressions: there was no more work to be had, and it would be years before anything would happen again in Drimelogue. They walked back towards town in hushed and straggling groups, some wheeling bicycles. One figure broke from the crowd and mounted his bicycle to push on towards the lakes where the solace and stillness he craved could be found.

Martin. She had almost forgotten him. So much of what she had once felt for him had died inside her now that her heart barely whispered when his name and face returned; all things must fade in time and what could live anyhow with nothing to feed on?

'Is there a drop of tea on the way?' He had returned to take his place at the fireside.

'There ... there is, Daddy. One moment now ...'

'You don't sound so sure,' he chided, stretching his legs out towards the fire which was hardly needed in the warm evening and had been set out of habit alone.

She remembered the letter again, her own words returning to taunt her: '*I miss you and I want to be with you.*' But they had never been answered.

She busied herself with cups and spoons, the rattle of metal on crockery reassuring Kelly that the tea was on the way. When she took the tray into him she noted that both of his socks needed darning, pink and bunioned toes poking through the worn cotton.

'Did anyone come looking for me at all?' she ventured a while later, but he did not answer.

'While I was gone, you know?' she tried again when the silence had ebbed.

He picked up the newspaper and shook it out, making a point of getting the fold straight, the pages fluttering like paper wings.

She leaned her bicycle against the wall of the house and went to knock on the half-open door. The interior was in semi-darkness, heavy net curtains obscuring any light the windows gave. The sweet smell of stewing apples hung in the air.

'Come in, Helen, come in,' Mrs Kane exclaimed when she came out from the kitchen to greet the caller. She wiped her floury hands on her apron and pulled out a chair for Helen to sit on. 'You'll have a cup of tea,' she insisted, busying herself with searching the cupboards for biscuits or cake to offer the visitor.

'We don't get many callers nowadays,' she said from deep in the kitchen. 'Not since he closed the electrical workshop six months back anyways.'

'You must be glad of the peace and quiet,' Helen offered, knowing how few callers there had ever been to this house.

'We're always happy to see a familiar face at any time of the day, Helen. You're always welcome.'

The house had not changed. The door to the workshop

stood ajar, a tangle of wires silhouetted against the window at the far end of the room where an outer door had once been crudely knocked through. Shards of bright metal were visible upon the floorboards. A clipboard roster hung on a nail above the workbench, the last recorded date probably months if not years past. She wondered where Mr Kane was now, if he had taken work elsewhere.

'Martin looked everywhere for you, you know,' Mrs Kane was saying as she came back into the room with a tray of tea and chocolate biscuits. 'He couldn't understand why you left the way you did. There were some that thought you were dead, until your father explained that you'd gone to live with your cousins in Dublin.'

Helen stared open-mouthed at Mrs Kane. She had never even considered that Kelly would offer any excuse but that she had disappeared. 'You're very kind,' she praised when the tray was set down before her.

'Martin was up and down to your house a few times before he got any answer at all.' The golden tea trickled into the cups one after another. 'He sent a few letters to the address your father gave him but as far as I know he never got a reply.'

'None of those letters reached me,' Helen whispered, her eyes wetting with tears. 'Daddy must have mixed up the addresses somehow.'

'It doesn't matter now anyways,' Mrs Kane sighed, and for a moment Helen imagined that Martin must have died such was the emptiness in Mrs Kane's voice. 'He got wind that all was not well in the factory and left for England last spring. He was in London for a while and then he found some work in a workshop in Nottingham. We got a card from him not so long ago and he phones his brother in Ballina from time to time.' Mrs Kane gazed over at the postcard on the mantelpiece, a humorous Robin Hood sketch. 'He seems happy enough.'

Helen turned the spoon idly around the bottom of her teacup while she listened to Mrs Kane talking about the other members of her family and how Mr Kane had got a contract with the P&T to lay telephone cables in County Louth. He came back on the bus every weekend and the money wasn't bad as long as it lasted. It made a change, she said.

Mrs Kane's house was the same as it had ever been but in spite of it everything had changed. The soul had been sucked from between these four walls. The house was clean and tidy and Mrs Kane was welcoming and easy company, but it was like a brilliant light that had nothing to shine upon.

On her way home the fields that had earlier been filled with sunshine were dark, as though a veil had been drawn across the sky. The clouds were slate-grey, Rosheen Lake as still and dull as poured lead. A pair of crows crouched in the roof-gutters of the empty factory, their tail feathers teased by the wind. A shed door slammed to and fro and Helen watched a young girl run down a path to tie the door back.

Kelly was inside when she got home.

'A foul looking evening we're going to have,' he announced as she began to scrub the potatoes, standing at the window in his stockings, hands plunged deep into trouser-pockets. The windows rattled as if on cue and Kelly cursed the weather in Irish. It had been so long since she had heard any Irish spoken that she didn't register it at first, but as she repeated his words to herself the rhythm returned. Her mother's Irish had been different. She remembered its clarity, borne of the classroom she had spent her days in, the language acquired in a teacher-training college in Dublin, sharp ring of consonants amid the softened vowels. Kelly's Irish came to him as naturally as instinct, the word's half-uttered and barely decipherable. It had been his parents' language but was no longer his own; English had been spoken in these parts for two generations now and the Irish was an echo of almost-forgotten history, heard only in classrooms and during the first Mass every Sunday. Still it returned to him, phrases and sayings that suited when nothing else would.

As the weeks wore on towards the end of that summer Helen took to cycling into Drimelogue and out beyond it again, to the boglands that were little known to her. Here men worked alone on the dark peat and a solitary Bord na Móna cutting machine lay stranded on a shelf of rock, yellow paint flaking from its rusted metalwork, the caterpillar tracks seized in defeat. She liked the wide expanse of the bogs, the almost limitless horizon, the sense that anything and nothing would happen there.

A man's head appeared above one of the cuttings. He straightened his cap and threw a *sleán* up over the lip and then lifted a very young girl out of the cutting. She flung her arms around his head while he lifted her, terrified that she might fall back into the cutting. When he let go she wobbled and steadied, her yellow dress collecting the breeze in its pleats. Her hair was fixed into pig-tails with red elastics. She kneeled down to pick some bog cotton but couldn't guide her fingers on to the white puff that the wind teased and she began to cry, her wail carrying across the bog.

Helen remembered the child she had lost, the part of her that was not meant to be. Why did it not want to live? *Why?* Sometimes she found herself wondering where its soul had gone, its spirit, the space it would have occupied in the world it had been turned away from.

The man emerged from the cutting and gathered the

little girl into his arms and her crying stopped. They set off across the bog to where a small van was parked at the side of the road.

In another direction out of town the road narrowed to cross a dam that separated two lakes. She watched her reflection in the water as she spun across, spokes flashing in the light, and on into a tunnel of trees, the road rusting with pine needles and rising towards a hill so that she would dismount and walk the bicycle until the gradient dropped again and the cycling was less of a chore. The sun filtered through the branches overhead, clouds of insects fizzing in pools of warm light. Mushrooms sprouted along the verges, grey and ghost-like in the shade of ferns.

The choking sound of an engine starting up broke through the peacefulness. Its pitch had risen to a heavy whine by the time she located the two men working the edge of a stand of larch trees a couple of fields away. The chainsaw faltered when it met the trunk of the first tree but soon gathered pace, the damp white sawdust spraying out across the dark soil of the tilled field. The men stood away as the tree began to fall, the slow arc of its descent coming to an end with a whoosh of leaves and snapping branches. One man set about the fallen tree with a bow-saw while the other took the chainsaw to the next tree. They would work all afternoon and evening until the trees were cleared. A fire would be set on the stumps and in a few months time it would be as though the trees had never been.

As she watched the men work she wondered if the stand of larches had been part of Martin's catalogue of local history and places. He had a name for everywhere. She remembered an evening in the spring of the year before when they had lain back on the long grass in a field that gave on to Rosheen Lake, the stars brightening in the indigo sky above them. Together they had listed the names of places they knew, deciding as they went which names they liked and which they did not. Helen had run out of names after a minute or two, but Martin could have continued all night, names drawn from a seemingly unending catalogue.

It would have saddened Martin to see the trees being felled and it saddened her the more to think of him and that evening beside the lake that could be recalled but not recaptured.

'You can't be all day in the house like this.'

Kelly had taken to commenting on her idleness when he found her reading the paper at the table or listening to the afternoon shows on the radio. Cooking and cleaning did not count as work in his eyes. 'Your own mother, God be good to her, was a teacher in her time, before she had a child to be rearing. She'd have gone back to it too, once you were reared, if she'd been given the chance.' He sighed and went back to rubbing dubbin into his boots, making small circle designs on the softening leather.

She had offered to help out in the fields but he had not wanted her help. They were his fields. The tomatoes and peppers that grew in the cloches had been harvested and sold at the market in Ballinasloe. Kelly had got a good price this year, and already there were grand ambitions for next year's crop, ambitions that would be dismantled as the winter wore on and the extra effort involved would destroy any attempt to improve on a good year.

'You should take yourself into Drimelogue and ask about for some shop work or the like. You won't be let fall into a rut around here.'

'I won't fall into any rut,' she countered. 'I've been looking already. I've asked at Ginn's and the Doorstep

Grocer but they had nothing.' The lie would appease him but she would have to go to the two shops now and ask for work in case he mentioned it to them in passing.

'The least you could be doing, I suppose,' he grumbled, folding the newspaper to do the crossword.

He was right, she thought as she watched his face bend towards the grid of black and blank boxes, it was too easy to grow lazy and fall into habits that would be hard to break out of. Lately she had taken to returning to bed once he had had his breakfast and was out in the fields, spreading the newspaper out on the blankets to read in the knowledge that he would not be back before noon unless the weather broke. Only in the afternoons did she take off on the bicycle, returning in time to start the potatoes and bacon she had prepared earlier.

But there was no work to be had for months. In late September she helped Kelly lift the potatoes, scrabbling about in the wet clay for the pale fleshy tubers, wiping grey slugs from the decaying roots, the potatoes collected into heavy brown sacks. Kelly came after her, pushing a pitchfork through the loose soil for any she had missed, cursing her whenever the tines speared a potato. He seemed to go out of his way to show her up, finding potatoes in places she had been over time and again for fear of failing him. She began to suspect that he was dropping them from his pocket but could not catch him at it.

Together they took the potatoes into the house to be stored. She watched him hoist each sack on to his shoulder and set off for the front door, one arm held out in the air like that of a tight-rope walker, his tensed body trembling but not yielding under the weight. When she tried to help by dragging a sack across the grass he shouted to her to stop, his thick fingers prying her hands away from the canvas.

'They'll be destroyed, girl! Destroyed altogether!' He settled the sack at his feet and bent to lift it up, pursing his lips in preparation for the effort.

'Go on in now,' he urged when the last sack was safely on his shoulder. 'You've done enough for the day. You could be getting the dinner ready for the working man.'

Autumn moved towards winter, the light falling from the evenings.

'The days are shortening on us, Daddy,' she remarked.

'Like every year,' he grumbled from the fireside. 'Year in year out.'

The convent stood on the slopes of a small hill beyond the dam where the two lakes met. She had passed it many times on her afternoon cycles the summer before. Two granite pillars gave on to a shrub-lined driveway up to the front door. Lawns and flowerbeds enclosed the grey- and cream-painted buildings. Beneath wind-stunted trees were small plaster gnomes fishing amongst the flowerbeds. Their eyes stared blankly out across the lawns, faces frozen in smiles, paint peeling from their beards and shoulders.

The metal doorbell buzzed dramatically when pressed and Helen almost leapt back off the granite step at the noise. Birds were going mad in the trees behind. It was some time before one of the Sisters floated up the parquet-floored hall to open the door for her.

'You're here for the assistant's position, I presume?' the nun asked, looking out past Helen and down the drive as she ushered her across the mat on the floor that read WELCOME.

'I am, Sister.'

The nun stood in the doorway and looked around at the grounds for a time. She muttered something about daffodils and closed the door.

'Sister Francis will see you in a short while. If you wait here she'll be along,' the nun said and withdrew down the hallway she had come, shoes tapping lightly on the floor as she went.

The hallway was lined with tall arched windows and a statuette of the Madonna and Child stood in the centre of every sill. Someone had washed the windows earlier that morning but had been unable to reach the uppermost panes which still held a film of grey dust. She imagined one of the Sisters standing on each of the sills in turn, hoping that the panes she missed would not be noticed. The hallway smelled strongly of the Jeyes fluid it had been mopped with, splashes of the disinfectant evident on the skirting boards. The sun came briefly out from behind the clouds and shone through the stained glass panels that framed the front door, tattooing the wooden floor with coloured light.

She remembered then the afternoon years before of her mother's funeral Mass when she had been left behind in the top-most pew of the church as her mother's coffin was borne back down the aisle. She had been left alone with nothing but the emptying shuffle of the mourners' feet on the wooden floor, desolate and terrified until the sun had found the stained glass stations of the cross, streaming through the windows to dapple the altar and walls with light. For a few moments she had escaped the sadness and tears to play amongst the luminous and miasmic pools. A sacristan had found her when he emerged to extinguish the candles and remove the flowers, taking her hand and leading her out into the world where her father waited, black-suited, weighed down by the day.

'You must be Helen,' Sister Francis enquired, bending towards her.

Helen had not heard her approach. 'I am, I am,' she blustered, shaking free the memory of years before.

'Well, if you follow me now we can be going through a

few of the details.' Sister Francis ushered her towards a door at the other end of the hallway.

Sister Francis was a tall and thin woman, her shoulders curved forwards so that her head seemed to protrude from her body. Her steps were slow and deliberate, as if each one of her long and delicate limbs had to be perfectly aligned before progress could be made. Her movements reminded Helen of a moorhen tracing its way across a bed of lily pads.

'Now then,' Sister Francis said when they were seated at either side of a desk in a room at the rear of the convent. 'You've applied for the job, have you?'

Helen nodded and explained that she had been looking for work ever since the factory had closed down.

'Needless to say we had more than our share of girls coming to us looking for work last spring.' Sister Francis proceeded to recount the names of the girls who had applied to the convent, remarking that a number of them had in their time been taught by the Sisters at the local convent school and that for those girls references would not have been required had a position been available at the time. But there was no paid work to be had at the convent then and in time the girls had moved on elsewhere. 'The lack of work takes the best away from us,' she said, drawing a line under Helen's name which was the day's only entry in a diary spread open on the desk. 'How is your father, Helen? I haven't seen him this long time.'

'He's well. Busy with the fields as usual.'

'That's good, very good,' the Sister purred, knotting her long and bony fingers together. From outside the window came the sound of clipping and soon another Sister appeared, cutting the dead blossoms from a row of standard roses. She dropped the brown-petalled flowers into a paper shopping bag as she moved along the row. As Sister Francis explained the work that the job entailed, Helen watched the other nun's progress, her arms reaching towards the uppermost blossoms, a few of which she could not reach at all. Helen wondered if this was the same Sister as the one who had cleaned the windows in the hallway.

It took her a second or two to register that Sister Francis had finished laying out the requirements of the job.

'Is that clear?' the Sister asked.

Helen nodded that it was, unsure of what she might be getting herself into.

'Your mother, God rest her, was a wonderful woman altogether,' Sister Francis began.

Helen had heard her mother's praises sung so many times before that it meant little to her now. It was something she separated from her own memories and thoughts of her mother so that they might not be dulled by the easy words of others.

'I remember when she used to come into this same office and sit at this desk, just as I am sitting here now, to look over the books for us. She had a great head for the old figures altogether, God rest her.' Sister Francis glanced at Helen's face for a second. 'I wonder,' she hesitated, 'if we might have some of the old ledgers with us still.' She picked her way across the office to a rack of shelves and pulled out a few thin stiff-backed folders.

'Here,' she said, opening the first folder out across the desk.

Helen recognized her mother's handwriting immediately. It had never changed, only the black ink had yellowed at the outer margins of the page. Each page bore her signature in the bottom right-hand corner: Elizabeth O'Shea. In another folder from a few years later the signature had changed to Elizabeth Kelly. Only here was the handwriting flawed: the 'Kelly' uncertain, the two 'l's tightly formed at first but assuming a clearer definition as the months progressed. This, Helen considered, must have mirrored how the marriage had been; those early months of uncertainty that grew into the knowledge that his life was also her life. That signature was constant to the end, all her will going into the checking of those figures as her health slipped away; Kelly waiting on the road outside the gate, the crossword folded across the van's steering wheel.

'Well now,' Sister Francis said when the folders had been returned to the shelves. She uncapped a fountain pen and wiped her hand across the open diary. 'When would you like to start?'

'Does that mean you're going to take me on?' Helen said, surprised.

'Indeed it does. I've no doubt that you'll be a credit to your mother,' Sister Francis smiled. 'And your father too, of course,' she added hastily.

A date for the following Tuesday was arranged and Sister Francis showed Helen out through one of the back doors and directed her from there towards the front gate. As she made her way around the side of the convent she noticed the nun who had earlier been dead-heading the roses tramping about a small vegetable plot, holding the hem of her habit clear of a pair of bright yellow wellington boots as she broke clods of earth with her feet.

'There's no butter,' he said when she came through the door. Boiled potatoes sat steaming at the edge of his plate, skins discarded on to a saucer, a pink wedge of boiled ham sitting amidst the bright green broccoli she had brought from Drimelogue the day before. The butter dish was empty, the last scrapings now melting on the edge of the knife held out in front of his face like a piece of damning evidence. 'How did you let it go?'

'I'm sorry, Daddy,' the refrain coming automatically to her. She had meant to buy some after the interview at the convent but with the excitement of getting the job she had forgotten.

'You know well I can't eat the potatoes without butter, or do you not have a head on those useless shoulders of yours?'

'I know, I know, Daddy. The Sisters in the convent offered me the job there and then and I forgot about the butter. I meant to get some.'

He spread his hands out over the plate like a priest at consecration. 'I can't be eating these now.'

'Daddy, they've given me the job and I start next week,' she repeated.

'I heard you well enough the first time, girl,' he rose. 'Now, is there any butter to be had in this house at all?'

'I'll go out for it.'

Before Helen was born there had been a shop at the gable of King's house, but it had closed after Mrs King had died suddenly of an aneurysm on the brain. As a child Helen had often looked over King's wall at the faded Kellogg's Corn Flakes, Dairy Milk, and HB Ice Cream posters that still hung forlornly in the dusty windows of the shop. Once she had crept up to one of the windows to peer inside and found the shelves and windowsills littered with the husks of upturned bluebottles and wasps, boxes of bathroom tiles and sacks of concrete stacked on the floor, the enormous glass sweet jars filled with screws, nails, washers, rawlplugs, and door hinges.

While Helen had been away, however, Mrs King's eldest daughter had returned with her husband and children to start the shop up again. The faded posters had been removed and replaced with shiny new adhesive ones, the window frames scraped and painted, the floor re-laid with a chequer-board of black and white plastic tiles, the shelves cleared and stocked with all sorts of things. In summer a white ice cream pennant fluttered above the door.

But Kelly shunned the new shop, resenting their bid for success in the face of his. The shop could be seen from the kitchen window of the house and Helen often found him leaning across the sink, hands planted on the taps to support himself as he craned his neck to watch the slow trickle of customers to King's Provision Store. He had warned Helen not to put any business their way if she could help it, but now she couldn't face the cycle into Drimelogue.

The shop was shut so she knocked on the half-open front door.

'*Anseo*,' came a reply from inside, and immediately the children's voices started up in the Irish their parents insisted be spoken at home.

Roisín King's husband came to the door, a cigarette cupped in his hand in the hope that it might not be seen, smoke emerging with his breath.

'Helen, *nach ea*?' he asked.

'*Sea*,' she said uncertainly, '*an bhfuil aon* ... I was wondering if you'd have a half-pound of butter in the shop?'

'Come along now, and we'll have a wee look for you,' he said, taking the keys from where they hung on the back of the door. The Irish disguised his accent but when he spoke in English his Belfast lilt came through.

There was a curious papery smell in the shop, like damp cardboard or plaster, as if the new flooring and paintwork could never erase those countless untenanted years. The old hinged counter remained and Roisín's husband went behind it to get the butter. Smoke from the cigarette still hung close about him in the stale air of the shop.

'We've a pound of butter here if you want it,' he said.

'Just the half would suit me better.'

'No harm at all, I'll cut it in half. Roisín will make use of the other half if no one else takes it.'

He set the block of butter down on the counter and

stood the cigarette on top of the till, the thin stream of blue smoke making for the open door. It was when he took out a knife and wiped its blade on his trouser-leg that Helen noticed how stained his hands were, the nicotine spread across his fingers and nails like a cancerous yellow bloom. She could barely take her eyes off his fingers as he folded the half-pound of butter into a square of grease-proof paper and handed it to her.

'There's nothing else you want now, is there?' he smiled.

She thanked and paid him and waited while he locked up. He took a packet of Major cigarettes with him before he left, stripping it of its wrapper while he waved her off. When she turned back at the gate she saw a match flare in front of his face.

Breathless from running home she unwrapped the butter into the dish and took Kelly's dinner from the warmer drawer in the range. She called him from the fireside and he set down the crossword. Silently she watched him eat. His anger at the lack of butter had not subsided and he would know that she had been to King's shop. Each time he knifed the butter she saw again the nicotine-stained hands and reminded herself to buy a pound of butter in Drimelogue the next day.

'When do you start?' he said later after she had taken his tea to him.

'On Tuesday, early.'

'It'll do you good to be up and about in the mornings for a change.'

'I'm up with the birds to make your breakfast anyway,' she retorted.

He looked across, the rim of the mug pressed against his lip, his expression admonishing her.

'Sorry, Daddy,' she whispered.

*

She bent her head against the rain which drifted and swirled about her face, moving in sheets across the fields. When she looked up from the road there was no seam of brightness on the horizon. The rain was down for the day. The lakes fizzed with falling raindrops as she sped along the causeway between them, the canopy of trees heavy with the weight of water, and when she reached the convent the driveway was varicosed with rivulets of streaming rain. She wheeled the bicycle up the drive, drenched, her head held back and her mouth open to catch the cool drops.

'You'll catch your death, Helen,' Sister Patricia exclaimed when Helen pushed in through the back door. She returned a minute later with some clothes from the laundry room. 'These were handed in for the poor. I'm sure God won't mind if you borrow them for the afternoon.'

Helen stripped out of her sodden clothes in the scullery, her footprints darkening the quarry-tiled floor. She had a momentary schoolgirl thrill at the thought of wearing only her bra and panties in a convent. She pulled on the charity clothes and took out her own to be dried.

'That's better now, isn't it?' the Sister said.

Helen agreed that it was but she resented having to wear the oversized trousers with the elasticated waist that slipped down over her hips and the knitted woollen sweater whose fibres made her skin feel raw.

When she went up to the top floor to see Sister Michael the old nun noticed nothing. Her eyes were like snowflakes, hard and hazy with cataracts. She peered at Helen for some time before registering that she was there at all, her eyes darting about all over the room. A gas heater behind the door beat out into the room so that the atmosphere was like that of an oven, the smell of the nun's decaying body filling the space. Helen would never get used to it.

'Hello, Sister Michael,' she said loudly. 'It's time for your food.'

'Hello! Hello!' Sister Michael answered in a high, reedy voice, her eyes still straining to focus on the girl who now stood over her.

She had shrunk even further, Helen thought. There was hardly any of her left in the bed now, her skin so slack that it seemed her bones might take it upon themselves to get up and walk away without her. Her face was like a walnut shell, so deeply lined that some of her features had completely disappeared. Her hair was dry and brittle, like Helen's mother's had been at the end of her illness, and wisps of it clung to the shoulders of her grey cardigan as if in the face of death they were refusing to let go of her.

The napkin had been cut from an old linen tablecloth and Helen unfolded it across the nun's chest and rested the plastic bowl of baby food upon it. She fed Sister Michael, spooning the glutinous paste between her dry and wheezing lips, scooping up dribbles which made their way down through the hairs on her chin. Every so often she had to stop as the the old woman hauled herself up on to her elbows to clear her chest, phlegm gargling in her throat before sinking again. And all the time Sister Michael's iced-over eyes held steady on Helen's face.

For years Sister Michael had cared for young babies in an orphanage on the outskirts of a nearby town, the illegitimate issue of teenage lust, incest, and accident. She had been heartbroken when the orphanage had closed, her life's work ended. The building was now a youth hostel with empty white flagpoles rising from the front lawn, bicycles leaning against the gable, fair-haired Europeans squatting on the doorstep.

'Your mother,' she began once the food had been taken, 'was the loveliest woman you could hope to meet,' frail voice sailing out through her dry mouth.

Helen switched off as Sister Michael's eulogy continued. From the moment she had set foot in the convent the nuns had made it their business to tell her about how good her mother had been. For them, the teaching of schoolchildren was an elevated state of being, the opportunity to turn young souls into the image of God. They spoke of her as if she had passed away just months before and not almost twenty years ago.

Sister Michael moved to lift herself up to clear her chest and Helen helped her, gently pushing the nun's brittle frame forwards as she filled her drowning lungs. She could feel the terrible rattle inside her and when she looked into the old nun's face after she had settled she saw there the unmistakable dread fear of death. When the Sister attempted a smile only a few uneasy tears came, slipping from her eyes to seep into her lined cheeks. She asked to be given her rosary beads which hung from the bedpost, the varnish worn from the wooden beads over the years, the silver chain subject dulled and bent. She closed her iced-over eyes and set to working her way through the litany of prayer, the mantra that would prepare her for the final journey, fingers working the beads, blistered lips thrumming together.

There was a small framed photograph on the window-sill. Yellowed with time that must have played upon the surface like heat so that the print was minutely cracked, it showed a young nun kneeling in a garden of grass and daisies, squinting into the lens. And ranged before her like trophy fish, five tiny babies, fists clenched to angry faces, legs kicking empty air. Helen set the photograph down and looked out of the window to escape its mute gaze.

The gardens lay neat and tidy in the late afternoon, save for the broken line of hedge trimmings along one border that waited to be collected, the undersides of the leaves brightening the shadows. She lifted the sash window a fraction and the scent of honeysuckle swarmed inside.

She remembered the evening she had stood on the bridge over the river and watched a vagrant woman drag a

Border collie along the foreshore. A vision of her lost child rose now as it had then, eyes open, barely formed hands reaching out for her, asking to be pulled forward into existence. But she could not reach for it. Had it lived, it might have been offered up, nameless and illegitimate, for adoption. Instead it was gone for ever, and perhaps her life was better now for that, but still she felt the tug of loss overpowering her.

When she looked up again it was to find her reflection in the glass, tears sliding so slowly down her cheeks that she felt nothing at all, only the waning of the pain and desperation that had risen inside her. It seemed so long ago now, another lifetime altogether, the memory as blurred as the edge of her vision was from tears.

Sister Michael broke into a hacking cough in the bed beside her, the coarse rattle of phlegm in her throat like an alarm call. Helen held a glass of water to her lips but she would not drink from it. After another attack of coughing, during which she again refused to drink, Helen straightened the sheets, the smell of the spirits used to treat the old nun's bedsores rising sharply from the mattress. A suction machine stood redundant behind the bedside table, the narrow blue hose dangling uselessly. After the first time Sister Michael had resisted any attempt by Helen to help clear her throat with the machine. In truth Helen preferred not to have to use the suction machine, the wet wheeze of the air pump and the sight of saliva and phlegm travelling along the tube disgusted her.

She went to shut the window. A nun had taken a rake to the hedge clippings and they stood in piles waiting to be collected into one of the old potato sacks.

'Emma.'

'But that's a girl's name, Daddy!'

COLM O'GAORA   230

'It was Emma or Triumph, one or the other.'

'Are they cars then?'

'Don't be making fun of me, girl,' he rose. The barley ran out between his fingers and down into the sack at his feet. He clapped the dust from his hands. 'Triumph's the easier variety to grow, but it's the Emma that'll keep the roof over our heads at the end of the day,' he explained.

He had spent the morning at a seed merchant's in Tuam, returning in high spirits with a few sacks of barley and a tin of powder to be mixed with water when the crop needed spraying. For weeks now he had forked and levelled the soil in his two fields, mixing in a half-hundredweight of spent hops he had been given in return for a day's loan of his van. The soil looked dark and rich, each field quartered by baling twine strung between straightened wire coat hangers so that the barley would not be scattered too closely together.

'Where will you sell it in the end?' she said as she watched him change into his old clothes in the hallway. He was too excited to retreat to the bedroom to change, rolling his trousers into a ball and throwing them in a corner while he jumped into the heavy brown tweeds he favoured.

'Minch's might take the lot if there's a good summer, otherwise I'll sell it to the same man I bought it from,' he said, unbuttoning his shirt.

She looked at his chest, skin the colour of pastry, whorls of hair upon his breastbone gone grey, only the arms looking healthy where the sun had tanned them. In time the skin would wither and slacken, become liver-mottled. She had not seen him like this for years. He was getting old, and with it his body admitted its own weaknesses in the face of age. It would be years yet before he would ever submit to it himself.

'It won't be wasted as horse-feed this time, girl,' he said, pulling the grey sweater down over his head.

She held out the bucket while he decanted some of the barley seed into it, folding the sack shut afterwards and leaving it inside the door in case it should rain. No rain was forecast, only the smallest of clouds drifting across the sky on a breeze that was barely noticeable. 'Perfect' he muttered, 'perfect,' swinging the bucket out in front of him and making for the fields.

All day was spent at the sowing, the seed scattered through funnelled fingers and lightly raked into the dark soil that still smelled of hops. Helen spent most of the afternoon sitting on the doorstep and reading a novel she had borrowed from the travelling library. The dog lay beside her, rising only to greet Kelly each time he came back to the house to refill the bucket. When she suggested that bringing the sack of seed out with him would be less effort he looked at her as if she were a simpleton, the seed rattling through a cloud of dust into the tin bucket.

Later she went into the house to set the dinner, taking the joint of over-salted ham from where it stood in a bowl of water and putting it in a pot of fresh water to boil. She chopped the cabbage into pieces and set it aside while she peeled the potatoes which were poor and would be mashed with sour milk.

Kelly was silent while they ate, drained by the sowing, stirring the meringue-like mash with his fork. This was the last of the potatoes stored in the loft. There would be none this year from his own land. As the excitement of the sowing subsided the anxiety would begin to take hold. His brooding silence filled the room as he ate, thinking back over the day's work. 'Is it the right month for the sowing or have I got it all arse-ways?' he muttered to himself between mouthfuls of mash. He stared into the plate as though it could provide an answer.

Kelly spent the rest of the evening carrying buckets of water out to the fields where he used a smaller bucket that had holes hammered into its underside with a nail to sprinkle the dry soil without disturbing the precious seed. As darkness fell he called her out to help with the threading of strips of tinfoil on to the baling twine that would keep the birds away from the seed.

'Come on, Daddy,' she tried again to encourage him to come back into the house. He went over the lines again and again, tearing another strip from the roll of foil where he imagined there was too wide a gap between one strip and another. The sun had long since disappeared beneath the horizon, the sky turned to ink, Kelly moving like a shadow amongst the lines of glittering foil. 'You'll be tired in the morning.'

'It could all be gone by the morning,' he retorted, checking the tension on the twine by plucking it so that it hummed gently. 'And where would I be then?'

'It'll be fine, you know it will.'

'What do you know anyways?' There was an anger in his voice now and she knew instantly she had taken her persuading too far. 'You've not woken to find that everything was gone, have you?' He had moved closer to her now and she could hear the hoarseness of his exhausted breath. The roll of foil twirled like a baton in his hand.

She turned back to the house and in a short while he followed her, one bucket clattering inside the other, the dog yelping with excitement as it circled him.

Lying in the darkness of the bedroom she listened to him moving about the house, the sound of his water in the toilet bowl, the sink filled and his face splashed clean, the scrubbing of a toothbrush. Finally the light in the hall was extinguished and his bedroom door closed, his clothes discarded on to the back of the chair at the dressing table. Helen tried to think what it would be like if he was gone when she woke in the morning, but so bound into the house and the fields was he that she could not even begin to imagine it. The thought disturbed her and she lay awake for a long while with only the sound of the foil strips chinking on the lengths of twine to accompany her into the night.

The tap on the front door startled her and she dropped the few carnations she had been arranging in a vase on the windowsill of the long hall.

'Yes?' she said, surprised to find a young man on the doorstep rather than another of the elderly women who often visited the convent to volunteer their help or old clothes and belongings for charity.

'I'm a nephew of one of the Sisters,' the young man said. 'I heard she's not well and I was hoping to get to see her.' He was tall and broad-shouldered. His hair was collar-length, longer than most men's, but it framed his face and his calm green eyes.

'Which Sister were you looking for?'

'Sister Carney.'

'That'll be Sister Michael then.' She stepped aside to let him in, locking the door after her. As she scooped up the spilled carnations and put them in the vase she explained to him that Sister Michael spent most of the afternoons asleep and that she could hardly talk.

'I just wanted to see her ... My name's Niall by the way.' He extended his hand and she shook it, feeling his fingers folding firmly about hers.

'I'll take you up to see her now.'

On the way up through the convent to Sister Michael's room Niall explained that he had been working on the sites in America for the last couple of years but that he'd had to come back soon after the Immigration Department had started asking for him at the foreman's office. He'd been home a few weeks and wanted to see his aunt before she got so bad that she wouldn't recognize him.

'She's slipped a lot, you know,' Helen cautioned. 'She mightn't know it's you at all.'

'I told my mother I'd come and see her, so it's for her sake as much as my aunt's that I'm here.'

The curtains were drawn so that the strong afternoon sun could not reach the bed where the nun lay. The room was still as death, sepulchral in the fuzzy light leaking through the curtains, the old woman's sighing breath rising and falling unsteadily. The stillness seemed to swallow everything that entered it, hushing their voices as they drew open the door.

Niall went to the bedside and looked at his aunt, his hands resting gently on the steel guard-rail, his soft green eyes tracking the sunken face he barely knew, the feeding tube taped to her nose with translucent blue tape, the rosary beads stark black against the starched whiteness of the sheets. Helen watched him, knowing by his expression that he felt little for the woman who lay dying and that he had only come out of duty to his mother.

She remembered the day she had visited Eamonn in hospital in London. 'You're good to come,' he had said when he saw her, yet in her heart she knew that she had not wanted to see him again but had visited because she felt she should.

It was different with those who were losing their hold on life itself, when the ebbing of their lives made the healthy feel guilty, as if they should take the blame for being spared.

'I think she's waking,' Niall whispered, stepping away from the bed as though in fear of the old woman.

Helen laid her hand on Sister Michael's forehead and the old woman open her eyes a fraction. Her cracked lips parted and Helen held the glass of water to them but she would not drink.

'Your nephew, Niall, is here to see you, Sister,' Helen

said as she leaned in and caught the sour decay in her breath. Death was everywhere in her.

Sister Michael tried to turn in the bed to look about the room but she had not the energy, and with her iced-over eyes she could see little anyway. Instead she blindly lifted a hand for Niall to take, the gnarled joints so disfigured by rheumatism that it was like holding a handful of horse-chestnuts. Her grip was fragile, the effort involved in lifting her arm showing in her quickened breath, and after a short while Niall let it rest on the sheets again.

In death, Helen's mother's hands had rested on the white sheets, tinged with blue but slim and healthy-looking, the skin soft and perfect, rosary beads laid across the shiny fingernails with their pale half-moons.

Helen went to wait at the window while Niall watched his aunt fall back to sleep, her eyelids closing, the tension leaving her body.

'There's not long for her now,' Helen said when he came to the window.

'How long do you think?'

'She'll hardly last the week.'

'I'll tell my mother to come and see her before it happens. She'd be upset if she didn't get to see her before she went.'

'I'll be expecting her.' Helen let the curtain fall back into place.

'Isn't there a great view altogether from up here?' Niall said, lifting the curtain to look out. The sunlight advanced at an angle across the floor until he stood in its way. 'You can see all sorts.'

It was true, although she had never really considered it, that the view from the top of the convent was marvellous. She looked down at the pair of glistening lakes, separated by the impossibly narrow causeway she cycled across each day. The steeple of a Church of Ireland chapel poked out from behind the trees at the other side of the lake, and beyond that lay the town, invisible but marked out by the pall of turf smoke that even on this warm day hung over the rooftops.

'Look,' Niall pointed, 'you can even see the line of the old railway.'

'Where?'

'Look at it there on the far side of the lake, between the trees and the water.'

She leaned in front of him and squinted as she tried to make out the old railway. He was very close behind her, the heat of him like something against her skin. She wondered, if she closed her eyes, would she hear his heart beating? She looked for the railway but could not find it. 'Ah yes, I see it now,' she lied. Her elbow touched some part of him as she turned away. 'We'd better leave her in peace,' she whispered, nodding towards the figure in the bed. The touch of him stayed with her.

'Who looks after the grounds for you?' he said when they reached the driveway. The bedding plants nodded their heads in a tickling breeze, the blank staring faces of the gnomes caught in the sun, the lawns a brilliant green.

'One of the Sisters does most of it, I think. It's nice to walk around in.'

She saw him to the gate and he promised to send his mother up to the convent in a day or two. She watched him walk off down towards the lakes, hair flowing about his collar, descending into the brightness until he had disappeared.

The fields were watched, nothing else could be done. Kelly prowled about the house like a tomcat, looking for jobs that needed doing when there were none. He scraped the paint from two window frames, cursing and swearing when the blow-lamp sent a crack running through the glass. He had to sit down on the floor to calm himself, the metal scraper pinging off the leg of a chair when he threw it across the room. It took him a couple of days to undercoat and gloss the frames and then he was looking for something else to do.

'Would you not fill in the trench out the back, Daddy?' she suggested as she set his dinner in front of him.

He did not answer, the meal taken in silence again, a newspaper fluttering in the strong draught from the doors left open front and back to dry the paint. He looked around at the newspaper gaily folding and unfolding its pages, as if his solemn gaze alone should cause it to stop, but he would not rise to still it with his own hand.

She dropped a book on to the fluttering newspaper.

'Christ!' he started.

'What, Daddy?'

'You made me jump, girl,' he fumed. 'It's like living with a bull in a china shop!'

'Now, now, Daddy,' she soothed, taking the empty plate from him as soon as it was cleared.

'Now nothing,' he stormed, pushing back the seat and tramping outside, picking up his boots on the way.

She watched him from where she took her own dinner at the table, doggedly making his way towards the fields as if his pace could shake off whatever demons troubled him, the dog trailing after him in the vain hope of getting the dinner scraps that had been forgotten in his anger.

The house was as quiet as the convent in his wake, only the front door moving uneasily on its hinges. The smell of paint had all but cleared. She could see him through the window, pacing the nearside of the wall that surrounded the first field, lifting and replacing the hat on top of his head for the want of something to do.

*

Days later everything had changed. A mind that had been blinded to all else was opened to the world when in the harsh and unformed light of dawn Kelly found his fields carpeted with thin filaments of pale green. He gripped the dry stone wall in excitement, lichen coming away on his palms, leaning as far into the field as he dared without bringing the stones over with him. He ran to the wooden pallet that he had once lifted from the factory forecourt and now served as a crude gate, pushing it back on its thick rope hinges and gingerly kneeling down before the barley like a man at worship. There was barely a half-inch of green shoot to be seen as he ran his fingers over the tender tips, their touch like static upon his skin. The aluminium strips looked like bunting to him now.

The few mourners stood around the grave as the priest began the last prayer, the litany of words doled out as easily to this passing soul as to the ones that went before and would come after, always the same. With repetition all import was as lost upon the living as the dead; yet comfort was to be found in the familiar.

'She was a grand age all the same,' someone comforted as they moved on through the other gravestones in the small plot tucked away in a shady corner of the convent grounds. Two workmen waited beneath an apple blossom, leaning upon their shovels, a cigarette passed from one to the other. They glanced at the mourners and then at the mound of topsoil. Soon they would set to work.

'You were right when you said she'd not last the week, Helen,' Niall said, dropping back from his mother and aunts to walk alongside her.

'I'm sorry that I was right.'

'Not at all. Wasn't it a relief when she finally passed away? Even my mother admitted as much after she visited her that last time. She said she didn't recognize her at the end.'

Helen looked up at the mourners who had reached the back gate. The Sisters were bidding the family goodbye, offering their condolences, Sister Francis's tall and wiry frame bent stiffly over as she shook hands one by one. Only a few close relatives had been allowed into the convent to attend the burial and the mourners would go now to Breffni's where the men waited with the children and other relatives. The men would order stout and whiskey for themselves, sherry and brandy for the women, and King's crisps and Corrib minerals for the children. They would stay there for the rest of the afternoon and into the evening, when the same priest would come in with the cards for the lottery that raised money for the local hurling and football club.

Their voices came tumbling back towards Helen and Niall, solemn expressions of sympathy entwined with the nuns' desire to be rid of the relatives so that they themselves could close around the wound like skin around torn flesh. Caught in conversation with Niall she had fallen behind the rest of the mourning party, and they were so far ahead that she found herself alone with him again. In a few moments the nuns would turn back from the gate and see her walking alone with him. When she had taken him up to see his dying aunt the week before it had been no more than was expected of her. This was different; they could read into it anything they wished.

'You'd better catch up with your poor mother there,' she started, gesturing towards the gate where the mourners had gathered. A grey cloud of midges hung about their heads, marking them out on the narrow path between the simple gravestones.

'She'll be fine,' he said, interrupting a story about one of the men he used to drink with in the bars in Boston. 'The rest of the family will be waiting for her in Breffni's, and it'll be easier on her once she's back with them. To be honest with you, she finds the nuns a bit grim.' He smiled, hoping that he hadn't offended her.

'Go on now,' she laughed, 'before I tell Sister Francis on you! Go on!'

He took off after his mother and her sisters, glancing back at her with an easy smile beneath his calm green eyes.

The nuns returned along the path, their shoes crunching harshly on the sharp gravel as though they were treading on broken bones. Sister Francis raised a weak, insincere smile as she came past and Helen caught the other Sister's words: 'She's her mother's daughter all right, turning heads wherever she goes.'

Helen watched the Sisters make their quiet way back to the convent building, the path taking them past the fresh grave where one of the workmen had jumped down into the hole to stamp the soil tightly around the sides of the coffin. He was only visible from the chest up, his lime-green sweater incongruously gay for the work undertaken, a cigarette pinched firmly between his lips as he trampled the soil his partner shovelled into the hole.

She had never heard it said that her mother was one for turning heads. Kelly had never remarked upon her mother's physical beauty and it had never struck her in the few photographs she had seen. She watched the nuns let themselves into the convent through the kitchen door. Sister Francis lingered for a second as she withdrew the key from the Yale lock, her long pale face turned towards Helen's for a second before she too went inside.

One of the workmen reached to help the other out of the grave, their arms momentarily trembling with the effort. 'Gerrup!' they yelled, laughing at some joke or other before setting back to fill in Sister Michael's grave.

*

Her gaze had always transformed the picture of herself into how she imagined herself to be, yet new knowledge was now brought to bear upon the face in the mirror that seemed not hers at all. She bunched her hair on top of her head and tipped forward so that some stray strands fell across her forehead, her eyes heavy-lidded as she squinted at herself. She parted her lips a fraction and bit them to raise the colour in them. She turned to the side and looked at her profile, a flat face and slender neck, small breasts, and a flat stomach. She had none of the curves of the swimsuit girls printed in garish colour on the pages of the *Sunday World*. A teenage thrill re-surfaced as she stretched her sweater collar down to expose a smooth expanse of shoulder, pouting sideways into the mirror. She let it spring back into place when the worn, grey-stained bra strap brought her back to herself.

'Who do you think you are at all?' she said to the empty room. Only the dog answered, setting up to whine after Kelly, who had taken himself off into Breffni's for the evening, the nervous throb of the van's engine shivering down the track to the road below, worn tyres squealing on tarmac smoothed by summer heat.

Her father's room was cool. Behind her hung his shirts, draped over the wire hangers that were hooked on every corner and ledge that would take them, the polycotton limp and empty of form like a skin that had been shed. A bedside lamp burned weakly through a heavily patterned shade, the room disguised rather than revealed. Still, there was enough light to see herself by, and the transformation of herself in her own mind was easier to achieve in such uncertain light.

The dressing table had long since been cleared of things, the facia ribbed and cracked by the influence of heat and water over the years, rings upon rings from hot mugs of tea and honeyed lemon on the rare occasions that he had been laid low by a chill.

She pulled out a couple of drawers stuffed with old seed

packets, balls of string, brass screws, jubilee clips, narrow strips of lead for roof tiles. Old newspapers occupied another drawer. She examined the dates and headlines. There seemed to be no reason that she could think of for keeping them. A few of her mother's things were scattered loosely in a shallow drawer in the centre of the dressing table: a lipstick charred by time, a Miraculous Medal gone fuzzily blue so that the Latin inscription was illegible, a powder puff that smelled only of the empty years it had lain there in the dry darkness.

Amongst other things there was a photograph that had turned almost completely in on its shy self, crackling like a reluctant leaf to her unfolding fingers, the surface splintering into nothing, but enough surviving for her to see her mother at the same age as Helen almost was now.

A formal occasion, the white gloves squeezed into one hand, black patent shoes, a herring-bone suit. One arm had disintegrated, and a black shape concealed the identity of the woman next to her, but her face, at least, was perfect. They were almost identical, Helen and her mother. Those eyes, that mouth with its slightly heavy topmost lip delicately curved and ribbed like the shell of some rare and beautiful mollusc. Now she recognized the same features in her aunt, her mother's sister who had once tried to persuade Kelly to let Helen come to live with her cousins. She had only tried to visit once in all the years since then, Kelly running her out of the place, her husband leaning against the Hillman parked halfway down the track like a getaway driver. In her aunt those same features had been consumed by age and a frustrated life. In death her mother's remained for ever.

The photograph all but disintegrated when she went to put it back in the drawer amongst the other things, curling over on itself as if to keep a secret that was already lost.

*

One by one the small, white onions were wiped on the clean glasscloth, polished like family silver before being placed in the heavy glass jars. When each jar had been filled he decanted a draught of vinegar from an enormous plastic bottle, the vinegar magnifying the tubers so that the tiny web of green capillaries stood out upon their surface. The tops were screwed on as tightly as he dared. He paid a penny to a shop in the village for each of the jars, 'taking them off their hands' was the term he used, and Helen helped out by steeping them in almost boiling water and turning them on to their necks on an old towel to dry.

As the barley occupied every inch of the fields there was little else for Kelly to be doing. The cloches were cleared of the courgettes and peppers by mid-August, the Wavin ribs standing black and bare now at the gable of the house like the upturned skeleton of a currach.

He took to carpentry for a mercifully short time, piecing together a unit to fit around the bathroom sink. Proudly he set the ZPII zinc shampoo bottles and Flash powder box on the shelf he had fitted beneath the basin. But he had not accounted for the damage water would do, pulling the joints asunder, nails rusting inside weeks, so that he took a hammer to the whole thing and destroyed in minutes what had taken him days. Afterwards, only his pencilled-in measurements remained on the wall beneath the basin.

Sister Raphael, who was responsible for the upkeep of the convent grounds, had taken to teaching Helen the Latin names for the trees, shrubs and flowers that filled the abundant acres the convent stood in. Helen had heard Sister Raphael reciting the names as she made her way along the paths that circled the main building, the snapping of the shiny secateurs trimming vowels from the longer names. *Ononis, Melilotis, Parnassia*. Helen picked up the words easily.

She found that they popped back into her head at strange times: at the kitchen sink when her hands were steeped in suds and her mind had drifted out across the stitched-in fields, the scattered pockets of sheep in the distance, the cracked tiles on the roof of King's shop where she had been only once and never again. *Saxifraga, Capsella, Leucanthemum.*

'*Digitalis purpurea,*' she once said in the van as they waited for two men to push a trailer through a gateway, the heel of Kelly's hand held hard on the horn while he glared at the men.

'What was that?' he said, the horn dying off, the men looking around in surprise.

'*Digitalis purpurea.* It's the Latin name of that plant beside the gatepost there.'

'That's a feckin' foxglove is all it is.'

'Same thing, *Digitalis purpurea.*'

'A foxglove.' The horn started up again louder than ever until the trailer was pushed through the gate.

A damson tree which stood within sight of the scullery window was the first sign of the end of summer, the tightly bunched fruit so swollen with juice that it stuck out at all angles from the branches that sustained it. The fruit began to fall, the white-dusted purple packages thudding on to the mown grass.

'*Damsonia,*' Sister Raphael muttered to herself as she lifted her head from a colander she had been scouring. Shaking the water and suds from her arms she went to fetch some of the Sisters. 'Helen, I'm glad I found you.' She tugged at Helen's sleeve. 'Be a good girl and tell the Sisters that the damsons are down, the *Damsonia.*'

The wasps were there before them, livid stripes upon the unbroken velvet of the fruit. The nuns beat them off with dishcloths, their faces reddened from the exertion and illicit excitement. Sister Raphael brought out the colander and they all worked together to fill it with the damsons. Sister Aidan popped one into her mouth and pronounced it a touch too bitter but the others ignored her. A milk crate was brought to stand on so that the uppermost branches could be reached and Sister Francis was called out from the office to help, her narrow limbs reaching slowly and deliberately out towards the precious fruit.

Great fuss was made as the jam was made, each Sister knowing from years of practice what needed to be done, but nothing would stop their clamour of excitement. Only evening prayers interrupted the hot work for a couple of hours, and by midnight the jam stood in two-pint jars on the windowsills to cool, the muslin lids tightly secured with thick elastic bands.

Helen was given a jar to take home with her the following afternoon. Kelly watched from where he stood at the edge of the first field as she left the bicycle at the gable and took the jar inside. 'What's that you have there?' he roared, but she pretended not to hear, his shout following her inside until he gave up.

When he came in later he was full of good humour, admiring the jar of damson jam, holding it up to the light and gazing through it, getting her to promise him the fine glass jar once the jam was finished.

'Do you remember the redcurrant jam we made years ago from the few plants we had out the back?' he asked. 'Wasn't it only awful?'

'I do, Daddy.'

'Like vinegar jelly it was.'

'And I thought you liked it.'

'I said I liked it on account of you going to the trouble of netting the plants so the birds wouldn't get at the berries, and you were only a wee thing at the time too. I didn't want you to be disappointed.'

'I thought it was horrible – I can still remember the taste of it.'

'It's as well for us both then that the redcurrants were destroyed the next winter or we'd have gone on fooling ourselves for ever.'

'It is,' she laughed, remembering the morning that she woke to fields christened with hard white frost, the redcurrants curiously black as though fire had taken to them.

The evening wore on, Kelly taking to interrupting the filling in of the crossword to share the memory of some incident with her. It had always occurred in her childhood, a knock or a fall she had had, a foolish schoolteacher, a pair of trousers the dog had once wrestled from a neighbour's clothes line and dragged back to the house. Her mother was never mentioned, as though their lives had only begun with her passing. In truth, there was nothing to be confronted with these memories that rested easily on them both.

Kelly turned the tuning dial on the radio, watching the unsteady progress of the ivory white peg behind the narrow glass panel. The speaker snarled with static and interference as he sought the station and when he found it he turned the volume slowly up, his head tilted away as if listening for sound from another source altogether. The polite tones of an English weather forecaster crackled into the semi-darkness of the room, the measured pace of his delivery like a nightbalm so that as she listened Helen felt her head grow heavy.

'It looks like the good weather is going to hold, girl,' Kelly whispered excitedly, rubbing his palms together.

'What, Daddy?' She had almost fallen asleep, the paperback she had been reading folded shut into her lap.

'Ssh, now. It's Valentia next, then Rockall.' He was poised, leaning forward out of the chair, the tips of his fingers pressed together to make a cage of his hands. A smile broke on his lips and his eyes brightened as the weather report was read out.

'I think I can wait another day at least before I start the cutting. The drier the barley is the better the price I'll get.' The forecast had moved north to Donegal and Rathlin Island and he was full of talk again. Weather always came from the south or west. 'You won't see me bringing a crop to the stables in Gort to sell as animal feed this year. It'll be as dry as old bones by the time it's loaded into the back of the van and there'll be no gentleman in a white coat from Minch's able to tell me otherwise this time around.'

'How long will the weather hold?' she asked, anxious that he not get carried away and his plans come to nothing. The winter would be unbearable.

'Long enough,' he said. 'I'll have it down in two days. Another day for drying and I'll get cracking on it. I'll tell O'Neill in the morning that I'll pick up the thresher Friday – I'll have him out of bed at dawn, the laggard!'

'How will you manage the fields in two days, Daddy?' She knew that there was almost a week's work in the cutting.

'I'll manage,' he sharpened. 'I've managed before and there's no reason why I won't manage again.'

'But it's a while since you had a go at it so quickly. You're not as young as you once were.' She was wide awake with concern for him now. 'Would you not start it tomorrow and take it a bit easier?'

The dial on the radio was turned up, reports from the North Sea coastal waters booming into the room filled with shadows, any argument impossible now.

He was standing amidst the fields when she set off for the convent the next morning, the barley a bronze colour under the narrow early sun. The ears swished to and fro in the gentlest of winds that was like a golden symphony to him. A benign smile hardly lifted from his lips when he raised an arm to wave her goodbye.

At breakfast he had not been able to sit still while she put the bacon, egg, and fried bread on the table for him, getting up to go to the window as if the fields might have vanished while he had his back turned.

'Your breakfast will go cold if you don't sit down to it,' she had warned.

'Let it,' he said bluntly from the window, his hands searching for loose change in his pockets to be busy with. An anxiety had come into his voice. So close was he now to achieving his goal that any mistake or misfortune could condemn the year's work to dust, return them both to another year of wanting.

As she set out into it, the clean clearness of morning erased all concerns. When she crossed the stream it was running slow and clear, long lines of weed weaving in the current, fry shoaled in the margins. The heron would have them later. She cycled on, rhyming off the names of the plants in the verges as she went, *Cirsium arvense, Tragopogon pratensis, Centaurea cyanus.*

Kelly worked on the front door which had been stripped of its blue paint a few weeks beforehand and had begun to look as if it had been dug up from some bog or other, the wood scorched in places where the flame had rested, scraped back against the grain in other places where his patience had been lost in the tedium of the task. He loaded and reloaded the brush with the grey undercoat as he went, spreading thick paint across the wood, rivulets coursing down the inside of his wrist. When he went to shake them from his skin a thin spray would issue from the brush and arc across the doorstep and down the front of the old shirt he wore. 'Merciful Jesus!'

he said each time, standing up to remark on the mess that would be forgotten the instant he turned his head to gaze at the barley ranked out in the fields.

When the outside of the door had been cloaked in grey he made himself a sandwich and a pot of tea, taking them out to the step with him. Blackie came and sat between his knees as he ate and drank. Kelly only noticed the clouds when he followed the dog's gaze out towards the horizon. The clouds were gathered there like great ships waiting offshore for a moment when the tide would turn in their favour. He hurried inside and returned with a kitchen chair to stand on so that he had a better view over the countless stone walls. He stood for almost half an hour, watching the movement of the clouds as they broiled on the distant edge of the sky. But there was no wind to move them anywhere and, becalmed, they dissolved as he cursed the brush that had dried hard in his hand.

The sun shone innocently. Once the brush had been loosened with petrol siphoned from the van he opened a tin of navy gloss paint and set to covering the front door, ignoring the streaks of grey that showed through from beneath.

The first drop fell like an exclamation mark upon the new paint. Another shattered into a multitude of shining droplets before his eyes. He stared, astonished. Another fell, and another, before a drop caught him on the back of the neck. In seconds there was rain falling on his head, his shoulders, and on the hands that reached to lay the brush across the gaping mouth of the paint tin. The sun still shone, brilliant and innocent, but a wind had risen and a lone cloud had navigated its way overhead, its grey curtain of rain trailing across the fields.

'Ah! for feck's sake!' Kelly ran for the gable of the house where the scythe waited, its blade already razor-sharp in preparation for this moment. He tested it with his thumb, smiling at the high rasp of it against his skin, before hoisting it on to his shoulder and making for the fields, Blackie running on ahead of him, infected by Kelly's own excitement.

The rain had long passed, the road dry again, only a few drops suspended beneath the laddered leaves of the roadside ferns. Nothing but a shower. It had been enough, though, to raise again the smell of the asphalt. Helen breathed it in as she cycled home, damp like the memory of so many summer days before.

Only a few yards' progress had been made when she arrived at the house, Kelly standing amidst the narrow clearing in the barley, his face coated in sweat and chaff. The instant he noticed her watching he picked up the heavy scythe and set to work again, the blade swung back and forth as it gathered and sheared through the sheaves of standing barley. Even she could tell by the stubble that it was hard work and that he was not prepared for it, the shorn stalks rising in uneven wedges from the soil. Kelly was lifting his head, dragging the blade with him.

'You've started then, Daddy!' she called, coming along the edge of the field to where the clearing started.

'I have,' the short words pushed out with his breath. The scythe swung heavily, his wrist twisting to control the travel. The barley shuddered and fell, and each time he reached to clear it from his path before swinging again. 'Just this minute,' he continued after a short while. 'I thought I'd make a start on it, and I'll have it cleared in no time at this rate.' He stood up and looked out at the horizon, wiping his palms on the seat of his trousers. His hands, softened over the course of a summer spent waiting, were already blistered and raw, a thumbnail split down the middle so that the pinkness beneath was exposed. 'Would you go in there now, like a good girl, and fetch me out a mug of tea and a sandwich?'

While the kettle boiled she went to the doorstep and watched him working the field. Every so often he turned around to approach the barley from another angle but each time it was the same and no rhythm came to carry him through the work. In his youth he had worked field after field, the scything motion as easy as instinct.

The kettle rattled dully on the range and she went in to make him his sandwiches, cutting the Cheddar into thick slices and laying it upon the buttered soda bread. The kitchen knife was sharp, honed on the same whetstone that he would have used to prepare the scythe. The whetstone had been handed down from father to son, folded into an old cloth cap for safe-keeping, the grey slab of stone wetted with spit before it would meet the blade.

What if he should have an accident? The scythe could pass through his shin and he would be crippled, she thought. What then? She could never look after him alone, locked up with the bitterness an accident would sharpen in him.

She wheeled the bicycle out to the edge of the field, lifting the bottle of tea off the handlebar and leaving it together with the foil-wrapped sandwiches on top of the wall for him.

'Good girl yourself!' he cried from the far corner where he had gone in the hope that the slight downward slope might make it easier for him. 'Are you off again?'

'I told the Sisters that I'd put in a few hours for them this afternoon.'

She cycled as hard as she could, bent over the handlebars to make herself smaller against the freshening wind. All around her the fields were down, farmers taking advantage of the good weather to cut before any risk of rain. Already the hay had been ricked. The women and children had been busy the previous weekend. Only Kelly was foolish enough to try to push it to the wire, yet she would do anything now to save them both. She pushed harder and harder on the pedals, the bicycle racing down the hill towards the factory that had been daubed with Republican graffiti, names and ages of hunger-strikers in the North that had died for an unknown cause.

The poor light inside the back room of the pub was filigreed with cigarette smoke. A weak bulb hung over each of two pool tables whose felt surfaces were pock-marked with burns and small tears. A youngster fired a cue-ball from cushion to cushion, the white ball searing the gloom, chipped varnish gleaming on the cue that was too big for his short arms. Each time the boy succeeded in hitting a pocket the cue-ball would rattle dully through the hidden innards of the table.

A jukebox fizzed with empty static in the far corner, youths collected like phantoms around its neon-lit playlist. Helen peered at them in the hope that the glow would illuminate one she recognized. An argument broke out about what to play next. AC/DC said one, while another insisted on Whitesnake or Motorhead. Pink Floyd, someone kept saying over and over again like a mantra. Eventually a tall shadow reached through the throng and spread his arms across the display and stabbed at the keys. 'Not again' came the collective groan, as the needle engaged and they mocked in unison: *'A year has passed since I wrote my note . . .'* The tall shadow melted back into the gloom and, like moths, the others converged on the display again.

'Yeah?' one of the youngsters greeted Helen as he struck the cue-ball.

'The man behind the bar said that Niall was in here.'

'Niall!' he yelled above the music. 'There's someone wants ya!'

The faces at the jukebox turned and the figure that

had been sitting next to the jukebox rose and came towards her.

'Helen,' he started when he saw that it was her, guiding her on ahead of him and through the bar to the street outside. She squinted at the brightness that was lost to all those inside. 'You should have got Mick to fetch me out,' he said. 'He should know better himself.' He pushed his hands into his pockets as if embarrassed at something. 'I was only in there myself to see if the lads knew of any work going.'

He had carried the smell of the back room of the pub out with him and it hung in the air about them, thick and stale. She didn't know what to say and the silence stretched.

'I'll speak to Mick before I head off home. You shouldn't have to be going in the back at all,' he added.

'You're not busy this afternoon then?' she asked.

'Things to be doing as usual, but nothing special,' he said, his forehead a puzzle of furrows. A question lay on his lips but did not come.

'I was wondering,' she began, 'if you might help out?'

'Sure. With what?'

'Daddy's only cutting the barley now and I'm afraid it'll kill him if he takes the two fields on by himself,' she blurted. 'He says there's rain on the way and the barley will be spoiled if it isn't cut straight away.'

More words, more fears came pouring out until Niall took her arms and steadied her. When she lifted her face he saw she was on the edge of tears.

'Come on, I'll borrow the brother's car and we'll be out there in no time at all.'

The Ford buzzed out the road, her bicycle rattling noisily in the boot where it had been tied with rope. At the factory they pulled over to tie down the lid of the boot which had worked free. The car smelled like the back room of the pub. The floor at her feet was littered with Champion spark plugs, light-bulbs, and swatches of greased paper. Niall apologized and explained that his brother was a car mechanic. The fields she had earlier cycled through reeled past her, the car bouncing over the bridge at the stream with the exhaust pipe scraping the road.

Kelly barely lifted his head as the car came slowly up the track towards the house. Only when it drew to a halt did he stop to watch the couple getting out and going into the house. 'Helen!' he roared but her name could not carry the distance.

'Slip into these old duds.' She offered Niall a pair of Kelly's old trousers.

'I've a pair of shorts on the back seat of the car. I'll jump into those instead – it'll be hot work. Have you noticed how close it is at all?'

'There'll be rain then, I suppose,' her voice rippled with anxiety.

'It'll hold for long enough to get the work done, then it can rain all it likes.' Niall went into the bathroom and pulled on the shorts and laced up a pair of his brother's steel-capped boots he had found in the boot of the car. 'There's no blade in the country that'll go through these boots then!' he laughed as they went to the gable for the second scythe.

She unfolded the whetstone as they went across to meet Kelly, who was already standing at the first wall.

'Daddy!' she called, running ahead when Niall slowed to rub the edge of the blade over the whetstone. 'Niall's going to help you cut the fields.'

'There's no help needed,' he rebuffed. 'I'm making headway into it by the new time. It'll be all but down by the time he's home in that car of his.'

'Mr Kelly.' Niall put out his hand but Kelly's did not move from the shaft of the scythe. 'You've made great time with that lot altogether.' Niall was careful to praise the little work that had been done.

The set of Kelly's face softened and he couldn't stop

himself from turning around to look at the narrow clearings he had made along two edges of the field, but still he said nothing. The breeze caught his collar and pushed it over where it set to fluttering against the film of sweat on his neck.

'It's awful close this afternoon, Mr Kelly,' Niall offered, and they both looked to the horizon where clouds had again begun to simmer.

'I'd better get back to it,' Kelly shortened, lifting the scythe and swinging it out in front of him. He made for the other end of the field.

When she went to him he warned her away from the scythe with a broad sweep of his arm.

'Will you not let Niall help out, Daddy? It'd all be finished in half the time.'

'I never asked for any help. There's no need for it.'

'Daddy! You won't get it done on your own. The rain will spoil it and then where will we be for another year?'

'Another year, is that it then?' he said quietly, stopping the scythe in mid-sweep. 'Another year of it, is that what you're afraid of girl?' He turned to her. 'Every year since your mother passed away is a year I've put before you.' His face was almost blue with rage. She could see words gagging in his throat. 'When I was let,' he added.

Her eyes were stinging with tears before she knew it. He picked up the scythe and swept it through the barley with more vehemence than ever before. She stood behind him for a few minutes watching him work away at the barley and the anger that boiled inside him.

'Are you still there, girl?' he said. He had advanced a yard at most. She was wiping her face with the sleeve of her cardigan when he turned to check on her.

'Look,' he said, nodding towards Niall who had come into the field but had stayed at the gate, teasing the dog. 'The lad doesn't even know what a day's work looks like, and I ask you now, who comes out to the fields in a pair of shorts?' He cocked an eye at her and she smiled. 'And would you look at the legs on him, like two straws hanging from a hayloft.'

Still her tears came. She looked at Kelly and was caught in his cold gaze, much as her whole life had been caught in it. He watched the ebbing of her sobs. She straightened and went to say something to him, but he cut in:

'I suppose there'd be no harm in him clearing the few yards around the gate before that stupid dog has it flattened with its tomfoolery.' He lifted the scythe and swung it in a wide arc through the crop so that she could come no closer and would ask for nothing more. He had set back into the work.

'Daddy says you can be clearing the way around the gate,' she announced to Niall, beaming as if some great gift had been handed to her by her father. 'He's afraid that Blackie will ruin the few yards with his play-acting.' The dog looked up at her when she mentioned its name, then disappeared into the barley.

'Get out of that, you hound, you!' Kelly roared, waving at the dog which turned and ran back towards the gate.

Niall took the scythe and swung it through empty air a few times to measure the balance of it. He adjusted the butterfly nuts to set the angle of the blade and tried again and again until he was happy with it.

'You know,' he started, 'it reminds me of the summers we had when I was a teenager and I used to stay on the cousins' farm for summer. When we were very young and knew little we'd be sent into the hay fields to clear the corncrakes, smashing the nests with sticks, the eggs tossed into the air like *sliothars*. We'd be spattered with bits of yolk and shell from throwing the eggs at each other. Then one year we were given sickles and scythes and sent to clear the corner of a fallow field that was knee-high with thistles.

There was no damage to be done there, and the next year we were given our place with the real men in the real fields. We thought we were made then.'

When he was happy with the pitch and balance of the scythe he set into the barley, cutting slowly at first until the rhythm found its way back to him. Soon large folds of barley were being laid out along the edge of the field.

'You're well on your way there, Niall,' Helen said when she brought out two mugs of tea and a plate of quartered sandwiches.

'I'm doing my best anyway.' He was glad to take the rest.

Kelly was still cutting away at the top of the field, bent over with the weight of the scythe, the sweeping movement of the scythe arrested by the bunching of the stalks on the dulling blade.

'God bless the tea,' Kelly praised, letting the scythe fall suddenly to the ground, the great curving blade pointed to the sky like a sundial. He put his hands on his sides and breathed deeply for a while.

The sun had begun to sink across the sky but still the other fields swum in a heat that turned the air to liquid. Barley dust was everywhere, caught in Kelly's eyebrows, stuck to the moisture on his lips and the sweat on his face and neck.

'It's awful close, Daddy.'

'It is,' he answered, but would not look up to the horizon where the rainclouds still threatened, preferring to work blindly on and not see that it might be all in vain.

From across the field came the shearing sound of the scythe as Niall went back to work.

'Has he that patch cleared yet at all?' Kelly asked casually, gazing at the ear of barley circling in his mug.

'He has indeed, and more.'

'And more?' Kelly started. 'Did I not say . . .' He emptied the dregs on to the stubble. The last sandwich was stuffed into the side of his mouth. He lifted the scythe, braced his legs and swung viciously into the barley.

Midges came with the dusk, vast clouds of them that rose so thickly from the soil that they seemed to take its dark colour with them. The light thickened and closed about the house and the fields as the midges fed on the sweat that slicked both men's skin. Helen stood at the door and watched them disappear into the gloaming as the sun began its setting, the shadows so long that they stretched into each other. Soon the day would become night and with it the work would have to end.

Niall had cut so much of the field that by now the two men worked within talking distance of each other, their backs turned. The sounds they made as they worked grew louder as they came closer to each other, Niall advancing up the gentle slope while Kelly came down it. The rushing sweep of the scythe as it reaped the barley and the barely audible backward glide of the blade, its blunt edge gently swept against the stalks as if in cruel forewarning of the destruction to come.

'We'll soon have it finished, Mr Kelly,' Niall said as he brought the scythe back to start another row.

'There's another field to be cleared yet,' Kelly said gruffly.

Later, in the near-dark, Niall stood aside and allowed Kelly to clear the last row of the field. 'You made great work there, Mr Kelly.' Again he was careful to praise the older man's efforts.

'Aye.' Kelly surveyed the field, the barley lying across the stubble like a thick blanket. 'We can only wait now and see if the rain holds off.' He looked up at the sky where nascent stars had begun to fix their place in the heavens. 'The worst part of the work has been done anyways.'

Niall took the scythes around the side of the house while

Kelly undid his bootlaces at the doorstep. The dog stood on the step and tried to lick his cheeks but the rough rasp of its tongue irritated: 'Get out of that!' The dog pushed away off the step, slinking off to lie beneath the wheel-arch of the Ford, where only its tongue showed in the dimness.

'There's tea on the table for the working men,' Helen enthused when they came in. The front room smelled of strong tea and bread. The jar of damson jam that Helen had brought back from the convent stood opened but Kelly would not touch it, preferring to devour slice after slice of soda bread with only butter to accompany it.

'They're a great pair of scythes altogether, Mr Kelly,' Niall said as a second pot of tea was set to draw. 'Where did you get them?'

'Here and about.' Kelly went in to fetch the whetstone which he carefully unfolded from the cap and set down on the table like a black block of butter, examining the edges for evidence that it had been forced against the blade. He wrapped it up again and set it on the mantelpiece. He slumped into the armchair, spreading the newspaper out to its full extent and proceeding to read through a piece that he had read before, sometimes glancing up to where Helen and Niall sat at the table talking in low voices for fear of disturbing him.

'I'm off looking for digs in Loughrea next week,' Niall announced.

'Why?'

'There's a rake of council houses going up there and there's plenty of labouring work to be got on the sites,' he explained. 'The mother wants me out from under her feet in any case. She got used to having one less mouth to feed while I was away, and the other brother will never leave home. What's there to keep me anyways?'

Helen's heart sank. That last sentence like a door

shutting upon another life. There was always the leaving, friendships and loves broken, all irrecoverable.

'Do you think you might be going soon?' she said casually.

'The sooner the better. I'd want to have a few pounds together before Christmas at any rate. They'll be expecting the same presents as I took home from the States with me last year.'

'They can't!'

'I've a reputation to keep up, you know,' he laughed.

Kelly shook the newspaper out and raised his eyes to the ceiling.

After a while their conversation ebbed. Helen asked if Niall would like more tea but he declined. They watched the moths beating time and again against the window pane.

'There was a lot of barley sown out east this season, Mr Kelly,' Niall offered.

The paper went limp and Kelly stiffened visibly in his chair. He mouthed something to himself and resumed his reading.

'Fields of it,' Niall continued. 'It's as well for them that risked it to have the good weather this year.'

'Is it now?' Kelly said firmly, dropping the paper on to his lap.

'It is,' Niall enthused, happy to have engaged Kelly in conversation at last. 'A week of rain at the wrong time and it would all have been spoiled.'

'Is that so?' Kelly feigned ignorance, waiting for the young man to lead himself into the trap.

'Aye. It's fierce fussy stuff, the barley. The price will drop after such a dry year, mind.'

Kelly picked something from the turn-up of his trousers and brought it to the table. He laid an ear of barley down in front of Niall. 'Do you know what that is?' he asked coolly.

'Barley,' Niall said, glancing at Helen.

'I was afraid you might need reminding.'

Kelly went to the window and looked out at the night.

'There's no call for that rudeness, Daddy,' Helen said angrily, but Kelly didn't want to hear and didn't turn around. 'I'm sorry,' Helen apologized. 'Daddy's tired after the day.'

'Isn't it about time you were making your way back home now, boy?' Kelly started from the window where he still stood looking out, hands squashed in his pockets, rocking back and forth ever so slightly on his heels. 'If you were to put the skids on you might be back at your bar stool in time for the last shout.'

'Daddy! After all the help you've had today!'

Niall rose from the table and took his jacket from the back of the chair. He lingered uncomfortably in the doorway between the front room and kitchen, as if waiting for something more from Kelly, but the older man's back was still turned. When Helen showed Niall to the door he said nothing in answer to the excuses and apologies she made for Kelly.

'There was no call for that, Daddy,' she said. The Ford rumbled off down the track. Blackie's shape could be seen against the glow of the rear lights as he half-heartedly chased it towards the road.

'After all he—'

'He'll be the better for it now,' Kelly cut in. 'The sharp edge of a tongue on a rough diamond the like of him never did any harm.'

'He's no rough diamond,' she protested.

'Did you ever hear the *ráméis* out of him. The get up of him and all. He might be king of the jukebox or the pool table back in Breffni's but he's no king of the fields.'

'He did his best, Daddy. What more can he do?'

'Aye, he did,' Kelly sneered as he turned away from the

window. 'Blackie! Blackie!' the shout ringing in the hallway and then fading almost to nothingness as he went off down the track in search of the dog.

All day was spent in the fields. She raked the first field while Kelly cut the second. The sky was overcast, clouds the colour of smoke that could darken within an hour and turn to rain. Sometimes he would come to the wall and urge her on and she would move the rake frantically to and fro, gathering the barley into long rows while he watched and warned her again of the rain that could fall at any minute. When he went back to the scythe she would slow and straighten herself, wishing for the still, hushed silences of the convent; the smell of rising bread in the kitchen; the dazzling colour of the flowerbeds.

As she raked she wondered where Niall was; in the back room at Breffni's she supposed. At breakfast Kelly told her that he had often seen Niall there, leaning up at the service hatch, asking for change for the jukebox or trying to persuade Mick to turn the television around so that he could watch it while he played pool. 'Where do you think all those dollars he earned in the States went?' Kelly mused.

It would be a while before she would see him again. She had taken a week's holiday from the convent to help with the fields. There would be no need to cycle into the town until the following week.

'Get on with it!' Kelly's shout burst from where he stood at the wall and she dropped the rake in fright. The field was almost finished. Soon it would be time to go into the house to make tea and sandwiches and then she would start on the second field, raking in the rows that Kelly had cleared.

*

A tractor and trailer were parked at the top of the track when she came out with the tea and sandwiches. She almost dropped the mugs and plate when she saw Niall scrambling down from the cabin and Kelly marching across the fields towards him. She ran, the tea spilling hot upon her hands, the sandwiches sliding back and forth across the plate. The dog set to barking then stopped to sniff the tractor tyres in turn before lifting its leg to one of them.

'Daddy!' she yelled but the two advancing men seemed not to notice her. She could hear Niall shout something out to Kelly, who stopped in his tracks and looked down at the ground for a moment. He looked up again, past Niall, at the tractor and trailer, and after a few moments he started roaring something at Niall who then turned swiftly on his heel.

'What's going on?' she panted, the mugs almost empty, her hands slicked with hot tea. The dog was trying to paw the white bread away from the ham inside the sandwiches which had fallen to the ground.

Kelly followed Niall on to the back of the trailer. The heavy throbbing of the tractor engine drowned Helen out and they worked as if their lives depended on it. Within twenty minutes they had the thresher assembled, Kelly shouting instructions at every opportunity while Niall worked in silence.

'C'mon, girl, we'll get cracking on that first field,' Kelly said. 'There's no time to be lost. C'mon.'

'Daddy?' she enquired but he was gone, off towards the cleared field where he began lifting stones from the wall and heaving them to one side. When a gap had been cleared Niall reversed the trailer into the corner of the field. Finally she was able to speak to him.

'It was the only way I'd get him to do it,' he explained when she asked what he was doing. 'I made him an offer he couldn't refuse – it's my uncle's thresher. His fields are

cleared and he won't miss it for a couple of days now.' He
nodded at Kelly who was raking in barley as if gripped by a
fever. 'He knows now he doesn't have a choice, otherwise
the whole lot would be damned to hell.' He turned to look
at the horizon where the rainclouds were stirring.

'All hands on deck!' Kelly shouted.

Helen helped feed the thresher while Niall cut the
second field. Slowly the trailer filled with barley, the chaff
blowing about in great flurries. When the first trailer was
full Niall took the van out to McDonagh's farm and borrowed a second. By seven o'clock the fields were down, the
trailers piled high with barley. They waited until the last
moment before covering the trailers with tarpaulins.

During the night the first thunderstorm broke over
distant hills. Minutes later rain began to fall, great drops of
it, thudding on to the tarpaulins and drumming on the roof
of the van. Thunder rumbled overhead like drums. Kelly
got up and went to look out. Every door and window in the
house rattled in its frame until the front door was closed
over again and he padded back to bed. Blackie barked and
whined, only settling when the thunder had moved on and
could be heard no more. Afterwards a thick steady rain set
to pattering on the trailer covers, reminding her of the sound
of rain on London pavements and the ticking of a bicycle
chain.

Niall arrived in the morning to take the barley to the
grain merchants. He waited in heavy yellow oilskins,
bemused, rain spilling from the edge of the hood, while
Kelly decided which merchant to honour with his business.
Eventually the decision was made; they would make the
journey to Minch's in Athy where a better price was paid for
good malting barley. 'There's no Emma going to end up
as horseshit this time around!' Kelly yelled into the rain as
he slammed shut the van door and followed Niall out to
the road, the wipers clearing a heavy film of water from the

windscreen. Niall waved from the window of his brother's Ford and tooted the horn a few times as they went out the road until the noise was drowned by rain.

They were gone two days. Only Niall returned to the house, Kelly stopping off at Breffni's to tell all and sundry about the price Minch's had paid.

'I suppose he was up to high-do on the way back,' Helen asked.

'He was indeed. I had hardly a minute's sleep in the B&B in Athy. As soon as I'd nod off he'd wake me again with some story or other, or wondering if he'd have got a better price elsewhere. Once there was daylight in the room I couldn't get back to sleep with his snoring.'

Helen found it hard to hold back a laugh.

'What are you smiling at?'

'I can just see the two of you in the room together and Daddy out cold on the flat of his back. There's no waking him if he's sleeping like that, you know. He'd take you to within an inch of your life if you were ever to wake him from sleep.'

'There were times I'd nearly have laid him out on the flat of his back with my fist if I'd had the guts to do it.' His clenched hand swung emptily through the air as he spoke.

'No doubt you would,' Helen giggled.

It was useless for him to be angry now and Niall joined in the laughing. Later, as the day slipped into evening and there was still no sign of Kelly, Niall recounted more of the stories Kelly had told him over the two days. Helen made him dinner, and afterwards he had scones with large dollops of the damson jam that Kelly had spurned. He was full of praise for the cooking and Helen was happy to cook for someone who appreciated her efforts, wishing she had had some fish or veal to offer him instead of the roast ham, broccoli, and potatoes.

'I must be getting back.' He rose from the armchair when she went to switch on the lamps. 'The brother will be wanting the car to take Madeline courting.'

She did not want him to go. Kelly would be the worse for drink when he came back, crashing into the house, full of himself, demanding.

'I might meet himself on the road.' He pulled on his jacket and brought his empty mug in to the sink. 'If I'm lucky,' he added drily.

She stood for a long time at the window, watching the rear lights of the car blurring into the night. When she turned away the empty plates on the table disturbed her, crumbs of the scones he had earlier enjoyed, the knife smeared with the damson jam he had relished. The napkin she had taken from her mother's box with a red rose embroidered into one corner lay loosely folded on the side plate where he had left it. She did not want to clear the table of these simple things that lightened her heart, but Kelly would be home soon.

The car had been parked outside Breffni's a few days before. With her heart thumping she had wheeled her bicycle across to say hello to Niall, his legs stretched out beneath the engine. 'Hello,' she had said, but it was not Niall whose oil-blacked face smiled back at her, but his brother, boiler-suited, the delicate machinery of a fuel pump poised in his oiled hands like the heart of a small mammal. 'Hello yourself,' he greeted, astonished at the way she blushed and almost burst into tears, running back across the road with the bicycle swinging this way and that.

Now it was Niall who was waiting at the convent gates, the car idling hoarsely.

'How's the ould fella?' He broke into a laugh.

'Don't let him hear you saying that!'

'I was wondering if you'd come out for a walk one of these evenings before the warm weather's gone altogether?' he said as soon as he had come around the car to her.

'Well . . .' she blustered. 'Why not? We might as well make the most of it, I suppose.'

They arranged to meet outside the gates on the Friday evening when she finished work, and she made her excuses to Kelly that the Sisters wanted her to stay on a little later. The sweet scent of the last of the honeysuckle that crowded around the convent gates hung heavy in the air as she walked out to wait for him, but he was there already, leaning against the railing of a green water pump, his father's old bicycle lying on the ground. They took the road that divided the lakes, crossing to the railway embankment that he had pointed out from Sister Michael's room a few months before.

Rust clung to the old railway line like a red moss. Most of the wooden sleepers had been removed and the long stretches of metal track now wove unevenly along the embankment that skirted the lake, where sunlight caught the broken-stemmed reed beds at the edge of the water.

'Do you remember the trains at all?' she asked.

'I don't, but my brother told me often about how they'd come here to lay coins on the lines and watch the train flatten them. They waited for hours the first couple of times, but then one of them looked up the timetable at the station and they hadn't to wait so long after that.'

They laughed at the thought of the schoolboys waiting for hours with nothing to look at but a few coppers on the railway line.

'I saw your brother the other day, working on the car. You don't look a bit like each other.'

'Everyone says that so I suppose it must be true.' He picked a flat stone from amongst the old ballast and skimmed it out on to the lake where it danced once, twice, and sank with a muted splash. 'I don't see too much of your father in you, now that I think of it,' he said.

'No. There's not much we have in common. Except a home perhaps.'

'And the fields.'

'God, no.' She stopped to look at him. 'The fields are his.'

'You don't share his temper anyways,' Niall humoured.

'That's for sure.'

'Did your mother look like you at all?' he ventured. 'I hear she was a schoolteacher.'

With a pang she remembered the photograph she had discovered months beforehand in the dresser in her father's room. Now it appeared in front of her, as if memory had projected it on to the surface of the lake. She could hear Niall apologizing: 'I'm sorry, Helen, I shouldn't have asked, only ...' The memory must have shown in her face, she thought, like the surprise of something sorrowfully new.

'I don't know, really,' she said softly. 'I don't remember her well at all. I was very young when she died, you know.' The words were trotted out, as if they were the very words her mother's death prepared her for.

A heron turned far out on the water, a grey smudge against the far-shore trees, lazy gait of the bird upon the lake whose surface was mottled like hammered metal.

'I know,' he offered. 'My own mother spoke of her from time to time. She was well known, and everyone was fond of her.'

'Thanks,' she said, but she was not grateful. The walk had been pleasing and simple until her mother had been mentioned. She had liked the easiness of his company, the reflective stillness of the lake, the warm evening seized upon. It had changed now, the lake looked suddenly deep, the reed beds shorn and rotted, the trees brown and lifeless where the waning sun caught their uppermost branches, his words like thorns. 'Shouldn't we turn for home? It'll be dark by the time I get in.'

'I'll show you the Abbey first,' he said. 'It's only at the bend, where the river comes in. Come on.' He walked ahead and she followed him.

The roofs had all gone and the thick stone walls rose gaunt and bare into the sky, like pieces of an incomplete jigsaw, fading sky showing through the empty arched windows. Cattle grazed around the walls but none, it seemed, would cross inside where the grass grew long and green. In places the walls were blackened where fires had been lit.

When Niall pointed out the inscriptions hewn into the flagstones that formed the floor of the old chapel she hopped off them with a shriek. Niall laughed but she was not happy to offend the dead.

She followed him up into the round tower, feeling her way along walls that had been smoothed by a multitude of hands before hers. Their voices rang off the thick stone walls as he told her about how he and his schoolfriends would dare each other to go further up the steps each time. One step higher than any of the others was enough to win the dare, and they would write their names in white chalk upon the highest step possible. Niall had always won because his long arms could reach to a higher step.

When they reached a sign that read: BOARD OF WORKS – DANGEROUS STRUCTURE Helen urged him to go no further. He teased her by pulling the sign aside and inviting her to lead the way to the top. 'No way,' she protested, clinging to the step for fear that he might want to pull her up. They were very close. The coolness inside the tower turned breath into clouds of vapour that rose upward into the spiralling darkness. She felt her heart beating fast, afraid that in the amplified space he might hear it. He turned and looked at her for a moment before moving back on to the step between them.

'I want to get back, Niall,' she said, and any spell there had been between them then was broken.

'Right so.' He guided her down and all the while she felt his eyes upon her back as though they sought to inscribe his name across her spine, like the chalked steps of his childhood and the names of the dead carved in stone.

On the way out he showed her the fish pool at the end of what was once the kitchen, a great stone bowl sunk in the floor where the monks would keep fresh the fish they caught from the stream. Its curving base was covered in broken glass and tin cans.

She was relieved to be back on the path that led to the railway with clear sky above her again and away from the blank staring windows of the Abbey and the choking gloom of the round tower.

'It was a great place when we were kids,' he said as they came away. 'We had great crack running courting couples out of it. You'd see them through a window, skirts lifted up and a bare arse heaving away for all it was worth. At the time we didn't know the half of what they were up to, but there'd be a great silence when you'd next meet them in the chip shop in town.'

They crossed the river, the water rattling amongst stones.

'Afterwards, when we knew the whole story, we'd sneak up as close as we could and watch them going at each other hammer and tongs before they got cold. We'd a great time looking back down the pews at them on a Sunday morning whenever the subject came up in a sermon, and that wasn't often.' They both laughed and the humour banished the shadow cast upon them by the old Abbey.

'*Trifolium pratense*,' Helen recited as they came past a burst of clover on the way back.

'What's that?' Niall asked and Helen explained how Sister Raphael had taught her the botanical names of countless plants and how she could rarely pass a particular flower, shrub or tree by without repeating its name to herself.

'Well,' he remarked, 'you never know when that knowledge might come in handy.

'Mocking is catching,' she laughed.

They walked on through the thickening light, the slow pace they had set themselves kept to so that the path seemed it could go on for ever.

'Will your father be at home when you get back?' he probed.

'He will if he's not already out looking for me.'

'Surely he'd leave you to your own devices. You're an adult after all.'

'Not in his eyes, I'm not,' she said. 'There's only one way anything should be done and that's his way.' She could see by Niall's expression that he was waiting to criticize. 'Often it's the right way,' she defended.

'Always?'

'Often is often enough.'

He knew not to travel any further along this avenue of conversation. She would defend until he was forced toward silence.

Gorse brightened the far bank of the lake and even in the fading light the last of the yellow flowers could be seen spread out upon the spiked branches like torn rags. Niall stopped at the water's edge where a line of stones ran into the lake for a few yards.

'I used to spend hours out on this point,' he said, stepping out along the stones until he could go no further. 'I'd come here with just the rod and an envelope of flies on an evening like this and cast for all I was worth.' He looked out across the lake as if he had recovered that feeling of being a child at the mercy of a great spread of water. 'The rod must have been three times higher than I was.' He smiled and swung his arm as if the rod was there again but no cleat appeared on the water's surface this time. 'Hours I'd stay here, not knowing how deep the water I was casting into was but too afraid of my own disappointment to find out.' He looked back at her standing at the point where the edge of the lapping water percolated through the stones. 'And do you know what I would catch?'

'No.'

'Bats. They'd come skimming across from the trees to pick up the flies as it got dark and get tangled in the line I had out. Christ, but they'd put up a great fight altogether!' His laugh broke across the water like the report from a gun. 'Taking the hook out of them was the worst part because they've skin like our own, as soft as anything, and you'd be afraid they'd die of fright in your hand.'

'That's horrible,' she said, turning to make her way back on to the path.

The stones rattled loudly and water splashed his trousers as he hurried back after her.

She listened to his efforts to catch up as she made her way back, cursing the water that darkened his jeans and the hoof-ruts in the soft verge that his shoes caught upon. She imagined him alone at the lake in summer evenings, the unwieldy rod like a spire against the sky, casting in vain for fish that had deserted the shallow margins before slipping up to the Abbey to spill his own urgent seed on the stones as he watched a couple's furtive lovemaking, the cries and whispers of their ecstasy like the despair of a bat he had earlier held in his palm.

'Sorry,' he panted, coming up behind her. 'I didn't mean to upset you.'

'Never mind,' she said, crossing her arms and bending into the approaching night as though it were rain to be got through. It was late and she was anxious to be home.

They found the bicycles back where the railway line crossed the road. The old signal box was ruined, the clapboard sides torn asunder to be used for fencing in fields all around. Iron levers poking out of a thick nest of nettles were all that had been spared in the plunder. Each autumn the county council would spread fresh tarmac on the old rails set into the road, and each winter frost would crack the surface so that by Easter the metal was showing through once again.

'I'll come back with you along the way,' he offered.

'There's no need.' But he insisted and in the end she was glad of the company. When he turned back she stopped to listen to the hoarse creaking of the saddle and the crush of the tyres on the roadside stones. She listened until he was gone and then she made her way up the track to the house.

The day for burning arrived, the wind finally turning to blow from behind the house, stiff enough to drive the fire without causing it to run out of control and send wide black fingers through the stubble that would leave gaps untouched which would then have to be torched one by one.

Helen saw the wedge of thick grey smoke drifting across the fields as she came home. She stopped the bicycle and got off to walk. Kelly would have her out spreading the fire with sticks, rooting the stubble apart so that the embers could burn down into the knotted roots. She hated the work, the cloying smell that stained her skin for weeks afterwards, the holes that appeared in the thickest of old skirts that Kelly tied with baling twine around her ankles, and worst of all the smell of her hair as it singed in the heat. When the hat was removed her head would always be covered in feathers of hair turned to grey ash. Once, when Kelly had soaked the hat in water she thought she could feel the droplets simmering and fizzing upon her scalp.

The burning was almost finished by the time she arrived, Kelly walking along the fire-line with a fork, poking about in the embers.

'You timed it well,' he said, turning his blackened face to her. A spark had eaten through the middle of one of his eyebrows and from it rose a thick smudge of ash where he had licked his thumb to wipe the spark away. The old dressing gown he wore over his duds was thickly coated in ash and down the middle of his back hung a complete stalk of barley that had in an instant been transformed into a grey and brittle carbon fossil.

'It was the soonest I could get away, Daddy,' she countered.

'Was it now?' he smirked. 'Go on in with you and get the sticks.'

The sticks were brought out, old fence posts that had been hardened by years of rain and sun which Kelly had then split and sealed, the ends hacked into a point with an axe. Together they beat the stubble with the sticks but the fire had been well set and in the end it was all done within an hour.

Kelly seemed disappointed to finish so early and once he had sent her back across both fields in search of lingering embers he called time on the work and they went back to the house. The sticks were rinsed and their clothes thrown in a basin to soak. Kelly took the first bath and left a thick black ring upon the porcelain for her to clear before she could wash herself. She cursed him as she watched the grey soap suds circling the plughole.

The smell lingered in the house for weeks afterwards. She would open a press or a wardrobe and the smell of burning would reach out to her, recalling the day and all the others of the years before it. She wished for the years of potatoes when there was no burning to be done, and the only smell that lingered was that of the spent hops that were brought to the village on the back of a truck from Dublin and portioned out in the Square, Kelly offering to scoop the leftovers from around the tyres and out of the corners as a favour to the driver.

Niall came to meet her at the convent gates more and more often as autumn moved towards winter, as if every evening spent together was to be their last, as if winter would take everything with its frozen embrace.

Sometimes Niall borrowed his brother's car and they drove to another town where they were not known and where they bought tea and drop scones in a shop run by an Englishwoman whose husband farmed salmon up in Killary Harbour. The big front room of their house had been converted into a teashop with half a dozen round tables and old, mismatched kitchen chairs plundered from a dump in Galway city. Helen and the Englishwoman shared memories of London but the Englishwoman said she did not miss it and would never go back. There was a bitter reserve in her voice which convinced Helen that the woman had not come to Ireland of her own accord, but Helen did not want to cause hurt by probing further.

When Niall did not have the car they often took that same path out along the old railway line, but they never revisited the ruined Abbey, Helen turning her gaze away from the grey tower that rose through the trees.

Once they followed the track out to an old railway station, its platform rotted to nothing, the skeletal columns and beams of the waiting room choked with creepers and ivy, the tiles long since plundered from the roof of the ticket office. Swallows had nested in the angles of the old rafters but the nests had already been abandoned in the flight before winter.

'Are they gone early this year, do you think?' she asked Niall.

'I don't know.' He shrugged his shoulders. 'Where do they go to anyway?'

She thought then of Martin Kane, who would have surely known if the swallows had flown early and to what continent they had fled. She wondered where he was now. She had not been past his family's house since she had visited his mother a few weeks after she had come home from England. She had heard nothing of him in the town.

'Are you all right, Helen?' Niall looked concerned.

'I'm fine,' she broke, rubbing her arms. 'Just dreaming. Don't you think it's getting cold?'

He breathed out and watched his breath cloud and fade into the dusk. 'I suppose so,' he said and they turned for home earlier than ever before.

On a Saturday afternoon Niall met her early from the convent. She had planned to leave before the preparations for the evening meal would start and in the end Sister Carmel sent her out before four o'clock and she found herself daw-dling at the gate, watching a flock of geese move about the lake, as if unable to settle for more than a minute in advance of their migration to the south. She felt as giddy as the geese, her limbs trembling and butterflies rising in her stomach as she waited. She had not seen Niall for almost a week, the length fallen from the weekday evenings so that there was no light to walk by. When the clocks were put back even these hours stolen from the weekend would disappear.

'Hello,' she said, getting into the car. She wanted to throw her arms around his shoulders and hug him.

He reached to kiss her gently on the cheek as he always did when they met. It was all she could do not to turn her mouth towards his so that his kiss would meet her lips rather than her cheek.

As they drove out around the lake she felt a wildness in the air that seemed to run also in her blood. Falling leaves raced into the windscreen, a mare shimmied at a fence and galloped away, its hooves thudding like heartbeats, a rabbit froze on the road for an instant before bolting for the safety of the roadside ferns. She recognized the shorn stumps of the copse that she had once seen two men clearing, the white scars of shavings across the tilled field that was stubble now. They said very little and she did not ask where he was taking her. She imagined that he did not know either.

They would always, it seemed, be drawn to water, the car turning off the road to track along a smooth river. Niall stopped the car so that they could read a memorial plaque which had been fixed to the side of a hump-backed bridge. A mansion house looked down on the river and bridge from its place on the hillside, framed by white paddock fencing, a herd of blonde Charolais cattle tugging on bales of hay, a Land-Rover idling at the front door. A boat fretted on its mooring where a landing stage had been built at the end of a cinder path that led down from the house.

'Isn't it just lovely here?' Helen remarked.

'It is, but if only I had the money they have,' Niall nodded towards the house.

'It's not everything.'

'Maybe.'

'Who knows if they're happy at all? There could be someone sick or bereaved for all we know. What difference would the money make then?'

'Well, it'd be a private ward and an oak coffin in any event,' Niall laughed, and they went on across the bridge and in through a wood where the light was shut out and everything changed. The mansion house was momentarily visible through the trees and then disappeared completely as if a blind had been drawn across it.

'They call it the Black Forest,' Niall whispered as the

car's tyres crunched across a mat of pine needles. 'They gave it the name after it went on fire a long time back and for years it was nothing but acres and acres of ashes. My grandmother says it was sparks from the old steam train that set it alight, so there's no fear of that happening again.' He wound down the window and the thick pine smell poured in.

He pulled the car over at a passing point. 'We can take a short walk before it gets too dark.' He helped her over a stile and into the trees. The ground was covered in dry needles that had turned a single shade of brown-grey. Here and there clumps of grass poked brightly through, like a green oasis. The whole interior of the wood seemed petrified, as if every quality of light had been sucked out to leave it like a sepia-tinted photograph. The silence seemed as endless as the forest. No birds sang and nothing seemed to move, as if the forest, like the light, had at one time been frozen.

She held tightly on to Niall's arm when he helped her over the stile and did not let go afterwards. They went on through the trees, blind as pilgrims.

'We'd better turn back soon,' she said when they reached a place where a tree that had come crashing through the canopy of branches lay across the path. It was if the forest had been torn open, clouds and the trail of a jet showing in the patch of sky above their heads. Poor light fell down through the gap, as if weakened by the journey through the trees, but still it brought some brightness to the rust-coloured bark, and the saucers of fungus sprouting from the joints between branch and trunk.

'We can wait here a little while,' Niall said sitting down on the fallen trunk. 'We'll be in the car long enough on the road back and anyway I'm glad of the fresh air.'

She sat down next to him and shivered. The cold beneath the trees had eaten through her coat and her teeth began to chatter. She leaned in towards Niall to steal his warmth and he put his arm around her. When she looked up at him he bent his face down towards hers and kissed her mouth. They drew away for a second as if recognizing each other for the first time before their lips met again. She felt the heat returning to her body, the wildness that had been in the air when they set out now gathering again. She sought his lips out with her tongue and then his tongue was probing her mouth too. She felt his hand reach for the buttons on her coat and she did not want to stop.

When he undid her shirt and pulled the bra up over her breasts the sudden cold spread goosepimples across her skin. They stopped for a moment so that he could lay his coat on the ground beneath her. When he entered her she felt the heat of him rushing inside and out again as he moved between her legs. Her fingers reached out and gathered handfuls of pine needles. Amongst them she found a pine cone. Her eyes opened to the cold wash of memory; a swan's nest, a gift given up at the roadside, the warmth of something that had burned in her for ages afterwards. She squeezed the cone as tightly as she could, closing her eyes again as if to blind herself to the returning memory.

He gasped her name as he came, coating her neck and breasts with quick kisses that felt like forest flowers blossoming upon her skin.

'Was there some pleasure in it for you?' he asked when they had lain in the thick silence for a few minutes after it was over.

'Of course there was, of course there was,' she reassured. 'There was every pleasure in it.' The cold came at her again, harsher now in the wake of the lovemaking so that she reached to pull up her coat that he had laid over them. He took off his sweater and spread it across her shoulders when he noticed how she shivered.

'Are you not cold yourself?' she asked. He sat up beside her, bare-chested, his trousers bunched around his knees. She stroked the filigree of hair that ran down from his navel and he looked back at her. She recognized the air of amazement that surrounded them, the suddenness of their lovemaking that had taken them by surprise.

'I didn't mean it to happen so fast,' he said.

'What?'

'Well, you know.'

'Don't be silly.' She touched his cheek with the back of her hand. 'It was as well that it happened now as any time. If we'd waited it might not have happened at all.'

The Charolais cattle were gone from the paddocked field when they came back over the bridge. Lights glowed softly in the windows of the mansion house. A child pulled back a curtain to peer out into the dusk. The Land-Rover swept up the drive and a woman in wellingtons got out to open the garage doors.

'They've a grand home to be getting back to,' Niall said as they came past.

'All the same, a home is what you make it,' Helen advised.

When they were out along the road a bit her hand began to hurt and she lifted it up into the glow of the dashboard lights. A pattern of tiny marks was etched into her skin, each raising a thread of dark blood where the edges of the pine cone had cut her. She looked out of the window, away from Niall so that he would not see the brightness that filled her eyes and fell slowly down her face.

They collected the bicycle from inside the convent gates and put it in the boot. The pub signs were flickering into life as they came through Drimelogue and Helen slid down in the passenger seat so that she wouldn't be seen when they stopped to let a tractor turn around in the Square.

'Are you afraid to be seen out with the likes of me, is that it?' Niall laughed as the car pulled away on to the main road again and she was able to sit back up in the seat.

'Not at all,' she said. 'But if word ever got back to Daddy that I was taking lifts in the car with you he'd never let me out of his sight. I'd be brought everywhere in the van.'

'He's going to know soon enough.'

'He'll be told when the time is right.' She laid her hand over his on the gear stick. 'The worst thing would be that he heard it from a stranger. He'd never forgive me.'

With the turning back of the clocks their evening walks ended, and they took to meeting after she finished work in the convent, the few hundred yards along the road that divided the two lakes stretched out to make every step count. The first time Niall reached to take her hand she refused it, afraid that someone would come along the road and see them, but the next time she slipped her hand inside his and swung his arm to and fro. There were days that Niall was called away for some casual work in another town or on his uncle's farm and she would still wheel the bicycle along the road, the dynamo throwing a limpid orange shape before her, the moon rising over the reed-fringed lake. She would wheel the bicycle until she had crossed the lake and at the old railway line where the steel tracks glinted in the tarmac-adam she would wait for a few seconds before mounting the saddle and cycling quickly home.

Kelly was not in the fields when she came home on the Saturday afternoon before Christmas. The warmth of the Sisters' Christmas pudding, and the memory of the tree and the decorations in the front hall of the convent were still with her. The old-age pensioners of the parish had spent the afternoon in the convent. The sacristan had borrowed the parish priest's Toyota to ferry them from their homes during the morning and now his evening would be taken up with bringing them back. The Sisters had been cooking and cleaning since Thursday morning in preparation for the Saturday and it had been a great success. The brandy enticed the old women to sing, and Thomas Mahoney managed to break into a rebel song before he could be headed off by Sister Michael who had been waiting for him to start but was called to the telephone at the wrong moment.

The house was cold, the range had cooled for want of stoking and in the front room the lights were out and the fire had all but smothered in the ashes. Kelly was asleep in his armchair, the newspaper spread across the floor where it had fallen. He was snoring gently, a thin dribble issuing from the corner of his mouth.

She took a couple of sods from the basket and set them in the fire, quietly encouraging the ashes through the grate with the poker. She took a sheet of the newspaper and spread it across the hearth and almost immediately the flames leapt high into the chimney, throwing into stark relief the angry and declaiming face of the Reverend politician on the second page. She held the newspaper up until his eyes began to scorch in the heat. A plume of smoke rose to the ceiling but at least the fire had taken again and would not have to be cleared and reset.

'Daddy.' She shook him gently awake when the dinner was ready, a steaming bowl of potatoes sitting on the table.

'Wha ... What?' he stammered, angry for a moment until he realized where he was. He wiped the dribble from his chin with the back of his hand.

'Your dinner's ready, Daddy.'

'Right you are, girl. Right you are.' He got up stiffly and came to the table.

Afterwards she brought in a jug of sweet whipped cream and warmed a measure of brandy in a tin mug on the range. She poured the brandy over three pieces of Christmas pudding she had brought with her from the convent and set light to it. The ghostly blue flame danced for but a few seconds. Kelly watched it die.

'Pudding gives me awful heartburn,' he said, picking up a fork and taking a mouthful of pudding. 'I suppose it can't be helped.'

'Daddy,' she said quietly when he had finished the pudding. She had been unable to finish her piece, nerves seeming to force her throat closed so that she could not swallow. 'You know Niall, don't you?'

Kelly glanced up from the plate where he had speared a final raisin on the end of his fork. 'I do. Why?'

'You know I've been doing a line with him since a while back.' Her words, so carefully thought out and rehearsed during the cooking of the dinner, seemed lost to her now. 'I should have told you that before, Daddy.'

Kelly's face darkened and he laid the fork back on the plate. He nodded. 'I have eyes and ears too,' he said and waited for her to continue.

'Well,' she blurted, feeling that she might be sick, 'Niall has asked me to marry him.' She felt tears coming to her eyes, her mouth dry, the tension pulling inside her chest. 'To be his wife.'

'I know what it means,' Kelly said coolly. 'I don't need it explained to me.' He got up and took his plate and fork into the kitchen, dropping them into the suds so that water splashed on to the floor. 'Is there a drop of tea on the way at all?' he said as he picked up the newspaper and sat back into the armchair. He looked at the scorch marks on the paper and then across at her, waiting for an answer.

'Yes, Daddy,' she hurried. 'There is.'

Part Five

THE DOG WAS slumped between the open back doors of the red van, ears twitching to scatter the flies that gathered in the corner of its closed eyes. Heat rose in plumes from the van and turned the fields beyond it into a fluid vision. The fields looked unreal, Helen thought when she went out to call the men in for their lunch, as unreal as if they were the landscape of a dream.

The men worked the big meadow below the house, the air thick with yellow pollen from the crop. Sweat beaded on her husband's shoulders, his hair lying in wet tangles on the nape of his neck. Every so often a slap rang out as he crushed insects that alighted to feed on the sweat. Kelly worked at equal pace alongside him but his slack and liver-mottled skin was dry and the insects did not trouble him. The men looked at each other when she called out to them and Niall raised his arm to let her know they were on their way.

'The rape'll be the making of us yet, Niall,' Kelly was saying as he came into the house. 'Mark my words.' He stood in the doorway for a moment to enjoy the coolness inside. A yellow halo of pollen marked the place where he had stamped his boots on the front step.

Niall propped the scythes up against the front wall and followed Kelly inside. 'Oh yes,' he agreed, ''twas the best idea you've had this long time.' He clapped Kelly on the back as they sat into the table.

'It's awful warm outside, isn't it?' Helen asked when she brought a plate of sliced beef to the table. The men sat with their knives poised over the rectangle of yellow butter just as the scythes had been poised over the crop of oil seed rape.

Niall withdrew his knife.

'You go on now,' Kelly said.

'No, you go on.'

Kelly took a corner off the butter and spread it on a slice of bread while Helen peeled clingfilm from the meat.

'It's awful hot,' she said again.

'Well,' Kelly began, pointing out at the fields with his knife, 'they said we'd make nothing out of the fields. Won't they look like right eejits when we go to cash the co-op cheque at the counter on Friday? Won't they?' He thumped both elbows on the table and looked at Niall while pushing a heel of bread and beef into his mouth.

'They will, they will indeed,' Niall humoured. He had had his doubts about planting the oil seed rape but with the crop almost harvested he was happy to be proven wrong. Other farmers had travelled out to examine the crop as it grew and at first Kelly had been delighted to show them around the two fields. When he realized that he was only helping them plan their own crops for the next season he refused every further request to visit the fields. A weekend was spent adding an extra line of stones to the walls around the fields so that nothing could be seen.

Niall picked up the salt cellar and shook it over the beef.

'There's a man likes salt! What! There's a man likes salt!' Kelly bellowed, a lump of half-chewed meat rolling over his lip and down on to the floor where the dog would later venture to claim it. When Kelly laughed his features creased and folded but his eyes were still on his son-in-law, waiting for a reaction.

Niall vigorously shook more salt on to the beef and Kelly laughed even louder, thumping the table again and again. The prospect of walking out of the co-op on Friday with the cheque held between both hands for all to see excited him so much that he could not contain himself.

Helen looked around at them and saw again the loose folds of flesh beneath her father's shoulder-blades, the twin freckles that had spread with age and gravity so that they were like two small eyes on his shoulders. She had cut his hair for him on the night before they had started work on the fields and now there was a crescent of angry red skin along the nape of his neck where she had trimmed it back hard with a razor. His hair had turned almost completely grey and only a very few dark hairs clustered about his ears. His freckled shoulders and slack-skinned back shook as he laughed out loud, the angry red skin creasing as he bent his neck to breathe in between laughs.

Niall looked across the table and caught her gaze. His eyes looked blank and humourless in the face of Kelly's mirth. She smiled weakly at him but his expression never changed. It was the same silent exchange that had taken place countless times in the twelve years of their marriage.

In a moment, as always, Kelly would notice and ask him what there was to be looking so glum about, and 'Aren't we the best little operation in the parish?' Then Niall would change in an instant, cracking some coarse joke he had heard in the hurling club's dressing room or in the back bar at Breffni's where he sometimes went to play pool. The joke would throw Kelly into fits of laughter, the plates and cutlery rattling on the table as his body shook. Niall was as trapped by fear as Helen had once been.

There was a small, hollow buzzing from beside the sink

where a bluebottle had dropped into an empty Guinness can. Helen came out with the men and shook the can until the fly escaped.

'At least it knows a good drop when it sees one,' Kelly remarked as the scythes were taken up again. They walked out of the shadow of the house and made for the fields. 'Blasted heat,' Kelly said, fingering the raw line on his neck. 'Blasted bloody heat.'

Helen cleared over after them. She noticed again the brown water stain that patterned the kitchen ceiling and which showed up more in the strong afternoon sunlight. The builders had been back twice since the house was built but each time the rain found another way through the roof tiles and on to the plasterboard below. For a long time after the stain had first appeared Kelly had mentioned it day in day out, bemoaning the poor skills of the roofers and claiming that no short-cuts were ever taken with the building of the old house. 'The best of everything' was what he liked to say, and for a while the phrase was adopted in his absence by Helen and Niall until eventually they forgot about it.

When she went to the back door to shake crumbs from the tablecloth Helen looked across at the old house whose lime-washed walls were no longer white but grey. The chimney pot had been sealed with an upturned metal bucket Kelly had once used to water his crops with, its bottom and sides peppered with holes so that it looked more like a colander. Paint flaked from the doors and window frames. She recalled the many afternoons Kelly had spent stripping and repainting them in years past, cursing and shooing away the crane-flies and ladybirds attracted by the heavy smell of paint. As a child she had prised the crane-flies from the doors with a pin, limbs as thin as hairs, wings like maps, their bodies sectioned like sticks of sugar barley.

Kelly had turned the old house into a repository for things that were broken or redundant but for which he intended some purpose. He had bought a job-lot of old Garda bicycles from a retired sergeant in Greenford with a view to restoring and then selling them to the university students in Galway. The heavy black bicycles had filled her old bedroom for years, chains clogged with rust for want of oil.

All sorts of containers were stored in the old house: steel barrels Kelly had pilfered from roadworks, a glass buoy found washed up in Salthill that was now used for storing seeds, numerous buckets of various fertilizers, the water tank he had removed from the attic and filled with sharp sand for spreading around the lettuces to keep slugs at bay. Things seemed stored like so many souls awaiting resurrection.

Helen and Niall had returned from their honeymoon in Portmarnock to find his armchair at the fireplace in the new house that still smelled of damp plaster. A bed was made up in the second bedroom that looked out on the fields.

'You've lived all your life in mine and I see no reason why I shouldn't see out my days in yours,' he had said with such firmness and confidence on that first night that they had been too afraid to go against him. Only the next day did they realize that he had gutted the old house, tearing out the kitchen cupboards, disconnecting the plumbing, and removing the internal doors. He would not and could not go back.

She folded the tablecloth and set it down on the dresser. She took a fat paperback from the shelf and tried to get into the story of a pair of women competing for the affections of the new vicar in their Gloucestershire parish, but the story was told in such a dull and wooden manner that she felt nothing for it and the afternoon heat sapped at her concentration as well as her energy. Irritated, she returned the book to the shelf and noticed that the sink had not been emptied. Circles of grease and breadcrumbs coated the surface and she reached in to check for lost teaspoons.

Later, she went out to the doorstep and sat down to watch the men.

'What'd I tell you, boy!' Kelly was roaring out in the fields, his voice coming clearly through the stillness of the hot afternoon. The heat could not blunt his mood. Niall answered him and although she heard him speak she couldn't make out what he was saying. Soon Kelly's breath began to run out and there was longer to wait between his shouts as he paused to lean on the scythe whenever he thought that Niall wasn't looking. Niall had caught him resting on the scythe during the harvest two years before and had said nothing for fear of angering Kelly. This year, however, the weakness would not go unexploited:

'Resting on the laurels already, are we?' Niall would taunt.

'This blade wouldn't cut butter,' came the quick reply. 'It's catching in everything and I have to stop to free it. We'll take the stone to them tonight and they'll be as right as rain in the morning.'

'Right you are, Kelly! Right you are!' but the words were barbed, and they both knew it.

She looked up at their dark shapes punched into the bright fields. Dragonflies passed across the tops of the yellow oil seed rape, their silver-blue wings busy like wound clocks. A pair of swallows darted from the roof of the house to feed on the dragonflies, intercepting them in mid-flight, their translucent wings drifting into the great mass of yellow like fallen ghosts.

While the swallows fed and the men laughed, she returned to the kitchen and filled the sink with hot water and set the men's shirts to soak. A new washing machine had stood in the corner of the kitchen since Christmas but her old habits died hard and at least, she comforted herself, the hand-washing killed time.

The rest of the afternoon was spent around the house

and in the small vegetable garden she kept outside the back door. She grew thyme and basil in small terracotta pots Niall had once brought her back from a business trip to Wicklow. Kelly disdained the taste of the herbs, but a leaf of basil was always folded into the ham sandwiches Niall took with him to work. While she weeded amongst the radish and lettuce plants the sun began to go down and the breeze-block frame of the house in Sweeney's fields cast its shadow across her back.

As he had grown older and slower, Sweeney had been unable to look after every field in his ownership and in the space of a couple of years holiday cottages had gone up on almost every plot of land he owned. Planning permission was only applied for once the houses were built. By then it was too difficult to refuse. In any case the county planning officer spent a fortnight every summer at Sweeney's lodge on the Erriff river, and a bottle of Jameson was delivered to his door each Christmas Eve. None would go against him. Except Kelly.

Kelly protested as soon as a JCB appeared in the field behind the house, the local councillor dragged from his bed and driven out to see the illegal foundations being laid. 'What'll be done about it?' Kelly had fumed, shaking his fist at the JCB driver, who cowered behind the controls but continued with the digging. 'I'll see to it,' the councillor said, getting back into his Nissan. 'You'll do more than see to it!' Kelly had roared, and for the next fortnight the councillor was roused from his bed at dawn until the building work was stopped. The JCB rumbled back across the fields and on to the road, leaving herring-bone tracks of mud and stacks of breeze-blocks that reached towards the sky like fingers.

I've no mind to be going at all,' Kelly blustered as he searched the kitchen for the cap he kept the whetstone in.

'What would I want to be going out on a drive for? What use is it to me anyways? What good would it do?'

'Here's the cap, the stone's inside.' Niall picked the cap off the windowsill and Kelly grabbed at it.

'Were you hiding it on me or what?' Kelly accused. 'It's a wonder you never thought of hiding it in the car where I'd find it during the *little drive*.' He drew the last two words out.

'Would you not come anyway?' Niall encouraged.

They had woken to find the oil seed rape coated in thick dew from a mist that was only beginning to lift. It would be hours before the sun would burn through and they could not begin to cut until then.

'No! There's work to be done for those that are willing to do it.' Kelly spat on the whetstone and began to rub furiously at the spit.

'We could drop into Breffni's for a bowl of soup on the way back,' Niall offered. 'The men would love to hear how the cutting is going. They'll be looking for all sorts of information.'

Kelly looked up, his thumb describing a slow circle on the black stone. He looked out at the mist which still touched the yellow heads of the rape. The sun had risen dully behind the clouds.

'Aye, a bowl of soup would be grand,' he said. 'It'd set us up for the day.'

When they went out to the car Kelly tried to caution against taking the car for fear that the roads might be thick with mist and that they might be too long getting back and the chance to clear the fields might be gone.

'Come on, Daddy,' Helen urged, holding the car door open for him to get into the back seat. 'Stop fretting.'

Kelly opened the passenger door and sat in.

'Daddy!' Helen sighed.

'I want to keep an eye on muck-o here, so's he doesn't get lost.' He smiled at Niall as he started the engine. 'Neutral then first, don't forget the handbrake,' he taunted.

The dog barked and yelped at the tyres as they rolled out the track. Its paws clicked on the door panel when it threw itself towards Kelly's face behind the glass.

'Poor Blackie,' Helen said, remembering how Niall hated having the distraction of the dog in the car while he drove.

'Stop! Stop!' Kelly said when they reached the road. The car lurched to a halt. He opened the door and pulled the dog up by its collar and on to his lap, where it set to licking his face and yawning.

'I can't have the dog in the car,' Niall protested.

'Are we going or what? The day'll be gone before we know where we are.' Kelly clamped Blackie's mouth shut with his fist.

They drove in silence until they came to the old cassette factory. The roof was long gone, the metal beams and corrugated steel now the fabric of barns and out-buildings for miles around. O'Donoghue had fashioned meal troughs for his goats from the roofing sheets and had not bothered to cover the old graffiti so that one trough had TIOCFAIDH AR LÁ in upside-down letters along its side. Ginn's now had a garage with a twenty-foot high roller-shutter door on the front if it. Much of the brickwork had been removed and put to similar uses and cattle could now wander across the broken concrete floor to where clumps of grass and weed grew between the cracks.

'Do you remember when the factory opened at all?' Niall asked as they passed. 'I was in America at the time – my brother tried to get work there as a fitter.'

Helen went to answer but Kelly cut in: 'Sure it was hardly there long enough for anyone to remember it at all.

Didn't I say before it opened that it wouldn't last more than a couple of years, and wasn't I right?' He turned around to glance at Helen. 'Wasn't I?'

'You never gave it a chance, Daddy. You had the lot of them damned to hell before they got going.'

'Was I right or not?' he cut in again.

'You were happy for me to work there while there was money going,' Helen sharpened. 'You took me out of school for it.'

Kelly glared at her and went to say something but stopped himself and turned back to the road, watching the telegraph poles glide past, the asphalt rushing under the car. Helen and Niall talked about the factory for a while but Kelly did not seem to listen, inspecting the dog's ears for ticks, flicking through a driver's manual he found in the glove compartment. He would do anything now not to have to engage them in conversation.

Niall slowed the car on a part of the road that had been newly re-surfaced, the stone chippings dancing in the wheel arches and setting the dog to whining and circling on Kelly's lap.

'Whist now, Blackie! Whist!' Kelly said, but the dog would not be still and grew more and more agitated so that he had to muzzle it with his fist until the old road surface was regained and the tyres ran smoothly.

'A couple of hours with a sweeping brush and those stones would have been cleared,' Kelly said. 'Can they not do anything right in this country at all?'

They turned on to the causeway that divided the twin lakes and then drove out past the convent which had been newly painted, the drone of a tractor mower coming from the grounds. A new primary school was being built beside the convent and there were men on the roof, tiles standing in jagged rows on the tar-paper that was tacked to the beams. Some of the nuns would teach there and Helen could imagine the Sisters making their way along the verge, bundles of copybooks clutched to their chests, black habits fluttering in the wake of speeding cars.

At the crossroads they turned to drive along the river that was low and knuckled with rocks.

'Do you remember the little bridge, Helen?' Niall asked as they slowed before it.

'I do, I do,' she said. 'And the plaque.'

The plaque had been removed or stolen, a rectangle of bare plaster marking where it had been. They both turned to look at the mansion house.

'Oh! God!' Helen gasped. The fine house had been reduced to a blackened shell, grey sky showing through its roof timbers, a chimney stack half destroyed. No one would now gaze through the huge windows at the gravel driveway, the river, the Black Forest beyond. The white paddock fencing was still intact but the field was empty of Charolais cattle and thick with nettles.

'Whatever happened, I wonder?' Niall said as he moved off the hump of the bridge to let another car pass by.

'Insurance,' Kelly said gruffly, not looking up. 'It was a Brady that owned it. He'd bought up a rake of pubs in Galway city and the banks were trying to close him down after the business turned bad. They say that in the end he let the banks have the pubs, torched the house, and retired on the pay-out.' Kelly let the dog out of the car and watched it run off along the road, chasing sparrows from the verges. 'Brady was clever enough, mind. He set the fire on Christmas Day and by the time an engine arrived sure the whole place was destroyed.'

'And he got away with it?' Niall exclaimed.

'He did, the blackguard. He's living up in Dublin these days, but the wife took the children to live with her parents. There was word that they're to be divorced in England.'

Niall parked the car and they walked down to the forest

together, the barking of the dog coming to them faintly through the trees. Kelly roared for it to come to heel but the forest seemed to swallow his words into its silence.

'The trees are that much bigger here that I'd hardly recognize the place,' Helen said to Niall. 'There's barely enough light to see by – no wonder no one ever comes here.'

'That's just as well,' Niall smiled, 'considering the last time we came.'

Helen frowned at him, knowing that Kelly, who seemed distracted by the whereabouts of the dog, would be listening to everything.

'You're familiar with it then?' Kelly asked.

'We are,' Helen replied. 'It's a grand place for a walk of an evening, but we haven't been here in a long, long time. We used to come here before we were married.'

'Is that so?' Kelly pondered. He seemed to soften, the stiffness falling from his shoulders, his chin dipping slightly as if he was considering the patterns the needles made on the forest floor. The dog's barking came more loudly now as it threaded its way back to them, but Kelly paid it no heed, crossing his arms as if to contain something.

A bird broke through the branches above their heads, the beating of its wings almost unnaturally loud. When Kelly lifted his head to look for it, Helen noticed that his eyes were wet with tears.

'Daddy?'

He lowered his head and turned quickly away, shuffling through the cones and needles. 'There's work to be getting back to,' he said without any conviction.

Helen went after him while Niall took off in search of the dog, peering through the dense-standing trees, calling its name.

'Daddy?' she asked again when she had reached him.

'Aye,' he breathed.

'Are you all right?'

He would not answer. His hands were sunk deep in his pockets as he walked, not looking around him but at the road ahead, as if there was something in the forest he did not want to see.

The sun was out when they emerged on to the road, all trace of mist erased from the day. The cutting could begin again. Kelly and Helen sat in the car while they waited for Niall and the dog.

'He'll be along any second now,' Helen encouraged, afraid that Kelly would be anxious to return to his fields.

'Let him take his time, girl,' Kelly sighed. 'Let him take his time.'

'Your mother, God rest her, used to love this walk herself,' he started after a while. 'The trees, mind, were so small then that you could see over the tops of them, but there was a lovely view of the big house on the hill and the land away towards the lakes there. We would walk the two miles to the train station and travel the one stop to Drimelogue just for the thrill of it. We never had to pay and your mother used to love it.'

Niall and Blackie appeared at the bottom of the road, the sun catching and marking them out against the dark of the trees. 'There they are now,' Kelly said.

Helen had not seen them emerge from the trees, so distracted was she by what her father had said, the sudden memory of her mother that had softened him and turned the day.

'When she was going from us,' he continued, 'I promised her that we'd take this walk again, but there was never the time.' He looked out at Niall and Blackie coming up the road, Niall's hands stuck in the front pockets of his jeans, smiling into the sunlight and laughing at the dog which was worrying a frog it had found in the ditch. 'But the two of you have all the time in the world,' Kelly finished without any bitterness.

'That was a grand walk all the same,' Niall said, getting into the car. 'I don't know where Blackie got to but he's covered in burrs.'

'Don't keep the man from the work anyways,' Kelly said.

'Hope and pray now that the weather holds for another day at least,' Kelly was saying as the men came through the door. The day's work was over, the sun sinking behind the distant hills and the sudden dew causing the dulled blades to slip uselessly against the stems of the oil seed rape. 'Another set of hands and we might have cleared the whole damn lot,' he added almost as an afterthought.

Helen looked up from the book of poems she had been reading as the men came in, folding it into her lap like some secret thing, its spell broken by the racket the men made in the house. Kelly tramped about the front room in his stockinged feet while Niall went into the bathroom to wash, the splashing sound of the water always strange against the tiles.

'Is it the books you're at again?' Kelly enquired, eyeing the thin green spine of the volume in Helen's lap.

She nodded, her head bowed as if in shame.

'Isn't there plenty that needs doing about the house to keep you busy without the books?'

'The house is clean and tidy, Daddy. There's nothing to be doing at all.'

Kelly stopped wiping his hands on a dishcloth and looked at her. 'Don't . . .' he started. 'Don't think you can answer me like that, girl. You haven't the measure of me yet between the two of you and don't you forget it.' He threw the dishcloth over the back of the armchair. 'I haven't heard you out with that vacuum cleaner thing this long time,' he said. 'God knows there was enough fuss and *ráiméis* about it when it arrived.'

'It sets the dog to howling, Daddy. You know that.'

'Blackie would get used to it soon enough,' he said, lowering into the armchair.

Yellow pollen had lifted from the soaking shirts, gilding the water's surface. She drained and refilled the sink, the wet cotton dragging along the back of her stirring hand like cold, dead skin. As she soaped the shirts she tried to remember the last lines of the poem she had been reading, but they would not come, as lost to her as if she had never seen those same stanzas that had been read and re-read in recent months, every element considered, the freighted words rolled around her mouth like something sweet. And still they would not come.

'It's a pity now that it's only the three of us you're washing for,' Kelly whispered over her shoulder.

'Dear God, Daddy!' she panted, pressing a wet palm to her chest in surprise. 'I didn't know you were there.' She could feel the weight of his presence. He was almost leaning against her. 'I thought you were in your armchair,' she defended.

'It's a great pity,' he went on. 'Another set of hands would make all the difference around this place in years to come.'

She tilted her head so that she could see his face, eyes searching her features, creased skin dusted with pollen, his breath thick and soured with regret. She looked back to the sink and said nothing, lifting a shirt from the water and running the bar of soap across the collar.

'It's a pity,' he said again, leaning closer to her so that she had to stop herself from pushing him away.

'It is,' she said, without regret, wishing only that he would leave her be. She had heard it too often before. Year after year he would punish them with it at harvest time, the season serving to remind him that in time *all* would be reaped and his fields divided amongst the farmers round and about. Their weakness had stopped his bloodline and denied him an heir. 'Forsaken' was a word he used often amongst them, mulling its biblical tones.

'But it can't be helped now, Daddy,' she said suddenly as he turned to leave.

'What?' He froze. 'What was that?'

'I said it can't be helped now, Daddy.'

'Is that so?' he breathed slowly. 'Is that so?' as if in search of other words that would cut deeper.

She shook desperately. She had said enough now. The taunt was his weapon against what had been denied him most and for years it had gone unanswered.

Kelly stood for a while, saying nothing, his head bent to his chest, his breath rising and falling like a pressure in the room.

They had tried for a child in vain. In the first years their lovemaking had been new and supple, drawn out through silent evenings as Kelly sat in the front room, the boundaries of their love explored while a crossword was filled, a weather forecast detailed, his footfall listened for, their gasps as they came stifled at the creak of a door or the barking of the dog. Later, the shadow of the wanted child fell upon them as they moved together upon the bed, joining time after time more in desperate hope than any conviction.

Niall came back into the room, wiping his bare shoulders and neck with a towel. Kelly pushed past him and went out to fetch the dog from the back of the van. 'Blackie! Blackie!' his shouts fading as he went around the house.

'What's going on?' Niall asked.

'Nothing.'

He took her hands from the water and held them in his. 'You're cold, Helen,' he said. 'Hands like mutton,' he smiled. She looked at his hands enclosing hers, strong and sinewed, veins and arteries standing proud beneath the skin; the hands that had wielded an all-important second scythe that first summer of the barley, fingers that had explored every inch of her, pressing upon her flesh as if sounding something out inside.

'Go away out of it,' she whispered. 'Mutton, indeed!' But her hands trembled in spite of herself and he saw that her eyes were wetting with tears. She drew her hands back and dried them on her apron.

'What did he say this time?' he asked.

'Leave it, Niall.'

'"Another pair of hands", is that it?' but she would say nothing against her father. 'Is that it?' he insisted.

She looked away, at the last bright curve of the sun slipping behind the hills and he knew he had his answer. The room plunged to almost complete darkness.

'He was on and on about it in the meadow this afternoon,' Niall stammered. 'It was all I could do not to take the scythe to him, you know.' Even in the near dark she could see the colour rising in his face. His was anger as hard as any Kelly ever had in him, but here it was too often let burn and eat away inside. He had never so much as raised his voice to her or Kelly, although both had often given him reason to. 'Will he ever stop?' he finished in exasperation.

Niall went out to the bedroom and crashed down on the bed, the old springs creaking with his weight. She heard the rustle of a newspaper being opened, the pages neatly folded over on each other until the crossword was a square of print before his eyes.

Cherry blossom had been out in the hospital grounds on the day they went to have Niall's test, the pink petals trodden into the tarmac of the car park so that they had turned brown. She waited while he went into a room and emerged some time later with a glass flask wrapped in blue paper. A nurse took the flask and labelled it, the pen slipping all the time in her gloved hand. Afterwards, Niall wondered if the samples hadn't been mixed up because his name was illegible. The truth was sealed into the envelope that came through the door a week later. They went together to see the doctor who told them that they could either adopt or foster children for six months at a time, but they wanted nothing of that and they left in the same silence that their later lives would endure.

Sometimes a vision of the child she had lost would come to her, as it had done that first time on a bridge over the River Thames, the grey tide filling as her heart emptied, the child's hands reaching out, its eyes tracking her face, looking for something that was not hers to give. The lost child was a secret folded deep inside her, but sometimes she wished it could unfold before her father, an answer to him once and for all.

The door to Kelly's room was closed, as always, when she passed it on the way out to the front step. Outside, Kelly was throwing a stick for the dog to retrieve. The stick made a quick whooping noise as it spun blindly through the darkening air and beneath it the dog panted softly, running to and fro. Kelly threw the stick again and again until the darkness had swarmed about them to swallow all but the flashes of white on the dog's legs and the red glow of a cigarette cupped in his hand.

The anger of earlier had subsided inside her, the edge blunted by time and habit. She looked at him now, his back turned to her against the night sky, framed amongst the stars as his life had been framed, not by any crime or great sin, but by the small mistakes that came to him day after day after day.

She heard the paper being thrown down to the floor in their bedroom. 'Will you wake me before he comes back in,

Helen? Will you?' Niall groaned as he stretched out on the bed.

'I will,' she called back into the house. She felt sorry for him, the week's work for Kelly that would go unrewarded and forgotten once Niall had returned to his desk at the computer software company he worked for. Every year was the same: the week's holiday held back until Kelly announced that the fields were ready to be cleared. The rituals were also the same: Kelly would insist that Niall hold a scrap of cloth soaked in methylated spirits between his hands on the night before the work would begin, for fear that his soft skin would split during the cutting and the work would slow. 'There's no hardening to be got from tapping away at them television things, Niall,' he advised. 'It's work that prepares you for nothing.'

'It's good work, Kelly,' Niall sharpened. 'I enjoy it.'

'I wouldn't be doing with it anyways. It's not fit for the likes of working men.' He tipped the jar of spirits on to the cloth and handed it to Niall. 'Ah, sure where's the ambition in it at all?'

'It's good work and good money in it too.' He squeezed the cloth and gave it back to Kelly. 'Good money, rain or shine,' he added, going in to get the whetstone.

For Helen the metal smell of the spirits marked the start of the harvest week, the cloth wrapped back into a paper bag for the next year, the sound of spitting as the men wet the stone before taking it to the blade.

A corncrake's rasping call broke the silence outside the house. When it called again the sound seemed closer, as if she could reach for and touch the bird. Kelly stiffened and the dog stood waiting at his feet. The corncrake rasped again.

'Blasted bloody bird!' Kelly cursed and threw the stick far into night, the dog checking for a second before beating out into the darkness. 'I'll take the pitchfork to its nest tomorrow morning if it's the last thing I do.' He knew she had been standing watching him all along but he did not turn to her. The corncrake rasped again but this time its call seemed more distant, as if it had already taken flight before the tines of Kelly's fork.

Helen did not doubt that the corncrake would be killed and its nest in the hayfield torn asunder. Kelly could show terrible callousness towards any creature, his anger allowed full reign against the utterly defenceless.

The first winter after she and Niall were married was a long and bitter one. For Kelly there was nothing to be done but watch and wait as the snow fell in sweeping drifts that filled the fields to the tops of the stone walls. He raged inside the house, looking for things to be doing when in the new house there was nothing. The van couldn't be taken out so the three of them would make the long walk into the village for bread and milk and other provisions, the conversation about the hard weather that began each journey trailing off into nothing within minutes, each watching their breath freezing in the air before them.

Once, as they passed Rosheen Lake, Niall noticed a pair of swans trapped in the thick ice. The swans sat a couple of yards apart from each other, slowly lifting and lowering their long necks, ice-bound. A fox appeared through the reeds in the margins of the lake and ventured out on to the ice, gingerly making its way towards the two swans. Helen stood at the roadside, transfixed by the scene, as caught by the moment as the swans were by the ice.

'Come on, will you?' Kelly urged. 'We'll catch our deaths if we don't keep moving.'

Niall let out a shout at the fox, waving his arms in an effort to scare it away. The fox skirmished for a second before resuming its steady progress. The swans turned to watch as it came towards them. Niall found a stone but when he drew his arm back to throw it Kelly grabbed and held him.

'Let nature take its course, boy!' he said, squeezing the stone from Niall's gloved fist. 'That fox is hungry too.'

Niall protested but Kelly dragged Helen on along the road as the fox drew closer and closer to the swans. There was hardly a sound as the fox attacked, only the rap of the swans' heavy bills on the ice as their necks were broken.

Kelly clicked his fingers to bring the dog to heel and the memory went from her, the bitter cold of that day almost impossible to imagine in the warmth of a late summer evening. He clicked his fingers again and the dog rose to follow him around the gable of the house. She heard the doors of the van scraping on their hinges and the heavy rattle as Kelly shut them again. The dog began to whine, like a thin keening for something it had lost. 'Whist now, Blackie. Whist,' Kelly said and the dog was quiet.

He brushed past her into the house, his breath thick with tobacco.

'Would you look at the boy!' he called to her from the door to their bedroom. 'Asleep already and the crossword hardly filled.' His voice was gentler now, not out of consideration for her sleeping husband but from his own exhaustion. He would be his usual self at the breakfast table in the morning, giddy with the expectation of the day that waited upon them. 'It's as well for him to get his forty winks now. With just the two of us to do the work he'll need every ounce of energy for tomorrow.'

Again he stood with his back to her, watching his own faint reflection in the glass of the kitchen window. He ran his hands back through his silvering hair, fingertips reaching to trace the arc of sunburn across the nape of his neck. His hands moved to knead the knotted muscles in his shoulder and as he bent forward the blunt knuckles of his spine pushed through his shirt. 'I'm getting old, girl,' he sighed. 'I'm getting old.'

As she watched her father rise and bend again she knew it was not age that he feared. What he feared most was passing on with nothing to go into nor leave behind; the fear of a future as empty as the white ghost of her husband's seed that had once passed often between them, the pale imitation of a new life.

Part Six

THE BEEHIVES BRIGHTENED as the day was born, lingering threads of mist dissolving in the face of the spring day, the wood slats as smooth and pale as candle wax. Later, when the sun had risen enough to warm the hives he would come to the window and watch the bees take flight, circling on the parapet for a few moments before taking wing across the fields. It was a long time since he had struggled into the old bee-keeper's suit which hung limply in a press behind the kitchen door, bone white, the face gauze repaired so many times that it was almost impossible to see through.

Helen collected the breakfast tray from his lap and took the napkin from where she had fastened it to the collar of his pyjamas.

'Are you all right now, Daddy?'

'I am, thanks be to God, I am.' He settled back in the bed, his shoulders trembling uncontrollably. 'Is himself taken off to work?'

'He is indeed.'

'He never said goodbye to me then.'

'Niall's always in a hurry in the mornings, Daddy.'

'He couldn't spare a second or two for me, I suppose.'

'He doesn't like to be late. You know what he's like.' She folded the napkin and put it in a corner of the tray.

He turned to look out of the window. He was losing his breath already. 'He might help me out to the hives later on. He's always promising.'

'He might, Daddy.' She left him in peace, gazing quizzically out of the window at the fields that were once all his own, but were farmed or left fallow by others now.

In another room, in a painted cot, a child, not quite eighteen months old, slept on its back, its arms flung up to frame its face, eyes tightly shut against the light leaking through the curtain.

Helen settled the blankets across his chest and whispered his name, Cormac, into the silence, leaning on the edge of the cot with its marks where the boy's first teeth had found purchase. Kelly had been pleased with the name that appeared on the adoption registry, but nothing else about the child which was a legacy in name alone. Whenever the boy cried he would take to shouting for it to be quiet: 'Can a man not have a minute's peace in his own house!' thumping the wall that divided them.

But one afternoon she and Niall had returned from a walk to find Kelly down on his knees in the front room, the child's hands held gently in his as it made its first stumbling steps across the carpet tiles, its face alive with laughing.

When the breakfast things had been washed and dried Helen took down her folder and course books and spread them out on the kitchen table. The latest study material from the university had arrived in the post, a thick volume of contemporary poetry which she leafed quickly through, pausing when a first line caught her eye:

> *The only legend I have ever loved is*
> *The story of a daughter lost in hell.*
> *And found and rescued there.*

She sat down to work. A bole of sunlight lanced the front room but left her untouched. She rose only once to seek out a book from the bookshelves beside the sofa. Her mother's books occupied the same shelf they always had, a series of Maurice Walsh and Neil M. Gunn novels whose spines had yellowed like rind.

At midday she looked in on him. He was lying on his back, asleep, his coarse and slow breathing soughing like wind in an autumn tree, his mouth open, looking for all the world like a dead man. It brought her back to the first weeks after the stroke had claimed so much of him, hour after hour spent at his hospital bedside, his head turned mutely toward the ceiling. Ever so slowly he had crawled back into life, his eyes opening for only a few seconds before shutting again, an arm raised and lowered, a word left half-formed on cracked lips, as if he was taunting them, hovering between life and nothingness.

'The fields! The fields!' he had finally and suddenly roared in the middle of the night, bringing the nurse pattering through the gloom of the wards to find him tearing at the drips and feeding tubes, terrified that they would drain him away.

They had brought him home a fortnight later and installed him in his own bedroom, always keeping an eye out for fear that he would break for the fields, the roaring and cursing that subsided into a muttered tirade against the world, a lifetime's loathing finally given voice. The jigsaw of his past returned fitfully, whole seasons revealed to him in an instant. 'Barley! Do yez remember the barley at all? Wasn't that a powerful summer altogether? Was it last year, was it?' His face twisted with wondering.

'Daddy,' she roused him gently, squeezing his shoulder. His breath was so sour she had to move away.

'What? What's that?'

'Daddy, it's just Helen.'

'Right you are, girl.' He straightened, squinting at the bright sky framed in the window, his whole face creased with the effort.

'Would you like a bowl of soup?'

'Soup?' he started, incredulously. 'But I never have soup for breakfast.'

'It's lunchtime, Daddy.'

'I've not had my breakfast yet.'

'But I brought you your breakfast . . . Don't you remember the boiled egg?'

'I know when I've not had breakfast,' he insisted. 'Run in there now and tell your mother . . . She'll know for sure. She knows how I like the egg done.'

Daddy, she sighed to herself. He was craning his neck to see the lids of the beehives and the fields beyond them. He liked it best when the bees swarmed and he could lie back on the pillow and watch the shapes they made against the sky. There was a spot of egg yolk on the collar of his pyjamas but she knew there was no use in pointing it out to him. Nothing would do him now but for her to bring him his breakfast.

After he had eaten he slept again, as he always did, and she could return to her books. In a fortnight she would be off to the university for a seminar: six days on the campus with other students, the freedom of the library, lectures and study groups, where she could free herself from the house, the hives, her father. The Masters she was studying for would help her get some teaching work in the college, there was even word of a university post going in the city. They would have to move then, to start a life in the city and leave the legacy of the fields to others. Kelly would be no part of it; a nursing home could be found if it was needed.

Already, Niall was counting down the days until she

left. 'Even with the harvests gone,' he complained, 'I still have to take the week off to look after him.' But he would never suggest that she not go. This year the week would be spent clearing the hives so that another farmer could take them away. The rough swath of grass they stood on would be rotovated, rolled, and sown so that they would have a lawn the following year. Kelly knew nothing of the plan. It was the last of the fields.

With the doors open she heard him get up, the frame clunking against the bedpost as he swung his legs over the side of the bed. There was the squeak of the rubber pads on the floor and after a short while the trickle of his water in the toilet. She stopped reading to listen, waiting for him to come in to her, his high wheeze riding the air, the hang-dog expression that sought only sympathy.

'How's the student?' There was little fire in him now. 'Always at the oul' books.' He stared at the carpet, reclaiming his breath. 'Like your good mother before you.'

'Is there something you want, Daddy?'

He looked across at her, holding her gaze for a second and pursing his lips.

'Can a man not get up for a wander now and again?' His skin was like paper, every feature drawn down by gravity, his hair frizzed out at all angles where it had lain on the pillow. His hands shook when they gripped the walking frame. He made his way to the window and looked out at the beehives.

The first of the worker bees had gathered on the parapet, circling the white wood. One by one they launched into the air, dipping low for a moment before soaring upwards. Soon they were lost in the landscape, but Kelly watched for them still.

Helen brought Cormac into the front room and sat him in a high-chair at the table where she could feed him while she read. His eyes were clotted with sleep, and often as not he pushed the spoons of custard on to the table. She scooped dribbles from his chin with the edge of her finger.

'Do you remember at all the swallows that used to feed on the bees of an evening?' Kelly said softly, working his way back to the table with the frame. 'Do you?'

'No, Daddy.'

He pursed his lips in frustration. 'I remember them well enough myself.'

He stood behind the boy and stroked the crown of his head, tickling the tiny earlobes with his thumb because he knew it made the child giggle. 'How's the little cuckoo today, then?' he asked. '*An chuach bheag, nach ea?*'

'Daddy! How dare you!' Helen protested. 'If only Niall could hear you, he'd take the frame from under you!'

'He would indeed,' Kelly scorned.

He tickled the child for a while longer before turning back to the armchair where years ago, before the stroke, he had often played cards on the stool. He played no longer. 'It's a terrible thing,' he was fond of saying, 'when an old man can remember his Confirmation suit, but nothing of what has been put before his own two eyes just a second earlier.'

He seemed caught in the memory of the swallows, his mind twisting and turning with their short wings. He gazed up at a picture of two sailing boats above the fireplace.

When he had finally settled she returned to her studying, filling lined foolscap pages with note after note, leafing through the books. Cormac slept in his high-chair, his eyes moving behind lids as thin as latex. The afternoon sank towards evening, the bole of sunlight drawn to one wall where it shortened and vanished.

When Kelly woke it was with a suddenness that startled her, the pages of a book flapping noisily shut.

'By Christ! It's getting dark already,' he exclaimed, looking about him, his hands gripping the edges of the armrests. 'I've been asleep the whole day. I'll never sleep tonight after that.'

'Don't worry, Daddy,' she said.

'Would it not have done you to wake me at all?' he accused.

'You've only been asleep a couple of hours. I brought you your second breakfast just before. Do you not remember the boiled egg at all?'

He looked at her, and as the lost hours fell into place his expression softened and his mouth opened and shut upon the words of his silent thoughts. He sat back in the armchair and gazed again at the sailing boats. His eyes began to well with reluctant tears that finally brimmed and fell across the creased landscape of his cheeks and he could do nothing to stop them.

Helen noticed the tears and could not bear to stay in the room with her father while he cried. She went into the kitchen and made noise by rummaging about in the cupboard beneath the sink. Here she found his old boots, encrusted with clay, the memory of their pounding upon the doorstep ringing in her head.

'Helen,' he called eventually, when his voice had recovered its strength.

'Yes?'

'Is there a drop of tea on the way at all?'

'There is, Daddy. There is.'